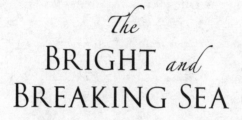

The
BRIGHT *and* BREAKING SEA

NOVELS BY CHLOE NEILL

THE CAPTAIN KIT BRIGHTLING NOVELS

The Bright and Breaking Sea

THE HEIRS OF CHICAGOLAND NOVELS

Wild Hunger   *Wicked Hour*

THE CHICAGOLAND VAMPIRES NOVELS

Some Girls Bite	*Biting Bad*
Friday Night Bites	*Wild Things*
Twice Bitten	*Blood Games*
Hard Bitten	*Dark Debt*
Drink Deep	*Midnight Marked*
Biting Cold	*Blade Bound*
House Rules	

"High Stakes"
novella in *Kicking It*
Howling for You
(A Chicagoland Vampires Novella)
Lucky Break
(A Chicagoland Vampires Novella)
Phantom Kiss
(A Chicagoland Vampires Novella)
Slaying It
(A Chicagoland Vampires Novella)

THE DEVIL'S ISLE NOVELS

The Veil   *The Hunt*
The Sight   *The Beyond*

THE DARK ELITE NOVELS

Firespell   *Charmfall*
Hexbound

The BRIGHT *and* BREAKING SEA

A Captain Kit Brightling Novel

CHLOE NEILL

Berkley

New York

BERKLEY
An imprint of Penguin Random House LLC
penguinrandomhouse.com

BERKLEY and the BERKLEY & B colophon are
registered trademarks of Penguin Random House LLC.

Library of Congress Cataloging-in-Publication Data

Names: Neill, Chloe, author.
Title: The bright and breaking sea / Chloe Neill.
Description: First Edition. | New York: Berkley, 2020. |
Series: A Captain Kit Brightling novel; vol 1
Identifiers: LCCN 2020025237 (print) | LCCN 2020025238 (ebook) |
ISBN 9781984806680 (trade paperback) | ISBN 9781984806697 (ebook)
Subjects: GSAFD: Fantasy fiction.
Classification: LCC PS3614.E4432 B75 2020 (print) |
LCC PS3614.E4432 (ebook) | DDC 813/.6—dc23
LC record available at https://lccn.loc.gov/2020025237
LC ebook record available at https://lccn.loc.gov/2020025238

First Edition: November 2020

Printed in the United States of America
3   5   7   9   10   8   6   4   2

Cover art © Rovina Cai
Cover design by Adam Auerbach
Map illustration by Cortney Skinner
Book design by Elke Sigal

War was a bitter scourge and curse;
Yet peace is, somehow, ten times worse.

HENRY LUTTRELL, *Advice to Julia*

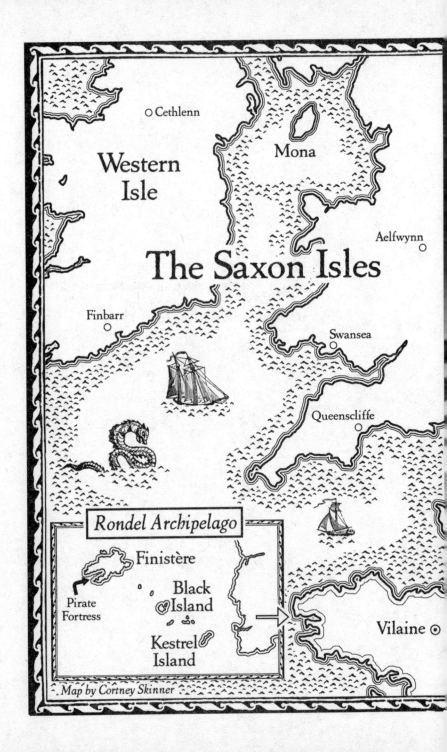

○ Cethlenn

Western
Isle

Mona

Aelfwynn
○

The Saxon Isles

Finbarr
○

Swansea
○

Queenscliffe
○

Rondel Archipelago

Finistère

Black
Island

Pirate
Fortress

Kestrel
Island

Vilaine ◉

~ *Map by Cortney Skinner*

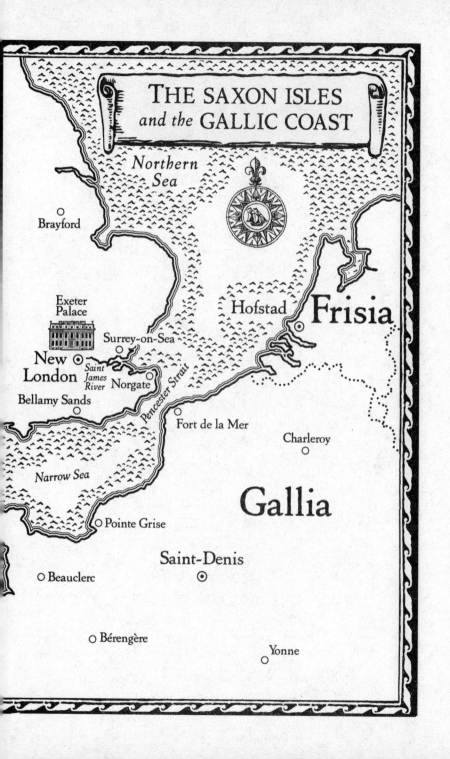

THE SAXON ISLES
and the GALLIC COAST

Northern
Sea

Brayford

Exeter
Palace

Hofstad   **Frisia**

New
London

Surrey-on-Sea

Saint
James
River   Norgate

Bellamy Sands

Pencester Strait

Fort de la Mer

Charleroy

Narrow Sea

Gallia

Pointe Grise

Saint-Denis

Beauclerc

Bérengère

Yonne

PROLOGUE

1812

War was a god, arrogant and proud. War was a human, earnest and ambitious. War was a child, petulant and demanding.

Gerard Rousseau, emperor of Gallia, knew its rhythm well. Knew the beat of soldiers' footsteps, the whinny of battle-tested horses, the look in the eye of a man who understood victory—or defeat—was already guaranteed. He didn't love war, but he loved to command. To place his mark upon a battlefield, upon those who served him. To be victorious, and to pull that victory from the bloody grasp of defeat. *To win.*

War was a means to an end. War was the tool that brought him control, power, people, territory. And with territory, magic. Magic buried inside stone and water and grassy plain, currents of power that feathered through the world like veins of gold through marble that could be felt by those who were Aligned to it. Some gave the lines a name: ley, aetheric, telluric. Some gave it an origin, said it was the fingerprint of the gods, the remnants of their physical touch upon the world.

Gerard didn't care how it came into being, or what name was given to it. He cared only for its potential . . . and for its possession. Whoever held the most land held the most magic. And whoever held the most magic held the most power. Literally and figuratively. He now ruled a large piece of the Continent, and intended to have the rest of it soon enough.

War was a game, and he was its master. Chess spread across oceans and continents. And hadn't he placed the pieces so very carefully across the board? A knight. A queen. A pawn. One at his side, one at his control, one unaware of the limitations of its position.

He looked down at the spread of maps across his campaign desk.

"At dawn," Gerard said to the man who stood silently beside the desk, awaiting the emperor's orders, "we move."

⁓

War was dirt and dust and exertion beyond exhaustion. War was time borrowed from death itself. War was escape from the strictures of obligation, a life narrowed to its thin, hard edge.

A mile away from Rousseau, a man lay in the slope of a dusty hill, his linen nearly the same color as the orange-red dirt. The land was scrubby, rocky, and not useful for much that he could see—except observing the enemy.

Rian Grant was one of Sutherland's observing officers, tasked with learning the land, finding Gerard's troops, uncovering their plans.

He wasn't Aligned, didn't care for phenomena he couldn't see or touch. But half the men in the twenty-member unit were. They could feel the terrain miles ahead, guide troops where to make camp, where to find water. One of the Aligned, a man named Bourne, had found the unit of Gallic soldiers, could feel the disruption in the currents of the earthworks they'd built to secure their position. Bourne had led them here, where Grant and his fellow officer, Dunwood, would listen and learn.

For two days, they'd watched Gerard's men eat, sleep, smoke, and drill, waiting for some sign of the army's direction and destination. The first night, they'd nearly been captured by sentries scouring the hillside for nosy locals or enemy spies. But the sentries tramped off toward the camp again, none the wiser.

Dunwood lay beside Grant in the dirt, spyglass to his eye, the metal scoured so there'd be no glint of sunlight to give away their position. "They'll be going west."

Grant snorted. "Copper says you're wrong. Again. They won't march directly toward the lines. They'll move around, try to out-flank."

Marcus Dunwood considered the bet, nodded. "I'll take that."

Four hours later, when the lines shifted and began to move west, Dunwood cursed.

"Why are you complaining?" Grant muttered. "You won."

"Only bet a copper, didn't I?" Dunwood shook his head with disgust. "I should have known better."

"Next time you will. Let's get the hell out of here."

⌣

War was full canvas, the drumbeat to quarters, the strike of blade against blade. War was honor and bravery beyond fear.

Two hundred miles away from Gerard's troops and Sutherland's officers, Lieutenant Kit Brightling was at the helm of the Isles ship *Ardent*, dark hair whipping in the wind as the ship streamed through high seas near San Miguel. She looked back, found the line of Frisian brigs—wide of beam and tall of mast— flying toward them with all sails. The *Ardent* had managed to stay ahead, but the brigs had more canvas, and they were gaining ground.

"Lieutenant, I believe it's time."

"Sir," Kit said to the woman beside her, whose eyes were concerned beneath a furrowed brow. Kit respected no one in the Crown Command more than Captain Perez. And she understood well the uncertainty in the captain's eyes.

Kit was Aligned to the sea, could feel the currents of magic that spun beneath the waves. Magic was energy, power; and humans were still only beginning to understand its scope, its potential— and the horrific costs of its misuse. Reading the stories told by the currents was harmless, as far as anyone could tell. Manipulating them—trying to shift them, to absorb them, to weaponize them— had been calamitous. Three months ago, Aligned Gallic officers had warped the current to the surface at Contra Costa, hoping to ignite it and send a current of fire through Isles troops. Ten thousand had died in the resulting inferno.

But Kit had found a path, a slender space between seeing and manipulating. A gentle grasping of the current, touching it just long enough to pull a ship into its arms—and speed the ship along its path. Too much, and the current would snap back—and break the ship in two.

Perez had been confident enough to let Kit try, her crew

trusting Perez enough to follow her orders despite the risk. And when they'd felt the ship fly, more than willing to try it again.

"Get ready," the captain said. "Hard to port when we're there. We'll come hard around," she added with a thin smile. "And drive right toward them."

Kit closed her eyes—easier to focus—and reached down through wood and tar and hemp to the water, deep and dark and swirling below, feeling for the shimmering current that crossed somewhere beneath them. Not directly—they hadn't been that lucky—and nearly a mile to port. But that was close enough . . .

"Starboard brig is gaining ground, Captain!"

Kit heard the shout from the waist, ignored it as her fingers began to tingle from the brush against the power, and reached farther, sweat on her brow as she drew closer to it. And then the heat of the ley line itself, the center core, bright and glimmering. The ship—an arrow; the current—a bowstring. The heat building, her skin damp with it, and she reached farther—just a bit more—until the current wrapped around her.

"Ready when you are," Perez said quietly, and Kit released fingers she'd clenched into hard fists, and then released the connection.

Like a loosed arrow, the *Ardent* shuddered and jerked forward, and Kit opened her eyes as lieutenants shouted orders and the ship made hard for port. She looked down at her hands, found a new constellation of spots, dark and minute, across her palms. Burns, the physick had said. Painless, but invariable, the scars of flying too closely to the magic.

"Let the canvas fly," Perez called out, and the *Ardent* roared forward against the breaking sea.

ONE

≈

There was a ribbon pinned to her coat, and a dagger in her hand. And as Captain Kit Brightling stared down at the little wooden box, there was a gleam in her gray eyes.

Two months of searching between the Saxon Isles and the Continent. Two months of sailing, of storms and sun, of crazed activity and mind-dulling monotony.

They hadn't been sure what they'd find when the *Diana* set sail from New London—the seat of the Isles' crown, named for the city rebuilt after the Great Fire's destruction—only that they'd almost certainly find something. It had been nearly a year since the Gallic emperor Gerard Rousseau was exiled to Montgraf, since the end of war that had spread death across the Continent like a dark plague. Gerard had finally been beaten back, his surrender and abdication just outside the Gallic capital city, Saint-Denis. The island nation of Montgraf, off the coast of

Gallia, was now his prison, and a king had been installed in Gallia again.

There were reports of Gerard's growing boredom and irritation with his exile, with the inadequacies of the island he'd been exiled to, with the failures of his replacement. There were rumors of plans, of the gathering of ships and soldiers, of missives sent across the water. Queen Charlotte had bid Kit, the only captain in the Queen's Own Guards, to find those missives.

They'd patrolled the Narrow Sea that separated the Isles from the Continent, visiting grungy ports and gleaming cities, trading for information, or spreading coin through portside taverns when tipple loosened more tongues. Then they'd found the grimy little packet ship twenty miles off the coast, not far from Pencester. And in the captain's stingy quarters, in a drawer cleverly concealed in his bunk, they'd found the lovely little box.

She couldn't fault its design. Honey-colored wood, carefully hewn iron, and brass corners that gleamed even in the pale light of dawn. It was intended to hold secrets. And given its lock—a rather lovely contraption of copper and iron gears—hadn't yet been triggered, it still did.

Secrets, Kit thought ruefully, were the currency of both war and peace.

"You can't touch that."

That declaration came from the sailor in the corner.

"I believe I can," Kit said, sliding the dagger into her belt and lifting the box from the drawer. She placed it on the desk that folded down from the worm-holed bulkhead, then glanced up. "It now belongs to Queen Charlotte."

"It already did," sneered the man, his teeth the same yellowed shade as his grimy shirt. His trousers were darker; the cap, which narrowed to a point that flopped over one eye, was the sickly green of week-old bread. "I'm from the Isles, same as you, and I'm to deliver that to her. You saw the flag."

"The flag was false," said the lanky man's captor. Jin Takamura was tall and elegantly built, with a sweep of long dark hair pulled back at the crown. His skin was tan, his eyes dark as obsidian in an oval face marked by his narrow nose and rounded cheekbones. And his gleaming sabre was drawn and currently at the neck of the grungy sailor.

Kit thought Jin, second in command of the *Diana*, complemented her perfectly—his patience and canny contemplation, matched against her desire to go, to see, to do. There was no one she trusted more.

"You've no papers, no letters of marque," Jin said, looking over the sailor's dingy clothes. "And certainly no uniforms."

"You aren't from the Isles," Kit concluded, "any more than this box is." She walked toward the pair, smelling the sweat and fish and unwashed body emanating from the smuggler three feet away. Baffling, since water, salty or not, was readily available.

Kit was slender and pale-skinned, with dark hair chopped to skim the edge of her chin. Her eyes were wide and gray, her nose straight, her lips full. She clasped her hands behind her back when she reached the two men, and cocked her head. "Would you like to tell us from whom you obtained it, and to whom it will be delivered?"

"It's for the queen," he said again. "A private gift of some . . . unmentionables. A fine lady like you shouldn't have to deal with that sort of thing."

Kit's brows lifted, and she glanced at Jin. "The queen's unmentionables, he says. And me a fine lady."

"Maybe we should let him return to his business," Jin said, gaze falling to the box, heavy and full of secrets. "And avoid the impropriety."

"Best you do," the sailor said with a confident bob of his chin. "Don't want no impro—whatever here."

"Unfortunately," Kit said, "we're well aware that's nonsense. You're smugglers, running the very nice Gallic brandy in your hold, not to mention this very pretty box. But because I'm a pleasant sort, I'm going to give you one last opportunity to tell us the truth. Where did you get the box?"

"Unmentionables," he said again. "And you don't scare me. Trussed up in fancy duds or not, you're still a girl."

At four-and-twenty years, Kit was more woman than girl, but she was still one of the youngest captains in the Crown Command—the Saxon Isles' military—and there were plenty who'd thought her too young or too female to hold her position. But she'd earned her rank on the water. At San Miguel, by finding deep magic, and reaching for the current just long enough to give her ship the gauge against a larger squadron of Frisian ships—and capture gold and munitions that Queen Charlotte was very pleased to add to her own armory. At Pointe Grise, she'd helped her captain avoid an attack by a larger Gallic privateer, and they'd captured the privateer's ship and the coded dispatches it was carrying to Saint-Denis. At Faulkney, as a young commander, she'd found a disturbance in the current of magic, and led her own squadron to a trio of Gallic ships led by an Aligned captain that had made it through the Isles' blockade and was racing toward Pencester to attack. Kit's ship successfully turned back the invasion.

"Am I a trussed-up girl or fine lady?" Kit asked. "You can't seem to make up your mind." She glanced down at the trim navy jacket with its gold braid and long tails, the gleaming black boots that rose to her knees over buff trousers. "Personally, I enjoy the uniform. I find it affords a certain . . . authority." She glanced at Jin, who nodded, his features drawn into utter seriousness.

"Oh, absolutely, Captain," said Jin, whose uniform was in the same style. "Should I just slit his neck here, or haul him up with the others? August said the dragons are swarming again. Sampson is strong enough to throw him over."

Sampson, another of Kit's crew, nearly filled the doorway with muscles and strength. He smiled, nodded.

That was enough to prompt a response. "I've got information," the smuggler said, words tumbling out.

"About what?" Kit asked. "Because I don't want to hear any further details about the queen's unmentionables."

"Gods save the queen," Jin said with a smile.

"Gods save the queen," Kit agreed, then lifted her brows at the smuggler. "Well?"

"I've information about . . ." His eyes wheeled between them. "About smuggling?"

That he'd made it a question suggested to Kit he really was as oblivious as he pretended to be.

She sighed, made it as haggard as she could. "You know, while Commander Takamura is quite skilled with that sabre, and the dragons probably are swarming—it's that time of year," she added, and Jin nodded his agreement. "Those aren't the things you should be really and truly worried about."

The smuggler swallowed hard. "What do you mean?"

Kit leaned forward, until she was close enough that he could see the sincerity in her eyes. "You should be afraid of the water. It's so dark, and it's so cold. And sea dragons are hardly the only monsters that hunt in its depths." She straightened up again, walked a few paces away, and pretended to look over the other furniture in the room. "Being eaten quickly—devoured by a sea dragon—would be a mercy. Because if you survive, and you sink, you'll go into the darkness."

She looked back at him. "I'm Aligned, you know. I can feel the sea, the rise and fall, like an echo of my heartbeat. I hear a tune just for you, ready to call you home." She took a step closer. "Would you like to be called home?"

She wasn't normally so poetic, or so full of nonsense, but she found getting into character useful in times like this. And it had the man swallowing hard. But he still wasn't talking.

She glanced up at Jin, got his nod. And then he braced an arm against the hull. Behind him, Sampson did the same. They knew what was coming. Knew what she was capable of.

She had to be careful; there was a line that couldn't be crossed, a threshold that couldn't be breached. But before that border, there was power. Potential.

Using her magic, Kit reached out for the current, for the heat and energy, for the ley line that shimmered below them in the waters. She touched it—as carefully as a violinist pressing a string—and the *Amelie* shuddered around them, oak creaking in the wake.

Her trick wasn't familiar to the prisoner. "Gods preserve us," he said, stumbling forward, face gone pale. Jin caught him by the collar, kept him upright, and when he gained his footing again, his eyes had gone huge.

"More?" Kit asked pleasantly.

"I don't know where it came from," the man blurted out, "and that's the gods' truth. I'm in the—I only make the deliveries."

"You're a smuggler," Kit said again, tone flat.

"If we're not being fine about it, yes. I pick up the goods in Fort de la Mer, and I get a fee for delivering them. I don't ask what's in the cargo."

Fort de la Mer was a Gallic village perched on the edge of the Narrow Sea in the thin strait that ran between the Isles and Gallia. It was a busy port for merchants and smugglers alike.

"Delivered to whom?"

"I don't know."

Kit cast her glance to the window, to the ocean that swelled outside.

"All right, all right. There's a pub in Pencester," he sputtered. "The Cork and Barrel. I'm to drop it there."

Pencester was directly across the sea and strait from Fort de la Mer. "To whom?" Kit asked again.

"Not to somebody," he said. "To something. I mean, there's a spot I'm to leave it. A table in the back. I'm to leave the box beneath the bench. That's all I know," he added as Kit lifted a dubious brow. "I deliver, and that's all."

Kit watched him for a moment, debated the likelihood he'd told the entire truth. And decided the Crown Command could wring any remaining information out of him in New London.

"Sampson, put him with the others."

The smuggler blustered as he was led away, muttering about prisoners' rights.

She glanced back, found Jin looking at her with amusement. "'*I hear a tune just for you,*'" he intoned, voice high and musical, "'*ready to call you home.*' That's a new one. And very effective."

"Total nonsense," Kit admitted with a grin. "Sailors like him don't care much for the sea. There's no love, no appreciation.

Only fear. One might as well make use of it." She gestured toward the box. "Do you think you can manage the lock?"

Jin just snorted, pulled a thin metal tool from his pocket, crouched in front of the box, and began to work the complicated arrangement of gears and cylinders. He closed his eyes, face utterly serene as, Kit imagined, he focused on the feel of the metal beneath his long and slender fingers.

He'd been a thief once, and very accomplished. But war had made patriots of many, including Jin, who'd used his spoils to purchase a commission. She'd met him at a pub in Portsdon, a lieutenant who'd just lifted from an arrogant dragoon the coins the dragoon had refused to pay for his dinner. The pub owner was paid, and the dragoon was none the wiser. But Kit had seen the snatch, was impressed by the method and the kindness. And was pleased to discover he'd been assigned to the ship on which she served as commander. That wasn't the last time his skills had come in handy.

"There's no ship that's floating but has a thief aboard," she murmured, repeating the adage.

Jin smiled as he tucked away his tool. "We are useful."

He flipped open the latch and lifted the lid, the hinges creaking slightly against humidity-swollen wood. And then he reached in . . . and pulled out a thick packet of folded paper. He offered it to Kit, and it weighed heavy in her hand.

The papers were bound with thin twine and a seal of thick poppy-red wax. But no symbol had been pressed into the wax, and there was no other mark of the sender on the exterior. No indication the packet was from anyone official. Except that it had been sealed into this very nice box with the very nice lock, and hidden away in the captain's quarters, such as they were.

She slipped her dagger beneath the wax, unfolded the papers. And her heart beat faster as she saw what was written there. Nonsense, or so it appeared. Letters and numbers made up words that were incomprehensible in Islish or the little Gallic she could speak.

The message had been encoded. That alone would have been enough to confirm to Kit it was important, even though it wasn't signed. But she knew the hand, as well—the letters thin and tall and slanting, here in ink the color of rust. She'd seen it. Studied it. Had captured more than one such message before the Treaty of Saint-Denis.

Gerard had penned this message.

She wasn't surprised; this had, after all, been the purpose of her mission. But that didn't douse her growing anger—not just that Gerard was sending coded dispatches in clear violation of the terms of his exile, but that conditions of his exile were comfortable enough to afford him the opportunity. He'd been an emperor, the monarchs had said, stripped of his crown and his glory. He would have known better than to try again. But ego and ambition were rarely so rational.

"Captain," Jin quietly prompted, and she handed the packet to him, watched his face as he reviewed, and saw the light when he reached the same conclusion.

He looked up, dark eyes shining. "It needs decoding, but the handwriting . . ."

"Gerard's," Kit finished, and they looked at each other, nodded. They'd found something. They'd have to wait for the message to be deciphered, but they'd fulfilled their mission.

It was one more mark in her favor, added to the column of miles and missions and nights beneath lightning-crossed skies. One more chance to earn some part of the life she'd been given.

Kit was a foundling who'd been left outside the palace by parents who couldn't care for her—or simply didn't wish to do so. The ribbon now pinned to her uniform—silk and well-worn—had been tied to the basket in which she'd been found. It was the only tangible memory she had of her childhood, and it had become her talisman, her reminder.

She'd been taken in by Hetta Brightling, a widow who intended to use her wealth and connections to house and feed girls who had nowhere else to go. Kit had been fed, educated, and brought up to believe in her own skills and the importance of self-sufficiency. And to Kit's mind, each victory for queen and country helped balance those scales.

But for every victory, there was a matching loss.

"This was bound for Pencester," Jin said darkly.

Kit knew from his tone their thoughts were aligned. Someone inside the Isles was the intended recipient of this missive. Someone inside the Isles was receiving correspondence from Gerard.

At least one of her countrymen was a traitor.

Jin folded the papers, handed them back to her. Kit slipped the packet into her jacket and centered herself, reached down through wood and wave to the waters below, to the bright current of power and let its presence—powerful and inexorable—comfort her.

And when she was steady again, opened her eyes. She had a crew to congratulate.

❧

A shrill whistle from one of the *Diana*'s lieutenants heralded Kit's presence on the *Amelie*'s deck, and all movement and chatter ceased, on both the captured ship and the *Diana*, which rocked alongside her. The *Diana*'s hull was a deep and gleaming blue, with a smart stripe of ivory just below the gunwale. She was rigged as a two-masted schooner, square topsails on the foremast. One hundred and twenty-nine feet of canvas and rope and wood. Kit thought she was the loveliest ship she'd ever seen.

The *Diana* dwarfed the *Amelie*, which had a single dirty sail now hanging limply from its mast, and its decking hadn't seen a holystone in years. Two months of searching, and the *Diana* had the boat in hand, crew contained, missive captured, in less than an hour. Anticipation hummed across the deck like a spark of magic, excitement rising as they looked at her, at Jin, watching their faces for a sign.

The senior officers gathered behind Kit and Jin near the helm. Joining them were Tamlin McCreary, Aligned to the wind (or so Kit believed), who stood beside Kit, red hair streaming in the breeze. Beside her, a man with dark brown skin and short, dark hair, and deep brown eyes behind round spectacles. This was Simon Pettigrew, the *Diana*'s pilot, navigator, and master of maps and intelligence. Simon charted the *Diana*'s course; Kit decided how best to get them there.

"Did we find something, Captain?" a brown-skinned and wrinkled man yelled from the *Diana*'s deck. August was the oldest member of the *Diana*'s crew, and wasn't nearly as spritely as he'd once been, but he knew rigging better than any sailor Kit had ever known.

Kit reached into her coat, then held up the dispatch.

The decks of both ships erupted with screams of victory, sailors and officers alike jumping and shouting with glee. Well, all but the corralled crew of the *Amelie*, who stood in a morose lump on the foredeck, pouting like disappointed children.

"You've all done the *Diana* proud," Kit said.

Some nodded, some touched their hands to the charms they wore on leather thongs around their necks. Their own talismans with bits of fire or grass or stone that had once been infused with the magic of their homes, even if the magic had long since drifted away. She slipped the papers inside her coat, fingers brushing the ribbon pinned there.

The cries of joy continued until a sailor called Banks shoved a sailor named Teasdale a little too hard, sending her tumbling to the deck. Teasdale popped up with an angry curl to her lip. But there was no room for anger among joy and relief and the exhaustion of the voyage. She put out a hand to Banks, and they shook firmly.

"Banks will probably pay for that later," Jin said. "Teasdale is the one who sewed Cook into his hammock."

"Cook had made hardtack tea," Kit said. "That's a punishable offense." She was a citizen of the Isles, by practice if not birth. Tea was a serious matter.

"And yet, he was not punished for the transgression."

"Not by me. He cooks our food. One must choose wisely. But Teasdale did the work for us."

"So, you're saying Cook is in charge of the ship." Jin's tone was dry, but he blinked, reconsidering. "Cook *is* in charge of the ship," he said, surprise tinged with resignation. "Which is why you allowed him to keep a goat in the guest cabin."

Kit found the word *allowed* a bit generous to her, but that just proved her point. She patted Jin's shoulder. "Better you learn early."

"And what shall we do with our prisoners?" Jin asked, gesturing toward August, who glared menacingly at the sailors and pulled a gnarled finger across his throat. Dramatic was August, but she couldn't fault his skills with a marlinspike.

"Mr. Smythe," Kit called out, and August jumped to attention.

"Captain!"

"While I'm certain they're intimidated by the very look of you," she said, working to hold her grin, "let's belay the throat slitting."

"Aye, Captain."

"Ensure we've taken all their weapons, and put them in our brig. Sampson on guard. Bring the coin, weapons, munitions back to the *Diana*."

"And that very fine Gallic brandy?"

"And that. A ration to the crew, the rest to Cook and the queen." Those close enough to hear the order cheered.

"And the ship?" Jin asked.

She looked back at the *Amelie*, contemplated towing it home, but decided the worm-eaten wood was hardly worth the trouble. "Let's waste neither the rope nor the explosives. Let her float."

When Jin walked away to relay the orders and coordinate the movement of goods from the *Amelie*, Kit turned to the rail, watched the horizon glow red and purple and amber, the sun rising through curls of flame. They were a hundred miles offshore, and the water looked slick and smooth. But she could feel the sea rising and falling like a song far below the surface of the water. That was its power, its magic.

She made her own homage. Reaching into her front pocket,

she pulled out a gold coin, ran her thumb over the raised silhou-
ette of Queen Charlotte's likeness.

"*Dastes*," she murmured, an invocation and a prayer, offering
thanks for the magic in the old language, and tossed the coin in.
And hoped the scales were balanced.

TWO

A day later, they were streaming down the Saint James toward New London.

Vessels sailed or rowed toward docks where goods or people would be unloaded, or back toward the sea to find more things to bring home. The *Diana* passed merchant quays where bags and boxes of rice and pepper plums waited to be sent to markets, where hardened crews finally dismissed from months of service dispersed to the larkhouses and pubs that lined the wharf, the shops waiting, eager as hungry fledglings, for their coins.

The weather was fine, the sky unusually clear and dry for spring, so there were more boats than usual crowding into the river. The wind was perfect—at their backs and off starboard— and they flew just enough canvas to make steady progress through the tangle of ships and barges toward the Crown Quay. Jackgulls darted among them, looking for scraps tossed by fishermen or for schools of fish feasting on the detritus that collected on the hulls.

Each time Kit returned to New London, she remembered standing on the banks of the Saint James as a child, mesmerized by the jungle of rigging. Hetta Brightling, who'd stood barely taller than Kit even then, had held Kit's hand as they watched ships sail downriver. Kit remembered the water, nearly the color of Hetta's favorite tea, light skipping across the surface as eddies whirled below. And she thought that she could . . . feel it. The first trembling in her chest, soft and low as a note from a cello. Slow and steady as water snaked toward the sea. And deeper than that, something brighter, thinner, hotter. With her mind, and with her hand, Kit reached out toward that line of power and, ever so gently, touched it . . . and felt the sea's answering shiver, like a ripple spreading outward.

Then she'd been jerked backward, pulled away from the water, and when she blinked back to the world, found herself staring into Hetta's brown eyes.

"You nearly fell in," Hetta had said, her breath coming short.

"There's something in the water," Kit said.

Hetta's brow had knit. "What? Did you find a treasure?"

There were often treasures along the river's shore, bits of pottery or coins hidden among the rocks and mud, lost a hundred or a thousand years ago.

"I don't think so." Kit had looked back at the river again, seen only the lapping of brown waves. "I could . . . feel it. It was cold and slow, and then it was hot and fast." Those were the only words she'd known to describe it. She put a hand to her chest. "It made a *thump* in here. Like a heartbeat."

She remembered Hetta had looked surprised. Kit hadn't been sure she liked the idea of Hetta being surprised by anything; Hetta had always simply *known*.

They'd eventually realized that Kit was Aligned, that the "thing" she felt had been the river's own magic. But it wasn't until some months later, when Hetta had taken the girls to Bellamy Sands, a beachside village on the southern side of the Isles, that Kit had realized the river's low song paled in comparison to the roar of the sea.

Now that song was fading in her ears as the *Diana* moved toward the Crown Quay, the deepwater harbor that sheltered several Crown Command ships. The sails would be hauled down, the hold unloaded of prisoners, of prizes, of crew members who'd almost certainly make for the nearest pub and the cheapest tankard of ale.

Kit had other priorities—namely, reporting to the queen and delivering the bounty they'd obtained from the *Amelie*. And as they neared the dock, Kit realized she wasn't the only one eager for news. A man and woman waited there, their polished uniforms crossed with the saffron sashes worn across their chests marking them as royal emissaries.

"Looks like they want to speak with you right away."

Kit glanced back from her spot near the helm. Tamlin stood behind her, feet bare and chewing a chunk from a rusty apple.

"Was that the last one in the barrel?" Kit asked, gesturing to the apple.

Tamlin grinned, swiped a freckled hand over her mouth. "Likely. Cook threw it at me. It's sweet. Bit mealy, though." She took another bite.

Kit lifted her brows. "And still you eat it."

Tamlin lifted a shoulder. "Fills the belly. I guess you'll go with them."

"I need to report what we've found. And responding to a summons from the queen is rarely optional."

"Of course it is," Tamlin said as she chewed. "If you prefer the stocks to the deck. But you probably don't." She tilted her head. "I don't think you'd look good in manacles."

"Not a good match with the uniform," Kit agreed. "They must have been watching for us, relayed a message from the watchtower. She wants to know what Gerard's about." Or there'd been developments while they'd been sailing, and those developments were secret enough that the queen hadn't wanted to reveal them in the mail exchanged between ships.

Tamlin took a final bite, tossed the core into the water, and looked back at her captain. "Whatever they say, don't forget your manners."

Kit's dark eyebrow lifted. "I'm as mannerly as my profession requires."

"We cavort with sailors, pirates, and felons."

"Only on the good days," Kit said with a grin. "Stay with the ship," she added absently. Without waiting for a response, Kit climbed down onto the dock, severing her connection with the sea. She'd have a hollow in her chest until she returned to the water. And that wasn't the only adjustment.

The rigidity of the boardwalk echoed in her bones with each step. And while the air still smelled of brine and carried the slosh of water against wood, the sounds and scents of the city were layered over it. Humans and animals and woodsmoke and cooking. And instead of the creak of hemp against wood, there were hooves against brick, the call of gulls, a sorrowful melody played by a busker in front of the customs house.

The emissaries stood at attention, hands clasped behind their backs, faces set in blank scowls.

"Captain Brightling," said the one on the left. "Her Royal Highness Queen Charlotte II requests your immediate attendance at the palace. We've horses." He gestured to three enormous creatures that stared at Kit from the end of the dock, chewing their bits with gargantuan teeth.

Kit Brightling had faced down typhoons, ships of the line, pirates, hunger. She didn't mind being aloft, wasn't nervous speaking to the queen, and had no qualms about leading her crew through storm or charge. But she had to work very hard to keep the dread out of her eyes.

It's not that she was afraid of horses. *She wasn't.* That would have been childish. She simply didn't *trust* them, and that was a matter of logic. They were larger than humans, had enormous teeth made for grinding, and could kill a human merely by lying on them. Putting one's life in the hands—hooves?—of a horse was simply bad planning.

Kit shook her head. "I prefer to walk." She was fairly certain she'd kept her tone mild.

"Walk, Captain?" The emissary on the right looked horrified.

"I've been cooped up on the *Diana*, so I'd appreciate the fresh air. And it's a scant half mile to the palace."

"Very well," said the one on the left. "Proceed inside. You will be met."

Before they could change their minds, she turned on a heel and strode toward the road, giving the beasts a very wide berth.

Not because she was afraid.

Because she was *wise*.

THREE

She might have preferred water to land, but there was something to be said for the markets of New London. Stalls lined the road that led to Exeter Palace, baskets overflowing with spices and fruit, pastries and pasties. One stall sold amulets and tokens, another cuts of mutton, a third the softly woven fabric from the Isles' northern reaches. People of a seemingly endless variety moved among them—tall, short; dark, light. Some had come to the Isles to escape the violence of war on the Continent, others as part of cultural exchanges instituted by King Richard, the queen's father, before his death. Diversified and open markets, he believed, were healthier and, therefore, more stable for the populous than economics based on few goods and colonization.

At the edge of the market, solid and stately, was Marten's, the coffeehouse where investors insured the cargo, placing bets on which ships would come back—and which wouldn't—and ringing the bell for each merchant ship that returned safely to port.

As she neared the palace, the stalls gave way to stately buildings where importers brought in goods from the Continent, and sent out goods from the Isles. Bolts of silks and good brandy coming in, wool and coal going out. The Unified Church of Isles, where the old gods had been exchanged for a unified being who created and spread the world's magic, stood across a busy road from the palace, its own silver bell chiming the hour as she passed.

Exeter Palace was long and white and columned, nearly eight hundred rooms that served as Queen Charlotte's residence in New London. It was surrounded by an imposing black fence over which curled the Saxon sea dragon in brilliant gold.

She was recognized by the guards—all of them members of the Queen's Own—and was allowed through the gate and into the grand rotunda of the palace proper. White stone marbled through with pale gray and gold covered floor to domed ceiling. The cavernous room was nearly empty but for a few who waited for instructions or meetings with the queen or her emissaries.

Kit glanced around . . . and found a friend among them. He stood near a potted palm at the edge of the room: tall and fashionably trim, with green eyes and a short crop of dark hair. Charles Kingsley worked in the Crown Command's Foreign Office for the Isles' spymaster, William Chandler. Kit's sister and closest friend, Jane, was convinced Kit and Kingsley were destined for wedding bells. Kit liked Kingsley, but she had no interest in marriage, in giving up the sea for domesticity.

Kingsley looked up as she moved toward him, and smiled warmly. She smiled back.

"Mr. Kingsley," Kit said.

"Captain Brightling," he said, and offered a bow as neat as his black tailcoat and waistcoat. "I didn't know you'd returned."

"Only just now," Kit said. "You're waiting to see Chandler?"

"I regret I'm unable to provide any details regarding my intentions."

Kit snorted. "You are, as ever, the soul of discretion."

"I could hardly work for Chandler without being so. Your mission was successful?"

"I regret I am unable et cetera, et cetera." Many knew of her position in the Queen's Own, but few were aware of her actual duties. Most believed she was little more than a courier, shuttling important messages to and from New London. She had delivered messages once or twice, when time was of the essence. But her missions were rarely so mundane.

King Richard had created the regiment to serve as his personal guards after an assassin was nearly successful in removing him from power. The king believed the attempt was aided by officers within the Crown Command, so to his personal guards he'd added a select few others who could undertake sensitive tasks without the Command's knowledge. Queen Charlotte had carried on the tradition when she took the throne after his death, and Kit had been inducted three years later.

Kingsley grinned. "Chandler should steal you away from the queen."

"I belong to the sea," she said, "and the sea belongs to me."

"Sailors always have a proverb at the ready."

"John Cox," she said. "*Cox's Seamanship* is very quotable."

Kingsley snorted. "John Cox didn't have a friend in the entire fleet, and spent most of his time at a desk penning that blasted book." He tapped a finger against his temple. "With intelligence officers, it's all brains. Learning what's worth the trouble—and what isn't."

"And what's worth the trouble?"

Kingsley laughed. "Little enough, as it turns out."

"Kingsley!"

They looked over. The man who approached in army red was pale and thin, with a scattering of freckles and short red hair. "We've just finished up here," he said, "and we're going to the Seven Keys. Come with us."

"Stanton. I've business today, but may join you yet this evening." He gestured to Kit. "Do you know Captain Brightling?"

He gave Kit a quick appraisal. "Oh, the queen's messenger, eh? With the good magic and fast ship? Always good to see a blue uniform. Our comrades on the sea, and all that. John Stanton. Foreign Office."

"Kit Brightling," she said, and didn't bother to correct his misperceptions.

"Captain Brightling has just returned from a voyage," Kingsley said. "Although she hasn't yet graced me with the details."

"The queen's concerns aren't mine to share," she said.

"So mysterious, the Queen's Own." Stanton's features screwed into something Kit guessed he considered serious. "You have quite the reputation."

"Do I?" Kit asked.

"For your . . . magical abilities," he said. "I, for one, believe there's too much emphasis on magic these days."

"Too much emphasis?" Kit asked mildly, hardly the first time she'd heard objections.

"Military action should be about physical skill. Mental prowess. Leadership and hardiness."

"I doubt Lord Sutherland would agree," Kit said. Sutherland was beloved in the Isles, the hero who'd chased Gerard across the Continent's southern peninsula—and had relied on Aligned officers to use the land to his advantage.

Stanton flushed, red rising high sharply against his pale skin. "Sutherland's use of Aligned officers is greatly exaggerated by those who have their own agendas."

Kit cocked her head. "Those who prefer to understand the topography of their battlefields?"

The flush deepened again. It was, Kit thought, rather like watching the sun rise and fall, spreading its colors across the sky.

"I find that anyone who decries magic," she said, now determined to see just how dark that flush would go, "either fears or misunderstands it."

This time, insult had him tipping up his chin defiantly. "I have no fear. I've earned my place by work and determination. Not by being"—his gaze raked disdainfully over Kit's uniform—"touched by some sort of conjuration."

Kingsley's eyes went hard. "I'm surprised, Stanton, that you'd have such old-fashioned ideas—or that you'd think it appropriate to voice them."

Stanton's brows lifted, as if shocked Kingsley would be so impertinent. "I'm late for an engagement," he added lamely, then walked away.

"I'm sorry for that," Kingsley said. "I hadn't known Stanton was quite such an ass."

"Beau Monde," she murmured. The Beau Monde was the Isles' most privileged class, its members born into extraordinary wealth and primarily concerned, at least in Kit's experience, with their own comfort and ease.

"Regretfully so," Kingsley said. "Although he's not usually quite so obnoxious."

Kit smiled.

"Captain Brightling."

They both looked over. The man who'd called her name was tan, his hair dark, his body compact and strong. Kess was the queen's closest adviser.

"If you'll come with me?" he asked.

"Of course. Kingsley," she said, glancing back at him.

"Brightling. Fair winds and following seas."

"I'm glad to see you've returned safely," Kess said as they walked down a wide marble hallway ornamented with portraits of previous kings and queens, sumptuous ermine pooling at their feet.

"Thank you. I'd intended to report immediately, but found emissaries waiting at the dock."

"There have been . . . developments," Kess said, confirming Kit's suspicions.

They turned into the anteroom, with its ladies-in-waiting and high gilt windows, and walked through it to the mahogany door—finely carved with a sinuous sea dragon—at the other end of the hall. A guard nodded at Kess, pulled the door open.

The walls of the throne room were the soft red of deep sunset, light dappling across them from the dozen crystal chandeliers that hung from the arched ceiling. At the far end of the room stood the golden throne cushioned in the same soft red, and bearing the queen's monogram—*CR* for Charlotte Regia.

Queen Charlotte sat her throne with grace and power. She was a stunning woman of thirty-three, with dark brown skin, brown eyes, and a straight nose above generous lips. Her dark hair rose like a wave above her golden diadem, and her aubergine dress was fitted low across her shoulders, marked by the saffron sash of Isles royalty and the sea dragon brooch that marked her as leader of the unified Crown Command.

Kess took his position beside the throne. Kit dropped her gaze to the thick carpet as she neared it, then dropped to one knee when she reached it. "Your Highness."

"Rise, Captain."

She did as commanded and held herself at attention, meeting the gaze of the ruler of the Saxon Isles.

The queen had inherited the throne from her father when he'd fallen ill in the midst of the war. She was the only child of an only child, and the duty of ruling the Isles had fallen to her in wartime at the age of twenty-eight. She'd managed the war with a savvy that surprised the king's advisers. And then she'd dismissed them.

"I was excited to learn of your return, Captain," the queen said. "Your mission?"

She wasn't wasting any time, Kit thought, and pulled the packet from her coat. The queen took it, opened it, and read.

And then swore. "Coded, but in his strange penmanship," the queen said. "Either a remarkable forgery, or another bit of arrogance. The treacherous bastard." She looked back at Kit. "Where was it found?"

"On a packet called the *Amelie*, Your Highness. Running under the Isles' flag."

"He would dare," she muttered.

"The *Amelie*'s captain told us the communication was part of cargo he picked up at Fort de la Mer. He was to leave it in a Pencester pub called the Cork and Barrel."

The queen's brows lifted. "Do you know it?"

"I don't, Your Highness."

"Then we will." She handed the packet to Kess, who slipped it inside his jacket.

There was movement to Kit's right. Her hand went instinctively to her dagger, weight shifting as she prepared to meet the threat. Two men walked toward the dais from a closing panel on the far side of the room. Given the queen's cool expression, they weren't unexpected.

Neither wore a uniform, just somber tailcoats and trousers. The first Kit had seen before, but never formally met. This was William Chandler, the spymaster. He was a big man, with tan skin and brown hair, a square jaw, and a face some would call rugged. And while his expression stayed mild, there was no disguising his confidence or his authority. This was a man in his power—a man who had the ear of the queen.

Kit didn't know the second. He was a tall man, with sun-kissed skin, his hair a sun-streaked brown brushed over a strong brow, his eyes a startling blue green.

"Mr. Chandler," the queen said. "I believe you know Captain Brightling."

Chandler nodded at her, expression cool. She did the same.

"Colonel Rian Grant, Viscount Queenscliffe," the queen said, gesturing to the other man.

Grant didn't look like a member of the Beau Monde, Kit thought, much less any viscount she'd ever seen. His shoulders were broad, and his body looked capable of action, not merely climbing in and out of a curricle to circle Victory Park. There was energy here, banked power, in such volume it seemed to charge the air in the room.

"Colonel Grant served as one of Sutherland's observing officers on the peninsula, and fought at Zadorra." Zadorra, near the river of the same name, was a town in Hispania not far from the Gallic border. There'd been brutal fighting there over hard terrain not long before the war ended. The casualties had been . . . severe.

"Colonel Grant," the queen continued, "this is Captain Kit Brightling of the Queen's Own."

If he had any thoughts about her presence in the room, they were well hidden behind a bland expression.

"Colonel," Kit said, opting for the title the queen had used.

"Captain." His tone was bland, as if mildly irritated to find her in his presence.

Charming, Kit thought.

"Now that you've gotten a look at each other," the queen said, "let's begin. I've asked you both here to deal with a very urgent matter. Marcus Dunwood is missing."

Kit knew Dunwood, at least by name. Like Kingsley, he worked for Chandler, gathering foreign intelligence abroad. She surmised Grant knew him, too, because he'd shifted beside her. Just the slightest movement, as if bracing against a blow.

"What's happened?" Grant asked, and his tone was grim.

The queen nodded at Chandler. "If you would."

"Dunwood had been serving on a sloop running cargo along the northern coast of Gallia," Chandler said. "Monitoring Guild activity."

The Guild was a Frisian association of the country's wealthy and powerful merchants. During the war, they'd supplied money and arms to Gerard in exchange for promised trade monopolies on spices, silk, and other goods.

"Monitoring them?" Kit asked.

"There was a downturn in economic activity following the end of the war," Chandler said. "Peace, as it turns out, is rarely as profitable. But trade activity is increasing again. More Guild ships leaving port, carrying greater cargo."

"Bound for?" Kit asked.

Chandler's lips curved, as if pleased by the query. "Everywhere they can manage it. We've identified no particularly unusual location or focus. And cargo moving into Guild ports has also increased. Wood, iron, hemp among them. Not, on their own, particularly unusual. They are required for many industries."

"But they are also useful in war," the queen said. "For guns. For ships."

Chandler nodded. "Yes. They've been very cautious. There's been nothing certain—documents or information—linking the Guild to Gerard, or to efforts to restore him to his former position. But the, shall we say, suggestive information cannot be ignored."

"And Dunwood?" Grant prompted.

"His last communiqué was received three weeks ago. Then, two days ago, the crew of the *Carpathian*—a privateer with a letter of marque from the Crown—found four injured sailors on a disabled sloop off the coast of Gallia, near Pointe Grise. They claimed to have been attacked, the fifth member of their crew taken."

"Dunwood was the fifth," Grant surmised.

Chandler confirmed with a nod. "The sailors stated the sloop's attackers had sought out and removed the crewman they knew as 'Paolo.' And thought it odd the attackers had referred to him as 'Marcus.'"

"They knew who he was," Grant said quietly.

Chandler nodded. "I'm sorry."

"You and Dunwood were friends," the queen said to Grant.

"We were together on the peninsula," Grant said. "He renewed his commission after Gerard's capture, and I returned to Queenscliffe."

And from the gruff tone, Kit thought it sounded as if he'd rather have remained there.

"You believe his identity was compromised," Grant said.

"We do," Chandler said. "By culprits we have not yet identified."

"There weren't many who knew of Marcus's mission, and even fewer his last location," the queen said. "And those who knew were members of the Crown Command."

That simple statement, and the accusation beneath it, cut through the room like a sabre.

"Which is why we're the only ones in the room," Kit said. "You believe there are traitors in the Crown Command."

"Yes," said the queen. And that word fell like a shadow across the room. They waited in silence for her to speak again.

"There have been traitors in the Crown Command before. My father removed many who'd been proven disloyal. Among them an admiral, a major general, and two agents in the Foreign Office. He installed a new minister and believed the Command secure." The queen's breath shuddered. Not with fear or concern, Kit thought, but with fury.

"Either he was wrong, or foreign agents have gotten their claws in again." She looked back at Kit and Grant, gaze burning with intensity. "I don't know who may have revealed Dunwood's name. But I will learn their name, and they will answer to me. Marcus has served the Isles for two decades. We will not leave him to molder or die while the rest of us sit in luxury. And that brings us to this meeting. The two of you will find him and bring him home."

The room went silent, and Kit had to work not to shift her gaze to the man beside her.

"The two of us," she said, hoping against hope she'd misheard the queen.

"Aboard the *Diana*," the queen said. "You will search for Marcus Dunwood, you will locate him, and you will free him."

Kit knew a command when she heard one. "Is there intelligence regarding his whereabouts?" she asked.

"The sailors believed Dunwood's captors were headed for Finistère," Chandler said.

"The pirate fortress," Kit said. "And, literally, 'the end of the earth.'" She knew the island's name and its reputation. It was the largest rocky island among many on the far western edge of Gallia at the boundary of the Narrow Sea. The archipelago was difficult to navigate, and the cliffs afforded a long view of the sea, which had long made it a favorite for pirates and privateers— including the Five, the famous pirate kings, who'd made their home in the fortress during the war.

"What would the Five want with Dunwood?" Kit asked.

"Money," Chandler said. "Even the Five aren't arrogant enough to sail directly into a Frisian port. So they take Dunwood back to Finistère, and wait for the highest bidder to retrieve him."

"Unless we get there first," Kit said, and Chandler nodded.

"Your Highness," Grant said, "the *Diana* is not a ship of war, and it cannot be sufficient for a frontal attack on a pirate quay. A larger vessel with guns would be more appropriate."

His tone—confident and cold—stoked Kit's anger, notwithstanding the fact that he was simply wrong. She'd yet to meet a soldier who could tell a staysail from a jib.

"Rescue missions require speed and maneuverability," Kit said, sparing Grant her most withering look. "Size is irrelevant, and guns are little use when trying to outrun another ship at full sail. The *Diana* is as swift as they come." Particularly, she thought, when I'm at the helm.

"You're a *courier*," Grant said. "That's hardly—"

"Grant," Chandler warned.

A warning Grant did not heed. "We cannot simply—"

"Colonel Grant," the queen said, her voice thunderous across the room. "Remember our conversation and where you stand."

His struggle for control was obvious, but he held his tongue. "Your Highness," Grant said tightly. And Kit would have given a few gold coins to be privy to whatever had been said between them.

After a moment, as if deciding she'd made her point, the queen shifted her gaze to Chandler. "It appears your suggestion we downplay the captain's position was perhaps too successful."

"So it appears," Chandler said. "Brightling isn't a mere courier, Grant, and the *Diana* no packet ship. Brightling fought at San Miguel, discovered the Gallic ships at Faulkney. And the *Diana* will do ten knots without magic—"

"Eleven," Kit corrected.

"Eleven," Chandler said with a nod and mild smile. "And with Captain Brightling's magic, considerably faster."

Grant looked at Kit. "You're Aligned?"

"I am," she said, eyes flashing and daring him to comment. But he made no response.

"And, as I mentioned, Grant is an able veteran with his own skills," the queen said to Kit, anticipating her silent objections. "You both have experience in battle in your respective forces. You have both shown resilience under pressure. You are leaders. And, although your present displays make me question my judgment, which I dislike very much, I believe you will complement each other." She looked at each of them in turn, an obvious threat in her eyes. "You will partner in this mission, and you will share the command."

It was Kit's turn to bristle. But she held her tongue.

"Sensible," the queen added, nodding in approval at Kit's control. "Given the need for dispatch, you will set sail tomorrow morning. The *Diana* will be provisioned this evening."

"How long will it take to reach Finistère?" Grant asked, and they all looked at Kit.

"Depending on seas and weather, and if we're able to maintain speed, about a day and a half."

Grant's features remained stony, his eyes hard. And there was something else there. Something deeper, darker. Nothing she could identify, at least not yet. But if she was to share her ship—and risk her people—she'd find out soon enough.

"The *Diana* is anchored at the Crown Quay," Kit told him. "You know it?"

"I do."

"Be there at dawn."

"Very well." The words were short, sharp. Bitten off, as if their taste were bitter.

Apparently satisfied they wouldn't mutiny, at least not in the throne room, the queen sat back, looked at each of them in turn.

"Find him," she said. "Find Marcus Dunwood, and bring him home."

FOUR

Kit strode back through the palace, anger building like a storm along the horizon.

She'd do her duty, by gods, because that's what duty was. Adversity, Hetta had told her daughters, was to be faced head-on, chin lifted, and fists raised. But she didn't want to haul a viscount across the sea. She didn't want to listen to his complaints or commands, or watch her words to avoid offending his sensibilities. Which might prove a problem given the state of the guest cabin . . .

She exited the palace, blinked in the sunlight, took a breath. She had sixteen hours, give or take, before the *Diana* was ready to sail again, and she'd use every damned minute of it. There was much to be done. First thing—get a message to Jin about the *Diana*'s mission. He had a wife and two children, and sixteen hours wasn't much to spend with them. But it would have to be enough.

"Flower, missus?"

Kit stared down into the grubby face of a small girl.

She was thin and young, her light skin dotted with freckles

(and dirt), and her hair was a mass of tangled curls cut just below her firm chin. Kit guessed she was eleven or twelve, and that she'd taken the flowers—and their earth-clotted roots—from the palace's front border.

Kit lifted an eyebrow. "I don't need weeds stolen from someone else's garden."

The flowers hit the ground, immediately abandoned. "I can also deliver things. Or carry things. Two bits."

Kit snorted at the price, but she didn't like the hollows in the girl's cheeks. "What's your name?"

Her eyes narrowed. "Why do you want to know?"

"I have a task that needs doing. An important message delivered, and I need to know the name of the girl delivering it."

"Louisa."

"Is that your real name?"

"Why wouldn't it be?" She held out her hand. "Silver."

Kit couldn't fault her courage, even if her prices were high. "Copper," she said, pulling a coin from her pocket.

The girl looked at her pityingly.

"You know the Crown Quay?" Kit asked.

"Where the queen's ships are."

"Exactly. I need a message delivered to the *Diana*. The message is for Jin, one of the ship's officers."

The girl pointed to the braiding on Kit's uniform. "Officers have gold on their coats."

"They do. I'll give you the copper to deliver it. And if Jin wants to send a message back to me, there'll be another copper waiting for you."

She watched Kit for a moment, nodded. "I can take a message."

"Good. The message is this: '*Diana* sails at dawn. CR will provision tonight. Go home.' Repeat it back to me."

Louisa rolled her eyes. "*Diana* sails at dawn. CR will provision tonight. Go home. Repeat it back to me."

"Very amusing," Kit said, and offered her the coin. The girl snapped it away, slipped it into a pocket of her short and dirty jacket.

"Do you know the Brightling house?" Kit asked.

Louisa's eyes widened. "Where the foundling girls live. They say a wee fairy lives with them."

Hetta was small, if entirely human. "If Jin has a return message, it can be sent there."

Louisa looked her over with obvious skepticism. "And I'll be paid another copper if I deliver that message."

"Yes," Kit said. "That's a promise from a captain."

With a nod, the girl sprinted toward the river.

⌣

Kit wanted a hot bath, tea with milk, a penny story, and a good biscuit. But there'd be no biscuits waiting for her in the Brightling house. Mrs. Eaves, the housekeeper, believed in mutton, hard-boiled eggs, and exceedingly dry toast. Spicy foods, she liked to say, led to spicy tempers.

Kit remembered she'd managed only a slice of meager toast while the *Diana* had slipped up the Saint James toward New London. And considering what she'd likely find at home, she thought of the stall Jin had shown her one rainy evening—and the dish she'd found there.

She passed the church again, then moved briskly through the narrow alley, past the stalls selling penny dreadfuls and romances, fried pastries and sugared fruits, to the counter where a woman in white, her dark hair a gleaming knot atop her head, seemed bathed in fragrant steam.

Kit put down a silver coin, and it was swept away, replaced almost immediately with a bowl of thick noodles in broth dotted with flecks of spicy peppers she knew would flay her tongue with heat.

And dug in immediately.

⁓

Two bowls later, when her hunger was finally sated and her mouth aflame, she strode down High Street to the building Mrs. Eaves had once called New London's premier temple of sin. Portnoy's Confectioners was a temple of puddings and biscuits and scones and desserts, a fantasy of sugar in glossy green boxes, and the pistachio nougats Kit loved most of all. She bought a box for her sisters, a paper cone of nougats for herself that she'd eat on the walk home.

New London became quieter as she walked toward Moreham Park and away from the bustle of shops and merchants, away from wagons hauling goods, and carriages waiting to disgorge their passengers for an afternoon of shopping. When she reached Francis Street, shade from towering oaks and elderwoods dappled light across the walk, and birds in the park proper chirped happily in the afternoon sun.

She stopped at No. 62. The familiar town house of painted white brick, with its gleaming black door, and round shrubberies behind the short black gate. A bronze sign, small and inconspicuous, posted beside the door was the only indication the town house was anything other than a typical residence. BRIGHTLING HOME FOR FOUNDLINGS it read in tidy block letters. EST. 1792.

One year after Hetta had returned from the Continent alone, having buried her husband on a high cliff near the sea.

Sir Harry Brightling had been a smart and canny man, born into "genteel" poverty before making money in some investment or other. He'd also been, at least based on the stories Kit had heard, a kind and generous man who'd loved Hetta to distraction. The Brightling house had been born of his wealth and her love, and bore the name he'd given her.

Hetta liked to tell her daughters that she hadn't needed to give birth; she'd only needed to find her children and gather them home. Seven girls were residents now—Kit, Jane, Astrid, Bettina, Georgina, Pari, and Marielle—all allowed to live in the Brightling house as long as they needed. In exchange for Hetta's financial and emotional support, they were expected to master their studies, learn and practice Hetta's Principles of Self-Sufficiency, and when they were grown, make a contribution— financial or otherwise—to family or nation.

Principle of Self-Sufficiency No. 1: Never take for granted the generosity of others.

Kit pushed through the low gate, took the steps to the front door, and opened it . . . to the sounds of combat.

She looked into the parlor. Two girls, identically dressed in white trousers and shirtsleeves, white masks on their faces, pointed épées at each other in the center of the room.

"Point," said one girl, stepping back and lifting her mask. Her pale face was freckled, her hair short and red, victory gleaming in her green eyes. "And that's a win for me."

The second swordswoman lifted her mask to reveal a markedly similar face, although her tight curls were pinned up at the back. "You cheated!" she said.

"Absolutely did not."

"I saw no cheating," Kit said, and the girls squealed, and launched themselves in her direction.

"Kit!" They wrapped their arms around her.

"How was your trip?"

"Was there treasure?"

"What about pirates?"

Bettina and Georgina were twins, and they approached everything with the same singular focus and vigor. And they craved adventure in the way of thirteen-year-olds who couldn't wait for the freedom to find it, and refused to accept the notion that Kit was a mere courier.

"We found what we were looking for," Kit said. "And I found this on the way home." She held out the Portnoy's box.

The girls looked at each other, nodded. Bettina took the box. Georgina ran to the doorway, looked into the hall.

"Clear," she said, and Bettina went to a corner of the room, dropped into a crouch. Using a fingernail, she flipped up a short plank of the floorboard, revealing a small compartment. She added the Portnoy's box, then pressed the floorboard down again and stood.

The loose board in the parlor had been a popular hiding spot even when Kit was a child.

"Cheeky girls," Kit said, when they both came back grinning. "Where are the others?"

"Jane is upstairs, as always," Bettina said, joining them again. "Pari took Marielle to the park. Astrid is calling on Mary Cartwright." Her tone dipped a bit at the last. At nineteen, Astrid was determined to marry her way into connections, wealth, and stability. Kit couldn't fault her desire for security, even if she didn't understand the desire to memorize the list of the season's most eligible Beau Monde members. Come to think of it, Astrid and Grant would probably get along royally.

"Get back to your practice."

"Come on," Georgina said, slipping her arm into Bettina's. "I'll give you one more chance to beat me."

Bettina snorted as Kit slipped through the long central hallway to the kitchen. And was stopped by a wooden spoon held at arm's length like the finest of swords.

"Halt."

Kit followed the spoon to the woman who wielded it. She was slender but strong, with pale skin and silver hair. Her dress was gray and starched so stiffly it might stand on its own.

"Mrs. Eaves," Kit said. And was glad her gift had been hidden.

Mrs. Eaves pulled the spoon back, looked down at Kit from nearly six feet of imposing height. "It doesn't appear you've eaten for a month. I hope you managed to feed your crew."

"The queen is frugal. We prefer to throw them overboard when they start complaining of hunger."

Mrs. Eaves's mouth thinned in obvious disapproval. But as much as Kit enjoyed their sparring—and surmised Mrs. Eaves did, too—there were other matters at hand.

"I sail again in the morning," Kit said, before Mrs. Eaves could voice that disapproval. "I'd like a bath after supper, please."

Try as she might, not even stoic Mrs. Eaves could hide the flare of concern that creased her brow. "You're leaving in the morning? But you've only just returned."

"Someone needs our help," Kit said, and felt the weight of the words and the obligation. Tomorrow, she'd don her coat, deliver a coin into the sea for luck and thanks, and command her ship and her crew into danger. But right now—in the warm kitchen of the house on Francis Street—she allowed herself a moment's regret, and a moment's gratefulness.

"In the morning," Kit said again. "And a bath this evening would be most welcome."

"Then it will be done," Mrs. Eaves said, and nodded stiffly. "I believe we've yet some of the lavender salts you enjoy."

"Thank you."

Their agreement dissolved the temporary truce, and Mrs. Eaves squared her shoulders again, narrowed her gaze. "What contraband did you sneak into my house?"

"I have no idea what you mean," Kit said, and slipped away.

The potting room, with its long table, tile floor, and views of the garden, had become the domain of Kit's closest sister, Jane.

It was a simple room, with whitewashed walls and chairs near the windows, perfect for reading. But that wasn't the kind of contemplation that most commonly happened here. Work was done at the well-worn table in the middle of the room. Jane had scoured the kitchen for bottles and jars and pots, had borrowed books from Hetta's library. And she'd directed her energies toward solving the mysteries of the world's substances.

She funded her studies and purchased new wares with the profits of the things she'd already invented. Solid soap that never diminished or dissolved. A fertilizer made of ground turnips and beets—the only appropriate use for either, in Kit's opinion—that nearly turned their small garden into a jungle. A paste that provided all the nutrition a body needed for an entire day's work—and that tasted as revolting as it looked.

Jane was two years younger than Kit's twenty-four years. She was tall and pale with blond hair, blue eyes, and a wide mouth. It was presently curved into a frown as she peered down at a thick book, used white gloves to carefully turn the pages.

It relieved Kit immensely to see her. But then she narrowed her eyes. "Are you wearing my gloves?"

Jane's squeal of delight rang through the room. "You're back!" she said, pulling off the gloves and running to her sister, wrapping Kit in an embrace. "I've missed you terribly."

"I've missed you, too," Kit said. "And those are my gloves."

Jane snorted. "You hardly ever wear them." She smiled slyly at Kit. "If you'd been here, I'd have asked you first."

"But since I wasn't, you helped yourself?"

"I had work to do."

"You might as well keep them now," Kit said. "They're probably soaked in deadly chemicals, and I have to sail again at dawn."

Jane's smile fell away. "We'll hardly have time to catch up."

"Then we'll have to catch up quickly," Kit said with a smile. "My mission was successful, my crew and ship are safe, and I'll be sailing tomorrow with a viscount. Oh, and I saw Kingsley."

"Did you?" Jane's brows lifted.

"It was a very brief meeting." She decided on sparing the confidential details.

"And how was he?"

"Amusing," Kit decided. "And he defended my honor when a soldier delighted in explaining that magic is nonsense."

Jane smiled approvingly. "Then Kingsley has better sense

than the soldier. Have you considered telling Kingsley that you enjoy his company, and suggesting he escort you to a musicale?"

Kit's mouth thinned. "I have no interest in musicales."

"No one of sane mind has an interest in musicales," Jane said. "That's hardly the point."

"Which is?"

Jane made an exhausted sound. "To spend time in the company of someone charming and handsome."

"In order to provoke an offer of marriage," Kit finished. "And as I also have no interest in resigning my commission to spend my days with needlepoint and social calls, I'd rather provoke a sea dragon. The cost is too high."

"Even for Kingsley?"

"For anyone."

Jane just sighed. "Where are you going tomorrow?"

"I'm sworn to secrecy," Kit said. "But it's a mission of utmost importance and valor."

"You're being mysterious again."

"I try to be mysterious at least thrice a day. It keeps the blood moving."

"Speaking of mysteries and missions," Jane said, moving around the table, "I have a little something for you to try."

Kit narrowed her eyes. "Do you think I've forgotten the vinegar candies? Fool me once, shame on you. Fool me twice, also shame on you, because I'm your devoted sister."

Jane picked up a velvet pouch that lay on a corner of the table. "So devoted you stopped by Portnoy's and didn't bring me so much as a nougat?"

Kit's eyes narrowed. "How do you know that?"

"You smell of chocolate."

"The twins have the package. Well concealed."

"Concealed in their belly within the hour," Jane predicted. "Hold out your hand, please," she said, when she'd reached Kit again.

Kit extended her palm, marked with the history of her Alignment, and Jane spilled the contents of the bag into it—two glass marbles, smooth and cold, and spun through with color. Kit held one up so sunlight shined through it, sending blue light glimmering across the floor. "They're beautiful. But why did you make marbles?"

"Thank you. And they aren't marbles. They're explosives."

Kit went completely rigid. "I beg your very serious pardon. You just dropped *explosives* into my hand?"

"I call them sparkers. They're quite inert. Unless you drop them."

Kit's expression was murderous. She hadn't planned on returning to a battlefield tonight, nor expected that her beloved sister would actually lob munitions at her.

"Just a bit of a joke," Jane said. "I mean, they are explosives, but dropping them won't do anything. They have to be triggered. There's a small depression in the glass. Press it until you feel the glass heat. Then throw it. *Quickly*," she added, as if Kit might need the incentive to put distance between herself and a warming explosive.

Frowning, Kit carefully lifted one from her palm. The glass was smooth but for, as promised, a gentle divot on one side that was slightly rougher than the other so it could be triggered even in darkness.

"I thought they'd be useful since the *Diana* has no guns, and your mission is certain to be dangerous."

Kit just looked at her. "I have no idea what you mean. I am a courier."

Jane's sigh was long and haggard and rather impressive. "Kit, you are a wonderful sister but a miserable liar. The queen is too smart to waste someone of your impressive talents as a watery messenger girl."

There was silence for a moment, as Hetta was the only one in the house aware of her actual duties, and Kit was honor bound to silence. A disappointment, as she was eager to complain about being partnered with an egotistical viscount.

"At any rate," Jane said, respecting Kit's silence, "they're very effective."

Kit lifted an eyebrow. "How effective?"

Jane's smile was wicked. "They'll blow a hole right through the hull of an enemy ship. So don't trigger it unless you intend to do serious damage."

Surely Kit could find a use for that.

FIVE

~

The Brightling house had plenty to commend it—the orangerie, with its fragrant potted citrus; the garden, nearly overburdened with peonies and boxwoods and roses. But the best room of all belonged to Hetta.

Her study was a museum, a library, a gallery. The walls were covered in books and folios that held prints of lands Kit hadn't yet had the opportunity to see. The chairs were leather and deep, and the tables held artifacts and stones. A globe stood near Hetta's claw-footed desk, an imposing, bulky piece of furniture covered in bric-a-brac and carvings. It was large enough, and Hetta was small enough, that she could have made a bunk out of it. She was not quite five feet tall, with pale skin and short hair, and brown eyes that saw much.

She'd summoned Kit, and sat beside that desk in a tunic of brilliant turquoise undoubtedly obtained outside the Isles, much to the consternation of Mrs. Eaves, who believed the clothes entirely too garish for a Saxon household.

A fireplace faced the desk, hanging above it a painting of her late husband in uniform, wearing a charming and slightly lop-sided smile, rather than the cool reserve usually shown in portraits. Sir Harry's hair was short and red and stuck up in tufts, and his cravat was slightly off center.

Hetta peered at Kit over her spectacles, then carefully put down the book and removed them. "Welcome back."

"Thank you," Kit said, stepping inside and closing the door behind her.

"Help yourself if you'd like some tea." Hetta gestured to a side table where a teapot and cup awaited. "Mrs. Eaves brought it in—well, I'm not sure how long ago. It may not be warm."

"Bergamot?"

"It is."

Kit touched a fingertip gingerly to the white ceramic pot. "Still warm," she said, then glanced back at Hetta. "Would you like some?"

"Please."

Kit poured two cups, added light sugar as Hetta preferred, and generous sugar and milk in hers. When she'd given Hetta the cup, she took a seat in one of the chairs in front of the desk, savored the first sweet sip.

"Oh, I've missed this."

"Run out of tea on board?"

"Milk," Kit said, opening her eyes. "We only had a bit iced down in the hold, and we had to drink it quickly."

"And how was your mission?" Hetta asked. When she wasn't raising children, Hetta assisted the Crown as an analyst of intelligence gathered by the Crown Command's Foreign Office. Hetta and Sir Harry had been in Gallia, seeking out useful information, when he'd died.

As with Kit, few knew of Hetta's real work, and they assumed she spent the majority of her free time like those who'd been born into the Beau Monde: at her leisure. They didn't know of her ongoing service, and believed she'd only been inducted into the Order of Saint James, one of the nation's highest honors, because she'd lost her husband.

"A coded letter in Gerard's handwriting," Kit said, and watched expressions stream across Hetta's face. Pride, concern, dismay.

"So much for the ban on communications," Hetta said. She sat back in the chair again. "I told them Montgraf was a poor choice. It seems imposing—the jagged peaks, inaccessible castle. But there's a village at the base of the mountain. A bit of gold crossing the hands of an eager villager, and much havoc can be wrought. Where was it bound?"

"Pencester."

Hetta nodded. "A disappointment, if not a surprise, to learn we've operatives in the Isles."

"And that may not be the only evidence of treachery. I'm leaving in the morning on a rescue mission."

Hetta stilled, teacup nearly to her lips. "Who?" she asked, and Kit could all but feel the dread that spilled into the air.

"Marcus Dunwood."

Porcelain rattled as Hetta lowered the cup and saucer again. "*Vas tiva es,*" she murmured. It was half question, half curse in the old language: *What have the gods wrought?*

Hetta sat quietly for a moment, brow furrowed and gaze staring as she considered, evaluated. "He was supposed to be in disguise," she said, after raising her gaze to Kit again.

"Compromised," Kit said, and saw the flash of temper in

Hetta's dark eyes. "He was captured on a packet and is believed to be in Finistère. I leave in the morning."

"I'll wish you fair winds. I suppose you've already been to Portnoy's?"

Kit grinned. "I can neither confirm nor deny."

Hetta sipped, rolled her eyes.

"What do you know about Viscount Queenscliffe?" Kit asked.

This time, Hetta's brows shot up. "The Grants hold that particular seat. As I recall, the family had financial troubles when the last viscount died. Two sons—the younger was a bit of a wastrel, and I believe there was some consternation about the older son's taking a commission."

Easy enough to guess Rian was the older son.

"Is the elder trustworthy?" Kit asked.

"I don't know enough of him to say. The family is generally well regarded, but for the lack of funds. Why do you ask?"

Kit cleared a bit of space on the edge of Hetta's desk—moving a box of pinned butterflies and a spyglass—and put down the cup and saucer.

"He is to accompany me on the mission," Kit said. "We are to lead it together, by order of the queen."

"As you're here," Hetta said coolly, "it doesn't appear you've been imprisoned for refusing her."

"She is my queen, and I'm not fond of treason." Restless now, Kit rose, wandered to the globe in its golden mount. She put a hand to the gemstone surface, felt the cold beneath her hand. Then spun it with a finger so the Isles whirled past, a dot in a great blue sea.

"I don't like having a member of the Beau Monde on my ship." She looked back at Hetta. "And I don't like involving in my mission a man I don't know, much less giving him partial control. Not when lives are at stake."

"The queen is young," Hetta said. "But she is not naive. She'd have had her reasons for adding him. And there's one easy way to confirm his motives."

Kit looked up, expecting Hetta to offer to send an inquiry.

"Ask him," Hetta said, amusement in her eyes.

Kit snorted. "I doubt he'll willingly confess to perfidy."

"Assuming he's involved in perfidy, which is unlikely." The cabinet clock sounded the hours ominously. "As you've an early morning, you might try to get some sleep."

"I should," Kit agreed.

"I didn't know you still wore your ribbon," Hetta said, gaze dropping. Kit looked down. She'd left her jacket unbuttoned, and a frayed end of ribbon peeked out.

"I do," Kit said, and fastened the buttons again. "As a reminder of how lucky I am, and Principle of Self-Sufficiency No. 7—The best of life comes from having earned it."

She walked around the desk, pressed a kiss to Hetta's cheek. Hetta covered Kit's hand with hers.

"The world is becoming dangerous again," she said. "Be as careful as you can."

"The world has always been dangerous," Kit said. "But some are better at hiding it. And there's too much of the world that I haven't yet seen to leave it so quickly."

She walked to the door, but paused by a shelf and pulled out a slim volume of adventure stories. She held it up to obtain Hetta's permission.

Hetta's expression was grim. "There are a thousand books in this room. Discourses on ancient philosophies. Treatises on naval maneuvers. And my children only want fairy tales and love stories."

"Because they aren't discourses on ancient philosophies or treatises on naval maneuvers," Kit said, and skipped out before she was treated to a lecture on the importance of intellectual breadth. That was Principle of Self-Sufficiency No. 8.

Ten minutes later, Kit was chin-deep in a copper tub of lavender-scented water, with a sweet in one hand and a book in the other.

She was home, even if only for a little while.

SIX

～

Kit slept fitfully in the stationary bed in the immobile house in the unmoving corner of New London. She was used to sleeping in the bosom of the sea, with the boat's gentle motion around her. Her feather bed was more than comfortable, but it still felt stiff after sleeping atop rolling waves for two months.

She woke to the sound of the cock crowing in the garden below, found the sky still dark, the wind blowing east. It would be a fine day for sailing.

Her trunk had been repacked, her boots polished, and her uniform brushed and hung. Mrs. Eaves could be a difficult master, but she was efficient beyond reproach, and handled her duties the same way Kit handled hers: with vigor and ferocity.

She smelled ham when she opened her bedroom door, and found the dining room empty but the sideboard full. Because time was short, she helped herself to breakfast, left notes for Jane and Hetta, and called a curricle for the trip back to the quay.

The Crown Quay was always busiest in the morning, when the light was pale and the shadows long, and ships were prepared for sailing, tide and weather permitting. The *Diana* gleamed in the morning light, sitting slightly lower in the water than she had the day before. The queen had been generous with the provisions, Kit thought, and she had no complaints there.

Jin and the crew were already on board, giving instructions to the sailors who washed down the deck, ensured the provisions were secured, and made the final preparations to sail.

Kit loved this part of every voyage. The stores were full, the crew was energetic, and anticipation seemed to charge the air. And since she'd gotten no return message from Jin the night before, she assumed most of the provisioning had gone smoothly.

"Good morning," Jin said, when Kit stepped onto the deck. "Fine breeze today."

"Very fine," she agreed, her body settling into the rhythm of the water. She slowed her breath, then reached down through wood and tar to the water below. The waves were softer in the quay, the river gentled by the harbor, and her connection was with the sea, not the river. But she could still feel the slither of the Saint James speeding toward the ocean, and the hot line of energy running beneath.

"If the wind holds," she said, coming to awareness of the deck again, "we'll have good sailing."

She glanced up at the bare masts, like trees above the deck, and found Tamlin already situated in the foremast top. Her eyes were closed as she faced the wind, the breeze blowing her red hair into a streaming pennant. As captain of the watch, and a woman who preferred the elements to conversation, she spent most of her time aloft.

"Had she any particular wisdom to bestow?" Kit asked.

"She doesn't like the taste of the wind."

That was a new one. "What does the wind taste like?"

"According to her, like 'green' and 'hot iron.' According to me, ill omens."

Tamlin had been born in the north of the Isles, a place of rocks and wind, and while she refused to call herself "Aligned," she understood the wind, could hear it, better than most. That was Aligned enough for Kit.

Kit frowned, glanced at the water. "Better to be safe than sorry. Has an offering been made?"

"Aye, when I came on board. I made the *Dastes*."

"Good." Her voice softened. "Did you get to see Nanae? The girls?"

"I did," Jin said, "if not for nearly long enough. Nanae sends her love. Saori won't stop asking questions, and Emi is crawling."

"I'm sorry your leave was curtailed. Perhaps we'll be exceedingly fortunate and this will be a fast and effective mission."

"It's difficult to be angry when a man's life is on the line."

Kit nodded, squeezed his arm supportively, and then scanned the deck. "I presume his lordship hasn't yet appeared?"

"Not yet." Jin smiled. "Is that what we're calling him?"

"We'll see what he prefers." Which would tell her a lot about Grant and his values.

"First impression?"

"Unenthused, to the point of growling at the queen."

"Unenthused?" Jin asked. "He doesn't want to help in securing Dunwood's release?"

"He served with Dunwood. Both Sutherland's observing officers. He told the queen our ship was insufficient and was led by a mere courier, so I suspect we're the objectionable bit."

"Beau Monde prig," Jin muttered, the words a curse.

"Beau Monde prig," Kit agreed. "I'm not any more enthused than Grant about sharing command—but the goal is finding Dunwood, getting him home."

"And not causing an international incident."

"If at all avoidable," Kit agreed. "Is his cabin ready?"

Jin's smile was thin. "Such as it is. Cook hung rosemary and lavender in the beams. So now it smells like rosemary and lavender and only a touch of wet goat."

"There was nowhere else to keep the damnable thing," Kit said. "I imagine we'll see if he's got his sea legs fast enough."

"While we're awaiting that, would you like to review the receipts?"

There were worse tasks aboard ship than paperwork, but Kit couldn't think of any at the moment. "Sarcasm is not an attractive quality in a commander."

"Agree to disagree," Jin said cheerily.

"Captain Brightling!"

The summons came from the dock. Kit and Jin exchanged a glance, then walked to the gunwale. Kingsley stood on the dock below, smiling up at her.

⁓

"Kingsley," Kit said, when she'd climbed down the rope ladder to the dock. "Come to see us off?"

"A voyage of my own," he said, and gestured to the packet anchored on the other end of the dock. It was the *Julianna*, a strong and sturdy vessel with eight guns to protect its passengers and crew.

Curious, she looked back at him. "Delivering information, or retrieving it?"

"One or the other," he said, confirming Kit's suspicion that he wouldn't answer directly. "I'm glad I caught you before you sailed. I wanted to apologize again for Stanton's boorish behavior yesterday."

"You aren't responsible for Stanton," she said. "But I appreciate the sentiment."

Kingsley smiled at the response, but then the cheer fell away, replaced by wariness and concern.

Kit looked back, found Grant striding toward them in buff trousers, dark boots, and a gray jacket over broad shoulders. He moved with purpose—and with the swagger of a confident man. But his expression was blank. If he had as little eagerness to sail today as he had yesterday, he hid it well.

Kit's guard went up. "Colonel." She didn't quite manage to hide the disdain in her voice. But she saw little point in concealing that.

"Captain," Grant said, then glanced at Kingsley from his several inches of additional height. "Kingsley."

"Grant," Kingsley said stiffly.

"You know each other?" Kit asked, looking between them, and seeing nothing of friendship, but animosity aplenty.

"We were acquainted during the war," Grant said, without elaboration.

Kingsley nodded, smile tight and obviously forced. "What's your business at the quay?"

"Just that," Grant said. "Business."

Kingsley waited for more, and Grant refused to oblige him. Kit wasn't certain whether the silence was motivated by his general obstinacy or because of some grudge between them.

A bell rang on the *Julianna*, signaling any remaining crew and passengers to board.

"I must leave you," Kingsley said, and made a short bow. "My lord," he said to Grant, then nodded at Kit. And as he walked past Kit toward the boat, whispered, "Be careful."

Surprised by the warning, Kit watched Kingsley walk to the *Julianna* and greet several soldiers who stood near the passenger gangway. And as he climbed the boarding ramp, he gave her a final nod.

What in the world, she wondered, was that about?

When Kit looked back at Grant, his brow was furrowed. "You and Kingsley are friends."

"Yes, we've known each other for several years," she said. "Do you object to the friendship, to me, or to Kingsley?"

His eyes flashed. "None of those are any of my concern."

"Absolutely correct," she said, and turned on her heel for the *Diana*.

"Captain aboard!" was called when she stepped onto the deck. Sailors came to attention, saluted.

"At ease," she said. "Continue readying the ship."

Grant climbed over the gunwale, straightened his coat, looked around, and then followed Kit as she walked astern toward the helm. She introduced him to Jin and Simon, and then to Tamlin, who'd come down to meet the baggage.

Tamlin looked him over, nodded, and then turned her attention to Kit. "She's soft, but steady. She'll get us downriver, but slowly, and she'll open up when we reach open water."

"She?" Grant asked.

"The wind, of course," Tamlin said. "But there's something odd there, too."

"A storm?" Kit asked.

"Nay, not a storm. I don't entirely know what it is." She opened her eyes, looked back at Kit. "Can the water not feel it?"

"I didn't feel anything odd," Kit said. "But we aren't to the sea yet. I don't hear the magic as strongly here. Let us know if it becomes . . . more odd," she decided on.

Tamlin nodded at Jin, then made a little curtsy to Grant before climbing barefoot into the rigging again.

Kit turned to Grant. "Do you need a nautical education?"

"I know this is the boat, and that's the water. Is there much else that matters?"

She refused the obvious bait. "We're a two-masted schooner. Foremast," she said, pointing to the mast in front, "and mainmast." She pointed to the second. "There are square sails atop the foremast; they hang from the vertical beams—the yards. The biggest sails on each mast are gaff rigged." She pointed up. "The gaff is the spar at the top, from which the sail hangs. The boom is the one on the bottom.

"Port," she said, pointing to the boat's left side. "Starboard," she said, pointing to the right. "Forward is front, aft is rear. While aboard, you're safest in your quarters," she continued. "If you're on deck, stay aft—in the back of the ship—behind the mainmast. You're least likely to be in the way."

"I could hardly be in the way when the queen has ordered me here, and to share in command of this mission."

"Unless you've become an experienced sailor overnight," she murmured, "you won't be directing the sailing of this ship." She gestured up to the stays, the shrouds, the masts, the sails, still furled like ivory cocoons dozens of feet above the deck. "But feel free to go up if you're so eager to assist."

The look he gave her was fulminating. "I don't need to prove my bravery."

"And I don't need to prove my skill. I'll show you your room," she said, not waiting for his response. "Jin, let me know when we're ready to weigh anchor."

"Aye, Captain."

She moved toward the companionway, heard Grant's footsteps behind her. The lower deck was darker, lit by lanterns and the sunlights that rose through the upper deck.

"My cabin," she said, pointing to the door at the end of the short passageway. "Officers' quarters here. And this is yours."

The room was narrow, with a bunk, a small desk and leather chair, and a gleaming porthole. The walls were whitewashed wood, a luxury given only to the guest and officers' quarters, including her own. His trunk had already been delivered and sat beside the desk.

Jin had been right. The herbs had nearly done away with the smell; the goaty reek was only barely discernable.

Grant's gaze traveled the room, the slender bed. He made no comment.

"Follow me," she said, and walked toward the bow. "Officers' mess," she said, pointing to her left, and then to her right. "And the galley."

A man with tan skin, black hair in a long queue, and a tiny mustache crouched in front of an enormous cast-iron stove. A long wooden counter took up the other side of the narrow space, with barrels as bookends. Ropes of garlic, bags of onions, and pans hung from the beams. A light breeze blew through an open porthole.

"This is Cook," Kit said.

The man grunted.

Grant nodded. "Mr. Cook."

"Not Mr. Cook," he said flatly, as if repeating a phrase he'd said too many times to bother enunciating. "Just Cook. If we're to be the mindless tools of a monarchy, we might as well give ourselves the names of those tools, aye? Might as well pretend to be the instruments of power and control."

"Cook is of a political bent," Kit said.

Cook snorted. "We'd all be political if we had the sense the gods gave a turnip. But not all of us are so gifted." He shoved wood into the stove from a small basket, then tossed in shavings and flicked in a spark from the tip of a flint. When the fire was lit, he closed the door again and rose, dusted off his hands. "Nothing wrong with a day's work, is there? With being a common man, a plebian man, working with his fingers and his muscles and his brains?"

"We're all workers here," Kit said.

Cook snorted, gave Grant a look. "Who're you?"

"Grant."

"Position?"

"Colonel," Grant said.

"Viscount," Kit corrected, and actually saw Grant's jaw clench.

Cook clucked his tongue. "Beau Monde, eh? More's the pity, as you won't be finding any aspics here. No towers of candied partridges or fricasseed whale, or whatever your kind eat."

"Not candied partridges or fricasseed whale," Grant said.

"Well, good then." Cook narrowed his eyes, then waved his hand in dismissal. "Get out of my light."

They reached the sailors' mess in further silence, the room empty given everyone was on the deck or in the hold.

"This is the mess for the crew. Used for meals and hammocks for those who don't fit in the forecastle. Every inch of space must be used. We have to carry everything we need—provisions, personnel, canvas, and rigging—with us. We may go days or weeks without seeing another vessel."

"Difficult to have a war, isn't it, when you're alone in the middle of the ocean?"

Kit stopped. "Are you intimating naval battles are imaginary, or that naval service is less arduous than that of the army?"

"I was making an observation."

"An insulting one." She pointed down at a closed hatch in the floor. "That leads into the hold." Then she gestured to the next bulwark, the narrow passageway through it. "That's the forecastle, where the rest of the crew sleep." She turned around to face him, found him standing nearly toe-to-toe, and managed her most imperious look.

"Perhaps," she said, when he declined to step back, "we should discuss our . . . joint command."

"Perhaps we should."

"My cabin," she said, then squeezed past him in the corridor, catching the faint scent of bay rum cologne. She liked bay rum, and was irritated that she'd now associate it with him.

She walked inside her cabin, holding open the door, and when he'd followed her in, closed it. He looked around, taking in the wall of windows, the desk, the built-in bunk, the round table and chairs.

"Let's be clear," she said, when she'd closed the door. "I don't much care who you are, or what you did before. I don't care about your title, or your connection to the queen. I do care about the safety of my crew, and the man I'm to rescue."

"You're very sure of yourself."

Kit's irritation flashed. "I'm captain of this ship, and that's my obligation to the crew. To evaluate, decide, order, and be sure. If I'm not confident in my decisions, I ought not be in a position to make them."

He cocked his head at her. "What, exactly, are you concerned I might do?"

"I couldn't possibly know what you might do, as I don't know you." And that, Kit thought, was what rankled her most. "But you've been deposited onto my ship, which makes you my responsibility."

She saw the flare of heat in his eyes.

"I am no one's responsibility but my own," he said. "And the *Diana* is the queen's ship, not yours. The queen requested I undertake this mission, and I agreed."

"Why you?"

"That's a question for the queen, isn't it?"

His tone was hard, a dare. If he'd been other than a colonel, a viscount, a man put here by the queen, she'd have knocked him down for insubordination. Unfortunately, that wasn't an option.

"It's a question for you, given you obviously loathe the idea of being on this ship with a *mere courier*." That she'd said the phrase again made her realize how personally she'd taken it. And she didn't know why. He was hardly the only person to think it; the story had been purposefully spread.

Grant's jaw clenched again. "I served my country dutifully. I have other obligations now."

"And yet, here you are."

"My reasons are my own," Grant said. "I will neither explain nor apologize for them."

Silence fell, brittle as glass. They stared at each other, commanders preparing for a battle they hadn't expected to fight.

She walked to the windows—it seemed important that she put space between them—and looked at the water. She knew there was more to pick at here, information Grant wasn't telling her that informed his reasons for being on her ship. Her ship. But she plainly wasn't going to learn them here and now, and there was no point in petty bickering with a viscount; Dunwood's life was more important than her own ego. Principle of Self-Sufficiency No. 5: Ego is less important than results. And right now, that one stung. Duty, she reminded herself, and brushed her fingers against the ribbon.

When she looked back at him, he was watching her carefully. That put heat at the back of her neck. That made her angry for reasons she didn't want to contemplate. So she ignored it.

"We don't know each other," she said. "And I suspect we wouldn't like each other even if we did. But that hardly matters, as the queen has put us together. So we find Dunwood and we bring him home. You can return to your estate, and I can return to my service, and we'll forget this entire irritation."

Grant looked at her, and hard, for a long moment. "Agreed," he said, then walked away.

For an entire minute, she stared at the ceiling, prayed for patience. "Gods save me from viscounts," she muttered, then followed him out.

"Status?" she asked Jin, when they reached the deck again.

"Ready," Jin said. "The door was closed, and I didn't want to interrupt your—"

"It's fine," Kit said, cutting him off. "Call the crew for the instructions, please. Battle stations aren't necessary." She wanted them close by so she could speak without the wind carrying her voice—and their mission—across the quay. Word would travel soon enough. This was the time for discretion.

"All hands!" Jin yelled, then whistled so sharply August dug a finger into his ear as if to dislodge the sound. The order was carried down the deck and through the hatchways, until footsteps began to pound and officers and sailors and gathered. Those already on board moved toward the stern to hear their instructions, learn what this sudden mission was about.

Cook was, as always, the last one on deck. When they filled the ship's waist, when hats were pulled off and crumpled into hands, she looked them over.

"Your leave was cut short," she said. "It was your duty to respond to the Crown's call, and here you are. It is believed a man loyal to the Crown, a man who has put himself in danger to protect her interests, has been taken by hostile forces. It is our job to find him, to rescue him, and to see him home safely. And that we will do."

"What's our destination, Captain?" August, as always, was the voice of the crew.

"We set sail for Finistère."

Eyes widened, voices murmuring excitement and approval. They were experienced sailors and understood very well the risk of a viper pit like Finistère . . . and the appeal.

"It will be dangerous," she said. "Our man is likely being held against his will, likely for the information he's gathered. Those who have detained him will not let him go easily. We may incur injuries—and worse—in the process of this mission."

She took a step forward, moving closer to her crew, and met each of their gazes in turn. Let them see the gravity of what they'd been asked to do, the importance of it. And the risk. She owed that to them, too.

"We will be quick," she said. "Fleet as foxes. Silent as doves on the wing. We will not fail."

"Hear, hear!" someone shouted, and the cheer spread across the deck.

"Weigh anchor!" Kit called out. And the work began.

SEVEN

When they were underway and streaming down the Saint James toward the sea, she gave Jin the helm, ensured he'd keep an eye on Grant, and went to her quarters.

She was obliged to document receipt of the ship's provisions and confirm her crew had come aboard, so they could be paid. Paperwork was one of the less enviable tasks of captaincy and, if she was being honest, one she ought to have completed before they'd left port. But she hadn't wanted to hold up the ship, and presumed the queen would forgive the delay.

It took two hours, and by then they'd reached the mouth of the Saint James—and the edge of the Narrow Sea. Kit put away the implements of this particular torture and climbed up to the deck. And felt a shudder of awareness as the ocean spread east before them.

Simon was at the wheel. Behind him, maps were spread atop the wooden cabinet that covered the mechanism connecting the wheel to the rudder below. A brass sextant kept them from blowing away in the wind.

Jin and Grant stood beside the cabinet. "How was the paper-work, Captain?" Jin asked.

Kit growled, glanced at Grant. "Colonel."

"Captain." His tone was as chilly as hers.

Probably irritated, Kit thought, that he wasn't actually steer-ing the ship. But he could learn to live with disappointment. She circled around to the maps.

"What have we got, Simon?"

When a waiting lieutenant took his place at the wheel, Simon moved to stand beside her. "Our present location," he said, point-ing to a spot just off the Isles' coast, then swept his finger to freckles of brown that lay on the other end of the Narrow Sea to their southwest. "And the Rondel archipelago."

The islands were spread along a diagonal that ran roughly northwest to southeast, arcing around the coast of Gallia. Dozens of cays and spots of land, five of which were large enough to be called islands, with Finistère the largest and most westerly.

Kit surveyed the map, the distance. She preferred open water to coastlines, as the current was faster there, the route straighter. And even after a year of peace, she was cautious around the Gallic coast. Privateers who held long-expired letters of marque still patrolled the waters, especially as the sea curved toward Finistère.

"South-southwest," Kit said. "And into the channel, away from the coasts. We'll adjust the heading, discuss our approach, as we near the island."

"Aye," Simon said, and began to mark a line approximating their route on the map.

"Prepare to make sail!" Jin called out. "Broad on the star-board bow."

At the order and those that followed, sailors ran to their positions, began the systematic process of spreading the rest of the *Diana*'s canvas. The foremast was climbed first; sailors scrambled toward the sky, one at a time, where they'd shimmy onto the yards where the sail was folded and tied.

This was Kit's favorite part of any journey, when they reached open water and the ship's great volume of canvas could be unfurled, pulled taut, to stretch against the wind.

As the crew worked the sails, Kit closed her eyes, reached down. The ship turned toward the Pencester strait, the narrowest point of the Narrow Sea, where Gallia sat only twenty miles from the Isles. The water was shallower here, still bearing the chill of the Northern Sea, but the current strong. Kit always felt the current most keenly here, and she wondered if there'd been some unremembered experience—something that had fomented her connection when she was a child—that had shaped her Alignment. Whatever the reason, she'd been grateful for it during the war, when the sea was crowded with enemy ships, and speed was a necessity.

She touched the current, an invisible cloud that swayed through the water like seaweed in the tide. And within it, the white-hot core, the concentrated filament of magic. As powerful and dangerous as always, but . . . She felt something else now, something different. A frizzle of energy at the edges, as if the magic itself were uneasy.

But she'd have to ponder that later, because the *Diana* swung to starboard. Kit waited until the ship and current were perpendicular, the arrow strung and bowstring taut. "Ready," she said quietly, and the ship seemed to stiffen, as if it could feel the tension of that waiting magic, the banked power.

"Aye," Jin said, their practiced response.

"*Now.*" The word was barely a whisper, but the crew—who understood the way of things—was silent when she said it. She let go. The current caught the boat, thrust it forward, and the shouts of her crew—thrilled at the burst of speed—had her eyes opening again.

And she found Grant at her feet, staring up at her.

She lifted an eyebrow. "Were you so impressed with a bit of magic, Colonel?"

"What in bloody hell was that?" Grant asked, taking Jin's offered hand and climbing back to his feet.

"An introduction to the *Diana*," Jin said, clapping him on the back. "Welcome aboard."

"Manipulating magic is banned," Grant said, adjusting his coat, "by international treaty and Isles law."

"That wasn't manipulation," Kit said. "It's a touch. Gentler and kinder." She extended her hand, palm up. "And I'm the only one who pays the price."

Grant pushed hair from his eyes, stared down at her hand. "Those are . . . scars?"

"Burns," Kit said. "Minute and mostly painless. And there because I become a temporary channel for the magic." But there weren't many, Aligned or otherwise, who were willing to take that risk. After her stint on the *Ardent*, she'd been asked to teach other Aligned sailors how she'd done it. A few had volunteered to try; few of those had actually succeeded. And fewer still had captains willing to risk their ships by engaging with the current so . . . intimately.

Brow furrowed deeply, Grant looked up at her, seemed

to search her face. "Hmm," was all he said, then he walked to the gunwale, fingers clenched upon the rail as he looked out at the sea.

"I didn't intend to knock him over," she told Jin.

"But nor did you warn him. And while I'd normally be perfectly agreeable with putting a member of the Beau Monde on his knees, I suspect he has some scars of his own."

"From the war, you mean," Kit said, head cocked as she watched Grant, and felt something heavy settle in her gut. "Damnation. Am I bound to apologize now?"

"I suspect the good colonel will adjust," Jin said, turning to look at her. "How goes the sea?"

"Swift and smooth. But there's something around the edges. Something is . . . disturbed."

"Disturbed?"

"Agitated," Kit said. "Uncomfortable. Like . . . a child that won't settle."

"Like the wind," Jin said. That had been Tamlin's assessment.

Kit nodded. She'd felt difficult seas before. Seas that burned with energy, sending waves nearly as tall as the ship's masts. This was different. And it bothered her that she didn't know the reason for it.

"I suspect we're feeling the same thing. But I'm not yet sure why." She looked up, where white canvas spread against brilliantly blue sky. "For now, the weather's clear and the wind is at our backs. Let's use the current while we can."

"Sea dragon!" came Tamlin's shout from the top. "Port bow!"

So many members of the crew rushed to port it was a miracle the *Diana* didn't simply roll over.

Hands on the rail, Kit stared at the water, trying to distinguish waves from fins.

Two silent minutes later, a serrated line of glittering crimson rose through the water a hundred yards away. It was the symbol of the Isles, the child, or so they said, of Arid and Kanos, born at the same time the Isles had been born, and from the same dark sea. Where the Isles received jagged peaks, sea dragons received those sharp and cutting fins.

A cheer erupted from the deck.

Grant, who stood beside her, glanced her way. "Why are they cheering?"

"Seeing the symbol of the Isles at the beginning of a voyage is a sign of good luck," she said. "It means the gods are on our side."

Hopefully, they'd stay there.

A few hours later, back in her cabin again, she was glad to smell savory things percolating. The deck bell rang, and she rose and stretched, then walked to the windows to look out at the sea. The sea was darker now, the water deeply blue, the waves low. They'd moved beyond the shores and into the deeper, colder ocean between the Isles and the Continent. Soon enough the water would lighten again, going turquoise as they neared the island and the danger they had no choice but to face. So there were plans to make. And should the worst occur, contingencies to consider.

She buttoned up her jacket, pushed her hair behind her ears, and opened her cabin door.

The scent of meat and herbs was welcome as a lover's kiss.

She walked to the officers' mess, the floor undulating rhythmically beneath her feet as the ship bobbed, and found the officers beginning to assemble around the table. Jin was already there, talking quietly with Tamlin, who'd tucked a golden feather behind her ear, a seabird's offering.

They moved to stand, and she waved them off. The *Diana* was a lovely ship, but she wasn't a man-of-war, and they'd all have bruised heads and shins if she required the ceremony.

"Good evening," she said, and took a seat at the end of the table. Then looked up as Grant stepped into the doorway.

"Everyone, Colonel Rian Grant."

"Grant will do," he said, and nods were exchanged around the table.

"Please," Kit said. "Have a seat. We try to keep the formality to a minimum."

"As long as Watson keeps her elbows off the table," Jin said, and the other officers laughed. Watson, one of her lieutenants, rolled her eyes.

Cook appeared at the table with a domed silver platter, and lifted the cover to reveal a roasted chicken surrounded by a rainbow of vegetables.

Kit nearly wept at the delectable smell and the sight of all that color. The vegetables wouldn't last, so they'd eat their fill while they could. They piled plates with food from bowls they passed. Grant, she noticed, watched how everyone else served themselves before adding meat and vegetables to his plate. She appreciated his attentiveness, even if she wished he'd forgo the air of superiority.

As if he could feel her stare, Grant looked up, met her gaze.

She managed not to look away—one didn't become captain without becoming expert in the steely stare. Neither shifted until another officer spoke up.

"We're really heading to Finistère, Captain?" The question was asked by Phillips, the youngest lieutenant on the ship. He was thin and pale, with a pointy nose and fluff of brown hair.

"We are," Kit said.

"Rats and smelly sailors," Tamlin murmured, nibbling on a crust of bread. "That's what you find in a pirate fortress."

"And this Marcus Dunwood is worth the trouble?" asked Lieutenant Hobbes. She was a capable sailor in her forties, with tan skin and dark hair streaked with silver. She'd continued sailing even after the war had ended, despite the merchant husband who awaited her at home.

"He's worth the trouble," Grant said, his voice, deep and grave, falling heavily over the room.

"I meant no offense," Hobbes said. "Merely that it's unusual to send an entire crew after a single man."

"I take no offense," Grant said. "I stated a fact. I know Dunwood, and he's worth the trouble. He has served the Crown in innumerable ways. We were observing officers for Sutherland on the peninsula, spent two years traveling together. And we fought together at Zadorra."

Silence fell over the room, the sailors struck by the weight of those words.

Hobbes cleared her throat. "I understand the fighting was hard there, at Zadorra."

"It was," Grant said. "We'd scouted the hills around the village, but rejoined Sutherland's brigade before the fighting began.

More than a hundred thousand soldiers waiting for battle. Our unit moved through the hills and around the city, intending to come around Gallic troops along a hairpin turn in the river."

Grant drank from his glass of wine, then put it down again, ran a thumb along the grooves in the crystal. "We caught up to them. Outflanked them. And attacked."

"It was . . . intense?" Phillips asked quietly.

"One of the bloodiest conflicts of the war," Grant said. "We fired across the river, and hitting our targets was nearly easy. Easier than it ought to have been for soldiers to kill one another." He ran a hand through his hair, sat back in his chair, as if resettling himself, adjusting to the discomfort of the retelling. "They turned soon enough, shot back. The fallen were all around us. Dunwood threw me into the mud, and I was furious he'd ruined my coat—which I'd finally gotten clean—until I realized he'd saved me from a sniper's bullet."

He looked up, stared at a high corner of the room, as if seeing a soldier on a hill again, rifle in hand, taking aim. The hand on the table fisted, knuckles white with tension and memory. And Kit felt worse about sending Grant to the deck this morning.

"He took the shot himself," Grant continued. "It grazed his shoulder, and he didn't allow me to forget that until the war was over." He smiled at that recollection. "Then we returned home. We've shared only a letter or two in that time, but I consider myself indebted to him."

"He sounds like a good man," Kit said. "And a good soldier."

Nodding, Grant unclenched his fingers, took another sip of port. "He is."

They lingered in the quiet, sipping their tea or port. And

then Kit leaned forward, linked her hands on the table. "We have a fast ship and a capable crew," she said. "And we're all curious about Finistère. But let's remember the danger. Let's be wary. Be prepared, and do what's necessary to help the man who's helped the Crown."

A figure appeared in the doorway. The *Diana*'s second mate and bosun, the highest-ranking nonofficer, offered an apologetic expression.

"Mr. Jones," Jin said to him. "Is there a problem?"

"My apologies for the interruption, Captain," he said, pulling off his cap. "But we felt the development was worth the trouble." He cleared his throat nervously.

"What is it?" Kit asked.

"We've found a rat in the hold."

"That's hardly news," Jin murmured, but went quiet when Mr. Jones pulled the quarry into view.

Before her, dirty collar pinched between Jones's fingers, was the foundling Kit had paid outside the palace to send a message. She didn't look any cleaner than she had the day before. But her little square chin was set, her eyes narrowed and determined.

Kit sighed, and made it count. "Hello, Louisa."

⁓

They sat her down in the officers' mess, where Cook offered her a bowl of stew and a small cup of milk.

The girl ate quickly, hunched over the food like it might be snatched away if she allowed the opportunity. That spoke wonders about her history, Kit thought, and felt a tug in her chest that might have been compassion or guilt. Or both.

"We could toss her overboard for violating the rules against fare dodgers," Jin said.

Louisa's eyes grew wide. "What's the rules against fare dodgers?"

"Commander Takamura means you've come aboard ship without permission or paying your way," Kit said. "That's a violation of the queen's orders."

"I had permission," she said, lifting her chin in that stubborn way. Then she shifted her gaze to Jin. "You invited me on board."

"To deliver a message. You were to leave when the message was delivered."

"You didn't tell me to leave." Her tone was prim, and Tamlin hid a laugh behind a not-very-convincing cough.

Jin merely looked at her, then at Kit, with mild amusement. "No," he said. "I suppose I did not. Nor did you expressly request permission to stay."

Louisa dropped her gaze to the stew, and didn't look nearly as pleased by it now.

"Why did you stay on board?" Kit asked.

Louisa lifted a shoulder but didn't raise her gaze. "I didn't have anything better to do."

"Your family?"

"Don't have one." She looked up, eyes fierce. "Don't need one, do I? I get along just fine."

She'd survived, certainly. But whether a child needed—or deserved—more than mere survival was a different matter.

"I can do lots of things," Louisa said. "I can carry things. Or find things."

"Both very important tasks," Kit agreed. But possibly better performed by a child safely onshore, not on a ship on a mission with a questionable possibility of success. "Mr. Pettigrew, will you please keep an eye on our charge for a moment?"

"Aye, Captain," he said, then turned to the girl, looked at her consideringly. "Have you ever seen a compass?"

"What's a compass?" she asked as he pulled the device from his pocket. Kit led the others back to her cabin, then closed the door when they were all inside.

"Well," Jin said. "This is an interesting surprise."

"You're acquainted?" Grant asked.

"She was waiting outside the palace after we spoke to the queen," Kit said. "I paid her to deliver a message to the *Diana*."

"She's a foundling?"

"I'm not certain," Kit said. "I presume so, but she wasn't exactly forthcoming regarding her background. If we were in town, I could take her to Hetta. But as it is . . ."

"She can't stay on board. It's much too dangerous for a child." Grant's voice had gone hard.

"Should I drop her into a boat and tell her to start rowing?"

"She's a *child*."

"Jin," she said, keeping her eyes on Grant. "How old were you when you first sailed?"

"Seven. I accompanied my grandfather, who was a fisherman."

Kit nodded. "I was punting down the Saint James at thirteen. The sea is dangerous for everyone; that makes it fair. She's old enough to be a cabin girl or general mate. And not all foundlings are lucky enough to have a safe bed and hot meal. The *Diana* is preferable to a larkhouse, a gambling hell, a life of picking detritus from the muck of the Saint James."

"Are you requesting a cabin girl?" Jin asked.

"Gods, no," Kit said quickly, shuddering at the thought of a person standing over her all night and day and asking what she wanted. That was a bit too Beau Monde. But there was always work to be done aboard ship, and they had food aplenty. Life onshore for a girl of Louisa's age, her size, would be no easier.

Grant made a sound of frustration.

"Welcome to life aboard someone else's ship," Kit said with heat. "It has none of the amenities of Grant Hall and you are, rather remarkably, not in charge."

"Sarcasm isn't helpful," Grant said.

"You should remember your own advice," Kit said. Then took a breath herself, because there was no point in arguing with him over this.

"This isn't an ideal situation," she said after a moment. "Especially considering where we're going or what we're doing. But it's the situation we're in, so we'll deal with it as best we can, and we'll protect her as best we can." And then she smiled, slow and sly, and looked at Jin. "Cook has daughters, does he not?"

"Six of them," Jin said with an answering grin. "And he's been complaining about needing more hands in the kitchen."

Kit nodded. "She'll share a cabin with Hobbes. She's easy with the younger crew members. Cook can teach her what he knows. But no knives," she said, pointing at him to emphasize the point. "Last thing we need is the little imp running around with a blade."

"Aye, Captain," Jin said, and they went back to the mess to deliver the news.

Kit took a seat at the table, and Louisa met her gaze squarely, if with a tint of suspicion in her eyes. She was a brave little thing, and Kit had to admire it. But the girl—for her own safety and everyone else's—needed to know who was in charge.

"You'll share a room with Lieutenant Hobbes," Kit said, glancing at the crew member. Hobbes looked visibly surprised, and not altogether pleased, but training and logic—which told her the crew's options were limited—had her nodding.

"And you'll learn to cook," Kit said, voice raised, and heard the echoing groan from the kitchen.

Louisa's gaze narrowed. "I get to stay."

"For now," Kit said. "If you can follow orders, which is necessary for every sailor on board this ship. Can you do that?"

Louisa watched her for a minute, face screwed up in concentration. Kit appreciated that she was actually taking the time to think about her answer.

"What if I don't?"

"Then we toss you to the sea dragons."

"No, you won't," Louisa said, with the gravity of a much older girl. "And what if the order isn't fair?"

Kit bit back a smile. Damn it all, but she admired the sass. "An order is an order," Kit said. "But we try very hard to make sure that our orders are fair. Because we're a kind of family."

The need that crossed Louisa's face was so plain, so bare, it made something in Kit's chest clench hard against her ribs. She had to resist the urge to sweep her into her arms, but understood well enough the distance she needed to keep in order to keep her safe.

"I can follow orders," Louisa said.

"Very well," Kit said. "Welcome aboard, sailor Louisa."

She grinned. "I'm a proper sailor now?"

"Not quite officially," Kit said. "First things first: You need a wash."

Years from now, Kit thought, they'd tell tales of the scream heard across the ocean.

EIGHT

K it woke before the sun had fully risen, stepped onto the deck as it breached the horizon. The morning blossomed, petals unfurling across the sky in orange and pink smears, casting brilliant light across the otherwise dark sea. Clouds were pale brushstrokes among the color, foretelling good sailing.

She wasn't alone; the sailors on the night's last watch were still in position, watching the sea or trimming the sails as the first mate ordered to follow the wind and keep the ship on her course.

Her gaze dropped from the horizon to the dark water that slipped against the ship's oaken planks. But the sea was calm, the wind fair, and the *Diana* slipped through the waves as elegantly as a dancer. *The wind moves the sea, and the sea moves the ship. The ship moves the sailors so the sailors don't drip.* A children's ditty she'd learned years ago.

She nodded at the mate, then went below, opening the rear hatch into the hold. She took a lantern from the passageway, and carried it down.

Inside the hold, she hung the lantern on an iron hook, slipped between barrels of coffee and sugar and tea to the hull on the port side. Here, alone in the hold and beneath the waterline, she was literally surrounded by the sea, by its story. She pressed her hand against the hull, reached out for the sea beyond.

She could feel its power against her palm, the pressure of water against copper and wood and iron. And the discord she'd felt yesterday had disappeared. The sea was calm again, the current shifting about as it always did, the core of it energized. For a moment, she wondered if she'd imagined it, had projected her own feelings about the voyage, the presence of a viscount, onto the sea. But then she remembered Tamlin's warning, the instability she'd felt, too. Either the magic had resolved its own crisis or, by traveling through the Narrow Sea, they'd sailed beyond it.

She would watch and listen. Because if the magic of the Narrow Sea had been damaged somehow, they'd be sailing back through it soon enough.

Kit gathered her officers in their mess when the watch bells were rung. Because she wasn't sure if he understood the bells or the watch, she rapped her knuckles on the door of Grant's cabin.

It opened immediately, Grant all but filling the doorway, broad shoulders down to booted calves. He hadn't shaved, or perhaps didn't plan to on a bobbing ship, so dark stubble traced the long line of his jaw. He wore black today, tailcoat and trousers, in sharp and elegant lines that Kit thought should have looked strange stretched across muscle, but instead looked regal.

"Captain," he said, gaze flat.

"Colonel. We'll be meeting in the officers' mess to plan the approach and rescue operation."

Those eyes flashed with temper. "I will be commanding the land operation."

She'd been considering an apology for failing to warn him about her magic. But his entirely Beau Monde tone had her rejecting that idea outright. "As my crew will be undertaking that operation, we will share that command."

"The lives of your crew are not the only lives at stake."

There was fury in her gaze. "I am well aware of the import of this mission. But this crew embarks on no operation that does not meet my approval."

"Then we'll have to hope you're sensible enough to approve it."

She'd nearly bared her teeth at him, when there was a polite throat clearing from the corridor beyond. "Captain," said Jin's voice.

She turned to find him in the companionway, perched on the ladder while waiting, Kit assumed, for her and Grant to come to fisticuffs.

"The officers' mess," Kit said to Grant. He closed the cabin door behind him with a snap, slid past her through the hallway, anger radiating like heat.

"I'm glad to see you're finally getting along," Jin said dryly, hopping down into the corridor.

Kit just growled. "Wind?" she asked, assuming he'd already spoken with Tamlin.

"Unworried," he said. "The sea?"

"The same," she said. "It will not fail us today."

Jin smiled with obvious relief. "Excellent. So it's only pirates to worry about then."

"And aristocrats," Kit added.

Cook's head popped out from the galley, hair damp from steam and heat. "Could use a good bit of class warfare now and again. It thins the humors."

"On that note," Jin said, offering his hand, "shall we away to the mess?"

"Let's," Kit said, and let him escort her down the corridor.

$\backsim$

The staff assembled, Simon placed documents on the mess table, topped them with a map of the island. It was a wide smudge of green and brown with a natural harbor on the southern end.

"Finistère," he said. "The largest of the Rondel islands, and home to the famous fortress of the five pirate kings."

"The Five," Jin said, "about whom the songs are sung. *'The Five of passions deep,'*" he intoned, *"'who bear the strength of ten men.'*"

"It's a miserable tune," Simon said. "But they've a fortress and island kingdom, so it must be true enough. There are cliffs nearly all the way around the island, with a few rocky harbors and inlets scattered here and there. It's dangerous—shoals, sandbars, and, so they say, the remains of a thousand ships that failed to make it safely through. They call it the Côte Sauvage."

"The savage coast," Kit translated, and Simon nodded.

"Land flattens toward the harbor. The fortress itself is here," he said, pointing at the crescent's center curve. "The building fits into rock cliffs behind it. It was abandoned a century ago, and re-settled by the Five." He moved his finger into the harbor in front of the fortress, drew an arc. "The dock is here."

"How many ships usually dock there?" Kit asked.

"Could be a hundred or a dozen, depending on who's telling

the tale. There's a trade zone here," Simon said, pointing to a spot on the eastern shore. "The island doesn't produce anything, so they allow commerce along this side of the island. It's the market for the entire archipelago."

"Do they have treasure?" Phillips asked.

"Good lord, man," Watson said, rolling her dark eyes. "Of course there's bloody treasure. It's a pirate fortress, aye?"

Phillips blushed.

"Watson's right," Simon said. He pulled off his spectacles, wiping away a smudge with a handkerchief he pulled from his jacket. "Any treasure there would be offered in homage to the Five—or taken by them. So if there's gold, it's in the fortress."

Phillips grinned, young and more innocent than Kit could ever hope to be. "Perhaps we'll find our charge and some treasure."

"We have a singular mission," Kit said firmly, and Phillips looked chagrined enough.

"If Dunwood's identity has been discovered," Grant said, ignoring the byplay, "he'd also be given to the Five. Would likely be in the fortress."

"Most likely," Simon said, replacing his glasses. "Mr. Chandler provided a sketch of the fortress's interior," he said, and placed it atop the map. The drawing showed three floors, inside a rectangle of stone with towers at each corner.

"Underground, first level, second level," Simon said, pointing at each in turn. "The entry is here," he said, pointing to the position. "I'm told there's a courtyard inside, stairways leading up and down. Down is the dungeon."

"Where Dunwood's likely being held," Kit said.

"Yes," Simon agreed. "The entry level houses kitchen, armory, stables. Second floor houses the Five. So how do you get in?"

"That would be for me to determine," Grant said. He moved closer to the maps, close enough that his body brushed hers.

Kit didn't enjoy being pushed aside, physically or metaphorically, and had to clench her hands against the urge to push him back and away, and remind herself why they were here—and that her crew was watching.

"Your proposal?" she asked, voice cold. But she refused to step back, to concede her territory. So they stood, side by side and, Kit thought, pretending very hard to ignore the other.

He pointed at the island's outer curve. "We anchor near here, climb up, and make our way across the island to the fortress."

"The cliffs are fifty to sixty feet tall, rough stone," Simon said. "Climbing would be difficult, and if you made it to the top, the island is largely flat with few trees. You'd have to walk across it, and you'd have virtually no cover."

"It would also look suspicious," Kit said dryly.

"Well, we can't simply march in and demand their captive," Jin said.

With smooth confidence that grated Kit's nerves, Grant studied the map with quiet contemplation. Then he pointed to the trade zone. "Here. We pretend to be traders."

"We can't sail into the free-trade zone," Jin said. "They'd recognize the ship."

"The *Diana*," Grant agreed. "But there's a smaller boat on deck, yes?"

"The jolly boat," Kit said.

Grant nodded. "You could anchor offshore on the other side of the island, and we could use the jolly boat, load it with provisions, pretend to trade them. And if we offered to unload the provisions," he said, shifting his gaze to Kit, "we could walk into the fortress."

There was a challenge in his eyes, a dare for her to insult his plan—or come up with a better one. The look thoroughly rankled. As did the fact that she couldn't think of one, because it wasn't an entirely awful plan.

"We could take the tea," she said quietly, and there were groans around her. The queen, perhaps acknowledging the canceled shore leave, had given them crates of her own blend.

"We'd have to wear disguises—perhaps clothes borrowed from the crew—and bluff our way into the fortress. But the Five will not simply allow us to stroll through the fortress to the dungeon and bring Dunwood out again."

"We'll have to fight our way through," Grant said. "Or create a distraction."

"The *Diana*'s appearance?" Jin offered. "We sail around the island, flags flying. That would certainly provoke a response."

Kit made a vague sound, looked at the sketch of the fortress again. It wasn't terribly detailed, and she didn't like her crew bearing the risk of limited information. "I've got explosives."

The officers went quiet, looked at Kit.

"Something my sister Jane created," she explained. "We can use them if necessary, but I'd rather not have to rely on them. We're attempting to remove Dunwood from danger, not make his situation more dangerous. We have to get into the dungeon," she said, pointing to the sketch again. "How are the prisoners held?"

"From the size," Simon said, "I'd presume individual cells. Probably barred or gated."

"We'll need a crowbar," Grant said. "Do you have one on board?"

"We'll find something," Jin said.

"It's possible, if not likely, Dunwood was injured in the taking, or may have been injured in his captivity. We may need to carry him out."

"Sailors are strong," Watson said, and curled an arm to show her biceps.

"Be that as it may," Kit said, "we should alert March."

"March?" Grant asked.

"Ship's physick," Kit explained. "Not officially; we're too small to merit our own dedicated physick. But she has skills in the area of healing and herbs."

"I'll do that," Jin said.

"What about exits?" Kit asked.

Simon pointed. "The sketch identifies a tunnel from dungeon to the shoreline. But in that environment, it's possible the tunnel is flooded at high tide."

"Or, given the ocean's power, that it's collapsed," Kit said. Silence fell as their joint leaders—Kit and Grant—reviewed the maps.

"It's possible this plan could work," Kit said. "It's also possible it may fail spectacularly." She looked at Grant. "What's your secondary plan?"

"We fight our way in," he said, "and we fight our way out."

"*Soldiers*," Watson muttered. "Always eager for a brawl."

"I've no urge to fight," Grant said, and the grimness in his voice had everyone looking at him. "Those who've seen the costs of war rarely do. But we're here for Dunwood, not for ourselves."

Kit was irritated that she didn't disagree with him.

In silence, she reviewed the plans, considered what he'd said, matched it against her own expertise. "We sail wide and to the north," she finally said, tracing a finger around the island. "We disembark on the western side, send the jolly boat around to the trade zone with provisions. While we're inside, the jolly boat should continue around the southern tip of the island, where we'll rendezvous, get Dunwood aboard, and sail home. Me, Grant, Watson, and Sampson will take the jolly boat."

"You should stay on the ship," Grant said to her, "in case you need to retreat quickly."

He may not have meant it as an insult, but it had the same effect—and had the officers narrowing their eyes at him.

"We do not leave crew behind," Kit said. "We sail together. Always."

"Your sense of honor will provide little comfort when Hetta is peeling the skin from our bones," Jin said, and took a sip of his tea.

"Hetta would never do that," Kit said with a grin. "She'd give the job to Jane."

❧

When their meeting was done, Kit went to the galley. She found Louisa sitting atop a chest there, holding a bowl as Cook cracked eggs into it. Cook looked up, nodded.

"Well, well," Kit said, feigning confusion. "Who is this?"

The girl looked up at her. "It's Louisa," she said, brow furrowed.

Kit frowned. "I don't think so. There was so much filth around Louisa it formed a cloud. You appear to be quite clean."

Louisa scowled.

"There she is," Kit said with a wink. "I recognize her now. What are you doing there?"

"I learned how to break an egg with one hand and say 'hell' in the old language."

Kit just sighed, looked up at Cook.

"Tiny Cook is a sailor," he said without apology. "She must learn a sailor's ways."

They'd see about that, Kit thought. But for now, there were other things to discuss.

She crouched so she could meet the girl eye to eye. "Louisa, I need to talk to you about something important."

"More important than steering the ship?"

"For now, yes." Kit considered how to say what she needed to say, how to impart enough fear in the child to ensure she understood the gravity of their situation without terrifying her.

"The queen has asked us to help someone who's in trouble—another sailor who works for the queen."

"Why is he in trouble?"

"Because he was taken by people who are cruel and greedy. They're also dangerous. And they don't want to let the sailor go, so they'll try to stop us. And they'll try to hurt us."

Instead of the fear Kit expected, anger crossed the girl's face.

"We should kill them with our sabres."

Brave and bloodthirsty, Kit thought. But there was nothing to be gained by hiding the truth. "We may have to fight," Kit said. "And they may fight back. But we have to get the sailor home safely—and we have to get you home safely. When I give you the order, I want you to go into the hold—the bottom of the ship—and stay there. Stay hidden."

"I'm not afraid."

"I know you aren't. I don't want you to stay hidden because you're afraid, but because I'm afraid for you. And if you're safe, I won't worry about you, and I can focus on the sailor."

Louisa didn't look entirely convinced Kit didn't mean to take away her newfound freedom.

"I can come out of the hold when it's done?"

"As soon as it's done. And if you'd like, you can even go aloft."

"What's a loft?"

"*Aloft*," Kit enunciated. "Up there, where Tamlin watches."

Louisa looked absolutely baffled. "Why would anyone want to go all the way up there?"

The eternal question of sailors who didn't care for the mast. "Some like the view. Some like the quiet."

"I like biscuits," Louisa said after a moment's consideration. Since Kit didn't disagree, she pulled a small tin from a shelf above the counter, opened it, and took out two pale butter biscuits.

"I do, too," Kit said, and offered one to Louisa. Under Cook's mutinous stare, they ate, smiling.

She'd just returned to the deck when the lieutenant at the helm held out the spyglass.

"Captain," she said. "You need to see this. There's a warship on the northern horizon, same bearing as us."

Kit was immediately prepared to reject the idea, but knew her people better. "A warship? Here?"

She looked, and swore aloud.

It was a gun brig, heavy with cannons. Kit counted six on the starboard side, and presumed there was an equal number on the port. Her hull was gleaming black, and no pennants or flags marked her identity. Two square-rigged masts, running with the wind—in the same direction as the *Diana*.

There would be plenty of boats and ships heading to Finistère. Traders with cargo, pirates looking for sanctuary, boats used by the Five to capture prizes. But this wasn't a civilian ship. It was too clean, too sharp, too well maintained. And it had gone to much trouble to hide its home country.

She offered Jin the glass so he could see what she did.

"Do you recognize it?" Grant asked. He'd come above deck, too, stood beside her at the gunwale.

"No," Kit said. "They've no flags, no name. But they're in a hurry. Running at full sail, heading in the same direction as we are, if just ahead of us."

"Guild?" he asked quietly.

"Very possibly," Kit said with a nod. "And probably heading toward Finistère to pick up the same cargo we're after."

"Dunwood," Grant said, and Kit nodded.

"They're very careful," she observed. "It's an unremarkable ship. Sturdy and well gunned, but not obviously Frisian or Akranian or anything else."

Akranes was an island of rock and ice northeast of the Isles, nearer the uninhabited frozen continent than New London. It was a small nation of contrasts—of jagged cliffs and green pastures, of waterfalls and smoking volcanoes. And its queen, Callysta, was one of Gerard's two daughters.

"They want Dunwood," Grant finished. "To interrogate, or to eliminate."

It was a small blessing, at least, that the ship hadn't given any indication it had seen the *Diana*.

"Captain?" Jin asked.

Kit considered, watched the horizon. "We're moving just faster than she is, so maintain course. We will not beat the gun brig at arms, so we will beat her with speed. We will get to Finistère first."

And we'll get to Dunwood first, she promised herself.

NINE

~

I t was just past noon when the call was made.

"Land ho!" Tamlin shouted, and Jin offered Kit her golden glass. She opened it, looked across the water to the point of darkness on the horizon, the water growing brighter as it neared the shore of the first island in the chain.

She offered it to Grant, who stood nearby, quiet and watching.

"Stay on course," Kit said. "If their lookouts see our sail, I want them to believe we're passing the island."

Jin acknowledged her command. "All hands!" he called, and the bell was rung, signaling all sailors, including those below preparing for a night on the watch, to their stations. And in the meantime, she had to prepare.

~

In her quarters, she changed into garments she'd borrowed from Tamlin. A shirt that had long since faded from crisp white to ivory, and a long vest of thin leather. From one of the lieutenants, scuffed but soft leather boots of doe brown.

She rebelted her scabbard, tied to her belt the small leather pouch containing the sparkers. Then she smeared candle soot across her cheekbones, her jaw. Just enough to look like a woman who'd come through some fire.

She came back above decks unrecognizable, and watched the quartermaster prepare to scold her for going below without permission. Until he realized who she was.

That was one success, at least.

"Captain," he said, "my apologies."

"Unnecessary," she said with a smile. "You're giving me confidence in my disguise."

He nodded, began to get very busy chastising sailors for their line-coiling skills.

Jin walked to her, offered a very beaten beaver hat that had become soft with time and damp, and at her nod, placed it on her head. He stood back, looked her over.

"You look like a . . . type of pirate."

"Your confidence is bracing, Jin. And I'm not wearing this." She pulled off the hat, sniffed it, held it at arm's length. "It smells like bilge."

"All part of the illusion," Jin said, but took it back.

Grant joined them, wearing a crewman's work clothes, the shabbier garb worn for messy work—caulking portions of the hull or deck to keep them watertight, or tarring the rigging to keep it from rotting. Trousers of cotton duck, a blousy shirt of linen, and a short blue jacket with a jaunty kerchief. He'd mussed his hair so it fell across his face, and, like her, had added a bit of candle black to his cheeks.

He looked entirely convincing as a sailor, and Kit didn't care to admit she found it rather attractive on him.

THE BRIGHT AND BREAKING SEA | 103

While she perused Grant, he perused her. "You don't look like a captain now."

"You don't look like a viscount. How did you come by the slops?" He just looked at her.

"The clothing," she clarified.

"I spoke with Chandler before we left. He suggested I might want attire that was less . . . titled."

"A good suggestion." She looked at Grant in the eye. "Finding Dunwood and getting him out is not likely to be easy. I need to know that—if we're caught, or injured, or the *Diana* is in danger, or Dunwood is already dead—that I can count on you. Can you handle yourself?"

"Yes."

She looked at him, kept looking at him.

"I am obviously not unskilled in combat," he said, and she felt a thrill that he'd been the one to blink first, to put an answer into that heavy silence. "That I don't want to fight doesn't mean I'm not capable of it. I've had enough of war, Captain. I've no need for more of it."

"And yet," she said, "you're about to engage in battle."

"That's different."

"Because it's Dunwood?"

"And because the queen requested it."

She understood duty, and could respect it. So she nodded, decided to give him the benefit of the doubt, as she'd do for the members of her crew. "Very well."

Watson and Sampson joined them in similar ensembles.

"Any questions?" Kit asked, and they all shook their heads. She glanced at Jin. "Have March prepare the crew's mess in case we have injuries. She can deal with them there."

"Already done," he said. "She's gathering her instruments of torture."

Watson lifted a hand. "If we're able to rescue Dunwood, and we were, theoretically speaking, to come across any pirate loot, would we be authorized to liberate said loot?"

"Under those specific conditions," Kit said, "it's probably best I not know of any loot-related activity. Understood?"

"Aye, Captain." She lifted a shoulder. "Odds seem low we'd run across that kind of thing, but a woman likes to be prepared, you know."

"Always," Kit said, and turned toward the sea.

They passed a dozen small islands, each a palette of tan and green and black, some nothing more than a spit of sand or stone.

There was no sign of the gun brig. Either it hadn't been headed for the island, or they'd beaten it here. Whatever the reason, Kit was relieved to find one less obstacle in her way.

As they neared Finistère, the water changed, lightened— became the color of rich turquoise. The island rose, black and gray, from that water like a table, the stone dotted with seabirds and scatterings of green that had found a foothold in crack or crevice.

"You were right," Grant said to Simon. "The cliffs would be . . . challenging."

"Sailors are uniquely adept at gauging the ease of a landfall," Simon said quietly, gaze on the landscape. "We've much practice at it."

But the cliffs were hardly the only threat. Smaller monoliths of rock stabbed up around the island like the points of a crown.

The waves were white between them, the spray ten feet above the surface. And gleaming among them, like jewels in the crown, were the bleached remains of ships that hadn't judged the shoals carefully enough. Bows and masts speared up, tattered flags and pennants shifting in the wind.

Kit didn't need to see her crew to know they'd be touching their talismans now, saying a silent prayer for the crew members lost to this graveyard.

They rounded the island, hanging as close as they dared, and neither heard nor saw any indication they'd been seen.

She nodded at Jin. "Bring us in so we can launch the jolly boat."

While he steered, Mr. Jones, the bosun, called out instructions to haul in the sails, slow the ship's forward progression.

"I'll be back," Kit said, accepting the time had come to give the promised instruction to Louisa.

Kit found her in the galley again, this time pounding her fist into a lump of what appeared to be dough.

Cook looked up, narrowed his gaze at his captain. "We don't have enough biscuits for you to graze them like sheep all day and night."

That he was the man in charge of biscuit distribution was the primary reason she didn't toss him overboard for insubordination.

"And that's a constant disappointment to me," she said. "We're nearing the island."

Cook's expression sobered, and he nodded. "Give me that, Tiny Cook." And he took the bowl from her, placed it onto the table where she worked, and then helped her hop down again.

"Remember what we talked about?" Kit asked her. "How it would be time for you to go into the hold?"

Louisa nodded.

"It's time now."

"Is that why you're dressed different?"

"It is."

After a moment of narrow-eyed consideration that was nearly as intimidating as the admirals to whom she reported, Louisa nodded. "All right. You have to be careful, though."

"I will be as careful as I can."

"I'll take her," Cook said, his tone softer.

It was the first time in Kit's memory that Cook had volunteered for anything outside the mess. But she appreciated the gesture and the care. Until they could get her back to New London, Louisa was their collective responsibility.

Keep her safe, she prayed, to any of the gods who might listen, who might have luck to spare for a child caught in a conflict that wasn't her doing.

The jolly boat was prepared. Small casks of rum and water were loaded as emergency provisions, then the bargaining chits—hardtack and tea. Then the boat was winched over the side of the *Diana*, and Watson and Sampson climbed aboard, took seats on two of the plank benches where oars would be extended over the hull. Kit motioned Grant on board, and then followed him in. But she turned back, held out her hand to Jin. Jin clasped her forearm, and they watched each other for a moment.

"*Tiva kass*," he said. It meant "gods' kiss," in the old language, a way of saying "take care."

"*Tiva kass*," Kit responded. "Lower the boat." She watched her sailors until she could no longer see them, kept their gazes until they'd disappeared from view. She committed their visages to memory; they would be her touchstone. The reminder, should she need one, of who and what waited for her. Of the crew that needed safe passage back to their homes and families.

Watson pulled a gold coin from the leather harness that crossed her chest, bearing throwing knives that, Kit had reason to know, she could aim with impressive accuracy. She kissed the coin, tossed it into the sea. "*Dastes*," she murmured as it slipped into the jewel-toned water.

"Do all sailors pay homage before sailing?" Grant asked, gripping the jolly boat's gunwale as they jerkily descended. He looked a bit green, Kit thought, and she understood the sensation. Not because of the smaller boat; though he'd be feeling the ocean plenty when they touched it. Kit didn't like being suspended in air. Having nothing beneath her between the hull of the jolly boat and the ocean's slick surface. She preferred land, with its unyielding stiffness, to nothingness.

"It's an unwise sailor doesn't ask the gods for safe passage," Sampson said. "And the crew of the *Diana* ain't unwise."

"No, they are not," Kit agreed, clenching against the final bounce as they hit the water. They unhitched the ropes, which the *Diana*'s crew began to pull in again.

Jin gave one final salute from the edge of the ship, then he disappeared like the rest.

Kit relaxed, settled into the ocean's undulations, and the oars were extended into the water. "Let's go find our man."

TEN

It took only minutes to reach the trade zone, as the waves pushed the boat toward the harbor. There'd been no need for Kit to touch the current, and a good thing, as the jolly boat was small enough that the force might have ripped them to kindling. But Kit listened to the sea the entire way, as if the connection might insulate them from danger, or save them from grinding against the tangle of rock and lumber.

They tied up under the narrowed gaze of the pirates who waited with their own vessels, or looked back from the dock, watching the new arrivals.

"Grant, with me. Sampson, Watson, stay with the boat," Kit said, climbing onto the dock. "And watch the tea."

Grant behind her, they walked across the weather-beaten planks and inspected the available wares with the narrowed gazes of suspicious buyers.

The merchants were mostly salt-crusted sailors with sun-lined skin, and the goods—bad food, bits of scavenged rope, meager weapons—weren't much of an improvement. The air smelled of overripe fruit and overripe bodies, and she had a sudden appreciation for the relative fastidiousness of Crown Command sailors.

Kit picked a merchant, a block of a man with tan skin, a bald pate, and eyebrows large enough to keep the sun out of his eyes. His offerings were limited, but the quality seemed good.

She approached him. Waited until he looked up and belched. And maintained her flat stare.

"If you're done with that, we've biscuit to trade."

The man snorted. "Don't need no moldy biscuits 'ere. Got more than enough."

Kit curled her lip. "Not moldy, you cur. Fresh from the Crown Command, and taken from a packet off the coast of Gallia." Best keep the details relatively close to some part of the truth.

"Don't want any biscuits," he said. "What else?"

Kit looked at Grant and frowned, as if debating her options. Then cursed under her breath.

"Tea."

Interest blossomed in the merchant's eyes. "From where?"

"Same packet. Headed right to the queen's own teapot. It's a bit too freshly acquired, if you catch my meaning, to sell on the Isles."

"How freshly acquired?"

"Thirty-six hours, give or take."

The man watched her for another moment, and Kit wondered if he couldn't see the thudding of her heart. Not in fear, but excitement.

The merchant held out his palm. "Sample?"

Kit opened a kerchief she'd filled with tea leaves, offered it. Hoped the man's palate wasn't so developed he could tell queen's tea from officers'. He held the kerchief beneath his nose, sniffed with a curled lip that said he was expecting to find something foul.

And closed his eyes in ecstasy.

Kit had to work to keep the triumphant smile off her face.

"How much?" he asked. No respectable merchant made the first offer.

Kit named her price, and the man snorted.

"It's tea, not opium."

Negotiations took ten more precious minutes, so Kit was fighting back impatience by the time they'd decided on a price, and it wasn't nearly as much as the tea was worth. But a little desperation worked in her favor, she figured, so she cursed, but nodded. "Fine.

"We'll get it from the boat," Kit said, and began to walk toward it. But Grant put a stopping hand on her arm, and his expression was mutinous.

"It's my damned tea, and I'm not handing it over to anyone without coin in hand."

The merchant snorted. "You're touched if you think I'm handing over coin for a kerchief of leaves. Could be a box of rat shit."

"And what would I be doin' with a box of rat shit?" Grant asked, disbelief in every word.

The merchant lifted a shoulder. "Don't know you, do I?"

"I know you're a big, dumb bastard won't give me my money."

The merchant's lip curled. "What did you say to me?"

Kit pulled her arm away from Grant. "Enough," she said, and the authority in her tone had both men looking at her with surprise in their expressions. Kit put a hand on her sabre, which had the chatterers around them quieting, watching. Probably hoping to see a good fight, if not jump right into one. She understood the need to play a role, but they were wasting time.

"We aren't handing over our merchandise without payment," she said. "Which means we're holding the tea until we get our money."

"I'm not hauling crates in this heat without more coin," Grant said. And before he could blink, Kit had her dagger out, its tip pressed at his crotch. She'd considered the heart, but this seemed much more piratey.

"I'm in charge here," she said, voice a low growl of anger. "You'll do as I order, or you'll be dropped a hundred miles off-shore for the sea dragons to eat. Is that clear?"

Grant expanded his nostrils as he exhaled with emotion. "Captain," he said, the word an obvious insult. And then muttered under his breath about unruly women.

"Get the crates," the merchant said. "The rest is up to the Five."

Grant and Kit walked back to the boat in what appeared to be fuming silence.

"You might warn a man next time you're going to point a dagger at his manhood," Grant said.

"Grab my arm again and pointing will be the least of your worries."

They reached the jolly boat, found Sampson lying napping in the sun, and Watson picking her nails clean with the point of a dagger. Kit kicked the bow. Sampson blinked and shot up. Watson flicked away some bit of grime from the tip of the knife.

Very convincing, Kit thought. "We've sold the tea," she said. "Hand it over."

Sampson rose, the boat bobbing as he moved from stern to bow, tea in his arms. "Good price?"

"No," Grant said with disgust, and gave Kit a look with matching disdain. "Can't trust a woman to negotiate."

"He's just angry I threatened him with castration."

Watson had to bite back a grin. "Did he deserve it?"

"Inarguably," Kit said as Sampson handed over the crate, then retrieved the other two, piled them on the deck.

"Sampson, with us. Watson, stay with the boat." Frowning, Kit glanced around, noting the eyes still on her. And the rather burly man and woman currently talking to the merchant, which told Kit the merchant wasn't sure of them despite their rather marvelous acting.

"Looking a bit hairy," she said, pursing her lips as if considering her options. "Watson, when the tide begins to turn, perhaps you'll find a reason to move to the other end of the dock, nearer the rendezvous location."

"Sir," Watson said, and began to chew thoughtfully at a hangnail.

Ready for their next act, they hefted their crates.

⌒

The burly pirates were gone by the time Kit, Grant, and Sampson reached the merchant. He looked them over wordlessly, then gestured them to follow.

The fortress hulked in front of them, as much vines and broken stone as actual structure. They walked the stone bridge in silence toward the arched entrance, as leather-skinned pirates sat or squatted along the edges of the bridge, with poles and string reaching into the water. One landed a fish the color of the flowers outside the palace, sunlight flashing across its scales like a mirror.

When they reached the entrance, the merchant walked to the guards stationed there, who both looked formidable.

She watched as they chatted, as the merchant and guards looked from her crew, to the trade zone, to the crates they carried.

They'd probably be allowed to enter the fortress, Kit thought. Perhaps make it as far as the courtyard. And that's when the trap would be sprung.

Kit gave a fake yawn, as if completely unconcerned and bored by the wait, made a show of looking around. "The first distraction is yours," she whispered to Grant.

"Appropriate," he said back, "given I'm in charge of the mission."

"Certainly," she muttered, "if one ignores the days of sailing that got you here." She glanced back again, feigned boredom. "What's taking so damned long?" she called out, and got a very rude gesture for her trouble.

"How long does it take to trade in tea?" she asked shortly when the merchant returned. "The tide will have turned before we finish this deal."

"You'll get your coin," the merchant muttered, and gestured them forward.

They walked beneath the stone archway, one of the guards falling into step behind them, and into a courtyard. It was open to the sky, the walls of the fortress's top story rising above it.

These interior walls were built of the same dark and pitted stone as the rest of the fortress, but that was the only commonality. The exterior was a warning; the interior was a celebration. The middle of the courtyard was a garden of greenery, with trees rising up toward the sky. Flowering vines in startling pinks and blues climbed around the columns that edged it, and stands of rosemary and dandy scented the area. A narrow pool of water ran through the space, golden coins glimmering up through the water, and at its head a golden cherub sculpture that relieved itself into the pool.

"It's not Exeter Palace," Grant said. "But it has a certain appeal."

"Don't need to be," the merchant said. "The Five's tougher than the queen and all the rest put together."

"So you say," Grant murmured. "You actually ever meet the Five?"

The merchant stopped, looked back at them with disdain. "Of course I've met the damn Five. Shut your mouth, or I'll shut it for you."

Grant snorted, and his voice was all arrogance. "You're welcome to try."

Something like anticipation gleamed in the merchant's eyes. He was obviously ready for a fight, but there was certainty in his expression now. He'd called for reinforcements, Kit guessed.

And they were definitely going to lose the tea.

"What the hell are we doing in here?" Kit asked, shifting the crate impatiently.

Footsteps began to sound from somewhere in the fortress, but the noise echoed off the stone so Kit had no idea of its direction.

"Ow! You son of an ox. Watch your damned feet! You'll break my damned toes."

Grant's voice rang out, and by the time Kit had turned to

look, his fist was flying. He hit the guard with a surprise jab that popped back his head, sent him staggering back. He might have regained his feet, but he tripped on a raised bit of stone, fell backward with a rattling *thud*.

And there was her distraction, Kit thought, hefting the box of tea. And with apologies to whatever kind gods had thought to gift sailors with it, threw it at the merchant.

She made use of her moment of surprise and pulled out her sabre as pirates (clean and dirty, respectively) swarmed the room like ants. The tea was tossed aside as Sampson and Grant took out their weapons. Sampson had a thick, short sword, Grant a pair of small, sleek blades.

The first pirate, unfortunate of dentition and shaggy of hair, came at her with his own gleaming sword. She met his thrust with a blow of steel against steel. He was a big man—more than six feet tall, and bulky with muscle. Rather logically, he appeared to believe he could simply break her in half. But Kit wasn't weak, and he wasn't her first pirate.

She knew to let him lead, to give him space to try to pummel her with that enormous broadsword. It clanged against stone, sending up sparks. She mashed his instep and dodged to the side when he tried to grab her with a meaty fist, and then brought her sword across his back. He screamed as blood welled, and turned back to her with murder in his eyes.

"Not today," she murmured, and brought her sabre up against his blows. Once, twice, thrice she blocked, each meeting of blades sending a shock of pain through her arms. Their swords crossed, he dropped one hand to grab her wrist, smiled in pleasure as she tried to writhe out of his manacle-like grip. He chuckled, looming over her.

She went limp, as if pretending to faint, sword arm falling.

Yes, the move was beneath her. But it was so very effective.

Instinctively, he released her wrist, intending to pick her up bodily. And dropped his sword arm. She slammed up with her sabre, striking the side of his face hard enough to have him wobbling backward and then stumbling over a pirate felled by Grant or Sampson.

He hit the ground, head striking stone with a *crack* that made her wince in sympathy. His eyes rolled back. She kicked away his sword, glanced around. Found Sampson pummeling a pirate with his bare fists, sword temporarily abandoned, and Grant engaged with another in a battle. His movements were sharp, crisp. Well trained and practiced, but not only. There was power there.

She didn't like being wrong again about his presumed aristocratic insufficiencies—and she enjoyed watching him fight more than she was comfortable admitting. So she looked away, was nearly relieved when another pirate approached, young and skinny, her hand shaking around her sword hand. Not feigning inexperience, Kit thought, but actually inexperienced.

Kit turned to face her, smiled. And held nothing back. She advanced, struck, slashing one way and then the next, forcing the girl to block blow after blow, to wince each time she managed, just barely, to avoid being run through.

Close, Kit thought, and kept advancing. She struck left, and the girl met the shot again. Time to finish this, Kit thought, and circled the sword until the girl's wrist bent backward and her own blade clattered to the ground.

The girl swallowed hard, then turned on her heel and ran.

"One way's as good as another," Kit said, then ran back across the courtyard. She reached it, and heard the floor shake as reinforcements were called in. She looked back, found the girl moving through the archway, this time with a dozen men behind her.

It was time to change the fight, she thought, and pulled one of Jane's sparkers from her bag.

"To the archway!" Kit said. "And cover your ears!"

Sampson, who knew how to respond to an order from a commanding officer, didn't wait for Kit to go first. He just ran.

Grant hesitated, and she saw the question in his eyes. But there was no room for chivalry here. He obviously thought better of it as his eyes flattened again, and he followed Sampson.

With more footsteps coming toward their flank, Kit turned for the archway, pressed down on the glass, and then tossed the sparker behind her.

ELEVEN

It was like she'd turned the world inside out.

They were through the courtyard when the sparker exploded, but even the reflected light on the facing stone was bright enough to put halos behind her eyes.

The fortress shook around them, sending the trio to the ground as stones rattled loose with a spray of fragments and dust. The sharp crackle followed by a bass *boom* was enough to rattle her heart in her chest. Kit had expected the sound of a cannon, but this was louder, deeper, richer, as if the earth had groaned in response.

For a moment, there was only a fog of smoke and the rainfall sound of small debris. Kit sucked in a breath. And then coughed it up again when smoke seared her lungs.

Kit wiped soot from her eyes and looked down, realized the lumps beneath her weren't upended stone. They were Rian Grant, his face streaked as hers probably was. She was draped across him, her elbow lodged just below his chest.

"I'm very sorry," she said, and climbed off, glad the grime hid her pinkening cheeks.

She shook her head to clear it, looked down at Grant. He was still on the ground, lips parted and eyes wide, staring in horror. Kit followed the direction of his gaze, found nothing but stone and rubble.

"Grant?" she asked, touching his shoulder. "Are you all right?"

He jerked beneath her fingers, but his gaze focused again, and he coughed, wiped dust from his face. "What the hell was that?"

"One of Jane's explosives," Kit said. "Self-contained combustible." She offered him a hand. And after looking at it for a moment, he took it, let her help pull him to his feet.

He ran a hand through his thick hair, now dusted with soot. "That's the second time I've ended up on the ground because of you."

"It's becoming a bad habit," she agreed. "Are you all right?" she asked again, quieter this time as Sampson climbed to his feet. "You seemed . . . startled."

"I'm fine. Just had . . . a moment. Of the war."

Kit nodded, hoped he was truly well, because this skirmish was only beginning. She looked at Sampson.

"Good?"

"Fine, Captain." He ran a hand across his soot-covered face. "Other than some scratches here and there, bruised knuckles."

There was movement behind them as guards and inhabitants rushed to the scene of the explosion, and those closer to the blast began to moan.

"Downstairs," she said, and pulled her sabre again. "Go."

This time, Grant didn't hesitate.

They took the spiral stone staircase, narrow, steep, and dark but for the flickering light of hanging torches, and descended. The scenery didn't improve, and Kit was glad when they spilled into a corridor. The dungeon split off in three different directions, and there were barred cells visible in all of them. The central corridor showed damage from the sparker—a hole in the ceiling and a pile of rocks on the floor, smoke slipping through the gap in a thin wisp. But it was still passable.

They'd have to split up. Kit didn't like it, but if they had any chance of finding Dunwood before the pirates realized where they'd gone—and found them—they'd have to be fast.

"Sampson, take a torch, go to the left. If you find him, signal us. If worse comes, get him out. Don't worry about or wait for us. Understood?"

Sampson looked down at her from his height, acknowledged the order with a grim nod.

She squeezed his arm, met his gaze. "We're all going to make it. I'm just telling you not to wait for us. We can get off the island separately, if that's what we need. But we will all make it off."

His hope apparently renewed, Sampson pulled a torch from the wall and set off down the left-hand corridor.

Grant was pulling another torch from the wall when she glanced back and caught sight of the crimson stripe on his sleeve.

"You're bleeding," she said, and didn't bother to ask before ripping away the sleeve, inspecting his biceps.

"It's fine. And I liked that shirt, and you're very presumptuous."

"The shirt was ruined anyway. It's not terribly deep," Kit said, ignoring him, looking over the stripe that crossed taut skin and hard muscle, and working hard to ignore the latter, "but it's big enough to bleed. It needs to be bandaged."

"It's fine," he said again, tone harder now.

Kit lifted her gaze to his. "And maybe you'll scar over quickly, or maybe you'll keep bleeding and lead a trail for the Five to follow. As you've proclaimed yourself the leader of this mission, which risk do you prefer?"

He growled, but ripped away the rest of his sleeve, handed it to her. She wrapped it around the wound twice, knotted it tight.

"That will hold until we're back." She glanced up at him, thought he didn't look much like a member of the Beau Monde now, with hair tousled and falling across his brow. "You don't fight like a viscount."

"I wasn't a viscount when I learned how to fight," Grant reminded her.

There were sounds behind them—shouts, footsteps. "Go," he said as she pulled the third torch. "You go straight. I'll go right."

"I'll tell you the same as I told Sampson—get out if you can."

"Like you said, I don't leave men behind."

Kit smiled slyly. "I'm no man."

⌀

Water dripped along the walls, and something—or some*things*—skittered across the ground. The general smell of illness and rot permeated the air, and put a sick sense of dread in Kit's belly. If Dunwood was down here, his condition was probably poor.

She ran through the corridor, passing a dozen gated cells. Many were empty—just stone and barred iron doors—although there was a scattering of prisoners, mostly men in various states of disrepair, who yelled as she walked by. Made offers. Asked for favors. She ignored their pleas. It may have been cold, but even if she'd had the urge to release a few dozen prisoners—which she did not—she didn't have the time or the resources to deal with them.

Dunwood was her mission. None of the inhabitants fit his description, and she hoped Sampson and Grant were having better luck. Else the intelligence had been wrong, Dunwood wasn't here, and they had no idea where he might be.

But then she reached the last cell, looked in.

A man lay on the floor, amid a scattering of rushes, the sweet smell of death even stronger here, and hope fell away like shattered glass.

"Dunwood," she said quietly.

It took a moment, but his head lifted, and he turned blue eyes on her. "Well," he said hoarsely. "Hullo, angel. Have you come to fetch me?"

"I have," she said, hope rising. Kit gave a whistle to signal the others, tried to push up the iron bar that kept the door locked. But it was halfway to rusted, and wouldn't budge.

Footsteps echoed down toward her, and she turned to face the corridor and whoever was charging toward them. And was actually relieved to see Grant.

"Sampson?"

Grant shook his head. "I've not seen him." He glanced at Dunwood, the bar.

"I could use some help," she said, and he stepped beside her.

"Crowbar," he said, and pulled it from his belt. He wedged it under the cell's bar, and pushed, grunting, until he'd broken through the rust and Kit could pull the bar from its brackets. She tossed it away, pulled open the door, and they rushed inside.

Kit dropped to her knees at Dunwood's side, put a hand against his forehead. "He's burning up. Illness?"

"Or could be this," Grant said, opening the man's shirt to reveal an ugly gash across his abdomen, the edges swollen and red. The sweet odor of rot lifted into the air.

"Just a scratch," Dunwood said, reaching out for Grant's hand with one of his own, and using the other to grip a token on a leather thong around his neck. "That you, Rian Grant?"

"It is, Marcus Dunwood. You've got yourself in a bit of a spot."

"Minor inconvenience," he said, and shifted his gaze to Kit, his eyes gleaming with interest. "And who might you be?"

"Your rescuer," she said.

"And a lovely one at that," he said with a wink.

"I see your infirmity hasn't changed your proclivities," Grant said.

"Oh, there's nothin' infirm about me," he said, wiggling his eyebrows.

"Given your current position," Kit said, "we'll politely disagree. But a poultice on that wound will fix you right up." But she looked at Grant, let him see the concern in her eyes. Cook and March could work a poultice, but they couldn't work a miracle.

"Typical," Grant said, climbing to his feet. "Lying around so I'm forced to rescue you."

Dunwood tried to snort, but managed only a weak cough. "Payback for all those times I saved you."

Grant and Kit looked up as noise began to ring down the hall. Sampson came running. "Heard the signal, but got turned around. Here now."

"We're glad of it," Kit said. "Meet Marcus Dunwood."

"Sir," Sampson said.

"No 'sirs' necessary, sailor. I'm just a soldier."

"We need to get him out of here," Grant said. "Tunnel should be to the right."

"It is," Dunwood said. "I can hear the waves when the tide's high."

"Then that's where we'll go," Grant said. "Follow me."

This time, Kit willingly obeyed.

~⌒~

Grant half walked, half carried Dunwood through the wet and stinking corridor toward the ocean. Kit walked first, Sampson last, both with blades extended. She concentrated on what she hoped was the sound of water on the shore nearby, and not just her own heart, beating furiously with the hope they'd manage to get Dunwood safely aboard the *Diana*.

She pushed back that fear, pushed beyond it. They had no room for it. Not now.

They stayed ahead of their pursuers as they followed the tunnel, but only just. The sound of mad footsteps behind them kept growing louder, faster.

The tunnel grew rockier and steeper, as if it were no longer part of the building, but the island itself. A vessel between heart and lungs.

She heard a grunt, a shuffle behind her, looked back to find Dunwood gripping his side, his face white as a sail, knees bent as his body buckled.

Grant cursed, bent his knees, and picked up his comrade as

tenderly as he might a child. He met Kit's gaze, and she saw the struggle in his eyes. Not from the physical exertion, she thought, but the realization his friend needed to be carried.

Many layers to this man, she thought.

"Arms around my neck if you can manage it," Grant said.

"Kanos's balls," Dunwood grunted through teeth clenched in pain, and managed one arm over Grant's shoulder. "Carrying me like I'm a helpless child."

Kanos was one of the old gods; he ruled the sea and the shorelines around it. Because of his fondness for women and aptitude for seduction, he was a favorite of soldiers and sailors.

"You weigh about as much," Grant said, shouts behind them as they moved forward again. "You need beefsteak and red dover."

"Don't care for fish," Dunwood said. "But aye, I'll take a beefsteak, good and bloody, when we're back in the Isles."

"At the Seven Keys," Grant said, naming one of New London's posh and exclusive men's clubs.

"Damned right."

"Captain," Sampson warned as the ground began to tremble.

"Faster now," Kit urged, and shifted to move behind Grant. The battle wouldn't happen in front of them, but behind. That's where she needed to be.

The tunnel shifted, curved away, then forked.

"Light!" Grant said, and continued toward the right, disappeared from view. "There's light up ahead. I can see water."

The sea, their savior. "Go," Kit said, "as fast as you can."

Grant looked back at her, sweat on his brow. Considered arguing, but moved.

"Dunwood," she said, a reminder of their mission. "Go."

Then waved everyone in front of her and followed them, gaze darting back as the noises grew louder.

The corridor grew brighter and brighter still, until Kit was squinting into brilliant sunlight. She emerged into sunlight and salt-scented air, the screaming jackgulls. The turquoise water was twenty feet beyond a bank of sand, of rock. And beyond that, the sails of the *Diana* waited, streaming toward the island.

She was, for a moment, modestly disappointed she hadn't been able to deploy her weapons again, and was on the verge of putting her sabre away, when men began emerging from the dunes like crabs.

Pirates stepped out from the corridor, led by a man with sun-kissed golden skin and coal-black hair, deep brown eyes that watched her with curiosity. His features were elegant, as were his clothes. The pirates wore their dirty and mismatched linen, most in bare feet and necks bound with amulets. He wore buff trousers and a linen shirt white as the sugar-colored sand.

The pirates had bided their time, waited for them to reach the likely exit, and trapped them from all sides. Efficient and elegant, Kit thought.

She wished she'd thought of it first.

"Back-to-back," Kit said, her heart beginning to thud in a new and different way now as Sampson moved to protect Grant and Dunwood.

She glanced back at the sea, and with relief found the jolly boat moving through the harbor toward their position. "Boat's a hundred yards away."

They had to get Dunwood to the boat, and then they had to get to the *Diana*.

"It would be best," Kit murmured, as the apparent pirate king strode toward them, "if we can get the pirates together."

She heard them shuffling behind her.

"So," the man said. "You're the ones who've destroyed my castle."

"If you're asking about the explosion, then yes. That was me. And you are?"

"Donal. And you?"

"Kit Brightling."

Donal looked faintly amused by the response. "I suppose that would be Captain Brightling of the lovely little ship behind you?"

Kit had to work not to show the bolt of fear that ripped through her, fear for her crew. But this wasn't the time to show weakness.

"As I'm facing you," she said, "I couldn't speak to what's behind me." And damn the fact that she wasn't in the water now, couldn't feel it moving. She took another step backward, nudging against Grant's back. And was relieved by his solidity.

"Clever," Donal said.

"Thank you. Where are the other four?"

"They have other priorities at the moment." His gaze raked Kit from head to toe. "I won the coin toss." He glanced at Dunwood. "It appears you're taking something that belongs to me."

"We're taking the man you've imprisoned without cause."

"I may be far removed from the Isles, my dearest captain, but I'm fairly confident spying is illegal."

Kit ignored that. "How did you come to have him?"

"A special delivery," he said with a smile.

More men gathered behind him, and he didn't bother to spare them a glance. Just smiled serenely at Kit.

"I prefer to be keeping him for myself, as I've plans for his . . . disposition."

"Yes, we saw the gun brig," Kit surmised. "Where's it from, Donal? Gallia? Frisia? Which country has paid the most for this particular treasure?"

"I've seen no flags of either of those countries," Donal said.

"It's near enough," Grant whispered, and Kit presumed he meant the jolly boat.

"Well, this is very disappointing," Kit said.

Donal's brows lifted. "What is?"

"That I'd enjoy conversing with you more, learning how you and your colleagues operate your kingdom. But I'm going to have to ruin it again."

His gaze narrowed as she took a step back, putting space between them. The pirates were still scattered, still holding their positions around the crew.

"Ready," she whispered to her men, then looked at Donal. "Goodbye," she said brightly, and threw the last sparker.

She'd aimed at the stone just above the tunnel, hoping the impact would throw out enough rocks to bring down most of the pirates.

It did, but sent her flying, too. She landed on her back in the sand ten feet from where she'd started, ears ringing and head spinning. She was going to need a nap. And possibly a good vomit.

She blinked at the sky until the voices resolved into shouts, the number of suns reduced to the requisite one. Then she climbed to her knees, looked back. What had been the opening to the tunnel was now a pile of rubble. Most of the pirates were on the sand, including Donal. Sampson was up, shaking his head. Grant was on his knees a few feet away, Dunwood still in his arms. And Watson and the boat were in the shallows now.

Dunwood opened one eye, looked around. "Now, that was a damn fine explosion."

Kit blew out a breath, climbed to her feet, plucked her sabre from the sand a few feet away. Then she strode to Grant. His eyes looked clear now, which was a relief. She guarded his back while he climbed to his feet.

"Run," she told him. "And get the boat moving toward the *Diana*."

"We aren't leaving you here."

"You won't have to, and that's a promise," she added when she saw doubt in his eyes. "I'll be right behind you." She held out her sword, making a wall of her body. And when a blade flashed to her right, she ducked, then spun, brought her sabre up and blocked the sword wielded by the pirate—a woman with sun-darkened skin and stringy yellow hair.

Metal sparked against metal, reflecting the blazing sun across the sand. They pushed off against each other, reset, came in again. The woman went high, bringing down her sword like a hammer. Kit stayed low, spun on her heel, and brought up the sabre against the woman's back, pushing her forward.

The woman stumbled, hit the ground.

Kit saw the shadow cross the sand, rolled forward just as the sword came down. It missed Kit, hit the woman across the chest. She screamed; the pirate who'd struck her grunted and pulled up his sword, flinging blood through the air as he moved for Kit again, apparently unconcerned about the sailor he'd nearly filleted.

"I've wondered about the loyalty of pirates," she said casually, dodging the man's overhead blows. He was big, but he was slow, and he signaled every move.

"Whether you're loyal to your comrades," she said, darting left, "or only to yourself."

He grunted, and Kit feinted right, then slipped left again, putting the big man off balance. She took her chance, kicking him over. He hit the sand, his sword flying forward. She grabbed it, stabbed the sand between his legs, neatly catching the crotch of his trousers to pin him to the ground.

Not a permanent end, but good enough given the whistle that split the air—Watson's earsplitting signal that it was time for her to follow. She pushed her sabre into her belt, turned toward the sea, and ran.

The boat was fifty feet out now. She pumped her arms and jumped into the surf, moving in a high-legged run through foaming water until it was deep enough.

And then she went under, diving into the waves, beneath them.

The human world disappeared, sounds swallowed by the soft murmur of water, the hard world traded for shifting green and white and yellow as light danced in the shallows. The surf was strong, but she could read her way through the rush of water against the shore, into the channels where the sea was smoother, slicker.

"It's like you were born to the water," Hetta had once said, when they'd determined the extent of Kit's Alignment. "Maybe born in it, swimming like an earnest little fish."

Kit believed it then, and she believed it now.

She swam toward the boat through water that deepened to a

crystalline blue, until she saw the white belly of the jolly boat above her. Then she breached the surface, sucking air, slapped the boat twice. The oars stopped, and Watson appeared over the side, arm extended.

"Captain," she said with a grin. "Welcome back."

TWELVE

K it joined Watson and Sampson at the oars as Grant held
Dunwood.

With every four feet they advanced, the sea pushed them
back two, as if helping the island contain them.

"Magic?" Grant asked.

"Much as I'd enjoy putting you down again, I can't touch the
current here," she said, heaving against the oars. "The boat's too
small for the force; it would break us to pieces. So we'll need to
do this the old-fashioned way."

Some pirates were running through the water; others dove in
to swim toward the jolly boat, just as she'd done. The gun brig
was nowhere in sight, but smaller boats had been launched and
were giving chase. If the jolly boat didn't speed up, they'd be in-
tercepted before they reached the *Diana*. And they needed to get
Dunwood on board.

"*Faster*," she said, watching a low boat painted an eye-searing
yellow that cut through the waves like a shark. They rowed
harder, faster, in perfect rhythm, until the *Diana* consumed their

horizon, and ropes were lowered. The jolly boat was tied on, and the crew began hauling her up as a *crack* issued from the fortress.

"Incoming!" came the shout from above.

"Down!" Kit said, and they ducked in the jolly boat, now hanging four feet in the air.

The cannon hit thirty feet off their starboard bow, sending an enormous plume of water into the air and jolting the jolly boat against the hull.

Kit lifted her head, looked back at the island. Found Donal atop the fortress, chest bare and thighs braced beside the smoking end of black iron cannon.

She bared her teeth. "Only children and cowards shoot cannons from shore," she said with disgust.

Dunwood chuckled. "You've got a lot of opinions there, Captain."

Grant grunted. "You don't know the half of it."

ᔐᔑᓂ

The boat was hauled up and over, Dunwood carefully lifted to the *Diana*, and the others followed him out.

March was waiting beside it, already in an apron. "Where shall we put him?"

"There's one empty cabin beside Grant's," Kit said. He deserved better than the mess. "It's small, but I don't imagine he'll complain about it."

"He won't," Grant said, and followed as the men carried Dunwood down.

Kit nodded, pushed water from her hair. "Everyone all right?"

"Right as rain, Captain," said Hobbes. "All hands accounted for."

Her favorite words. "Then let's get the hell out of Finistère."

"Make sail!" Jin called out, and sailors rushed to the foremast to climb to the yards and let fly the topsail. Kit ran forward to the mainmast, joined the line of sailors hauling the halyard to raise the mainsail—the largest of the *Diana*'s sails.

"Ah, the captain's on the line now!" called out one of the midshipmen. "You'd better heave to, my mates, lest she outhaul the rest of you!"

Hand over hand, inches at a time, they raised the spar that held the sail, and felt the canvas catch the wind, the *Diana* shudder in response. The sail was sheeted, made tight against the wind, and sailors ran to other sails to finish the work.

The sail raised, Kit walked to the stern, watched as they put sea between the ship and the island. And for the first time in hours, she took a breath.

It would take time before they were completely clear of the archipelago, but Kit had additional business.

"Keep us moving," she told Jin. "Into the deep and away from the shoals. I'm going to check on Dunwood."

"Aye," Jin said.

She went belowdecks, where the air smelled of vinegar and cabbage, then to Dunwood's cabin. Grant stood outside it, looking in from the doorway. She saw fear in his eyes when he acknowledged her presence, but he managed to hide it before moving aside so Kit could get a look.

Dunwood was in the berth, his torn and dingy clothes switched for clean linens, presumably borrowed from one of her crew. March kneeled beside him, helping him drink from a wide bowl.

"You've a visitor," Dunwood said as March dabbed his face with a wet cloth.

She looked back. "I don't think they're for me," she said, rising. She put the bowl on a small ledge built into the hull. "Let me speak to the captain about the crew, and I'll be right back." She stepped out.

Dunwood probably didn't believe the lie, but he didn't make an argument.

Kit gestured March and Grant into her cabin, waited until the door was closed. "How is he?"

"I've sponged some of the filth off him," March said, "although he was surprisingly modest for a spy. New clothes, and I've cleaned the wound, put on a bandage. Managed to get a bit of broth in him. But the wound is bad, and he's still feverish. We're using vinegar compresses, trying to cool him down. But the illness has set in deep. I don't know if he'll recover."

"He'll recover," Kit said, forcing hope she didn't really feel into her tone. It was her job to be honest, but a good captain always erred on the side of hope. Without it, what was the point of the monotony, the effort, the danger, the trials? "His condition is what it is," Kit said. "But we'll do whatever we can—whatever must be done—to bring him through it. He's our responsibility."

"Aye, Captain. Of course."

Kit looked at Grant, got his nod, and opened the door again. "Get some food," she told March.

"I will," March said. "The old fogy wants to talk to you anyway."

"I can hear you," Dunwood called out, although hoarsely.

"I know," March said, then grinned at Kit and Grant. "I like him. He's a good bit of sass."

"Sass he has in abundance," Grant agreed.

Dunwood muttered something about respect from the younger generations.

March left them, and Kit and Grant squeezed inside. Grant sat on a small chair near the bed; Kit stood beside him, and together they nearly filled the space.

"So, 'Paolo,'" Grant said, crossing his arms. "What happened?"

Dunwood tried to chuckle, but the sound was hoarse and graveled. "I presume Chandler told you some of it, or you wouldn't know that name, much less be here."

"He said you'd been on a cargo ship, monitoring Guild activity along the coast."

"How'd they realize I was gone?"

"You didn't report in," Grant said. "Your fastidiousness saved you there. The *Carpathian* found the other four members of your crew."

Even though Dunwood was injured, the light in his eyes was clear. "They're safe, the others?"

"As far as we're aware," Grant said. "What happened?"

"A Gallic damned privateer is what happened. I thought at first he'd gotten lucky, running the coast and looking for whatever he might find. But no privateers or pirates should have known my name."

"Someone told them who you were," Kit said.

"Someone from Crown Command," Grant added.

Dunwood nodded. "Aye. They provided my name, my alias, where I was likely to be found. Word traveled, as it does, and the privateer found me. Ship name of *Chevalier*. I was considered a bit of very dangerous cargo in peacetime, spy or no. Not something they'd haul right into Frisia. So they brought me to the Five at Finistère and sold me to Donal, as he was the only one smart or stupid enough for it."

Grant leaned forward. "He interrogated you?"

"Aye. Asked me what I was doing on the *Sally*, that was the sloop's name, what had I seen, what I knew. I gave nothing up," Dunwood said. He coughed, holding a hand over his bandaged wound as he did.

When he swallowed hard, Kit picked up the bowl, offered it. When he nodded, she lifted his head—burning with fever—with one hand and held the bowl in the other. He swallowed twice, then turned his face away. Kit put the bowl down, then put the damp cloth across his forehead.

"Thank you, angel."

Kit nodded, moved back behind Grant, and found a softness in his gaze she hadn't seen before.

"Not often I have two pretty girls to care for me," he said, closing his eyes and breathing deeply. "Although that doesn't help much with the fever."

"I'm sorry for it," Grant said. "Sorry it took so long to find you."

"No point to being sorry for that, is there? Life will go as it does. Waste of time to wish for what's not."

"You always were a pessimist," Grant said.

"And I'm never disappointed with what comes. But we've business to continue, which needs to get done before I'm off this boat—however I'm taken off. I'm sure Chandler told you Frisia's gone very busy. Trade in, trade out. Makes the Guild very happy, as peacetime wasn't nearly so profitable. Gerard takes power again, they figure to capitalize on the markets. And they'll help in that regard as much as they can." Dunwood opened his eyes, looked at both of them in turn. "That's the sticking point, aye? The information everyone craves."

"What is it?" Grant asked.

Dunwood looked at Kit for such a long time she began to worry they'd lost him in the middle of it. "You're Aligned?" he asked finally.

Kit nodded. "I am. To the sea. Are you Aligned?"

"Gods, no," he said with a grin. "But I've spent enough time on the sea to know when someone has the connection." Dunwood shifted his gaze to Grant. "We didn't see much of the light touch under Sutherland."

"And a pity that," Grant said.

"Oh, aye. The land and the people suffered from it." He looked at Kit. "You know of Contra Costa."

"I do," she said.

"The Allies and the Isles saw Contra Costa as a tragedy. But Gerard thought it a lesson. Word is, he believes he lost the war because the Allies were better with magic. Had more of it, understood how to use it. He's been, you might say, ruminating over it. The loss. The magic. Getting angrier, say the island staff. And the Guild is encouraging him. He reckons he can reclaim his throne—and use magic to get him there, and damn the consequences."

"How?" Kit asked.

"With ships," he said. "I've not heard any details, only that the ship has something to do with magic. Some new kind of man-of-war, and the Guild has promised a squadron to Gerard. The first, it's said, is near completion."

"Where are these ships being built?" Kit asked.

Dunwood coughed again, and this time Grant rose, helped prop him up to make the breathing easier. "Dungeon's hell on the lungs," Dunwood said, when Grant had offered him a drink. Compassion again, at least for a fellow soldier, an old friend, and a man in obvious pain.

But for now, she had to put aside compassion. Because if Dunwood was right, and she had no reason to doubt him, they had to move, and quickly.

When Dunwood was settled again, he shook his head. "I don't know about where, other than not in Frisia. That would be too close to violating the treaty."

"Gallia?"

"No. Same problem, aye? It would invite too much attention."

"We have to get home," Kit said. "We have to tell the queen, warn the Crown Command. The shipyard has to be located and destroyed."

She turned to head back to the deck—to give the order to make all possible speed—when the ship's bell began to ring, calling all the sailors to their stations.

Kit cursed. "Damned pirates. Stay here," she told Grant.

"I'm coming," March said, running toward them. "I can stay with him."

"Aye, you can," Dunwood said with a leering wink. But his mouth was hard. He understood danger, and duty. "Put Grant to work," he said to Kit. "No sense in the wastrel lazing around down here when there's work to be done."

"I'll be back," Grant promised, and put a hand over Dunwood's and squeezed. And the men looked at each other with the kind of intimacy and tenderness born of hard times and deep trust.

She made for the companionway, Grant rushing behind her. And upon reaching the deck, shouted, "What is it?" to anyone who'd answer.

"That," Jin said, voice flat and gaze on the sea.

Kit followed his gaze, and swore.

The gun brig from Finistère was behind them, all sails flying, and giving chase.

THIRTEEN

W here the hell did they come from?" Kit asked, grabbing the glass Jin offered her as sailors ran to their posts, ready for instructions.

But she could surmise the answer—the gun brig had swung around the far side of one of the archipelago's islands, was rounding the downwind side of it. The ship was a mile off the *Diana*'s port quarter and gaining ground. Every sail had been raised, or was being raised, and it flew like a bird across the water.

Tamlin dropped to the deck and ran toward them through the currents of sailors.

"Why would it attack us?" she asked. Her hair was windblown and tousled, her cheeks pink from breeze and sunlight, and her eyes wide.

"Because of who we have on board," Grant said. "They want Dunwood."

"Or his information," Kit agreed. "Or to destroy the entire lot of us and make things much easier for themselves and Gerard. Let me think," she added, and walked to the stern, looked over the sea in their wake. The ship and its contingent seemed to inhale, as if silently holding a collective breath for her response.

The *Diana* was fast, and although they'd put out plenty of canvas to leave Finistère, there were sails to unfurl yet. But the gun brig had cannons. It didn't need to overcome the *Diana*; it only needed to get within firing range. And that particular threshold was growing closer: Kit growled as the gun brig unfurled stunsails that extended horizontally over the hull of the ship like wings of canvas.

"The Guild can march right into the sea," Kit muttered, then looked up, took in the canvas already on the ship, considered the wind, the water.

Fully rigged, the gun brig would probably be faster on a straight run. They were downwind, and if the sea and wind stayed steady, even with all canvas flying, they might not be able to outrun it. It would be close, and she didn't like close.

But the *Diana* was more maneuverable, and speed could be negotiated. So she closed her eyes and reached out for the water. She could feel the tension created by both ships. The water thin and churning in the shoals that surrounded the islands, deeper and smoother in the waters offshore. Those were the faster waters. But, again, if they couldn't win at speed, they could win other ways.

She opened her eyes, found Simon nearby. "Get me the archipelago map. Tamlin, get back in the top. Let us know if the wind's going to change. Jin, all hands and keep us flying."

The bell was rung. Seconds later, the sailors who weren't already on deck emerged from the forecastle, began spreading to their stations.

By the time Kit turned back to the cabinet behind the wheel, Simon had the archipelago map spread atop it. Kit surveyed it, reviewed the distance between their position and the two next-largest islands: Black and Kestrel.

"What are you thinking?" Grant asked, standing beside her. And for the first time, he sounded curious, not as if he was preparing for criticism or argument.

"That we can't beat them running downwind, and we can't engage them," she said. "They're probably faster and obviously armed. As much as I'd like to let them get closer and take them with steel, it's too risky. We have to get Dunwood home. But we may be able to outsail them.

"We're here," she added, pointing at the spot just northeast of Finistère. Then she looked up, glanced at the horizon. Black Island, the next in the chain, was south of them, and several miles off the port bow. The opposite of the direction they needed to travel—northeast and toward home—but the diversion would, she hoped, be temporary.

"If they can use the islands to hide," she said, "we can use them to escape." She looked up and at her officers. "The gun brig has a deeper draft. It's all those damn cannons and shot. And I suspect they're eager enough, desperate enough, to chase us, but we have the advantage in shallow water. So let's use the shoals to our advantage."

"You want to trick them into following us into shallow water and grounding themselves?" Grant asked.

"That's the idea." They'd had some luck today, and she hoped it would hold. "I'm thinking . . ." Kit began, and traced a finger along the route she had in mind, snaking in and around the islands.

"Won't they have the same maps?" Grant asked. "And know we're ultimately headed home? They could simply wait for us."

"Maps, yes," Kit agreed. "But they won't follow us all the way to the Isles—not without a declaration of war—and they don't want to risk losing Dunwood. If they want to catch us now, they're going to have to play by our rules."

She moved in front of the wheel, looked over her crew. "We're going to let them chase us," she called out, loud enough that the sailors could hear. "But we're going to set the course. We're going through the shoals, and need to be careful and cautious. She's armed, and she may fire when we tack, when we expose our flank. That's a risk we'll have to take. Our mission is to get Dunwood home," Kit said. "And by Kanos, that's damned well what we'll do."

"For Dunwood!" the crew called out, fists raised in the air. "For the Isles!"

Nodding, she looked at Jin. "I want every available bit of canvas hanging on this boat. If there's a jib, staysail, stunsail, pair of filthy trousers, it should be attached and hanging."

"Aye, Captain," Jin said with a satisfied smile, and the relay of orders began. Men were already on the foremast yard to unfurl the square topgallant, and she was sheeted home, tightened against the wind, masts and rigging creaking as the *Diana* surged forward.

The process was repeated—canvas raised or unfolded, lines tightened, the *Diana* offering mild complaints against the tension on her hull, but increasing her speed all the same.

Kit's smile was slow and satisfied, and her heart began to pound again. She understood the stakes, understood the risk. Understood the likelihood that she, or some of her crew, would be injured. But they'd do it with sails flying, charting their own course. And there was little more that a sailor could ask for.

Except, in this case, for a viscount.

She looked at Grant. "I need you to be my eyes."

He blinked back surprise. "Pardon?"

"It's easier to read the water if I close my eyes—shut out the distractions. But I could use someone to give an eye on our visible location. I need Jin giving orders, Simon at the wheel. That means it falls to you."

Grant lifted a brow. "Not entirely flattering, being third choice."

"Third on a ship of nearly two dozen," Kit pointed out, "and an army man at that. So it's really quite a compliment."

"In that case, I can hardly decline." His tone was mannerly, but there was a glint in his eye. Amusement or eagerness, she wasn't sure. He moved to stand beside her.

"We're ready, Captain," Jin said, and Kit gave one last look at the gun brig, the castle of canvas. And prepared to ground it.

"First tack is around Black Island," Kit said. "Hard to port on my mark." She glanced at Grant. "You recall which side is port?"

"You're terribly amusing. And yes."

She smiled at him. "Excellent. And hang on. These turns are going to be tight."

He nodded, the same battle readiness in his eyes as the others', and looked ahead.

Kit put a hand on the steering cabinet to steady herself, closed her eyes, and drifted down as the crew went silent, waiting for her command. Deep water to port, shallower to starboard, the current stochastic and broken among the rocks and the remains of ships that finally had run out of luck.

"We're nearing the channel between the islands," Grant said.

"I can feel it," she said quietly as the current sped, magic filling the deeper void between rocky outposts. The *Diana* would need to thread that channel just so, and she waited . . . then a bit more . . . for the timing . . .

"Three . . . two . . . one." Her words were quiet, her concentration intense. "Mark."

They tacked hard to port, the *Diana* keeling, deck tilted, as she pushed against ocean and inertia, and putting their side in the scope of the gun brig.

She knew the gun brig would take the chance and fire, because it was the same thing she'd have done. Kit felt the sea brace, contract as if repelled. And understood its reaction immediately.

"Incoming!" someone called out.

"Brace for impact!" Jin shouted, and she could hear the shift of wood and canvas as sailors ducked.

Two shots flew toward them, the sound following behind. She opened her eyes, watched the ball strike the water twenty feet from the hull, sending spray into the air that doused the sheets, but doing no damage.

"It's tacking," someone called out as sailors rose again with shouts of victory; firing at that angle would be useless. But this was only the *Diana*'s first turn. There would be others, and the gun brig would push closer for a better shot.

Which was exactly what Kit wanted. She settled her shoulders, closed her eyes again. "Grant?"

"Black Island on the starboard side."

"Straighten her out," Kit said. "North-northeast until my mark."

"Aye, Captain," Jin said, and the course was shifted until the ship was upright again, no longer leaning into the hard turn.

"We're past Black Island," Grant said a minute later.

"Kestrel next," Kit said. And reached for the water again. The shallows around Black Island had been almost neatly distributed, like a crisp crust around the isle's perimeter. But Kestrel was different, less uniform.

"Too shallow along the southeastern side," she murmured, feeling the high ridge of rock and coral. "Keep her in the deep," she said. "It's rougher here."

"Aye, Captain."

"We're two hundred yards offshore," Grant said. Kit could hear the cacophonous scream of seabirds from an island she surmised was covered with them.

"Stay the course," Kit said, pushing forward until she pushed through the water, and felt the ridge just off the island's eastern shore.

"There's a reef," she said. "We'll tack south around Kestrel between Kestrel and Black, then north-northeast. And if we get close enough without losing our own keel, we'll lead them into it."

"How close?" she heard Jin call out, concern in his voice.

"We may scrape a few barnacles off the hull," she said with a smile, eyes still closed. "But if they're focused on stopping us before we get into the Narrow Sea, this is their best opportunity. They may be foolish enough to risk it. Given they're chasing an Isles ship without a declaration of war, they're foolish enough. Jin, douse the stunsails. Let them get closer."

There was no hesitation, regardless of the danger of the order. "Aye, Captain," Jin said, and the order went out. The crew understood naval tactics, but still didn't relish the idea of slowing down with a cannon-loaded ship behind them. But they trusted their captain as much as she trusted them.

The stunsails were hauled in, stowed, the *Diana* slowing.

"We're coming up on the edge of the island," Grant said.

"I can feel it," Kit confirmed, its bulk like a blank spot in the water, an absence. The deep channel between and beyond. And beyond it, shallow water and the jagged reef, diamond sharp.

"We'll be within their firing range, so stay ready, and stay careful."

Shouts of "Aye" came from the deck, and then it went silent again but for the rush of water, the creak of rigging.

"On my mark," she said again. "Three. Two. One. Mark."

The order was made, the *Diana* heeling again as she was brought sharply south-southeast around the island.

The gun brig took its shot almost instantaneously. Kit felt the concussion, the air tightening as shots exploded toward them.

"Incoming!" was shouted again, and the crew braced.

Kit opened her eyes. The first struck the hull with a *crack* that Kit could feel through her bones. Wood and men flew through air now smeared with smoke and the acrid scent of gunpowder.

The second flew through the gunwale, sending splinters flying like arrows. It bullied through rigging and then fell through the deck.

"It's tacking," Simon called out.

"Have March see to the wounded," Kit told Jin. "And get Oglejack downstairs to check the hull."

Kit wouldn't worry about that, not now. Not when the damned gun brig was still bearing down on them. Kit loved speed, but she was impatient, and she was particularly losing patience for a vessel making an unsanctioned attack on her ship—damaging her ship and hurting her people—in international damned waters.

"Kanos's balls," she muttered, and wondered if she should have thrown a dozen coins into the sea when they'd left New London.

"This is it," she called out, focusing again on her job and closing her eyes. "Grant?"

"I'm with you. I can see the chop ahead—the water's lighter."

As was the magic, Kit thought, the current was choppier again. Beyond them, to port, was the reef, just offshore. She needed to find the threshold around it, and sail just along that line. And then tempt the gun brig into crossing it.

She waited until they were close, until sweat covered her brow and coral seemed to prick at her fingers. "Three . . . two . . . one. Mark."

They bore toward port, the ship creaking like an old woman, listing in the turn.

Kit opened her eyes, looked back. The gun brig cut in just behind them, aimed at the *Diana*'s flank—its position just slightly farther north. If it wanted to fire again, it would have to sail right over the reef.

Both ships took a risk. Both ships hoped the benefit would outweigh the cost.

Kit saw the spark as the gun brig fired. "Incoming!" she screamed, but the sound of the cannons drowned her voice.

Three shots this time, whistling . . . and then there was chaos.

One ball glanced off the port bow, tore through rigging, and had the flying jib flapping. The other hit forward near the forecastle, shattering glass and punching another hole through the deck.

Kit watched in horror as the third struck the top portion of the mainmast, just above where Tamlin perched. A *snap* broke the air like lightning, and the topmast split away, taking sails and rigging—and Tamlin—with it, plunging into the sea.

"Man overboard!" someone called as the *Diana* listed to the side, pulled down by the weight of sails and rigging and wood.

"Cut it away!" someone yelled, and fear gripped Kit's heart like a fist. She took off toward the bow, but Grant, long legs pumping, was faster, looked over the gunwale.

"She's in the rigging!" he called out. "And she's holding on. Don't cut it away—haul it in!"

Kit forced herself to trust him, to join the line of sailors who heaved, arm over arm, to pull up the tangle of rope and wood.

And then Grant was reaching out, and he and Sampson pulled Tamlin over the side. Her eyes were wide, her skin even paler than usual, her red hair wet and streaming.

But she was alive.

"*Dastes*," Kit said, refusing to think how close they'd been to tragedy, and reminded herself to throw a coin later.

"Take her down to March," Kit said as Sampson scooped Tamlin in his arms. "And get the mess cut away. Keep anything worth salvaging." And because she still had a crew to lead, trusted Sampson and March just as she'd trusted Grant, and went back to the helm, looked back at the gun brig.

"Status?"

"Still moving, Captain," Jin said.

"Anytime now," Simon murmured.

They heard the grinding crunch across the water, looked back to see the gun brig lean, then come to a full stop as hull and coral came to blows. And coral won, even as the masts began to tilt, the sails still full of wind.

There were shouts of glee from the *Diana*, shouts of fury and fear from the gun brig as they ran for the masts, prepared to cut them down to keep from tearing their ship apart.

"Take that, ya bastards!" August said, shaking a fist in victory. He finally got one right.

FOURTEEN

Kit stayed on deck until the sails were no longer visible, until the topmast and rigging were cut away. And then she wiped her brow, looked down at the streak of soot on her shirt, and realized she was filthy from the explosions.

They'd been attacked—an Isles ship—during peacetime. She'd need to relay the entire tale to the queen. But since they had no way to get that message off the ship at present, there were more critical matters to see to.

"Jin, you have the helm," she said, and didn't wait for his response. She went below, wincing at the ache in her ribs as she climbed down, moved swiftly forward where the ball had struck. She needed to check her injured crew, but if the *Diana*'s wound wasn't stanched first, none of them would make it home.

She made her way forward. By the time she reached the forecastle, she was sloshing in ankle-deep water.

The ship's carpenter, a tall and thin man whose skin and hair were nearly the same ruddy shade, was nailing a barrel head atop the *Diana*'s hull. The sky shone through the splintered wood, and water dribbled through as the waves rushed by.

"How bad is it?" she asked as the others in the room came to attention.

"Captain," Mr. Oglejack said. "The patch'll keep most of the water out, but I can't keep her entirely dry. Not at sea."

"Because you'd have to pull out the entire plank."

"That's it exactly, Captain. We can fill in a bit more," he said, and gestured to sailors near the bow who were unraveling old rope into thinner cords, which they'd drive into the gaps with a mallet.

"Hold's still dry," Oglejack continued, "and there's more work to be done, including the topmast."

"Do we have a spare yard?"

"Aye, several, and we can fix that right enough, but we're tackling the structural problems first."

"A good plan, and good work. Keep at it, and let Jin or one of the lieutenants know if you need more men or supplies."

"Aye, Captain," he said, and turned back to his people. "Wells, not like that! For gods' sake, you've got to take to it like a lover. Gently, man. Gently."

Good for Mrs. Oglejack, she thought, and headed aft.

Humans still had much to learn about the workings of the body. And Kit was never more certain of that proposition than when she stepped into an onboard surgery. But the mess was empty of people now but for March, who'd begun to clean up the detritus of healing.

"How many limbs did we lose in here?" Kit asked, swallowing down instinctual horror at the blood on the floor.

March glanced back. "Captain, sorry. I didn't hear you come in." She still wore her canvas apron, and now it was smeared and streaked with soot and blood. And probably worse.

"No lost limbs," she said as she scrubbed blood from beneath her short nails. "Lieutenant Phillips was struck in the head by a good chunk of the rail; he's unconscious but resting. Ms. Teasdale took a pretty large splinter in her side. I was able to remove it, and she's resting with a poultice. Most of this is hers," she said, nose wrinkled. "Tamlin's a bit dizzy yet, and Mr. Cordova's got a fairly serious broken arm. They're all in their respective berths. The other injuries are minor." She held up a finger. "Oh, but for one human bite."

Kit just stared at her. "I'm sorry. Did you say—"

March's eyes twinkled with amusement. "Aye, Captain. A human bite."

"But we didn't engage with the enemy that closely. They didn't get near the *Diana*."

"Oh, aye," March said again with a widening grin. "But August got a bit excited running about during the chase, and he slipped on the deck. And when Ms. Fahri tried to help him up, August clamped right down on her ankle with what remains of his teeth."

Kit looked skyward. "For gods' sake."

"August told me he had worked his family's farm during the war," March said. "Missed out on what he calls 'the good fighting.' So he takes every fight a bit more seriously than he ought."

Given he would have been in his fifties during the war, Kit

wondered what work he might have done, or what "good fighting" he'd have been allowed to do. She'd never assigned him to an away team, and they'd sailed together for nearly a year. Maybe that was part of the problem. Maybe he needed a better outlet.

She shook her head to clear it. August was the least of her concerns right now.

"Let me know if anything changes," Kit said, and felt suddenly tired. The adrenaline had drained away now, leaving her empty.

She walked out and moved down the corridor. She found Grant still in the small chair in Dunwood's cabin. But instead of Dunwood's pale but smiling face, she found an empty bed.

All the breath left her. "He's gone."

"It was the fever. It happened fast."

That was something, at least. She'd seen her share of sailors who hadn't had the luck to go quickly.

"I am so sorry," she said, though those words seemed insufficient. "So very sorry."

"I'm sick of war," Grant said. "I was sick of it before. And sick of it more now." He put his head in his hands, ran his fingers through his hair, and kept them there. "I didn't want to be here, on this damned boat. I have other problems to solve, my own concerns. And I certainly didn't want to have failed him. Damnation," he said, and sat up again, rested his head against the wall behind him. "Damnation."

Kit had been a sailor long enough to hear the sound of one near the end of his figurative rope—and that it was her job, her responsibility, to pull him back. She'd also learned enough about Grant in the last few days to figure how to do that.

"Self-pity won't bring him back."

"Leave me be."

"I won't. And as this is my ship, you've no authority to order me about."

Slowly, he turned his head to look at her. "Is this the time to flaunt your rank, *Captain*?"

"If the other option is you stewing in self-blame, then yes. Grieve for your friend, rage at the men who took his life. And then prepare for what's next."

"Is it easy to be so cold?"

She looked at him. "Never," she said, her tone smooth. "But I'm the captain. I'm not allowed to stop, not allowed the luxury of dwelling on my failures, no matter how cruel they are."

Grant dropped his head back again, squeezed his eyes closed.

"We left New London within hours of learning of his capture," Kit said after a moment. "We sailed with all possible speed—and magic—to Finistère, and we got him out of that gods-forbidden fortress. He did not die in the hands of enemies in a stinking dungeon. If he was to go, I am glad he went here, in warmth and comfort, and in the company of a friend."

After a moment, Grant opened his eyes. "Do you truly believe that?"

"I do," Kit said. "But that I believe it doesn't make me feel any less miserable for having been unsuccessful in saving him."

Grant nodded, stared mournfully at the empty bed.

"We'll meet in the officers' mess to discuss our next steps," Kit said, and turned for the door to give him time to find balance again.

"Brightling."

Kit stopped, looked back.

"Thank you."

She nodded, and left him to his grief.

~⌒~

Kit checked with Cook, learned Louisa had followed her promise and stayed in the hold until he'd fetched her again. Kit found her in a chair in Tamlin's small quarters, both of them sitting cross-legged on the bed and looking at a book.

Although no sailor was expected to be on duty at all hours, Tamlin rarely left the top. Kit couldn't recall a time she'd seen Tamlin in her room to do anything but sleep. And she'd never seen anyone *in* Tamlin's quarters; companionship wasn't something Tamlin often sought out.

But Tamlin read the pages aloud—a story about pirates, it seemed—and looked absolutely enthralled in the tale.

"Ladies," Kit said, and they both looked up.

"Captain," Louisa said gravely. "I'm working on my letters and learning about a pirate queen."

"Is she?" Kit asked, glancing at Tamlin.

"Best to stay below until all business was done above," Tamlin said.

"It's always good to improve one's mind," Kit said. "I love to read, especially romances."

Louisa's nose wrinkled. "Stories with kissing are disgusting."

"Hmm," Kit said noncommittally. "I'm told you did very well during our battle."

"You're my captain now, so I have to do your orders."

"Very well done," Kit said. And now that their mission was done, and they'd be returning to New London, she thought she ought to talk to Louisa about her future.

"Louisa, I wanted to speak to you about where you'll live when we return."

She caught Tamlin's raised brows, but kept her gaze on Louisa.

"I'll live on board with you and Cook and Tamlin and Lieutenant Hobbes."

"None of us will be staying on board. When we're between missions, we go to our houses or our families. I know you told me you don't have a family, but is there someone whom we should tell that you've made it safely home?"

Louisa's expression shuttered. "I don't have anyone."

"No mother or father?"

"My mother is dead. My father ran away to hell and damnation. That's what the nun said."

"The nun?"

Louisa pressed her lips together, but that was enough information for Kit. She surmised Louisa had lived in a foundling house run by the Unified Church. She'd have been well cared for, and taught rudimentary reading and writing, but would have been subject to strict rules that Kit imagined didn't sit well with Louisa. But still . . .

"When we get back to New London, shall we take you back there?"

"No." Her answer was quick and hard. "They're mean. And I have friends outside."

Literally outside, Kit thought, where children huddled together in make-do shelters and searched the Saint James mud for bits of coin or things to sell.

"Hmm," Kit said. "What if I knew of a different place that you could stay? A place where other girls without families lived."

Louisa looked utterly suspicious. "Like where?"

"Like the Brightling house, where I live."

"Where the wee fairy lives?"

"She's not a fairy, just a bit more wee than you or I. And yes, she lives there with me and our housekeeper and my other sisters." Kit leaned forward conspiratorially. "There are lots of us."

"Would I get to go on the ship and still be a sailor?"

"We'd have to discuss that."

Louisa looked away, blinked as she appeared to diligently concentrate. "Could I maybe meet them and decide?"

"I think that could be arranged."

"All right, then."

One question answered. Now, to speak to Hetta.

"He died," Louisa said. "The man you tried to rescue."

She didn't want to have this discussion with a child, even as she suspected Louisa understood tragedy as well as any adult. But Kit thought everyone deserved honesty.

"Yes, he did," Kit said. "He was hurt when we found him, and although we brought him back and took care of him, he didn't survive. We're going to have a memorial on board, and he'll be given to the sea."

Louisa looked toward the hull. "Isn't it cold down there?"

"Deep down, it's cold. But he won't feel it, or any pain. Not anymore."

That was for the rest of them to bear.

∽

Dunwood was sewn into canvas; by Isles tradition, a small pocket had been sewn just above his heart for a golden coin to give him safe passage. Hats were held in hands, Jin said the necessary words, and when it was done, silence fell across the deck again.

Afterward, Kit made her way to the officers' mess, sat down at the table. Jin joined her, took a seat in silence. Cook came in, gave them both a dour look, and put cups and a teapot on the table. With a curl of his lip, he turned on his heel and stalked away.

Kit looked down at the pot, sniffed the air cautiously. The steam that wafted from it smelled of roadside weeds and shoe leather. "He's angry we lost the tea."

"He's angry we lost the tea," Jin agreed. But they both needed the boost, so by unspoken agreement, he poured "tea" into the cups.

Grant came in. Seeing him again in his pirate gear, arm bandaged, reminded Kit that she was still dressed as one. She hadn't had time to clean up or change.

He sat down heavily.

"Tea?" Jin asked, sipping from his own cup, and barely hiding his wince.

Grant sniffed the air. "Is that tea?"

"It's been referred to as tea," Kit said.

He paused, then shook his head. "I prefer a more identifiable beverage, thank you."

"I'm sorry for your loss," Jin said, and Grant nodded.

"Thank you."

"You didn't expect to fight again," Jin said, and Grant looked at him, surprise obvious in his face.

"No," he said. "I didn't."

Jin nodded, sipped, grimaced. "Every soldier and sailor has a limit. And I imagine how quickly we reach it depends on the things we've seen, the things we've done. The things lost while we were away."

"That's very wise," Grant said, and looked at Kit. "And not the first wise thing I've heard today."

Kit took that as Grant's version of an apology, and thought there was something lighter in his voice.

"I've heard there's a hole in the hull," he said. "Can we make it back to New London?"

"Yes," Kit said, sipping her brown water. "If the weather cooperates, and the sea cooperates, and the patch holds, and the condition of the injured doesn't deteriorate."

"And if the gun brig doesn't get free and find us," Jin said.

"And that," Kit agreed.

Grant cleared his throat. "I think I may be able to assist."

Kit looked up at him. "Assist?"

"Rather than sailing straight to New London, we can make for my home, Grant Hall. Queenscliffe is a small village, but there's a harbor, and there was some shipbuilding activity during the war. The shipwrights could repair the *Diana*, or at least enough to make the trip home, and I could arrange for a physick for the injured crew members."

Kit considered it. They weren't too injured, too broken, to sail safely back to New London. She didn't have permission to delay her return. But if the pirates gave chase—or if the Five sent another squadron—they wouldn't have a chance.

"There's an inn?"

"There is," Grant said.

Kit nodded. "The sailors, those who aren't injured, can sleep on board, or at the inn if they've money to spare. And we'll need a horse to send a message to New London. To the queen."

"I'm sure we can find a horse."

If the horse, she thought, didn't find them first.

FIFTEEN

The *Diana* moved slowly, her gait off balance, the sea pressing hard at her hull. But they eventually made it to the high cliffs that marked the Saxon Isles' southern shore.

On the deck, in a cool breeze and pale sky, Kit and Jin made plans. They decided Jin would stay with the ship and oversee the repairs. Kit would accompany the most severely wounded to Grant Hall. Louisa would stay on board until they reached New London, assuming Hetta agreed to the idea of meeting her.

The water soothed as they slipped into the bay, then sailed across it to Queenscliffe. The small village of pale stone and mortar buildings perched above a narrow harbor lined with more stone. The wind faced them now, so they threw a line to a man on the docks and winched their way toward them.

"Make anchor," she ordered when they'd reached their destination, and then dropped onto the dock with Grant.

A man, short and bowlegged, came toward them. He wore sturdy trousers, a vest over a linen shirt, and a cap with a low bill.

His skin was suntanned and windburned, his hair a frizzle of gray that poked in tufts beneath the cap, which he tipped as he approached them.

"Mr. Bailey," Grant said.

"M'lord." He and Grant exchanged small bows.

"This is Captain Kit Brightling of the Crown Command," Grant said.

"Jefferson Bailey at your service, Captain." He shifted his gaze back to the *Diana* and winced at the damage. "Looks like you've run into a spot of trouble."

"We did, and we're on an urgent mission for the Crown. We need as much repair as can be done, and quickly."

"Of course. M'lord," he said again to Grant, then walked to the edge of the dock, scratched his stubble as he looked over the ship.

"I'm going to send a message to the house," Grant said to her, "make the arrangements for the wounded. I'll meet you back here when I'm done."

Things were so easily arranged, Kit thought, when one had money and position.

She nodded, watched him stride up the stone steps that led from dock to street and smile at the townspeople who'd gathered, curious at the commotion. Then she walked to where Mr. Bailey crouched, gaze narrowed at the hull, her own footsteps ringing across stone.

"Took some shot, did you?" he asked.

"We did," Kit said. "Fourteen-pounders."

Surprise widened the man's eyes. "Are we at war again?"

"We aren't supposed to be," Kit said dourly.

"Aye," he said. "And you can't go bumping through the waves with a hole as big as that. Lucky she's above the waterline. Any damage beneath?"

"Not that's caused an unusual leak."

"We'll see," he said, his tone growing absent as he reached out, stroked a hand across the hull. "She's a good ship. Tide goes down, we'll see more of what ails her."

"How long do you think the repairs will take?" She braced herself, thinking he'd say several weeks, and fearing she'd have to leave Jin and the *Diana* here and travel back to New London by land.

"How solid do you want it?"

"Solid enough to return to New London with all hands against a fighting sea."

"Two days? Maybe three?"

That would have to be good enough. Kit nodded. "And the Crown will see you fairly compensated for your work."

His nod was absent now, as he was peering again at the hull. Time, Kit thought, to leave him to get started.

~ᴑ

A wagon arrived for the wounded, and a horse for the lieutenant who'd send Kit's message to the queen. The carriage that came for Kit and Grant seemed timeworn, the black paint chipped, the gilt gone dull. Not what she'd have expected of a viscount's transport, although the horses seemed sturdy enough. Which was the only compliment she was willing to give a horse.

"I'll be back in the morning," Kit assured Jin. "Although I don't like to leave the ship."

"Captain's prerogative and punishment," he said with a grin. "You get to sleep in a softer bed. But you have to be mannerly in the meantime."

Kit's lip curled. "I know."

"And you'll sleep better if you know your people are being cared for. We probably won't sail back to New London without you. Probably."

"Insubordination is also unattractive in a commander."

"Again, agree to disagree," Jin said, and squeezed her shoulder. "Beware the lady's maid. She might add fripperies to your coat or ribbons to your hair."

Kit shuddered, and resigned herself to discomfort.

Kit had seen thousands of miles of the Isles, but mostly from the deck of the *Diana*. She knew shorelines and harbors and fjords. She didn't know much about the countries beyond their ports, but she was fairly certain Grant Hall would be considered magnificent even by a seasoned overland traveler.

It was two long stories of stone in shades of ivory and umber, a matching row of narrow windows with white mullions on each story, and a portico with four pairs of columns in front. The roof of dark gray slate rose to a gentle pitch, where more white windows and nearly a dozen chimneys made their home.

"Front of the house was intended to be formal, impressive, imposing," Grant said.

"I'd say it's all three. It's lovely."

"Thank you," Grant said, his tone softening. "It's home."

Kit sensed Grant meant to give the word its most complex meaning. Not just the seat of his family, the place of his birth, but the place where joys and tragedies and all the things in between had occurred, had soaked into the ground.

The carriage pulled to a stop, and Grant jumped out, offered Kit a hand, which she declined. "I'm fine, thank you."

They walked toward the portico, and Kit could see the flaws that had been invisible at a distance. The stone on the right side of the house was darker than the rest, as if in need of cleaning, and some of the glass in the windows was broken. She didn't know much about green things or growing them, but the bit of a garden she could see from the walk appeared to need shaping.

"There's work yet to be done," Grant said, and climbed the steps to double doors of paned glass, flanked by windows as tall as the doors, which, Kit guessed, could be opened to let in the breeze. "My father passed during the war, and the estate . . . suffered."

Much more there, Kit thought, but wasn't surprised that he didn't elaborate.

Grant opened the door, walked into the foyer. Kit followed him inside . . . and goggled. If her house was comfortable, Grant Hall was palatial. Cherry panels covered the floor, walls, and coffered ceiling of the foyer. The facing wall bore a long cabinet with carved doors topped with candles and crystal, presided over by four portraits of men with long wigs and dark robes above. Light poured in from the windows along the front wall, so the wood seemed to glow from within.

The sides of the room bore three tall archways. Beyond the archways were atriums with tapestry-covered chairs and crystal and gilt clocks, and winding wooden staircases with carved balusters, the treads covered in thick carpets. More portraits hung on the pillars between the archways; ancestors with white collars and concerned frowns, hands on important books or the arms of velvet-covered chairs.

Her first country manor, she thought with a smile, and an impressive start for that particular list. She'd expected to see fine things in the home of a viscount, but she'd also expected hard formality. A cold and sterile chill in the air.

The house smelled of resin and leather and lemon, and the faint scent of Grant's cologne. There was a sense of history and warmth, and Kit wondered if this was why Grant had been eager to return—and so angry about having had to leave in the first place.

"Welcome to Grant Hall," he said, moving to stand in the middle of the room and gazing up at the portraits, their subjects seeming to watch him from their lofty heights.

"Thank you for the invitation."

There were clicks on the wooden floor, and a white blur raced toward them.

Grant whistled. A small white dog, square and compact, sat and gazed at Grant a few feet away, tail wiggling in apparent delight. For a moment, there was only the dog's joyous anticipation. Then Grant whistled, and the dog leaped into his open arms and began to make a feast of his face.

"This is Sprout," Grant said, but was so obviously relieved to see the little dog that she wasn't sure he'd have heard any answer she bothered to give.

Something had relaxed in his face, a tension relieved. She watched with amusement as he scratched the dog behind its ears until its back leg shook with joy. There was something sweet, if strange, about watching a dangerous man giving love and attention to a very small dog.

A man and woman, probably in their forties, appeared in the doorway. Both had pale skin; both wore servants' dress. The man was of average height and on the thin side, his hair dark and thick. The woman was shorter, blond hair up beneath a lace cap, her curves tucked into a gray dress with a gauzy fichu.

Grant tucked the dog under his arm. Its tongue lolled happily, clearly content to be in the arms of its master again.

"My lord," the man said, looking equally as pleased to see Grant at home again, if with much less wiggling.

"Mr. Spivey. Mrs. Spivey," Grant said. "This is Captain Kit Brightling of the *Diana*."

They exchanged polite nods.

"You received my message?" Grant asked.

"We did, sir. The physick is on his way, and we've gathered some materials. We've just now put them in the schoolroom, and moved in the spare beds. We thought Captain Brightling might enjoy the viscountess's rooms, given they're empty."

"That's fine," Grant said, then glanced at Kit. "There's room and light and . . . facilities in the schoolroom. And I'm sure you'll be comfortable in the suite."

Kit doubted that very much. "A cot in the schoolroom with the others would be more than sufficient."

Mrs. Spivey looked appalled. "Well, that won't do. You're a captain. You should have a nice place to sleep."

Nice, Kit thought, was relative. "There's no need to go to any trouble."

"Well, it's no trouble to use a room that already exists, is it?"

Mrs. Spivey's tone made it very clear she neither expected nor desired a response—or any further argument from Kit. So she nodded, accepting the loss.

"Was it a very fierce battle?" Mr. Spivey's dark eyes gleamed. A little bloodthirsty, Kit thought, which loosed some of the tension in her shoulders. She understood bloodthirsty.

"Very fierce," Kit said. "Although, with Lord Grant's assistance, we were victorious."

"Well, of course," Mrs. Spivey said, and smiled beatifically at Grant. "He's a very brave one, is our colonel."

"Very brave," Kit said. "And he has a bandage that needs replacing."

Mrs. Spivey's eyes went wide with concern. "Bandage? You've been injured, sir?"

"A scratch," he said, giving Kit a flat look. He hadn't wanted them to know he'd been hurt. He either didn't want them to worry, or didn't want to deal with the hassle.

"Later," Grant said. "I'll keep until then." He looked around the foyer. "Where's Lucien?"

Mrs. Spivey looked at Mr. Spivey, who appeared markedly uncomfortable. "He's . . . not in residence, sir," Mr. Spivey said. "He said he had urgent business in New London." Mr. Spivey's tone was cautious, and he shifted his gaze meaningfully at Kit, as if uncertain how frank he could be.

Grant went utterly still, a predator poised on the edge of violence. "He promised me—" Grant cut himself off, turned away, and stalked across the room, anger obvious in the hard set of his shoulders.

"Lucien?" Kit asked quietly.

Grant jolted at the question, as if he'd forgotten she was still in the room. "My brother," he said. And that was all he said.

The younger brother, Kit surmised. The one Hetta had called a wastrel. "I see."

"Mrs. Spivey will show you to your room. I have some business to attend to."

"Of course," she said. And he moved into the corridor. It was obvious he wanted to be alone, to deal with whatever it meant that his brother was in New London. But there was one thing that had to be said.

Kit followed him, had to move briskly to keep up with his long strides, found him heading toward a closed door, dog still tucked beneath his arm.

"Grant."

"Brightling," he said, and sounded defeated. "I've neither the interest nor the inclination to discuss the Crown Command at present."

"Thank you," was all she said. And she was amused by the suspicion in his eyes.

His brows winged up. "For what?"

"For this. For the wagon and the horse and the care for my men. It's obvious you've other concerns, but you offered your home to them, a solution for the ship. So on behalf of the Crown Command, thank you."

For a long, quiet moment, he simply looked at her, and she couldn't begin to name the emotions behind his eyes.

"You're welcome," he said finally, then walked into the room and closed the door behind him.

Mrs. Spivey led Kit up one of the staircases to the house's second story, and then to a wide paneled door of pale blue.

"The suite hasn't been used since the viscountess passed," Mrs. Spivey said, pulling out a chatelaine of keys and bobbles, and sliding one into the wide paneled door.

"That would be Colonel Grant's mother?"

"It would," Mrs. Spivey said, then opened the door and stood aside so Kit would walk in. "A well-loved woman, was she."

And a woman with lovely taste, Kit thought, walking into the room.

The sitting room was chalky blue, with a fireplace of blue stone flecked with bits of silver. The paintings in this room were landscapes—windblown cliffs and sunsets—silk and velvet settees and chairs with embroidered cushions. A wall of windows fronted by deep, padded seats threw light across the room. The sitting room led to the bedroom. The same blue paint and fireplace, more beautiful landscapes, and the largest bed Kit had ever seen, a silk canopy rising over it.

"You should find everything you need," Mrs. Spivey said. "But if don't, you'll likely find us in the back of the house. The kitchen stays warmer than the rest," she said with a smile, "and we don't have the staff—not these days—to keep upstairs maids at the ready. But we do what we can. I've not spoken to my lord about it, but he doesn't usually dine formally at supper. But there will be a sideboard with plates, should you be hungry."

Kit didn't have much appetite, and wanted a good night's sleep more than anything. But she nodded politely. "I'm sure that will be lovely. Thank you very much."

When she was alone, Kit looked back at the rooms. At the pretty luxury. The viscountess, whomever she might prove to be, would have a glorious set of rooms when settled into Grant Hall. Whom would Grant want? Undoubtedly someone beautiful—he was too handsome, and probably too particular, to settle for anything less. Someone titled, probably with funds, given the repairs that still needed to be made. Someone mannerly and eager to settle into routine.

She walked to the bed, traced fingertips along the silk counterpane, then walked to the window, did the same with the silk and velvet curtains. Rain had begun to fall, spilling raindrops across the glass. Through it, she could see the grounds that stretched beyond—lawn and trees and gardens. And not another house or human in sight.

This would be a very lonely life, she thought. To be a woman alone in these rooms in the cavernous house, which in turn sat alone in the park and far from the village. There would probably be books and embroidery, and the interruptions of tea and luncheon. Perhaps a ball or party now and again during the season. To Kit, it seemed a very small life. A very confined one, despite the sheer amount of space. She couldn't imagine giving up the sea, the freedom, the camaraderie, the discovery, and exchanging it for this . . . empty beauty, she decided.

But that was neither here nor there. She was a guest, only here for a bit while the *Diana* was being repaired. And for the first time, it occurred to her that she'd return to New London without Grant. Their mission was complete, and just as she promised Grant his first day on board, their involvement was at an end. Much to her surprise, she wasn't entirely pleased to realize that. No point in dwelling on it. (Principle of Self-Sufficiency No. 4:

Learn from the past; don't dwell on it.) So she let the curtain fall again, adjusted her coat, and went for the door.

～⌒⌒

She walked down the corridor, followed the noise of chatting to a room on the right. It was a bright and open room, even on a rainy day, with wood floors and high windows along one side. Chairs and small desks and settees had been pushed against the walls, and four small beds had been placed in a row in the center of the room to make a kind of infirmary.

Phillips, Cordova, and Teasdale were on the beds. Cordova sat up, cradling his arm in its make-do sling, and the others reclined. All were still in uniform.

A barrel-chested man with neatly trimmed white hair and beard, wearing a dark coat and trousers, was directing two women in apron-covered dresses about bandages and cleaning wounds. She walked inside, but the physick straightened his shoulders and stared at her with small, bright blue eyes.

"No," he said, in a tone that promised he was accustomed to being immediately obeyed.

"Excuse me?" But she stopped.

The man walked toward her, waving her back. "No. We are caring for individuals in precarious health. There will be no interruptions, no visits, until we ensure they are comfortable."

"I'm their captain," Kit said, in her most captainly tone.

"We aren't on a boat."

Kit couldn't fault that logic. "When can I see them?"

"At a time which is not now," he said, and shut the door in her face.

Grant had arranged for her trunk to be taken to the house, and she allowed herself the luxury she couldn't afford on board—she changed into her nightdress. Beat to quarters might be called in the wee hours of the morning, and she needed to make a swift appearance on deck. Which meant she'd either have to waste time changing into her uniform, or appear on deck in a filmy linen nightdress and wrapper. Which would almost certainly have violated several Crown Command protocols—if the Crown Command had considered the possibility of captains mustered in their wrappers. Even *Cox's Seamanship*, which devoted an entire chapter to the boiling of mutton, had nothing to offer. So Kit avoided the problem and slept uncomfortably.

But tonight, there was soft muslin and freedom of movement. And an upsettingly large bed in a voluminous room in a sprawling country manor.

She lay on her back, sheet drawn to her chin, and stared at the ceiling. It was too damned quiet, and it was too damned still. There was always noise on the ship. People or waves or wind or canvas being reefed or unfurled. The din of the watch bells. The shuffle of the watch being changed.

Even Moreham Park had its noises. Merchants coming or going, street sweepers about their work. Rustling trees, barking crows, whining cats. And in her house, a sister staying up entirely too late or waking entirely too early, or Hetta rushing to the palace, or Mrs. Eaves stoking fires or preparing breakfast.

Here, there was only silence. There were several people in the house—Grant, the Spiveys, surely a few more staff—but she

couldn't hear any of them, or anything else other than the occa-
sional sigh of the house settling around her.

Maybe it was different for Grant, who'd been raised in this
kind of quiet, in this kind of space. And likely would be different
for the woman he ultimately chose.

She tossed for an hour, then rose and went to the window,
could see nothing but stars in the darkness that stretched outside.
Thinking a walk might do her good, she pulled on her wrapper
and slippers, and made her way downstairs. The house was dark
but for a glow from a room in the far corner.

She walked toward it, peeked inside, and found Grant, jacket
abandoned, stretched in a leather chair. Sprout, the little dog,
was curled beside him. Grant's study, she guessed.

Grant looked up suddenly, eyes wide. "Captain."

"So sorry," Kit said. "I couldn't sleep, and I saw the light . . ."
She turned, hardly in a state of dress appropriate for chatting
with a bachelor viscount, but heard footsteps behind her.

"Wait," he said, and she sighed, turned back.

He glanced at her ensemble, raised an eyebrow.

"I couldn't sleep," she said again. "I hadn't planned on company."

"And yet," Grant said, moving back into the room. "You're
welcome to join me. The fire and whiskey are very agreeable. But
I'll understand if you prefer a chaperone and"—he glanced back
at her nightwear—"alternate clothing."

She was angry that pink colored her cheeks, and glad that it
was dark enough that he couldn't see her face. She was a ship's
captain, for gods' sake, and didn't need a damned chaperone.
She'd done her time in a forecastle berth where there was little
time or space for modesty. She was clothed, wasn't she? Perhaps

not for tea with company, but for warming oneself in front of the fire? Perfectly acceptable.

"I'd appreciate a drink," she said, chin lifted.

"Very well," Grant said with a knowing smile, and gestured toward a chair. "Have a seat."

She walked inside. His study was dark cornered, with leather chairs and sparking fire, a table for gaming, a desk for business, and books lining the walls. Not entirely unlike Hetta's office, she thought.

"Grant Hall is beautiful, and this room is no exception."

"Largely beautiful," Grant said. "Partially decrepit." He moved to a table that bore a collection of crystal glasses and decanters.

Kit moved to the facing leather chair in front of the stone fireplace, fire roaring, and sank in. A moment later, Grant brought her a small glass of amber liquid.

"Thank you." Kit accepted the glass and sipped—and was welcomed by warmth and smoke and smoothness. "Well. That's rather impressive."

"It's a family favorite," Grant said darkly.

"You've been working on the house?" Kit asked.

He nodded. "My father had debts—became, I think, careless after our mother died. The house wasn't maintained the way it ought to have been. I've been trying to put the estate back in order, but that work is obviously not complete. I've learned any number of new skills along the way. Creditor juggling, masonry repair, the cost of curtains."

"You were fighting when your father passed?"

"With Sutherland," Grant said with a nod. "My brother managed the estate while I was gone. Or was intended to do so."

"That would be Lucien."

Grant took a sip. "That would be Lucien. He was nineteen when I left. By the time I made it home again, the house was in further disrepair, the notes from creditors still piling up."

He finished the rest of his whiskey, put the glass on a side table. "He drinks and he gambles, both without success. There are times when his particular demons do not haunt him, and he is a smart and charming fellow then. But the demons seem to inevitably find him again, and lure him back in. Now they've lured him to New London, and I imagine there will be more creditors to contact, more debts to negotiate, more repairs to delay."

"I'm sorry," Kit said.

"As am I."

"You said your mother died?" Kit asked.

"A few years before my father," Grant said. "She loved growing things. The gardens outside were her design, and primarily her work. It wasn't fashionable—not for her to work in dirt or dirty her hands. But she didn't care."

"She sounds like a very formidable woman."

"She was. I miss her dearly."

The words echoed in the space. Even here, the ceilings rose nearly twenty feet high.

"Was it lonely to grow up here?" Kit asked. "The house is so large, and I didn't see another for several miles."

"We weren't lonely as children," Grant said. "We ran a bit wild across the estate, made a fortress of the orchard, harassed our tutors. But then my mother died, and Gerard took power. I wanted to fight; Lucien didn't. My father was opposed to it—my being the first son and all—so I went to my uncle to fund the commission.

My father and I were angry at each other when I left, and I was on the peninsula when he died. The house feels lonelier now."

"I'm sure he'd appreciate the work you've put in to set it to rights."

Grant's expression was hard, his brow furrowed as if he wrangled with memory. "I very much doubt that, Brightling."

Rain began to fall, knocking hard against the window. Kit thought of her gothic romances, which were usually tales of an emotionally haunted man in a spiritually haunted abode. Grant Hall and its master might qualify.

"A few giant wolfhounds might help liven the hall," Kit suggested with a smile. "They're quite common in stories of lonely cliffside estates."

"Are they?" he asked, obviously amused, and looked down at the dog nestled in his lap. "Sprout doesn't have a wolfhound's build, but he does have the confidence of a much larger dog." He looked up, watched her for a moment. "Do you know much about your family—before Hetta, I mean?"

She hadn't discussed her family with Grant, but if her surname hadn't been clue enough, he'd probably have looked into her background before they sailed. Probably interviewed Chandler about her, just as she'd done with Hetta.

"I have no memories of my parents," Kit said, finishing her own glass and placing it beside Grant's. "Not my mother's face, or my father's laugh. I don't know if she liked to garden. On the other hand, while I'd not say it's better to be a foundling, being one does avoid some of the familial complications."

"Surely you and your sisters have disagreements."

"Well," she said with a smile. "There are seven of us."

"Seven," Grant said with a chuckle. "So many women in one home. The rows must be terrible."

Her flat look had him holding up a hand. "Apologies, Brightling. I couldn't resist."

The quiet fell again. The fire crackled, as the wind swirled outside, and Kit realized this might be one of the last conversations she'd have with Rian Grant now that their mission was done. And she found that disappointing, as she'd rather gotten used to their sharp repartee.

"I suppose you'll be returning to New London to find your brother? I mean, I've the sense you weren't entirely confident he'd return in a timely manner."

Grant grunted. "That was diplomatically said. And yes. I likely will, if he's not returned before you sail."

"You're welcome to return with us. Although you may prefer a faster method."

"I've not yet decided which I would prefer."

Something in his tone had her looking back at him. She found his gaze on her, intense and warm. "It's a fairly easy decision," she said, gazing back. "To sail or not to sail. I will always choose to sail."

"Always? You've no wish for anything beyond a ship and a star?"

She smiled at the reference to *Cox's Seamanship*, and gave Grant silent accolades for it. "I wish for many things. Pistachio nougats, safety for my family, Gerard's eternal incarceration. If you mean my future, I've no desire to give up my captaincy or my ship. And I've yet to meet a married woman allowed to keep them."

"You've such a negative view of marriage?"

"I've a negative view of the requirements that women play at being helpless to attract a wealthy man, and exchange meaningful activity to become accessories, like a soft rug or a charming vase, once married. Is that what you want, Grant? A viscountess of fine breeding and connections who can support your life of gentlemanly contentment?"

He looked at her for so long she had to force herself to keep from breaking his inscrutable gaze. "I find my desires are somewhat more . . . variable."

"But then," Kit said, "you're a viscount. You're allowed to be variable." She looked back at the fire, let her mind drift back to the present. "Do you really think Gerard is building warships?"

It took a moment for Grant to answer. "I have no reason to doubt Dunwood or the information he obtained—or the arrogance of Gerard or the Guild. I suspect you'd know more about shipbuilding than me," he said wryly, "but I'm aware it requires space, workers, materials."

"Wood," Kit said. "Hemp. Pitch. Iron. All in large supply."

"The more people," Grant said, "the more opportunities for gossip, for word to spread. Which is likely how the information came to Dunwood in the first place." He sighed, ran a hand through his hair. "And if Gerard's handed a new navy, what can be far behind?"

"War," Kit answered grimly. "More needless death. More needless destruction." And with that grim thought, she rose. "I should go back to my room. Try to sleep."

"All right," Grant said, rising. "Do you know the way?"

"I'm sure I can find it. Good night," she said with a nod. "Thank you for the drink, and the conversation."

"Kit."

It was the first time he'd said her name, and there was something in the tone—a kind of grim understanding—that had her turning back. "Yes?"

"Whatever comes. Be careful."

She nodded, retreated into darkness from more talk of war.

In her room, she took the coverlet from the bed, trailed it into the sitting room, and climbed onto the window bench. She pulled the curtain closed around her, and in her small fabric cocoon, tried not to think of the future.

SIXTEEN

She woke at dawn to find the rain gone, the sun just above the
horizon, the sky smudged purple and orange.

She washed her face and dressed in her spare uniform, then
searched out the schoolroom again, only erred once while tra-
versing the labyrinthine wing. The door was open, as were the
windows, and a fresh breeze blew inside.

She checked on her sailors, found them all awake and sipping
on tea. She began to walk into the room, but the physick glared
back at her before moving from Teasdale's bed to Cordova's.
Teasdale offered her a wave; Kit waved back.

"He's a good physick."

Kit nearly jumped at the voice, turned to find Mrs. Spivey
behind her.

"His manner's a bit cold," she continued, "but he's delivered a
dozen children and cured twice as many fevers."

"As long as he helps them, he can have whatever manner he
likes," Kit said.

"Good morning."

They glanced back, found Grant in the corridor. He'd gotten a shave, and his jaw was scraped clean again, square beneath his dark brows and turquoise eyes. He wore deerskin breeks with his dark boots today, and a greatcoat in the same honeyed color.

"Grant," she said.

"Captain," Grant said. "How are the patients?"

"Improving, it appears. Although the physick has not deigned to speak with me, nor am I allowed to enter the room."

Grant nodded. "I thought you'd want to drive to Queenscliffe to check on the ship. I've a curricle harnessed."

She felt immediately calmer at the thought of returning to the ship, the water, if only temporarily. Less so at the thought of climbing into a death trap to get there.

"That's kind. But if you have estate concerns that you need to manage, I'd be happy to walk."

He raised his brows. "It's four miles."

"I enjoy a good walk," she said. On her own damned feet.

"At present, the *Diana* is my estate concern. And I can collect some items Mrs. Spivey needs from the village, which will save her the trip."

"In that case, I suppose I have no other option."

And gods help them both.

⁓

She'd thought of curricles—in the rare instances she'd been forced to consider them—as dares. It was as if their designer had decided two horses simply weren't dangerous enough on their own, so added a rickety bench balanced on narrow wheels at their back.

If Grant noticed her white-knuckle grip on the seat, he managed not to mention it.

They reached the village, and villagers emerged from buildings as the curricle passed, then watched from the dock as Kit made her way to the *Diana*. The hole in her side was bigger now, and Kit couldn't hide the wince, even though she understood the reason. They'd need clean edges for a clean patch, not the irregular tear made by the cannon.

You can't get through the thick, Kit thought, hearing Hetta's voice recite Principle of Self-Sufficiency No. 9, without going through it. This, at least for the *Diana*, was the thick.

Grant stopped to chat with villagers, and Kit continued through them, could feel their curious stares, could just see their approving nods at the periphery of her vision. Then she put it away, climbed the rope ladder with the swiftness of a salty hand, and chuckled at the mild applause.

"Captain on deck!" someone shouted, and the sailors above came to attention.

"At ease," she said, and looked around at the work underway.

Mr. Oglejack had indeed found a spare yard, and had set sailors to work planing it down to replace the lost topmast. Damaged decking was being pulled up, the pitted gunwale being sanded.

Jin was chatting with Simon. He looked up, caught her eye, and came her way.

"Captain," Jin said. "Been a while since we've had a fancy lady on board."

"Hilarious as always," she said dryly, and was relieved to return to the company of those she knew and understood. "How's the crew?"

"Very well, m'lady," Jin said, and made a little bow.

"I will write you up for insubordination."

"Perhaps you could request a servant prepare the documents for you?"

"Hilarity," she said. "Report."

"A few crew members had too much tipple last night, but the town's full of sailors who outdid ours in drink, so that's something." He gestured toward the high street of shops. "The bakery reportedly makes a very good meat pie. I hear there's still a bit of coin to be spent. As long as that's the case, they'll be very welcome here."

"We need the repairs finished by the time it runs out," Kit mused.

"As you can see," Jin said, "the villagers are skilled and efficient. They found more hull damage beneath the waterline, but nothing as big as the hole."

"The hold?"

"Still dry, or at least no wetter than usual. The hand pumps are ready, just in case, but we haven't had to use them yet. How are the patients?"

"They've a very skilled physick. And while I would never admit this in his presence—or Grant's—he's rather bossy."

Jin just looked at her.

"Insubordination," she called out, and headed for the stairs.

❧

Kit found a hive of activity in the forecastle. At present, Mr. Oglejack and Mr. Bailey were involved in a heated discussion over how tight to make the wooden plug they'd prepared.

"It will swell when it hits the water!" Oglejack said. "If it's too snug now, it'll pop right out again."

"And if it's not tight enough," Bailey said, "it'll pop out before you leave the damned harbor."

When the sailors realized Kit had entered the room, the din quieted for a moment, then picked up again at twice the volume as each man tried to sway Kit to his side.

Kit stared at them blandly until they stopped shouting.

"Thank you," she said in the ensuing silence, and looked at Mr. Oglejack. "While I think you'd be absolutely right if the hole was beneath the waterline, it may not swell enough above to keep the plug seated. So seal it now but"—she said, holding up a hand as she saw a fresh barrage being loaded—"in the event Mr. Bailey and I are both wrong, we should have an extra plug that we can plane down and use if the first one does, as you said, pop."

Neither man looked especially pleased by the result, which Kit figured was a pretty good sign she'd done the right thing.

She checked the hold herself, then went back to the deck to watch the work, when someone called her name.

"Captain."

Kit refocused, found Mr. Oglejack on the deck a few feet in front of her with one of the village carpenters, a piece of decking, and a wooden box of tools. And there was plain discomfort on Mr. Oglejack's face.

"Yes?" she asked.

"You'll beg my pardon, but the, well, the pacing is making it a bit hard for us to accurately plane the decking."

She looked around, realized she was the only person standing in this part of the ship, and didn't remember having walked here. She'd been pacing, something she did only when working things over. A marauding water buffalo, Astrid had once called her.

"Pardon," Mr. Oglejack said sheepishly, cheeks blushing.

"No, it's my fault," Kit said with a smile she forced into place. "I was thinking, and hadn't realized I'd stepped into your workspace. My apologies, gentlemen." She went back to the helm, crossed her arms, and felt her foul mood returning.

"Irritating your own men?"

Kit refused to look at Grant. "I'm observing their progress."

"I'm aware," Grant said. "But your very fine carpenter is right; they won't get as much done with you hovering over them like a governess."

"I don't hover," she said crisply. "I lead. I *manage*."

"You're slowing their work."

This time, she bared her teeth at him. "And what else am I supposed to do? Learn to cook pasties? Perhaps a bit of embroidery while Mrs. Spivey brings me tea and biscuits."

Grant's expression stayed mild. "If she's biscuits, have her send some up for me, as well. And I'm fairly certain you can't tell a needle from thread."

"I've mended a shirt now and again," she said, sounding defensive even to her ear.

"Impressive," Grant said, a corner of his mouth lifting. "If you've no antimacassars to tat, perhaps you could take a walk around the village, or the grounds of Grant Hall. There's a lovely view of the sea from the hills behind the garden at Grant Hall. I've some business here, but you can wait for me. Or you can pace back on your own."

She growled, even as she knew hovering wasn't going to help. And besides, women in the penny romances were always going for walks on the moors or by the ocean or across a hedged ground. An enemy was nearly always lying in wait to ambush them, but they usually enjoyed walks up to that point. She could try a meander. Maybe it would help her burn away some of the excess energy.

"Fine," she said.

"Captain."

She looked back at Grant.

"If you reach the sea, you've gone too far."

She took the same road back, marveled at how much she could hear when the noise wasn't damped by speed or hidden by the clomp of horses and the squeak of wood and leather. The sky was overcast, and birds tittered nervously, as if expecting the sky to break open. Insects whirred and buzzed in the air, and frogs she couldn't see made sounds like drums farther away.

It took just over an hour to reach Grant Hall, and seen from the ground it might have been a public park. The lawn seemed to stretch in all directions without end. There was an enormous pond stocked with darting orange and black fish, hedge gardens that needed trimming, with green walls twice as tall as she was. A labyrinth of herbs. Fields of wildflowers. And acres of closely cropped grass that led toward the sea and the echoing waves.

On a hillock of some of that grass, she passed a wooden building shaped like wheat sheaf, wider at the bottom than the top, but easily thrice as large. A barn stood nearby. A wooden door was closed, the side path leading to it well-worn and flattened, but she could hear what sounded like grinding from inside, and there were several large round stones propped against the building. A gristmill of some kind, she guessed.

She kept walking, and the ground became rougher as she neared the sea, cratered rocks interspersed with moss as green as peridot, tiny white flowers adding softness to the craggy land-scape. And then the stone fell away, and blue stretched into infin-ity. It churned white along the rocks below her, deepened in color to the horizon. The little peninsula leaning forward into the wa-ter so blue was the only thing she could see below.

She closed her eyes against the wind, let it break against her, and listened for the song of the sea. The sea was a hundred feet below, its song just as distant. But even from above she could hear the faint melody, turbulent as water battled back rock and stone. It was a war—not just between landscapes—but between magic. The fluidity of water, the urge to move, to go faster, to slick through currents. The solidity of stone, standing tall against change, against capriciousness. And between, in the foaming wa-ter and water-smoothed rock, was the battle line.

She felt the ground rumble, for a moment wondered if she'd managed to touch the magic without even being in the sea. And then she looked back.

Grant galloped toward her on an imposing black horse, fast enough that his hair blew back in the wind, his coat flying out be-hind him like a cape.

"Hello," he said when he reached her, his turquoise eyes glinting.

"Hello," she said, and looked warily at the beast who'd borne him. It was big but lean, its coat was so deeply black it seemed to shine blue in the sunlight, and its mane had been carefully braided.

"Would you like to ride?"

Her *no* was perhaps a bit too quick.

"You run headlong into a battle with pirates, but a horse dis-turbs you?"

"They have bigger teeth."

Grant blinked. "I suppose that's inarguable." Before she could move away, he hitched a leg over the horse, hopped off, and shifted the reins over the horse's head. "Come then, Captain. I'll walk back with you, and stand between you and this vicious creature." His coat lifted in the breeze, and he looked as much the commander inspecting the battlefield as gentleman preparing to negotiate a grassy heath.

Kit looked at the horse from behind her human barrier. "What's its name?"

"Her name is Cordelia."

Kit also didn't understand giving horses human names. It was just unnatural. But she wasn't going to say that aloud, and admitted to herself that Cordelia was a handsome horse, as horses went.

"Hmm," Kit said noncommittally. But if she praised it, it might move closer. So she tried her best to ignore it. "There's a building not far from here, shaped like a cone. What is it? I thought perhaps a mill, but it's nowhere near water."

"It's a gristmill," Grant confirmed. "But it uses magic, not water."

She stopped short, looked at him. "It's siphoning magic? That's incredibly dangerous. And illegal."

He gave her an exceedingly bland look.

"I don't siphon magic," she reminded him, and held up her palms. "I only touch it."

"The gristmill doesn't siphon, either. As you'll recall, I understand the dangers of magic as well as you do."

The image of Grant on his knees, shock and concern in his gaze, flashed in her memory.

"Right," she said. "How does it work?"

"It doesn't—not yet. But it will. We're in the gods' palm, you see."

That was one of the old stories—that the magic had been unequally spread across the world as the gods battled for supremacy. When Kanos, the god of water, finally bested Arid, the god of stone, Kanos had fallen to his hands and knees in the sea, grabbed at the earth near the shore, imbuing sea and shore with magic.

"The soil in this area is thin," Grant said, "the bedrock beneath it abundant in magic. The magic here has a vibration."

Her brows lifted. "Really?"

"So I'm told," Grant said. "Is there no vibration in the sea?"

"There's an energy," Kit said. "But it flows, just as a current of water, and the speed and strength vary. How are you using the vibration?"

"We've built a cellar," Grant continued. "A wide well that goes down to the bedrock. A stone from the surface is placed on top. The vibrational difference between the two moves the top stone against the bottom and, we hope, will grind grain between them."

Kit considered that for a bit. "That's rather ingenious, isn't it?"

"It will be if we can get it to work correctly. We're still trying to find the right stone."

That explained the bevy of them outside the building, Kit thought. "I've never heard of anything like this before."

"That's because it's the first time it's been attempted. There's a water mill on the neighboring estate, but the river's course changed, and the mill's virtually useless now. If this effort is successful, it would mean a great deal to the village."

"I suppose even a viscount can have a good idea occasionally."

"Be careful you aren't too generous with the compliments," Grant said dryly. "Your crew may think you're going soft."

                          ⁓

They reached the house, coming around the back this time, and Grant offered the horse to a stableman who ran out from a nearby building. They made their way inside, found Mr. and Mrs. Spivey in the foyer, staring through the front windows.

Mr. Spivey turned back. "My lord, there's a carriage coming up the drive."

"Oh?" Brows arched, Grant moved to the windows, looked outside.

A carriage pulled in front of the house—glossy gray with crimson accents, driven by a pair of bay horses.

The driver hopped down, opened the doors, and a man emerged, tall and thin as a rail, with pale skin, curly brown hair, and a cheerful smile. He wore all black, though his waistcoat was patterned with small dots and his cravat held a fluffier knot beneath his long face.

"Well, that's very timely," Grant said, and moved to the door. "It's the Howards. Mr. Howard is the inventor of the gristmill."

Curious, Kit followed Grant outside.

"Grant!" said Mr. Howard when Grant reached him. He pumped Grant's arm. "Good to see you again. So glad you've returned safely."

"Matthew. Good to see you as well."

Matthew turned back to the carriage, offered a hand to the woman who emerged. She took it in a gloved hand and stepped down. She was as petite as he was tall. Light brown skin with a cap of short, black hair peeking from beneath her bonnet.

"Tasha," Grant said, and bowed over the gloved hand she offered him. "You look radiant, as always."

"And you're charming as always, my lord."

Then the pair of them turned their eyes to Kit.

"Matthew and Tasha Howard, this is Captain Brightling of the Queen's Own."

"A pleasure," Matthew said, offering her a bow. "It appears the repairs on your ship are coming along."

"She appears to be in very good hands," Kit agreed. "And it's lovely to meet you."

"Your *Diana* is a beautiful ship," Tasha said.

"The queen's *Diana*," Kit said. "Mine only for the borrowing."

Tasha smiled. "Spoken like a true sailor."

"And Tasha would know," Grant said. "You may know Tasha's father. John Lawrence."

Kit blinked back surprise. "*Admiral* John Lawrence?"

"He is," Tasha said with a smile. "So I know how to judge a good bit of clinking and a neat bowline."

Kit smiled.

"Let's go inside," Grant said, and extended his hand toward the door.

They moved into a parlor Kit hadn't yet seen, with buttercup-yellow walls and wide windows facing the back garden. By the time they took their seats, Mrs. Spivey was wheeling in a tea tray.

"You're a marvel, Mrs. Spivey," Tasha said, taking a cup and saucer and a thin golden biscuit. "Thank you so much."

Unable to decline fresh tea with milk, Kit took a cup, added an extra splash for good measure.

"My father always said he couldn't get enough tea with milk when he returned from a mission."

"It becomes a luxury one grows to appreciate," Kit said, and sampled one of Mrs. Spivey's golden biscuits, found it crisp and sweet and a perfect foil to the hot tea.

"What brings you by?" Grant asked, when everyone had been served.

"The gristmill," Matthew said. "The granite wasn't successful. It doesn't turn so much as shiver atop the bedrock."

Kit considered that. "Where was the top stone from?"

"The cliffs near the village," Matthew said. "Why do you ask?"

"Kit is Aligned to the sea," Grant said, and she nodded.

"The flavor of magic can be quite different from one geographic area to another, even from county to county," Kit explained. "If you use a stone from another part of the Isles, that difference may produce a stronger effect."

"Well," Matthew said, putting his teacup on the table. "I hadn't known there might be such a nuance. There's a boy Aligned in the village, but he's new to the, well, practice, I suppose you'd call it. If we can get it to work—and I'm feeling quite energized now—we could build mills all over the Isles."

"I understand you're just getting started," Kit said, "so there've been no ill effects from the mill. But more of them, all operating together, could have a more profound impact on the current. It could be dangerous."

"We've yet to get one to work," Matthew said. "So we're a long way from a mill in every county. But I take your concerns to heart." His expression sobered. "I wasn't in the war, but I've friends who were, and of course Tasha's father knew much misery. I don't take magic lightly."

Kit nodded, knew there was little else to say about it now, but still unable to shake that lingering unease.

"So, Kit," Tasha said, turning toward her, teacup balanced carefully on her lap. "How do you entertain yourself when you aren't at sea? Or perhaps on board the ship, as there must be slow times between fights and battles. Do you draw, or perhaps play music?"

"Neither, I'm afraid. My sisters have the talents there. I tried embroidery once, but put the needle through my sister's finger, and that was the end of that. I do enjoy reading," Kit added. "Especially penny dreadfuls and romances."

"Oh, I *love* a good dreadful," Tasha said with a grin. "Murder and drama and perfidy. They're absolutely delicious. Everyone deserves a bit of adventure now and again."

"Hear, hear," Grant said.

Tasha looked at Grant. "And what do you like to read? I've seen your beautiful library; you've plenty to choose from."

"I'm not a great reader," he said. "When I do, it's usually to do with the finances of the estate."

"That sounds like dull stuff," Matthew said.

"There are more interesting tasks," Grant agreed. "If I'm lucky, Mrs. Spivey lets me count the rutabagas." That got a chuckle from the Howards. "And lest Captain Brightling give herself insufficient credit, she may not be much with embroidery, but she captains a ship very creditably."

"A compliment from Rian Grant," Kit said, sipping her tea. "That must have exhausted your entire reserves."

"Oh, surely you're being too hard on Lord Grant," Tasha said. "He always has a lovely word."

"Captain Brightling and I are acquainted by our professional connection," Grant said, watching Kit over the rim of his glass. "There is a certain required formality."

Mrs. Spivey came to the doorway, then moved to Grant, whispered something in his ear that had him smiling. "A lovely suggestion," he said, and looked at the others. "Mrs. Spivey has inquired if you might stay for dinner?"

Tasha looked hopefully at Matthew, but he shook his head. "Thank you for the offer, but we should get back. There's work to be done before the day's out—and I'd like to pen a message to some friends in New London about stone." He looked at Kit, smiled genially. "I think you might have something there. And I thank you for it."

Kit nodded, and hoped she hadn't just set in motion a wave that couldn't be stopped.

～～～

Friendly goodbyes were exchanged, and Grant waved away the carriage as it scritched down the rock drive.

"They seem like lovely people," Kit said.

"They are," Grant agreed. "Given her father's position, Tasha could have every convenience in New London, but she decided to stay near the village where she grew up. They have a house not far from town." He looked at Kit, brow furrowed as he studied her face. "You needn't worry. He wouldn't harm anyone intentionally."

"The soldiers at Contra Costa didn't mean to harm their own," she pointed out. "That mattered little to the thousands they killed, which is why manipulating magic was banned."

"And you know as well as I that the tide will turn again,"

Grant said. "Such things are inevitable, particularly if some enterprising soul figures how a bit of gold could be made."

"You think the mechanization of magic is inevitable," Kit said.

Grant considered that. "I think humans look for every advantage they can find." And before she could argue, he took her hand, looked at the dark dots across her palm. "Every advantage," he said, lifting his gaze to hers.

"I don't manipulate," she said, and pulled her hand away.

"You don't," he agreed. "But neither will you be the last to use it for your benefit—even if the benefit is the safety of others."

Kit didn't like it, but knew he was right. Which was precisely why she needed to get out of Queenscliffe, to return to New London. She needed to talk to the queen and Chandler about the warships possibly commissioned for Gerard, how they might use magic, and what the Isles could do about it.

"There's business I should see to," she said. "Logs and correspondence to write. I should go take care of that."

She gave him a nod, but didn't wait for his response. And as she strode to the majestic staircase, rubbed her fingers against her tingling palm.

SEVENTEEN

Another day passed, with more logs and messages and unsuccessful visits to the sickroom. Teasdale and Phillips healed enough to return to the ship. Cordova's arm became worrisome, so they sent him back to New London, accompanied by the physick, for care by the Crown's own medical staff. Hetta sent a message about Louisa, indicating she'd be pleased to meet the girl upon her return to New London and requesting they stay safe in the meantime.

Kit had paced her way through Grant Hall, walked every corridor in each wing three or four times over, waiting for the *Diana*'s completion. She'd even considered going back to New London with them, but couldn't—and wouldn't—leave her crew to fend for themselves when the *Diana* was repaired, especially if the gun brig was waiting for them offshore.

And she didn't think the physick would let her in the carriage.

On the morning of her third day in Queenscliffe, the message arrived from the village. The repairs were complete, and it was time for the *Diana* to sail.

Her relief was as physical as it was emotional, a weight lifted from her shoulders. She could return to New London, to her family, put Dunwood's death behind her, and prepare for what came next. She was ready for her next mission.

Still.

There'd been memorable moments in Grant Hall, with the whiskey and the cliffs and the little dog, the conversations she'd shared with Grant. She could admit he'd surprised her; he wasn't the type of titled gentleman she was used to meeting. That wasn't to say that she liked him, or that she needed more adventures with the Beau Monde. But she'd almost become accustomed to his being a member of her crew, and she could admit to a bit of sadness that she was leaving this place and what she'd found here. It had been, she thought, a kind of interlude. A lifestyle she hadn't experienced before in the bustle of New London. And one she wasn't likely to soon forget.

She traversed the foyer, found Grant in his study, standing before a lectern with a ledger propped upon it. He scanned the contents, Sprout cradled in the crook of one arm like a baby, utterly content now that its master was home.

Grant didn't look back. "Over here, if you would, Mrs. Spivey."

"I'm not Mrs. Spivey, but if you're having tea, I'd love some."

He showed no measure of surprise, cool as he was. But smiled at Kit as Sprout eyed her narrowly. "Brightling."

"Grant. I've come to let you know the *Diana* is ready. I'll be leaving to the village as soon as the carriage is ready."

"Horses?" he asked, setting the dog on a chair. It turned once, returned promptly to sleep.

"Trunk," Kit explained. "I've no interest in dragging it four miles back to town."

Grant nodded, frowned, seemed to be adjusting his thoughts. "To be honest, I thought the repairs would take a bit longer." He looked up at her. "I suppose this would be goodbye."

Something about that tightened her belly, and Kit refused to think overmuch about it. That was Principle of Self-Sufficiency No. 3: Plan for the future, but live in the present.

"It is," she said, and stepped forward, hand extended, all courtesy and proper etiquette. "Thank you again for everything you've done."

Grant watched her for a moment, then offered his hand. "You're quite welcome." They shook, and all but jumped apart when Mr. Spivey stepped into the doorway, paper in hand.

"Er, pardon me, sir, ma'am," Mr. Spivey said, looking between them. "There's a message for the captain. A sailor brought it; he's waiting outside. He says his name is Sampson."

"Yes, thank you," Grant said, and stepped back, put space between them.

Kit took the paper. It was heavy and thick and sealed with maroon wax stamped with the outline of a sea dragon. Probably her new orders from the queen, and more excellent timing.

"Thank you, Mr. Spivey," Kit said. "Please ask him to wait."

She slipped a fingertip beneath the wax, walked to the window as she opened the folded pages, scanned them.

The queen first acknowledged the intelligence they'd gotten from Dunwood, expressed her regret over his death, and offered her condolences to Grant.

"The Guild denies any aggression against the *Diana*," Kit read. "They say the gun brig was not an authorized vessel of the

Guild or its constituent merchants or countries. That's nonsense, but not unexpected given the care they took to make it unidentifiable.

"They also decoded the dispatch from Gerard," she continued, then lifted her gaze, looked at Grant. "The one we delivered just before you came into the throne room."

Grant nodded, crossed his arms, brow furrowed as he listened.

"They've not provided the details but for one reference that didn't make sense, even with decoding. It discussed a university on Forstadt." Forstadt was an island just off the Frisian coast.

"There is no university on Forstadt," Grant said, "or much of anything else. The island is held by the Frisian throne in trust so kings can hunt there in peace. Other than a lodge, there's nothing but trees and game animals."

"So we are led to believe," she said. "But there'd hardly be a point in coding the discussion of an island if it's not being used for some secret and nefarious purpose." She thought of the conversation she'd had with Grant her first night in the manor house, about Gerard and war and ships . . . and shipbuilding.

"You said Forstadt had trees," Kit said. "It's close to Frisia, but separate from it. Secluded. Gerard knows of its existence, and found it important enough to discuss—coded—in a dispatch to a foreign ally."

She watched understanding dawn in Grant's eyes. "Shipyard?"

"Possibly," Kit agreed. "Entirely speculation—but the queen appears to be of a similar mind." She held up the message. "We're to sail to Norgate, where we'll be met by a trio of frigates." Norgate was a village on the tip of the peninsula that jutted into the

Narrow Sea below New London. "Once we've rendezvoused, we're to sail to Forstadt, with the *Diana* using whatever magic will aid us to arriving swiftly, and investigate activity on the island."

Grant went very still. "Did you say 'we'?"

She inclined her head. "You're to sail with us."

"With you," he said, and held out his hand for the papers. She wouldn't normally have handed over an assignment from the queen, but given he was part of the mission, there seemed little point in hiding it from him.

She offered it, and he read in silence in front of the window, his fingers clenched around the letter so tightly she thought he might simply rip it up. "I can't leave again. Every time I leave, something falls apart. My home, my family."

Kit stayed quiet, as she could think of nothing comforting to say.

"I'll tell her now," he said, half to himself. "I'll pen a response, tell her events are too important here, and I cannot go."

"And she'd have you at the palace to answer for your refusal," Kit said. "Which won't help your estate."

Grant cursed, tossed the letter onto a side table, strode to the fireplace. He rested an elbow on the mantel, ran fingers through his hair, put the other hand at his waist. "We aren't supposed to be at war, and I'm not supposed to be a soldier. Men aren't supposed to die in my arms. Not any longer."

She'd seen death before Dunwood, as had he. And she knew how wrenching it was. How each death seemed to rip away a bit of the soul. But there was a reason that price was paid. Duty, obligation. And she'd learned enough about Grant in the last few days to understand those qualities were as important to him as they were to her.

"If we succeed in this mission," she said quietly, "we may stop a war. We'll save lives."

"A direct strike," Grant said quietly. "Right across the heart. You have excellent aim, Captain."

"And as much as it pains me to say it, you make a relatively credible soldier."

He shifted his gaze to her, brows lifted. "That pained you?"

"I don't care to compliment members of the Beau Monde," she muttered.

"I'm aware." Grant closed his eyes, rubbed his temples. "How long to Forstadt?"

She considered. "From Norgate, give or take two days. About as far as Finistère, and again depending on the wind and weather. I expect we'd go back to New London, so if your brother hasn't returned in your absence, you could look for him there."

"Damned convenient, that," Grant muttered, then sighed. "Mrs. Spivey," he called out, and given she darted right into the room, Kit guessed she'd been listening outside the door.

"My lord?"

"I'll be accompanying Captain Brightling to the *Diana*. It appears the queen has more use of me yet."

Her smile fell away. "Oh, again, my lord? We were going to make a treacle tart this evening. One of your favorites."

That managed to pull a smile from him. "As I doubt the queen would care overmuch for the excuse of my staying to eat it, you'll have to enjoy it on my behalf. I presume Captain Brightling would like to leave as soon as possible."

"Please," Kit said.

"I'll need my trunk again, and I've some messages that will need to be sent."

"Of course, my lord," she said, and they heard quick footsteps as she rushed down the hallway.

"She's going to hold this against me," Kit said. "Your leaving again."

"Probably," Grant agreed. "You can make it up to her by sailing quickly."

Fortunately for Grant, that was always Kit's goal.

⁓

Kit quickly penned a message for Jin, advising him what she could of their next mission, and gave it to Sampson so the crew could be readied for what came next. When the trunks were packed and loaded, Kit and Grant bounced in the carriage for the return to Queenscliffe.

"You jump every time the carriage does."

"The sea is smoother," Kit said.

"Hardly," Grant said, long legs spread across the carriage, and offered a wry smile. "It's not because you've a fear of horses?"

"I don't fear them." *She absolutely feared them.* "I know my place, and theirs. And my place is where they are not."

"Mm-hmm," Grant said noncommittally, then glanced out the window. "Do you know why it's called Queenscliffe?"

"I can surmise the reason for the 'cliff' bit," Kit said.

"I've heard sarcasm isn't an attractive quality in a single young woman."

Kit snorted, both at the sentiment and because she'd said nearly the same thing to Jin. "That would be incorrect. It's a very attractive quality, as it enlivens long walks and lonely days at sea."

Grant rolled his eyes.

"Queenscliffe?" she prompted.

"Queen Morgaine, before she became queen, toured this place."

"I know her story," Kit said. "There aren't many queens who led warships."

He smiled. "No, I imagine not. Morgaine disembarked at the village, where she was to tour the surrounding towns and meet her subjects. But the weather changed, so she and her ladies were forced to take shelter at a castle on the cliff. It's gone now," he added. "Has been for nearly a century, after storms battered the cliffs, dropped the stone right into the sea. But it stood while Morgaine visited. It was a cold, lonely place, with the wind whipping through the hallways.

"One day, Morgaine was hungry, so she walked through the castle to the kitchens below, looking for an apple. And nearly screamed when she ran into a young man with dark hair and green eyes and a strong and honorable way about him."

Kit snorted.

"'Hello,' said Morgaine. 'Hello,' said the young man. And the storm roared for six more days, and they spent that time together and grew to love each other. Morgaine dreaded the clearing of the weather, for she would be forced to leave the young man and continue her travels as queen. One morning, the sky dawned clear, and Morgaine, lovesick and sad, went to find her beau and wish him goodbye. But she found he'd already traveled on, knowing he had to let her go. They say we have mists and fog now because she cried copious tears for her beloved."

Kit lifted a brow. "Queen Morgaine married a Gallic duke and had four children."

"So she did," Grant said with a grin. "*Afterward*. And she was a good and steady queen. But they say her heart lies still at Queenscliffe, and she never forgot the boy she met here, whom she loved till the end of her life."

None of that had appeared in Kit's history books. She narrowed her gaze. "Is any of that actually true?"

"It's true to the tale my governess told me. Although I recall she was trying to encourage me to eat porridge at the time. Horrid stuff."

"For once," Kit said, "we agree."

They reached the village proper, children playing in front of stone cottages, and linens flapped in the breeze, probably refusing to dry in the damp mist. They reached the street above the dock, and Kit was relieved to see the *Diana* below, albeit with a new stripe of honey-colored wood where the ball had struck her side.

Kit boarded to the waves of the villagers while Grant conducted a bit of estate business in preparation of his leaving. On the deck, Kit found energy and anticipation. Her sailors had enjoyed a few nights ashore, and were ready now to return to wind and water.

"Captain," Jin said.

"Commander." She nodded at Simon, checked the mast, and found Tamlin's hair streaming in the wind. "I take it she's comfortable with the new topmast."

"She is."

"The patch looks well."

"Mr. Oglejack is confident she'll hold to Forstadt. He's less confident about the return. But we've extra lumber and ample pitch, should we need them."

That would have to do. "Were we able to resupply?"

"Yes, although Cook was not enthused about the meat selection, so prepare for a week of mutton."

Cook would, at least, spice the mutton, so they'd manage.

"Other than that," Jin said, "we're ready. Oh, and the receipts for the repair have been delivered to your quarters and await your review and signature."

"How dare you," Kit said, but without enthusiasm.

Grant came over the gunwale like an old salt, on his arm a basket of something that smelled incredibly tempting.

"So that's how it is, aye?"

Kit looked back at Jin, found amusement in his eyes. "That's how what is?"

"The very friendly look you gave the colonel there."

"I gave no one a look." And even if she had, it was perfectly reasonable to appreciate the fine cut of a tailcoat.

"Mm-hmm," Jin said noncommittally, and glanced at the basket when Grant joined them. "What have you got there?"

"Meat pies," he said, and pulled back the gingham cloth, revealing crescent-shaped rounds of golden pastry, steam rising from a small hole in the top shaped like a bird.

"Those are lovely," Kit said. "And very kind of them."

"They are, and they are," Grant agreed. "And I know from experience they taste as good as they look."

"I can take those to Cook."

They looked down, found Louisa standing in front of them, arms outstretched and little eyes narrowed with purpose. Kit had considered—again—sending her back to New London by carriage, but since the *Diana* was ultimately bound for New London and Louisa had followed instructions during their last round, she decided to give the girl another opportunity.

"Thank you," Grant said, and offered her the basket.

"Those aren't to go into Cook's personal supply," Kit said, and Louisa batted innocent eyes.

"I don't know what you mean." And before it could be explained, she'd disappeared into the companionway.

"Are we going to regret giving those to her?" Grant asked.

"Probably," Kit said. "Now that we're all here, let's get to sea."

She walked to the gunwale, looked out at the water. The harbor seemed smaller now than it had been when they'd arrived with the wind at their back, and they had no such luck today. And it was far too narrow for her to risk touching the current; she could get the boat moving, but she didn't have enough control over where it ended up to risk it here.

"We'll have to winch our way out." Winching was so anticlimactic, and not the heroes' exit she'd prefer to give to the villagers who watched avidly, waiting for canvas to fill with wind. But not even Tamlin had that power, so it would be a slow crawl out of the harbor.

Kit and Grant joined the work at the capstan as lines were thrown to one cleat at a time, the ship winched to that spot, and then the line was thrown again. It was hard and slow and painstaking work. But while less glamorous than leaving the village under full, crisp sail, it was a necessity.

They were able to make sail when they reached the bay, the jibs set to the cheering of the villagers as the *Diana* and her crew streamed toward open water.

⌇

They briefed the crew on this second mission, found significantly less enthusiasm about sailing to a tree-laden Frisian island than a treasure-laden pirate fortress. Although she'd walked away from Finistère with none of that loot, she understood the sentiment.

Kit found the sea as calm as she'd left it several days ago, and was soothed by the connection, which was a balm to conflicting emotions she'd rather not consider. The course was charted, the receipts reviewed—the villagers valued their work very highly, she found—and the sails unfurled for the voyage to Norgate. Maps were hardly necessary given that the crew were intimately familiar with the Isles' coastline, but Simon reviewed them for form. They were forced to tack against a hard wind that refused to turn in their favor, which slowed their progress, even when Kit steered them toward favorable currents. The wasted hours added frustration, as Kit had wanted to arrive before the trio of ships. It set a certain tone, she thought, to be in position and waiting for the others.

While the sailing wasn't easy, it was no more eventful than usual. They watched a school of dolphins in the surf, more than a few jackgulls, and the faraway spouts of whales savvy enough not to go near a naval ship.

Not eventful . . . except for the crawling unease that Kit began to feel the farther east they sailed. The sky was white as if the color had been leached away. And beneath them, chaos.

She stood near the helm, hair blowing across her face in the hard wind, trying to pick out the magic's song. But there were intervals—pauses—when it felt as if the current had stuttered. Not unlike she'd felt on the way to Finistère. And the sensation was so strange, so unusual, that she wondered if she was the only one feeling it.

She opened her eyes, found Grant's and Simon's gazes upon her. "I'm going aloft," she decided.

"Aloft?" Simon asked, head cocked.

"I want to talk to Tamlin, and I want to talk to her in her . . . territory," she said for lack of a better word. She glanced at Grant. "Would you like to go?"

"No. I'm fine on the ground," he said. "Or what stands in for it."

Kit nodded, began to make her way across the boat, rising and dipping in the water, toward the foremast. Sailors jumped out of her way as she moved, and watched—she thought with pride—as she began to climb the shroud that angled toward the mast, and then swung over to the mast itself. The sea's motion was more pronounced aloft, the mast swaying back and forth as the ship rolled, and she had to close her eyes only once to keep her bearings. Then it was hand over hand until she reached the plank just below the topmast that served as the fighting top. Tamlin sat facing the bow, one leg curled around a rope for stability.

Kit narrowed her gaze. "Are you eating a meat pie?"

"Yes," Tamlin said, and took another bite. "You want?" she asked, holding out the remainder.

"No," Kit said. "Why did you get one? They were supposed to go to Cook."

"Ah," Tamlin said with a wag of her finger. "That's your problem there. Never let Cook get his hands on the good stuff. He's stingy."

"Louisa gave it to you," Kit realized.

Tamlin grinned, mouth full, and swallowed hard. "We're friends."

"I'm glad of it. And I'm coming up," Kit said, and Tamlin slid to the edge of the plank. Kit slid in beside her, and grabbed a line with white knuckles as the top rolled a good thirty degrees. But the view—so much sky, so much water—was well worth it.

"Sometimes hard to remember why we do this," Tamlin said quietly. "I never forget when I'm up here."

"No, I bet not." Kit glanced at her, looked her over. "Your head?"

"Fine as ever," Tamlin said, then ate the last of the meat pie, dusted her hands. "Yours?"

"Fine," Kit said with a smile, and hoped that was accurate. "The wind. Is it off?"

"Can you feel it?" Tamlin's voice held both surprise and relief.

"Not in the wind. But in the sea, yes."

"There's a strain in the magic."

"That's it exactly," Kit said, and understood well that mix of surprise and relief. And worry. "The current stutters, as if it's . . ."

"Broken," Tamlin finished. "Aye."

"Have you felt this before?"

Tamlin looked at her. "Not since we left the Isles for Finistère."

Kit nodded at the confirmation. So it was geographic. Some phenomenon that existed nearer the Isles' southeastern coast than the southwestern. "I've not felt it before that," she said. "And how many times have we sailed the Narrow Sea?"

"Many, and aye, never before. Are we going to investigate it?"

"Not now," Kit said. "Not while we've a mission to complete." Unless their mission had some relation to it, but Kit couldn't see how. Forstadt was hundreds of miles away, and the current between wasn't a straight line, but a network of them, a lace of magic woven into the water itself.

"We'll be meeting the squadron soon," Tamlin said. "Other captains are usually much less fun."

Kit opened her mouth, closed it again. "I'm not sure if that's a compliment to my demeanor or an insult to my leadership."

Tamlin lifted a brow, closed her eyes in the sparkling sunlight. "It's an insult to them, that's for sure."

"In that case, thank you." She made ready to climb down the mast again, glanced at Tamlin. "If anything changes, let me know."

Tamlin opened her eyes, and her gaze on Kit was direct. Tamlin saw the world, Kit knew, in a unique way. But she took her position very seriously. "Aye, Captain. I will." Then she looked back toward the sea, eyes closed again. "Perhaps it's a small thing, and this is the end of it."

But it was only the beginning.

EIGHTEEN

S ails ho!" was called just after dawn when they rounded the
peninsula to Norgate. Kit made what minimal ablutions she
could—splashed water on her face, brushed her hair, downed the
tea that Louisa brought to her door—and buttoned her uniform
jacket.

Grant was already on deck, nodded at her as she joined him
at the gunwale.

Three frigates, long and low and triple-masted, sailed swiftly
toward them. The frigates were admittedly impressive ships—
rugged and loaded with guns—all three painted dark blue with
glinting golden accents and carved golden figureheads.

"The *Divine*, the *Lucida*, the *Delphine*," Kit said. Not just
frigates, but three of the biggest and strongest in the Isles' fleet.
The queen was very concerned about what they might find on
Forstadt.

"Make for the *Lucida*," Kit said, referring to the ship in the
middle. And then felt for the magic again, and didn't care for
what she'd found—even more chaos than the day before. More

stuttering, as if the magic thrashed against a captor. And either the magic or her frustration on behalf of it made her head ache.

"The current is worse," she said quietly, hoping not to alarm the crew any more than necessary. "I'll need to tell the captains."

"What can be done about it?" Grant asked.

"Nothing I'm aware of," Kit said. "But it is . . . unnerving."

Simon at the helm, they made the final journey to the rendezvous, and sails were doused as the *Diana* coasted toward the *Lucida*.

"Come aboard," called out a lieutenant in a tricorn hat, beckoning her onto the ship, which loomed a good ten feet over the *Diana*'s rail.

"Hmm," Jin said quietly, while Kit considered the request.

Grant looked between them, puzzlement in his face. "What's wrong?"

"The queen authorized the *Diana* to lead the way with magic, so the other captains should visit us, not the reverse. It is unusual," Jin added. "And disrespectful."

"Do you need backup?" Grant asked.

"I believe I'm safe from three commissioned captains," she said, but her tone was hard. "If things change, I'll give a signal. Otherwise, hold her steady."

Coordinating her movement with the rocking of the sea, Kit bounded across four feet of water and over the gunwale to the *Lucida*'s weather deck—to the cheers and whistles of her crew.

She was led by the lieutenant across the weather deck to the ship's plush stateroom, which held a table with ten cushioned chairs and a sofa beside. Both messes on the *Diana*, she reckoned, would have fit in this single room.

The ships' three captains—Preston, Smith, and Thornberry—awaited her at the table, along with a steward perched behind it, quill and notebook at the ready. The captains were dressed formally, gold gleaming, blue wool brushed, hair arranged just so. Two men: one tall, one short. Both with pale skin. Preston, shorter, with tidy gray hair. If memory served, he was the *Lucida*'s captain. Thornberry, with dark hair that swept forward nearly to his eyebrows, was the taller of the two. He had the *Divine*.

Smith, of the *Delphine*, was the only other woman in the room. She had pale skin, short steel-gray hair, and green eyes.

None of them rose from their seats when she walked in. Preston and Thornberry looked her over and, given their smug smiles, apparently found her lacking.

Kit steeled herself for condescension, and continued tamping down her anger.

"Welcome aboard the *Lucida*," Preston said. "Have a seat."

She considered staying on her feet, but decided that would make her feel as if she were reporting to the trio, so she kept her smile casual, slid out a chair, sat fluidly down, a woman in utter control.

"Thank you," she said, and glanced at them in turn. "You may not yet be aware, but the magic in the Narrow Sea has, for reasons we don't yet understand, become erratic. We realized it felt unbalanced when we left New London for Finistère. As we moved southwest, the sensation disappeared, and the current seemed normal again. But the imbalance has returned again as we've come east. The magic is uneven and breaking, which I've not experienced in my many years of Alignment."

The men exchanged a knowing look. "Now that you've

brought up magic," Preston said, "perhaps it is best we start by clearing the air."

"'Clearing the air,'" Kit repeated.

Preston nodded. "We thought it best, as professionals, to speak plainly about the involvement of magic in this mission. We're aware you are Aligned. While we understand that magic and Alignment can have a certain . . . role . . . in sailing, we have decided all strategic decisions in this particular mission will be determined based on Crown Command protocols and our experience. Not magic."

There it was, Kit thought. The gauntlet tossed. They'd "decided"—without her input and despite the fact that they wouldn't even know about the ship but for the *Diana*'s efforts.

"You've decided," Kit echoed blandly.

Preston linked his fingers together. "Correct."

"And you're aware the queen specifically ordered the *Diana* to make use of the Alignment of its crew?"

Preston sighed wearily. "Kit—"

"Captain Brightling," she corrected. "We are colleagues, and this is not a personal discussion."

His jaw worked. "Captain Brightling," he corrected stiffly. "I think we can all agree, as experienced professionals, that there is no precedent for a captain as young as yourself, much less in a glorified packet ship, to determine the fate of three frigates based on the hunch of one of its officers. That cannot have been what the queen intended."

"Glorified packet ship," she said quietly, offense obvious in her tone.

"You're young," Thornberry said, ignoring it. "And given you've obtained the rank of captain, and you're a very becoming young woman, I'm sure you have some . . . talents." But his tone—and the fact that his gaze settled on her chest—said he doubted her talents had anything to do with sailing. "Nonetheless, this is not some"—he searched for a word—"dalliance in the Narrow Sea."

Kit gave him a look of disgust. "I doubt the Frisians at San Miguel would call their encounter with me a dalliance, nor were they overly concerned with my attractiveness."

"The *Diana* isn't a frigate," Smith put in quickly, as if trying to remedy the obvious offense. "It has no guns."

Kit shifted her gaze to the woman. "Precisely. If the queen meant for us to join this mission for our arsenal, we'd have been a very poor choice indeed. Which means she intended us for other tasks. And there is no mere 'hunch.'"

Preston's mouth thinned. He was probably not used to being challenged, much less by someone he deemed completely inferior. "We sail based on intelligence and science," he said, with an air of determination. "Not magic."

Nor, apparently, the queen's express orders.

They bore the same rank as she did—all captains. But they'd sailed longer, and they sailed larger vessels. And their experience apparently hadn't brought much wisdom.

"So, to be clear," Kit said, "you believe it is strategically wise to ignore not only the queen's orders, but the obvious changes in the sea's magic?"

"We read her orders differently," Thornberry said.

"And the Aligned members of your crew," Kit said, ignoring him. "Have you asked them? Inquired if they've sensed any change?"

"There are none who are Aligned on my ship," Preston said. "I don't allow it."

More likely, Kit thought, his Aligned sailors simply refused to admit it. "Dunwood said the Guild intends its ships to utilize magic."

"There's no hard evidence magic is involved. Gerard would be happy for a navy of his own regardless."

"I doubt Dunwood would have spun the tale from air," Kit said dryly.

"Perhaps he misheard, or was misled," Preston said. "Or perhaps you did. That would hardly have been the only failure at Finistère. Not a terribly successful mission, was it?"

Preston knew where to strike, Kit thought, and she couldn't fault his aim. But she'd made what peace she could with Dunwood's death.

"Given we rescued Dunwood and preserved the intelligence he'd gathered, and this mission exists only because of that intelligence, I'd suggest Finistère was quite successful. You'll know, of course, that he incurred grievous wounds and fell ill before we arrived, and was quickly removed to the *Diana* and treated there. If there's a new cure for fever of which we aren't aware, please do share your expertise."

Thornberry opened his mouth to respond, but Preston put a hand on his arm. "We are, of course, devastated by the loss of such a fine Crown asset. But this decision has been made, and it has been made by officers who have considerably more experience than you do."

She let silence fall again, and looked at each of them in turn. They all met her gaze; Preston and Thornberry without hesitation, and Smith with at least a small morsel of apology in her eyes.

Refusing to acknowledge magic was shortsighted and foolish. And then a thought occurred, one that Kit didn't care for.

There was a traitor in the Crown Command—someone who had given up Dunwood's identity and position—to support Gerard's plans. Could Gerard have hoped for a better response from the Crown Command's officers to a mission intended to thwart those plans—giving up one of their most useful tools?

She didn't have the stomach to dwell on that possibility, so she filed it away to ferment. In the meantime, she worked to keep her voice exceedingly calm.

Kit rose. "This is a mistake. I object to this course of action, and that will be noted in my log. You may, of course, make whatever decision you deem appropriate as to your ships. You captain them, after all. But I am not part of your crew, nor am I on your ship, and I am not beholden to your authority. The queen has given me orders, and I will follow them in the manner I deem most appropriate, including by use of magic."

"Be careful, *Captain*, that you don't place your own ego over the needs of the Crown."

"*Thornberry*," Smith muttered, a warning. But Thornberry's predatory smile was unapologetic.

Kit paused, glanced back at him, her expression quizzical. "Be careful, Captains, that you do not confuse your own arrogance with concern for the queen or the Crown."

And she left them staring.

Kit held her tongue until she'd reboarded the *Diana*, and the crew stifled any questions they might have asked when they saw the look on her face.

"Make sail and follow the squadron," Kit said to Jin. "You have the helm."

"Aye, Captain," Jin said, lifting his brows at the order, but wise enough not to challenge it.

She went below to burn away the better part of her anger, given she suspected the captains would have told the *Lucida* sailors to watch her and report back about her reaction. She wasn't going to give them the satisfaction of seeing a tantrum.

She opened the door to her cabin, found Grant sitting at her table, and stared at him. "What in gods' names are you doing in my quarters?"

He looked up from his small book. "I heard you stomping on the deck and presumed you'd want to discuss our mission."

She just growled. "I do not stomp."

"Then I withdraw my comment. Your strides are purposeful and intentional. I was waiting here in anticipation of the captains' behavior being less than genteel. I surmise I was correct."

"'Less than genteel,'" Kit repeated in a mutter. "There was no discussion, no debate, no dialogue. There was dismissal. Orders were handed down." She took a seat at the table, told him what they said, what they'd done.

Grant's dark smile made her feel better. "And yet, they live?"

"Running through fellow captains is generally frowned upon."

"Yes, I can see how that might negatively affect morale. I don't know Smith," he said. "I know Preston and Thornberry, albeit as aristocrats, not sailors."

"That's enough, I imagine."

"It is." Grant frowned, crossed his arms. "They refuse to use magic, despite the intelligence that the Guild is using magic to support Gerard. And despite the queen's orders?"

"They read the orders differently, they say. And see no point in listening to the whims of females—queen or captain." She frowned. "Could it be them? Preston or Thornberry? Could they be the traitors?"

Grant's brows lifted. "You're asking if either of two highly regarded captains in the Crown Command are passing information to Gerard?"

"Ignoring the evidence of magic manipulation will benefit him."

Grant considered this in silence. "Are you aware of the Prefects?"

She frowned. "University prefects?"

"*The* Prefects," he clarified. "It was a secret society created in the drawing room of some posh New London home, I'm led to understand, by men who doubted a queen could effectively rule the Isles."

"Created when Richard died," Kit guessed, and Grant nodded.

"Charlotte was young and beautiful and smart and very, very savvy. But she did not have the same ties to the titled as her father. She didn't see much point in them," Grant added, "which led many of the titled to contend she was incapable of effectively ruling the nation."

"And yet they live?" Kit asked with a smile.

"The queen is aware of their existence, but decided to exercise her will by ignoring them and turning her attention to being a good regent. The club no longer exists formally, but many of the members share the same views—that her decisions will never be sound because she is female."

"And Preston and Thornberry were members of this society?"

He nodded.

"Little wonder they think me incapable of performing my job. Or that their intellect is superior to mine. But Smith is a woman, and she made no argument. Granted, even women in positions of authority don't always—can't always—challenge the usual state of affairs."

Grant linked his hands on the table. "What's your true concern?"

"That we'll discern something they don't. That I'll feel something in the sea, or Tamlin in the air, and they'll ignore it to the detriment of their crews—and mine."

"At least you have one thing to look forward to."

"What's that?"

His smile was wry. "When it all goes to hell, you'll have the satisfaction of knowing you were right."

"If their behavior hurts my crew," she said, "hell is what I will rain down upon their heads. That's a promise. And, Grant?"

He lifted his brows.

"If I find you in my cabin again without my permission, they won't be the only ones facing hell."

NINETEEN

Kit let the frigates take the lead; they did have the guns, after all. The *Diana* stayed within the ships' draft, watching and waiting . . . and listening while the gaps in the current became more frequent and larger, as if parts of it had somehow been chopped away.

They hadn't yet needed to run, not with Preston and the others in front. But concern she wouldn't be able to call upon that power if the need arose had her trying it . . .

. . . and faltering.

There simply wasn't enough power to push the *Diana*—not even within that thin electric core. With each mile, the magic grew weaker, and her head pounded more fiercely. And it hadn't escaped Kit's notice that each mile was drawing them closer to Forstadt.

"Forstadt has to be the source," she said, staring again at a map of the Gallic and Frisian coasts, as if some detail, some obvious cause, would suddenly snap into her attention. "But how can magic break?" Kit asked, and not for the first time. "Either it is, or it isn't."

"There are nulls, yes?"

Startled at the sound of Grant's voice, Kit looked up, found him standing beside her, his brow furrowed. "What?"

"Areas without magic. You said it wasn't evenly dispersed."

"Yes," she said, and rubbed her temples, as if that might dislodge the tension, "but this isn't a null. Nulls are common; the magic simply doesn't reach there. But this is . . . an absence. There was magic here, but it's been diminished. It has faded."

"Have you eaten today?"

"I—what?"

"You've been staring at that map for nearly an hour, and I don't think you've left the deck in several."

"I'm fine," she said, even as she realized her stomach rumbled with hunger and the ache in her head was pulsing. "I'm fine. I just . . . need answers," she said, and scrubbed at her face. "I need to understand how something far distant from our location is breaking magic—diminishing magic—here. I need to know why. Until I know, I can't prepare my crew."

"The Guild could be facing the same problems."

"The Guild might well be *making* the problem," she corrected. "Dunwood said the Guild is building a new ship intended to use magic. The dispatch identified Forstadt as an important island in the effort to put Gerard back on the throne. The magic gets fainter as we move closer to Forstadt. We put those things together, and the Guild has created a ship that breaks magic, either intentionally or inadvertently. And there's nothing I can do about it, no damned protocol I can follow that will give me any better insight."

She paced to the stern, looked out over the sea and the wake that trailed the *Diana*. "If I don't know the cause, I don't know how to protect us—to protect them. I don't care for that."

"To be out of control?" Grant asked, and the amusement in his voice irritated her further. "No, I imagine that doesn't fit you especially well. And while I'm far from being a skilled sailor, I'll remind you that you aren't a captain because you can follow protocols, but because you can make good decisions in times of crisis, even with limited information. Trust yourself, even if you can't trust the magic."

She looked back at him, gaze narrowed. "That's remarkably sensible."

"So is having tea. I understand Cook has reserved a meat pie."

That was enough to have her moving.

⁓

She ate and filled, at least, the hole in her belly. But it didn't clear away the worry. If the Guild's activities were responsible for this, what horrors might they face next? She thought of gristmills and mechanization, and wondered if the world was on the cusp of something very, very dangerous.

Two hours later, she got a taste.

The wind stopped. The sea went glassy. And without the wind to fill their canvas, four ships lay still and silent in the water.

The doldrums, sailors called it, because a sea without wind led to melancholy and fear. Sailors lived in awe of the wind and relied on its mercy; its absence spawned the fear that somehow, this time, the wind would not return, and they'd be stranded. Utterly helpless.

It wasn't the first time she'd experienced the doldrums; it was common enough. They'd been becalmed before, had faced days without wind. But this was different, as the wind wasn't the only thing affected. The magic was a bare pulse in the water.

So even as the Guild's shipwrights made progress on their weapon of war, the queen's fleet sat in the middle of the Narrow Sea.

The windless air was as oppressive as wet wool. Every hatch and porthole on the boat was open, but there wasn't breeze enough to push air through them. Uniform jackets were discarded in the first two hours, and Kit's hair was still damp from a trip into the hold, where she tried without success to feel a current strong enough to give them options.

"There is no wind," Simon said, wiping his brow with a handkerchief, "and you said there's nearly no magic. Can those be related?"

"Manipulating magic can affect the weather," Kit said. "But I don't know if that's what's happened here. There's no way for us to know until something changes, until something happens." And until then, they had to bloody wait.

She was still in pain—couldn't deny the absence of magic, or the weather was affecting her physically—in addition to being angry and irritable. She wanted to blame this on someone—preferably Preston, Thornberry, and Smith. But they hadn't taken the wind. Maybe, if they'd listened to her warning, heeded it, Kit could have steered them toward a different course. But maybe not. Maybe this was unavoidable. Maybe they'd be stuck here for a week while the Guild continued its work.

Mr. Jones tried to keep the sailors busy during the long hot day. They touched up paint that had been scraped off during the battle with the gun brig, tarred the rigging. And to keep morale from disintegrating completely, she allowed the crew breaks to swim, to cool themselves in the water.

While Kit paced, Grant kept mostly to himself, staring across the flat sea or reading in his quarters, his pent-up energy almost palpable. It was ironic, Kit thought, how much of the *Diana* was absorbed in working off excess energy, and the sea's own was lacking.

And still, there was no wind.

They waited through a sticky night, and into a dawn that blossomed brilliantly red. Terrifyingly red.

"Well," Jin said as they watched the coloring horizon. "I suppose the pendulum would swing."

"What is it?" Grant asked, and the question marked him as a soldier, not a sailor.

"Red dawn," Kit said. "It means a storm is coming."

"It will bring wind, at least?" Grant asked, looking back at Kit.

"Given the color of the sky, more than we'd want," she said, and glanced to the mast, watched as Tamlin flew down a line to land on the deck. She ran toward them, looked at Kit.

"She'll blow fierce," Tamlin said.

"How large?" Grant asked.

Kit looked back to the west, still touched by darkness and stars. "We won't know until it hits us." She looked back at Tamlin, forced herself to ask the question. "Does your head ache?"

Tamlin's eyes went wide. "Aye, a bit. Yours?"

"Aye. Weather or magic?"

Tamlin lifted a shoulder. "Who's to say? All manner of strange things afoot."

The next strange thing, a message from the frigates, came twenty minutes later.

A boat approached: Preston, Thornberry, Smith, and four sailors who pumped the oars while the captains sat, stiff-necked and prideful. She made them come to her. She waited, and she watched.

"Captain," Preston said, when they'd crossed the gunwale, distaste in the curl of his lips.

"Captains," she said. "Let's adjourn to my quarters." She turned on her heel without looking back. "Jin and Grant, with me. Simon, you have the helm."

"Aye, Captain."

She climbed down and walked into her cabin, presumed the other captains would at best find it quaint, and more likely shabby and stifling. But they were poor strategists, and they'd come to her ship, tails between their legs. So she didn't much care about their opinions.

They walked inside, Jin last, and he closed the door. The heat began to build immediately. She gestured at the table, but no one sat. Grant and Jin waited at the door, stone-faced. The captains looked miserable and angry. And a little bit afraid. Good, Kit thought. That was the first sensible emotion they'd displayed since this mission began.

Thornberry, cheeks red and beads of sweat on his face, looked mutinous. "You did this."

Kit lifted her brows. "I beg your pardon?" That wasn't what she'd expected to hear.

"You used some charm, some spell, to affect the sea. You will fix this immediately so we can be on our way." He actually pounded a fist on the table.

"You were angry, and the wind diminished," Preston said. "There's an obvious connection."

She couldn't help it. She'd intended to keep a straight face, but the possibility, the theory, was so ludicrous that she couldn't stop the rolling laughter. That they looked violently insulted by her amusement just amused her further.

"So," she began, when she managed to control herself, brushing away an errant tear and straightening the hem of her jacket. "Rather than admitting you were simply wrong, you've decided I have the ability to stop the wind using the magic you don't really believe in. And I used that ability so we can sit here, dead in the water and working through our provisions, just to irritate you?"

"You reacted poorly to our concerns," Thornberry said, a defensive snit in his voice.

"I was furious at your ignorant comments," Kit clarified. "And with ample justification. You ignored my warning."

"We made an educated decision."

"All evidence to the contrary," she said, gesturing to the becalmed sea. "You made a decision based on your own prejudices against magic, against female captains, against me. But, at present, that's beside the point. A storm is coming."

"We can see the sky very well. We're prepared for a spot of rain and thunder." Thornberry's tone was that of a parent to a naive child.

"Not a spot of rain and thunder," Kit said. "You're aware there's nearly no magic in our present position? That it became weaker as we moved from the Isles—as we've moved toward Forstadt?"

"Nonsense," Preston said.

"Its strength—and absence—is measurable and verifiable. The effect of the island? Admittedly conjecture," she said. "It may be chance, fate, that we've swung from doldrums to looming storm in a matter of hours, or they may be connected to that magic, to something that's happening at Forstadt, or in Forstadt's direction."

Smith, frowning, crossed her arms. "There is precedent for magic overuse affecting storms."

"There is," Kit agreed. "But it takes much to affect the currents to the degree we've seen, much less the weather."

"So you admit you did this," Thornberry boomed, and Smith rolled her eyes.

"Enough, William," Smith snapped. "That's enough. Captain Brightling didn't create this situation any more than you or I."

"You suspect the storm will be severe," Preston said.

"I do," Kit said. "I think its formation was not wholly natural, that there are too many connections to ignore. I think we must be prepared."

"We could turn back," Preston said. "Seek shelter."

"We aren't turning back," Thornberry said.

"And in what wind?" Smith asked. "The wind may not return until the storm is upon us."

"So we wait out the storm, or we continue to Forstadt," Preston said. "I believe—"

"You've had more than enough time to provide your opinion," Smith said, her tone cutting, and Kit wondered how much blathering the woman had been forced to endure.

"When the wind returns," Smith said to Kit, "you can select the course. We will follow."

Preston prepared to argue, but Smith held up a hand. "It is time," she said, and with some authority. "Had we been attentive to the magic in the first instance, we may not be facing this hardship."

Kit waited, looked at her. "You will follow without argument?"

"Discussion is to be expected," Thornberry mumbled.

"Not any longer," Kit said, and made her decision. "We won't have time to get ashore before the storm breaks. We've already lost valuable time while someone, it appears, is manipulating very substantial magic. If there's any hope of stopping the Guild, this ship, more chaos and ruin, we have no choice but to make for Forstadt." And gods willing, the cost of that decision wouldn't be higher than she could bear.

"But I'll warn you," she continued. "If what we believe is accurate, the path will not be easy. You should prepare your boats and your crew for the worst. And rest assured that if anyone on the *Diana* is injured because of further idiocy from these vessels, I will personally see that you never set foot on a Crown ship again. Now," she added, "get off my ship."

❧

"Do you think they believed you?" Jin asked when they returned to the deck to watch the captains ride back to their ships.

"I think Smith believes me. I suspect Preston and Thornberry are incapable of believing I'm correct about anything. Probably because I have breasts."

"Do you?" Grant asked, brows lifted in an expression of perfect innocence. "I hadn't noticed."

"Amusing," Kit said.

"Preston and Thornberry are pigs," Jin agreed.

"Pigs, at least, provide ham, which affords them some merit. I can't say the same for the captains. Ring the bell, please, Commander. We need to alert the crew."

She waited at the helm while they assembled, sailors experienced and new, from the Isles and beyond. And she hoped she could keep them all alive.

"We can all see a storm is coming," she called out, and several of them looked to the northern horizon, to the dark clouds that hovered there, grew. "The sea's magic's been disturbed. Broken, for lack of a better word. We don't know what's affected the magic, what's broken the sky. But we suspect they're connected by Forstadt."

There were whispers and grumbles across the deck.

"The storm is north of us," she continued, "and moving east. Forstadt is to our northeast, which presents a certain . . . dilemma." Some of the crew chuckled, as she'd meant them to. If the wind wouldn't break the tension, she'd have to.

"We must get to the island," she said. "We must find the ship. And if they are manipulating magic, harming the current, we must stop them. We cannot wait for the storm to pass. When the wind returns, we will sail northwest, and hope the storm will pass us by. But we'll almost certainly catch the edge, and the edge is likely to be bad enough.

"We're all frustrated and angry, but we have to stay alert, and we have to be prepared. When the weather turns, it will turn quickly, and it will turn hard."

She glanced at Cook, who'd taken time from his stove to join the crew above deck. "Did you hold back brandy taken from the *Amelie*?"

Cook's eyes narrowed to slits. "Why do you say that?"

She gave him her flattest stare. "How much?"

He chewed on the answer for five full seconds. "Four bottles."

"You keep one," she said. "The other three are for them." She looked at the crew. "A round for everyone at dinner."

"Back to work," Jin called out as sailors cheered their good luck.

She looked back at Cook. "We'll need Tamlin above. Can you keep Louisa safe below?"

There was no argument, no sarcasm. Just honesty, gravity. "I will," he said, and she nodded. When he returned below, she found Grant. "Can we speak?"

He nodded, followed her into the companionway, and then downstairs. Sailors who weren't on watch were still moving belowdecks, so she gestured him into her cabin.

"You're in pain," he said, when they were inside and the door shut behind them.

She looked back at him, brows lifted. "Pardon?"

"You're in pain. I heard your question to Tamlin, and I can see it in the set of your shoulders. The magic?"

"I don't know." And it hardly mattered. "Can you swim?"

"If need be."

"Need may be," she said. "The sea will be high, and the wind will blow. You're going to need to find a spot—preferably below—and stick to it."

He just shook his head. "All hands, you said. I'm one of the hands, and I'll stay above."

"That's more than you're obliged to do," she said.

"I believe I deserve better than that insult, Brightling. Why do you think so lightly of soldiers?"

"Because Sutherland was an ass," she said without hesitation.

And for the first time, she saw Rian Grant's full grin, and was nearly bowled over by the power of it.

"Is that amusing?" she asked.

"No. It's accurate. He's a fine soldier. And an ass."

She bit back a smile. "And why don't you trust sailors?"

"Because Worsley was an ass."

Admiral Worsley had led the Isles fleet at Barbata, the decisive naval battle in the war, and had succumbed to injuries he sustained during the fight. She'd never met him, but knew him as an excellent strategist, good commander, and philandering husband.

"But a fine sailor," Kit said.

They smiled at each other for a moment, and then the watch bells sounded, drawing them back, and her smile fell away. "Be prepared to swim," she said, and walked back to the helm.

The wind began to blow at dusk, and that shift was enough to loosen some of the ache in her head.

Lanterns were lit on the *Diana* to guide the way, and she led the squadron northwest as clouds continued to swell. Lightning jagged across the sky, and the air chilled, haze covering the stars, so they could see only the bob of lights on the frigates behind them, like seabound fireflies.

She'd already decided she'd stay on board for the duration; the crew would stand their watches as long as conditions permitted, but it was her burden and responsibility to see them through the storm. And Cook gave her the tin of biscuits. So that helped.

"It will be soon," Tamlin said when she'd dropped to the

deck, apparently scenting the biscuits on the wind. And stuffing four into her waistcoat before climbing the mast again.

Kit reached out for the magic. Faint, she thought, and fading. No longer a torrent of power, but a rivulet. No longer a song, but a whisper.

The rain began at midnight. It was, at first, a relief. Sailors of every watch stood on the deck, letting fresh water rinse salt and sweat and grime from their bodies. But then the rain fell harder, drops that struck skin with punishing intensity. And the wind followed suit, from a breeze to a gale that sent sailors onto the yards, scrambling to lower the square sails. The jibs were furled, the topsails, the staysails, until the foresail was the only canvas still standing, and that only to give them some pretense of control.

There was too much risk that a lamp might roll and break, fire escaping through the ship. So the lanterns were doused, the cooking fires extinguished on all four ships, leaving them in the blending darkness of water and sky.

The waves grew higher, the furrows deeper, so the *Diana* rose twenty feet at each crest, dropped into each trough, water slamming into the bow and flowing back in a torrent with each rise and fall. Sailors held to masts, lines, shrouds, gunwale to keep from washing into the darkness and the deep. The water was frigid, sailors soaked to the bone even beneath oiled canvas.

Simon worked the wheel, Grant beside as they pushed rudder against ocean to keep the *Diana* pointed into the waves. If a wave struck her broadside, it could push her over. She'd roll into the cold dark water, and they'd all go under. At the edge of the Northern Sea in the dark of night, the rates of survival would be low.

Kit reached out to the magic as much as she could, grasping for what whispers of the current remained to pull the boat out of the clutching, white-fingered waves.

No storm could blow forever, she told herself, over and over again, as if the repetition would give it power.

The world became visible again each time lightning flashed across the sky, illuminating clouds that seemed thick enough to hold. She watched one of the frigates ride the crest of a wave that seemed high as the palace itself and then drop down and completely disappear from view. She held her breath until she saw its masts, stark against the clouds and whitecaps once more.

The wind continued to roar, long enough that even the terror, that sickening undulation, became monotonous. It was impossible to determine their position, and she had no way to judge the storm's spread or their nearness to the island—assuming the tempest hadn't thrown them completely off course.

They made it three hours before the lines snapped and the main boom tore free. Canvas flapped, and warnings were shouted as the wooden beam—nearly sixty feet of wood—pulled down lines and rigging.

And then a shadow and a scream . . . and a *splash* heard clear against the wailing wind.

"Man overboard!" came Tamlin's voice, the words diving between raindrops toward the deck.

Kit and Jin ran to the gunwale on the starboard side, nearly hit the water themselves as wind and sea pushed the *Diana* toward port.

"It was Watson!" Hobbes screamed over the wind. "She pushed me down and out of the way, but the water hit her and she just went over!"

Kit felt worn through and hollow, but there was no other choice. She pulled off her belt and scabbard, pushed them into Hobbes's arms. Then boots and jacket, skin steaming in the frigid wind.

Then she heard Grant behind her. "What are you—" he began, but she was already up, perched on the gunwale in her stocking feet.

And then she jumped.

TWENTY

The water was frigid. Kit's muscles tightened in response, fighting back against the onslaught of cold. But in the bosom of the sea, the pain was easy to ignore.

She was surrounded by darkness, but for the faint and shifting lines of milky light at the surface. She turned in a circle, squinting into shadows, and saw nothing. Watson might have been directly in front of her, and Kit wouldn't have seen her. So she reached out for what current remained.

It was there, that bare and sickly whisper, but her reach was broader, more refined, underwater. She could feel the crackling now, tingles against her palm and beating at the back of her skull, and tried to ignore the sensations, to focus on what the current told her . . . the dark shadow of the *Diana*, bobbing above them, wrinkling the blanket of the sea's surface. And beyond it, a dozen yards away now, the smaller shadow, body still, but not yet buoyant.

Watson.

There might still be time. Hope flared, mirrored by the lightning flash above her that turned the dark water turquoise, sparkling like a precious gem.

Kit was close enough to the surface that the water was still rough, still thick with wind and friction, still frigid with cold. Each kick increased the pressure in her lungs, but she ignored it, made herself focus on Watson. If Kit didn't manage this, Watson wouldn't have a chance.

Kit reached her, eyes closed and hair floating, the need for air a tightening band around Kit's chest. Kit shook her, got no response. Kit grabbed her hand, prepared to make the upward push. And for a moment, felt the lure of the sea calling her back. It was a trick of her Alignment, she knew, made stronger by the lethargy that cold and air deprivation was bringing.

She could stay down here, was her absent thought, where the song was constant, and where she would be surrounded by magic, buoyed by it.

But she knew that was folly, that she didn't belong to the sea, no matter her connection. Her body longed for the surface, and she had to bite down on her tongue to stanch the instinctive demand that she open her mouth underwater, breathe in.

She squeezed her fingers around Watson's wrist, nails digging in to ensure she'd keep her hold, and she made her silent *Dastes*. And she reached out once more toward the power, this time looking for the quiet spot—the least turbulent water—or the updraft that would help push her to the surface, show her the way toward wind and sky. She found it, another shadow against the slightly brighter current, and used her last energy, the hand that pulled Watson clenched and shaking.

She broke the water like a sea dragon, sucking in air, managed rain and seawater with it, and pulled Watson's head above water, thumped her back.

"Watson!" Kit shouted, feet scrambling to stay above the cacophonous waves. "Breathe!" Two hard taps to the face, then one more thump on the back, and Watson was coughing.

Kit hardly had time to cry out in relief before arms pulled Watson up and away, and more arms grabbed Kit's and pulled her out of the water. Wood scraped her ribs before she landed hard in the swaying jolly boat, soaked to the bone.

Lightning streaked across the sky, illuminating Grant's face. He still held her arms, his eyes the same color as the jeweled water. The rain still fell, and he was soaked, water streaming through his hair, down his face.

Maybe it was because of the cold, or she'd been below too long. But all she could think was that he looked like a god of the sea, furious and strong and silhouetted against the swells.

"Kanos's balls," he said. "Are you insane?"

That wasn't a very godlike question, Kit thought, and coughed up seawater, pushed wet hair from her eyes, and gave herself a moment to retrieve her senses.

"I'm captain of my ship," she managed between great and glorious lungfuls of salty air. "I don't lose my sailors to the sea."

To other men, to cannon, to blades, perhaps.

But not to the sea.

※

The seas were so high, the troughs so deep, that it took half an hour to get everyone back into the boat; all considered it a miracle they survived the trip. By the time they reached the *Diana*'s deck, bodies steaming in the cold and wet, the rain had begun to diminish, the thunder sounding more sporadically. They'd passed the edge of the storm—or it had passed them.

Jin stayed at the helm while Watson was taken to her berth, and the rest of the damp sailors were shuffled into the officers' mess, wet coats and boots pulled away, bodies wrapped in blankets, hot tea offered around. All the sailors but Grant, at any rate; Kit wasn't sure where he'd gone.

She warmed her hands around her teacup, and when she finally found the energy to lift it, wept at the taste. It was the good tea, the queen's tea, and Cook had added so much sugar it nearly made Kit's teeth ache with joy.

She took another heartening sip, then turned an eye to Cook, who watched with concern from the doorway. "I knew you'd held some back," she said.

Cook simply lifted a shoulder. "Emergency rations. This was an emergency. I'm glad you are alive."

"I'm also glad I'm alive," she said.

Grant appeared in the doorway when she'd just finished her cup of tea, wet shirt replaced with a dry one, untucked and sans coats, his hair tousled and damp. Not the state of dishabille a viscount typically adopted on land, she guessed. But there were different rules at sea. Which is how she justified not looking away. There was just . . . so much of him.

"We need to speak."

Kit lifted her brows at the tone, hard and angry, presumed he had thoughts about the frigate captains or Forstadt. She was ready for dry clothes, so she nodded and rose, unwrapped the blanket she'd been bound in, and left it across her chair to dry. Then she walked to her quarters, looked longingly at the bed. Fatigue was dragging at her now, and she nearly jumped when Grant slammed the door.

Slowly, she looked back at him. "Problem, Colonel?"

His eyes flashed at her use of his title. "That was ridiculously dangerous."

"Going into the water?" Kit asked, running a hand through her still-damp hair. "It was dangerous, but not ridiculously so. You saw me swim at Finistère. I'm a better swimmer than Watson. Better to take the risk to save a life."

"Is it?"

She looked up at him. There was something different in his eyes now, and she wasn't sure what it was. "If it's my life I'm risking, absolutely."

He stared at her for a moment, then stalked to the other end of the room, turned his angry gaze on the windows.

"The storm isn't going to stop just because you give it one of your glares."

He looked back at her, brows lifted. "Excuse me?"

"Your glares," she repeated. "You have a way of looking at people as if you'd like to march them right into the sea. And right now, you're giving the sea the same look."

"There are many people who need to be marched right into the sea," he said, then added, "Seven minutes."

Kit blinked. "Seven minutes?"

He stalked back to her, looked down from his height. There was no bay rum now, just salt and linen and something she could only describe as male.

"You were in the water for seven minutes," he said. "I counted. I'd taken my jacket off. Didn't have my watch, so I counted. Seven minutes is a very long time."

It was a long time, Kit thought, and didn't know how she'd managed to hold her breath that long. Maybe the cold, maybe the adrenaline, maybe the effects of the magic. *Probably* the effects of the magic, but not his concern.

"I'm sorry that you had to wait—that everyone had to wait. I've been the one waiting before, and I know it's difficult. But I'd do the same thing again. It's my job."

"Hardly. I know plenty of officers who'd define their roles much more narrowly."

"I'm not one of those people." She glared at him. "And given you walked into a pirate fortress to save Marcus Dunwood, I know you aren't, either."

"This is different."

"Why?"

"Because it is!" Grant's voice, heavy with concern, boomed against wood and glass, and before she could comment, his hands were on her arms, the contact shocking.

And then his mouth was on hers, and he was pulling her closer, and her body snapped against his like a sail pulled taut, every one of her nerves singing with the contact.

For a moment, she heard nothing but the ocean, the roar of the sea in her ears, and felt equally as comforted and breathless as she had beneath the waves. That familiarity eased her way. Kit moved closer, kissed him back. His groan was primal, victorious, his body a hard line of temptation.

His kisses were skillful—teasing and passionate. She'd been kissed before, if not often, and understood expertise. And she'd read enough penny novels to understand what could come next, and was as confident he'd be as skilled a lover as he was a kisser. So it took entirely too long for her mind to return to reality; he'd fogged her brain just as the sea had done. She stepped back, breaking the contact, putting space between them, and leaving a cold chill across her skin that she didn't like. So she moved backward again.

"We can't," she said, shaking her head. "You cannot kiss me. And I certainly can't kiss you."

Gods, but she wanted to. She wanted to grab that hair and push him back against the wall and have her very particular way with him. But she didn't. Couldn't.

Grant glared at her, frustration obvious. "Why the bloody hell not?"

"Because you're a—" Brain fogged, she simply waved her arm in his direction.

"A viscount?" he asked dryly.

"Yes. That. A soldier, and a member of the Beau Monde, and the future husband to a viscountess. And I am certainly not a viscountess," she said, with all the vehemence she could muster.

"No argument there," Grant muttered.

"You've an estate and horses and Spiveys and a village. I have a ship and a crew and a million miles yet to sail. And even if all of that weren't true, we're attempting to stop a global effort to put a dictator back on the throne."

"But that's your only objection?" His voice was exceedingly dry, and the sound she made was mostly a growl.

Grant looked at her for a moment, jaw clenched. And then he gave a stiff nod. "Very well." He walked toward the door, just close enough that their arms brushed.

She knew he'd done it intentionally. And that her knees actually felt weak at the contact made her furious at both of them.

"I've a dagger and sword," she murmured, a reminder.

He slammed out of the room.

"Viscounts," she muttered, meaning to make it a curse, and sat down at the table. She ran her fingertips across her lips, which still tingled from the abrasion of his unshaven skin, and indulged in a very dramatic sigh.

She was tired enough to sleep while standing, or on the deck, or on the forecastle floor. But even after the storm had shifted, the rain more akin to an Isles afternoon shower, she refused to leave the helm.

"We're on a mission," Kit said again, wondering if she was the only one who recalled that particular fact, and nearly pulled her dagger when Grant grunted nearby.

"You can sleep now," Jin said, expression mild, "or you can sleep when we get to Forstadt. Which do you prefer?"

Because she couldn't argue with that logic, she agreed to go below in exchange for his promise to wake her if the storm changed direction, or the frigates broke rank, or the island was sighted.

And when she reached her quarters again, and closed her door, she nearly fell into her berth.

TWENTY-ONE

S he slept for six hours, and woke squinting in sunlight, still wearing her clothes from the day before.

By the time she made it to the deck, Simon was at the helm, sailors on watch undertaking their morning tasks. She didn't see Grant, which was probably just as well.

The wind was at their backs and just off port, the frigates in their tidy arrow behind the *Diana*, and the sun rising above the bow and over the bank of clouds along the eastern horizon. That was the storm, now bearing down over Frisia; she hoped anyone else on the water had time to prepare.

"Captain," Simon said as she looked over the ship, checking for storm damage and finding none—or at least none that hadn't already been repaired while she slept.

"Good morning," she said. "Everything looks to be in fighting trim."

Simon nodded. "Once the rain slowed, the storm moved quickly. We're forty miles out from Forstadt by my reading."

"Which is always accurate," she said, and squeezed his shoulder. "Thank you for the sleep."

"Thank you for Watson," Simon said.

"How is she?"

"Good," he said with a smile, then gestured toward the bow, where Watson upbraided a seaman for a very sloppy hitch.

Her ship was in order, her crew was safe, the sun was shining, and the wind was in their favor. There was little more a captain could ask for. Unless she was Aligned.

Kit glanced at the water. The sea was breaking, but it was bright, diamonds shimmering across its surface. Then she reached down, expecting to feel the current bright again, and found it . . . gone.

Not just broken. Not just pale. And not a null where there'd been no current. It was absent, its loss leaving a mark in the sea, in her mind.

She looked up toward the horizon, toward the direction of Forstadt.

What the hell had gone on there?

In silence, Grant and Jin and Simon and Kit—and Tamlin in the top—watched as a long green smear came into view toward the east. A low island of dark trees, wisps of fog drifting through them like serpents. No sails, no ships. And no sign of any recent habitation on the island.

But that was wrong. Not just because of Dunwood, of the dispatch, but because of the magic—or absence of it—leading them like an arrow to this place.

"Captain?" Simon asked.

"Circle it," she said. "And keep a hard eye out for sails."

"Aye," Simon said with a nod.

They found what they were looking for on the eastern shore, protected as it was from the pounding waves of the Northern Sea—an inlet and sandy cove marked by the framework of scaffolds that would have held a ship in the process of its construction.

And there was no ship.

Kit cursed the captains, the weather, the damned Guild. But forced her anger down. They needed information, and she needed satisfaction regarding the source of the magic. They'd have to explore the island for that.

"Here," Kit said as they rounded the inlet, had gone as close to the shore as they dared. "Signal the frigates to prepare their boats. We'll meet on the cove."

The sails were doused, the anchor weighed, the jolly boat prepared for launch.

"Jin, Grant, and Hobbes, with me. Be careful and be ready." She looked at Simon. "You have the helm, and the same instructions. We're close enough to Frisia and Aleman both that we need to be careful. Any sign of sails, of trouble, and you signal us."

"Aye, Captain," he said. "We'll keep a watchful eye. You do the same."

Kit's small team piled into the boat, were dropped down into the water, and rowed toward the island.

Hobbes and Jin climbed out of the boat first, hopping down into foot-deep water. They pulled the boat onto the shore, found the sand hard packed, probably from the storm, a frilled lace of shell and seaweed several yards inland where the storm tide had reached.

Without waiting for the other boats, Kit climbed a wall of sand cut in by hard waves. The land above had scruffy grass and small shrubs, and led to a forest of trees. The storm damage was obvious. Detritus washed ashore, leaves stripped from the nearest trees.

And at the edge, the scaffolding she'd seen. Or, she belatedly realized, what would have been the scaffolding.

A dozen enormous wooden posts would have supported a boat during its construction. But only half that were still standing, and they looked like they'd been burned about the edges, which were charcoal dark. The rest were on the ground, scattered among chunks of wood and sawdust and bits of frazzled rope. They looked charred, too, and Kit imagined they'd have been smoking if the storm hadn't doused the fire.

"*Vas tiva es,*" she heard Hobbes say, and looked up, as the taste of smoke—round and acrid—scratched the back of her throat. She wasn't Aligned to the land, but—maybe because she was so close to the water—could feel that the island's magic had been spent. Stripped away, just like the current.

Kit walked to Hobbes, would have asked what she'd found, but could see it for herself.

A man on his stomach, dead for at least a day or two, Kit guessed. She wasn't sure what had done him in, not without moving him, but there were burns on his back, arms, legs, where simple and worn fabric had been burned away, left his skin singed.

"There are more," Grant said behind her. "We've counted four. All look to be workers here."

"Burns?" Kit asked, without looking back.

"Yes," was his simple reply. And he extended his hand. In his palm was a charred bit of metal, a round disk that could be folded over to slip onto a collar, through a buttonhole. She could just see the outline of an imperial eagle.

"A Guild trade token," Kit said. A badge of protection and affiliation worn by Guildmembers.

Grant nodded, slipped it into his pocket. "One of the men was wearing it. The Guild is responsible for this."

"Captain," Hobbes said, voice quiet and stuck through with fear, "what happened here?"

"I'm not entirely sure," she said. But she had an idea, because she knew what had happened at Contra Costa. She looked back at Grant, and saw the same knowledge in his face.

The other boats had landed, sailors dispersing to search the island. "Captain!" one of them called out, gesturing Preston closer. Unabashed, Kit and her crew followed, and found the sailor standing near a darkened circle of earth twenty feet across.

"A fire," the sailor said. "They were burning wood?"

"No," Grant said. "They weren't burning anything. At least not on purpose."

She could see Preston prepared to interrogate, to ask for more information, but she ignored him, looked at the sailors. "If any of you are Aligned to land, can you sense the magic here? Can you feel it?"

There was silence as sailors looked busily at the ground, the sky. Not entirely surprising, Kit thought, given Preston's attitude. And Thornberry's was probably similar.

"Jackson," Smith said, "you've a land Alignment. Can you feel anything?"

A young man with dark skin and hair, looking slightly abashed at being called out, nodded firmly. "Captain. There's no magic here."

Smith's brows lifted. "Is your Alignment so different?"

"Sir, my place is different than this—I'm from near Thornpole—but I can still feel the magic here, or what magic there would have been. But it's . . . gone." He looked at Kit. "There's a shadow where it was. A void. But no power."

"I understand," Kit said. "Thank you."

"Captain Brightling," Preston said impatiently. "Would you like to enlighten us?"

His tone, impatient and prim, said he didn't believe anything Kit had to say would be enlightening in the least.

"Contra Costa," was all she said, naming the battle in which thousands had been killed because Gallic soldiers had tried to use the current as a weapon of war.

Preston's eyes lit with anger. "Leave us!" he said, the words a whip of sound, and sailors scattered.

Hobbes and Jin looked at Kit, and she nodded. They moved to stand with the others. Grant, for his part, made no move at all.

Then Preston turned on her. "How dare you. An officer cannot throw out those words whenever it suits her whim. You will incite panic in the ranks."

She felt, more than saw, Grant braced against the insult. "It doesn't suit my whim at all," she said calmly. "It's a fact."

"Nonsense," Thornberry said. "They wouldn't dare try to manipulate magic again, not given the losses."

"There is only one loss Gerard cares about," Grant said. "That of his own throne. His soldiers, his sailors, were fungible. They were pawns."

"The island had magic," Kit said. "The magic is gone not just from here, but from, to varying degrees, the water several hundred miles away." She gestured to the wrecked scaffolding. "A ship was built here; the ship is now gone. And a catastrophe occurred here, one that scorched the earth, blew apart the dock, killed the workers." Who were now confirmed to be members of the Guild, but she kept that thought to herself, as she still wasn't certain of the captains' motives.

"You think the ship pulled in the island's magic somehow," Smith said. "Used it as fuel."

"A ship cannot sail with magic alone," Preston said.

"Not before," Kit said. "Or maybe we've entered a new era, a new time, and they've figured out a way to use the current as fuel in a more consistent manner. And with devastating side effects."

Thornberry snorted his disdain. But Preston's gaze had narrowed. He might not like it, but he was smart enough to understand the wisdom in what she'd said.

"And the doldrums?" Preston asked. "The storm?"

Kit gestured toward the destruction. "Caused by whatever was taking place here. Wounding the magic of the land, the sea, affects them both in multiple ways, including weather. There were similar effects at Contra Costa, and the magic required to move a large ship would be substantial. The consequences would be catastrophic." They only had to look around to see that.

"This is all speculation," Thornberry said. "Nonsense from a female trying to puff herself up."

"Reasonable speculation," Grant said, and Kit saw Thornberry's eyes flash, probably angry a civilian had dared challenge him.

"And as I'm the only soldier here," Grant continued, "and

likely the only one who saw Contra Costa firsthand, I suspect you've no cause to argue with her conclusions."

He was at Contra Costa, Kit thought. And had said nothing of it, despite knowing the possibilities of what they'd sailed into. Her sympathy matched against esteem.

"The timing," Smith said, frowning. "The storm just happened. They couldn't have evacuated so quickly."

"If we're right, the storm followed the taking of the magic," Kit said. "That means they launched the boat before we left Norgate." And likely had been testing it before then.

"You think they knew we were coming," Smith said. "They made their preparations, evacuated the island so there'd be no evidence of who committed this violation of the treaty, and left on the ship. Or with it."

"Or they feared they wouldn't reach Dunwood before we did," Kit said, "so they launched."

That might have been true. But she thought it far more likely someone at Crown Command had learned about their mission and sent a message to Forstadt before the *Diana* was repaired, before she rendezvoused with the squadron.

Silence fell, heavy and uncertain.

"We should be careful," Kit said. "And we should be sure. We need to search the island."

To that, at least, the captains made no objection. They split into groups to search the quadrants of the isle. Kit led her people down a path that moved inland. Many of the trees near the shore had been cut for lumber, but the forest thickened as they walked. The path eventually led to a meadow, where they found a barn with a pointed roof and long, low buildings that looked to her like barracks. Empty now, but for the detritus of those who'd lived and worked here.

They searched for two more hours, but found nothing else useful. The activity, the effort of building a new kind of warship, had been focused along the coast. What evidence they found was collected, gathered for transport and analysis in New London, before they joined the other captains at the shore again.

"We've found what there is to find," Smith said. "We should make for New London immediately."

"Agreed," Kit said.

"What about the ship?" Grant asked. "Ought we not search for it?"

"It's had several days' head start," Kit said, "and could be anywhere by now. Most likely, if this was a test of its magic, it has moved inland, toward the coasts where it will have protection from storms and snooping eyes."

"And if we send frigates snooping along Frisian or Aleman shores," Smith put in, "we may create more problems than we solve."

Grant nodded. Kit could tell he didn't like the idea of leaving the warship free and in open water, but nor did she trust the frigates to report to the queen alone.

"We'll lead the squadron home," Kit said. "Arrow formation, just as before. And be wary. It's unlikely we'll find either the gun brig or whatever was built here along the way, but be wary."

"We'll handle the report to the queen," Thornberry said, tone conciliatory, as if he were doing Kit a favor. More like, Kit thought, he was hoping to get to the queen before she did in order to spin his tale of heroism.

"Do as you will," Kit said. "I will, of course, make my own report."

Thornberry's face went hard. "That won't be necessary given—"

"I wasn't asking," Kit interrupted. "Given your doubts about magic, it would hardly be appropriate for you to report on it."

Thornberry and Smith walked away. Preston stayed where he was, and looked down his titled, narrow nose at Kit.

"Impudence is unbecoming in a young officer. Particularly a female."

"Arrogance is unbecoming in an old officer, regardless of gender. So I suppose we both have things to complain about."

With that, she walked away, and left him staring after her.

"That appeared to be a relatively peaceful discussion," Jin said from the polite distance they'd stood and waited for Kit to commune with the captains. "At least until the end."

"Peaceful enough," Kit said. "Is he still staring angrily?"

Jin made a less-than-subtle glance in Preston's direction. "Yes. Did you dare have an opinion of your own?"

"I was impudent," Kit said with a snort. "Which, I'm told, is unbecoming in female officers."

"That was . . . regrettable," Jin said.

"The words, yes, although I doubt he's capable of the emotion. In any event, we've agreed it's time to leave. Not that they had much choice."

"Given we found Dunwood, the dispatch, and the former shipyard?" Jin asked with a narrow smile.

"Given," she agreed, "but let's not award the medals yet. We've leagues to go and a pair of egoists between us."

Kit and the others were walking back toward the boat when someone called her name. She looked back, found a woman jogging toward them. She had pale skin, a sturdy body with square shoulders and a lean waist, and silvery-white hair, short on the sides and swooping high over her crown. Her eyes were bright and sharp, and she wore the plain blue jacket of a midshipman.

"Apologies for the interruption, Captain, but could I have a moment?"

"Of course," Kit said with not a little curiosity, and nodded for the others. "Get the jolly boat ready."

"Could we, perhaps, speak over the rise?" the midshipman asked, gesturing toward a more secluded spot.

"All right," Kit said, suspicious but curious, and they walked toward the tree line.

The woman waited until they were alone. "We just wanted to let you know—we believe you were mistreated."

Kit raised her brows. "Was I?"

"I don't like to speak out of turn; my family has been Crown Command for three generations, and I understand and respect chain of command. But there are four of us Aligned on Thornberry's ship, and we know when we're being asked, if you'll pardon the expression, to shovel shit."

Kit glanced at her uniform, noted her rank. "You speak frankly, Midshipman . . . ?"

"Cooper, ma'am. Midshipman Cooper of the *Divine*. And I rarely speak otherwise, ma'am." That grin was cheeky again.

"You're one of the Aligned?"

"I am, sir. To the land. I keep my head down, and I'll do as

I'm ordered; we all will. But we serve the queen, and the Isles. We just wanted you to know."

Kit inclined her head, watched Cooper rejoin her crew. Kit understood chain of command, and had a deep distrust—if admittedly an indoctrinated one—of people who broke that chain. But she also understood duty and honor, and she sympathized with Cooper's frustration, and not just because Cooper was agreeing with her.

She turned to walk back to the boat, and as she cleared the small rise, found Grant, Preston, Smith, and Thornberry stood a few feet away, oblivious to her presence. It would have been the polite thing to alert them.

But she wasn't that polite.

⌒

"Lord Grant," Thornberry said. "I'm surprised to see you've affiliated yourself with Captain Brightling. Aligned, and a foundling. Unknown connections."

Rian's brows lifted. "A foundling who's become a captain in your service, Thornberry, with an Alignment that appears to have solved the puzzle laid out here."

Thornberry's stance went rigid. "Now see here—" he began, but Grant held up a hand.

"I see more than you'd probably prefer. I see ego and arrogance. I see two men who decided to play a game instead of following the queen's orders."

"We had no way of knowing—"

"But you did," Grant said. "The queen gave you instructions, and Kit told you the details. You chose not to believe her. Because she's younger than you? Because she's a woman? Because she's

Aligned? She nearly died during the tempest to save one of her crew. Jumped overboard—into the sea during that storm—to save her. She has more bravery than you can even comprehend, much less summon. Perhaps the next time you decide to ignore the queen's orders, you'll remember that. And perhaps when the queen learns the truth, you'll commit that particular lesson to memory."

Preston's eyes went hard and cold. "I hear your brother's been gambling again," he said, gaze scanning Grant's face, as if looking for weakness. "Pity if those debts were called in, wouldn't it?"

Grant met Preston's gaze. "If you have issues with my brother, take them up with him. At present, you're speaking to me. I'd wager that I have more connections than you, Preston. And mine are substantially higher."

"You can't threaten me."

"Oh, I can. And back up the threat besides. But a threat won't do Captain Brightling any good. And she's the one who deserves the praise here. So I'm willing to forget your mistake," Grant said. "If you are."

"Meaning?" Smith asked.

She, at least, was willing to negotiate.

"If you want to discuss the ships' delay in finding Forstadt in your reports, you blame it on the weather. Or mast problems. Or any number of issues related to the sailing of vessels in foreign oceans. You will not, as I surmise you are wont to do, fill those reports with claptrap about imagined magic. And if you fail to heed this," Grant continued, cutting off Thornberry's sputtering, "the queen will very quickly discover the truth, as will Admiral Lawrence." He leaned forward, smiled. "His daughter's a good friend."

"We'll be circumspect," Smith said quickly, shutting off Preston's rant with a pointed stare. "Assuming Captain Brightling offers the same consideration."

"I'll speak with her," Grant said. "And you'd best hope she does."

～

Kit was still staring when he turned back, found her standing nearby.

"Nosy, aren't you?" he asked when she reached him.

"Curious," she said. "And I didn't want to interrupt."

He looked dubious, which was fair.

"What you said . . ." she began.

"Was the truth."

"You know as well as I there's truth, and there's *truth*. You've protected the reputation of my ship and my crew. So I'm forced, again, to say thank you."

"You're welcome. If Thornberry and his ilk are indicative of your interactions with the Beau Monde, I begin to understand your distaste."

This was dodgy territory, Kit thought. "I've known few. None, at least in my experience, would have thought to defend me."

"That's a pity," Grant said coolly.

"You were at Contra Costa," Kit said, and Grant nodded. "You didn't mention it."

"There are some things better forgotten."

Kit nodded.

"Captain," Hobbes called out, and they looked over together, found Jin in the boat, Hobbes holding it at the waterline. The frigates were preparing to sail.

Grant looked at her expectantly, and Kit had the sense she was meant to say something to clear the air, but had no idea what that might be.

"We should go," Kit said finally, and they walked in silence to the boat.

TWENTY-TWO

The sun was surprisingly bright in New London, and there were crowds along the Saint James watching as the ships returned to port, canvas flying.

Kit waved, and let her sailors do the same as they slid slowly toward the Crown Quay. They had enough wind to make it in without assistance, thank the gods, and cozied to the dock as delicately as an alighting dove.

"The queen?" Jin asked as the crew weighed anchor, began to take in the sails.

"The queen," she agreed. "And I've a favor to ask you." She looked over at the mast, where Louisa stood with Tamlin, who was pointing up into the rigging. Explaining the parts of the ship, Kit guessed.

"You want me to take Louisa to Hetta."

Kit smiled sheepishly. "Could you? I trust you the most, after all."

Jin snorted. "You trust virtually no one and in no significant amount."

"Exactly," Kit said. "That means you're the most special of them all."

Jin sighed. "I'll take her."

"Thank you. You might consider inviting Tamlin for the trip. They seem to have connected. And when that's done, go home and see your family. If there's more to do, I'll send a message."

"Try not to adopt another foundling in the process," he suggested. "The ship's becoming a bit crowded." He offered a handshake of goodbye; Kit took it, and it quickly evolved into an embrace.

"And try not to mortally wound the captains in front of the queen," Jin said. "You know she deplores gore in the throne room."

"What about a mere scrape? A light flesh wound?"

His lips twitched. "Perfectly acceptable."

They'd agreed to meet at the palace, and given the likelihood of backstabbing and treachery, Kit was determined to arrive early. For that reason, and that reason only, she agreed to the hackney Grant hailed off the dock, led by two brown horses with bowed backs and bored eyes.

Feigned boredom, obviously. She knew they had plans.

They arrived before the captains, found Kess waiting outside the throne room doors. The queen had been watching again.

"Welcome back," he said, then looked at Grant. "I'm very sorry about Dunwood. He was a good man."

Grant nodded. "He was."

At the sound of quick-march footsteps on stone, they all

glanced back. The captains strode toward them, and very proper nods were exchanged.

"Now that we're all here," Kess said, "let's not keep her waiting." And he opened the throne room doors.

The captains all but pushed their way to the front of the room, to line up first before the queen.

"Confident, aren't they?" Kess murmured.

"They are not acquainted with self-doubt," Kit said.

"Nor self-assessment," Grant added.

"And you're content to let them lead the dance?" Kess asked.

Kit glanced back at him. "I'm content to trust the queen."

That was all she needed to say.

❧

Kess took his place beside the queen, who wore a dress of saffron taffeta. The sleeves were short and the waist high, and a collar rose at the back of the neckline to brush the cloud of dark curls that framed her face.

Chandler stood nearby, watching as they entered, considering, evaluating.

"Captains," the queen said, when they reached the dais. "Grant."

*Your Highness*es were murmured.

"I understand your mission was successful." She looked at each of them, lined up like children prepared to report to their governesses, eager for attention. All but Kit, who was content to watch and wait.

"Captain Preston," the queen said, without shifting her gaze from Kit. "Report."

"Your Highness," Preston said. "The squadron confirmed Forstadt was the site of a shipbuilding operation."

"Was?" the queen asked.

"There was evidence of shipbuilding on the island. But the ship was gone. There were several dead men, some evidence of a fire."

"Dead?" Chandler asked.

"Killed, it would appear, by fire or explosion."

The queen's brows lifted. "A ship, dead men, a fire," she said, steepling her fingers. "You haven't mentioned magic. Dunwood's intelligence indicated the Guild hoped to incorporate magic into their design."

Preston's lips thinned. "No, Your Highness. I'm not one of the Aligned, nor did I see any direct evidence of the same on the island. I prefer to sail the old-fashioned way."

He was an unapologetic liar, Kit thought, if one who carefully calibrated his words. He hadn't "seen" evidence, so there was no such evidence. Despite what Kit had said. Beside him, Smith shifted, but made no move to correct the assertion. Because she'd changed her mind, Kit wondered, or had been rolled over by the others?

"With slaves or serfs doing the rowing?" The queen's voice was utterly smooth, the chill in her eyes devastating.

Preston didn't bother to hide his apparent disgust at the truth, or the fact that she'd cornered him so neatly. "With skill," he said, the viper no longer hiding behind pleasantries.

"I believe seeing and understanding magic, much less incorporating it safely into one's sailing, takes considerable skill," the queen said. "As does sailing into Finistère and surviving the trip. Any confirmation of Guild activity?" she asked, before he could argue.

"No, Your Highness," Preston said.

"Yes, Your Highness," Grant countered and, with Kess's nod,

moved forward to offer the trade token he'd found. The queen took it, and Kit saw the fire light in her eyes, along with the anger.

Kit watched the other captains, saw confusion give way to surprise, then fury. But Kit saw no guilt or deception. Skilled actors, she thought, or legitimately surprised at the connection.

"A trade token," Chandler said, when the queen offered it to him, then looked at the captains, watched them, too.

"We were not apprised of this evidence," Preston said, directing his expression toward Kit, "and cannot verify its authenticity."

"I can," Kit said unapologetically. "It was found on one of the deceased sailors."

The queen nodded. "And magic?"

"Your Highness," Kit said. "On the way to the island, the amount of magic in the sea current, and the stability of that magic, steadily decreased. We also experienced doldrums, unusual for that portion of the Narrow Sea, and a severe storm. We arrived at the island to find what remained of a shipyard, evidence trees had been chopped for lumber. No ship was present. And the magic had, we believe, been stripped away. We believe magic was manipulated, and harshly so, on the island, possibly to fuel that ship, given Dunwood's statement. We believe, as at Contra Costa, the manipulation of that magic caused the resulting decrease in magic on sea and land, and the doldrums and the storm, and some sort of explosive activity that destroyed most of the scaffolding, felled trees, and killed several of the workers."

Silence fell.

"We disagree," Thornberry put in. "Magic cannot be used to fuel a ship, and any comparisons to Contra Costa are overblown."

The queen nodded, but she made no other indication of surprise or concern. No shock at the possibility magic had been so profoundly manipulated despite the storm, the lingering malevolence on the island, and the possibility Gerard had found a new and powerful weapon.

She shifted her gaze to Grant. "Colonel?"

"I have nothing to add to Captain Brightling's statement, and concur with her analysis."

"Thank you, Colonel." She looked at Preston, Thornberry, and Smith. "We appreciate your service and your swift investigation of this matter."

"Your Highness," Preston said with a little bow, but made no move to leave. Instead, he slid his gaze to Kit.

The queen's brows lifted. "You have been dismissed, Captain Preston."

The trio managed not to grumble, but made their little nods and exited the room with anger in their strides.

"Well," she said, when the door closed behind them. "I suppose those who aligned with the Prefects will have plenty to talk about this evening."

The sarcasm in her voice broke the thick tension in the air.

"My offer to destroy what remains of them stands," Chandler said.

"And it is a thoughtful offer," said the queen, with a hint of a smile. "But I must decline." She turned her attention to Grant and Kit. "Now that we have cleared the room, let's discuss your next mission."

"*Our* next mission?" Kit asked, and could feel Grant bristling beside her.

The queen nodded. "Mr. Chandler."

Chandler straightened. "As you're aware, the dispatch Captain Brightling located has been decoded. In addition to referencing Forstadt, it arranges a meeting, tonight, at the pavilion at Lambeth Gardens. The dispatch's intended recipient is to deliver certain requested information to his or her contact."

"What information?" Grant asked.

"It wasn't discussed in the dispatch," Chandler said. "Given the lengths taken to organize this meeting, it's presumably important. To ensure the meeting would proceed as planned, we delivered the dispatch to the Cork and Barrel as directed."

"Clever," Grant said.

"I'm glad to hear you think so," the queen said dryly. "Given that you've returned with ample time to prepare, you will attend the gathering tonight and you will surveil the meeting. Together."

The room went silent in the aftermath of that announcement.

"Together," Kit said. "At Lambeth Gardens. With the Beau Monde and the strolling and the fireworks?"

"And the meeting of traitors," Chandler said. "The pavilion, during the fireworks. You will confirm the identities of the spies and capture them, if possible."

Kit admitted to herself that dressing up for an evening at Lambeth Gardens looking for perfidy could be interesting; she'd enjoyed playing a salty trader at Finistère, after all. But with Grant, and in the wake of the kiss and the lingering awkwardness?

"Captain Brightling is not trained in espionage," Grant said.

"And you aren't trained in compliments or pleasant conversation," Kit said with amusement, "but I suspect we'll both manage."

The queen's lips twitched. "I believe Captain Brightling has amply demonstrated her ability to adapt to circumstances—and viscounts."

"Why us?" Grant asked.

"As a viscount, it's perfectly reasonable that you'd attend an important social event, and unlikely anyone would suspect you had ulterior motives. And, frankly, given the delicate nature of this issue, and the presence of traitors in the Crown Command, we must make use of a limited pool of assets."

A bit less entertaining, Kit thought, to have been the only option.

"You'll need an escort," the queen said. "In order to fully maintain the illusion, and lest you should be accused of improprieties."

"Notwithstanding cavorting with pirates," Grant said.

"Notwithstanding," the queen agreed, and looked at Kit. "Captain, perhaps one of your sisters would be agreeable?"

Kit imagined Jane's amusement at following them around Lambeth. "I imagine one would."

The queen nodded. "While the event will be, shall we say, lighthearted, I do not need to remind you of the gravity of this situation, nor the risk if the spy is not apprehended. We do not know how much information has already been given to Frisia, the Guild, or Gerard, but we do not want more to fall into their hands. And as to the magic . . ."

She looked at Kess, at Chandler. Both of them nodded.

The queen sighed, linked her fingers together, and looked back at Kit. "Let us be frank. We agree with Dunwood's conclusions and your suspicions regarding the magic used by the new ship. We believe you were correct that the ship used magic as some sort of fuel. We were aware that Gerard was interested in utilizing magic, despite Contra Costa and the terms of the treaty. We were aware," the queen said again, "in part, because we also have an interest in developing magic as a tool of warfare."

For a full minute, Kit just stared at her queen, the woman who commanded her, whom she'd bowed to on innumerable occasions. And the woman's last words, *magic as a tool of warfare*, echoed in Kit's head. She was torn between bafflement and fury.

"We lost thousands at Contra Costa," Kit said quietly. "There were dead men on Forstadt, and we nearly lost sailors in the Forstadt storm. Manipulating magic, the current, carries a cost that is too high for us to bear."

"And the deaths caused by prolonged war?" the queen said. "Is that cost too high?"

"Heat, famine, the ruin of the soil, volcanic activity."

"Millions dead or missing before Gerard was stopped at Saint-Denis. You may believe his means of conducting war—past or future—are immoral. I tend to believe that war is immoral, and a queen allowing deaths that could have been prevented equally so." Her tone was scalding now, her eyes just as hot. "So before you decide what cost is too high, be sure you've done the calculations."

"Your Highness," Kit said, taking the reprimand.

"You're dismissed," the queen said, and left them in silence.

"Are you all right?" Grant asked, when they were outside the throne room in the chill of shadowed marble.

"I've just argued with the queen, so no."

"That's not what I meant," he said. "'Magic as a tool of warfare,'" he repeated. "You went pale when she said it."

"Maybe it's naive to expect we hold ourselves to higher standards than Gerard."

"It's not. But let us thank the gods we aren't in her position. And do our best in fripperies and silk tonight to stop Gerard before we need to deal with magic."

"Fripperies and silk," Kit said, lips curving at the mild insult in his voice. That felt comfortable, as if he'd moved past the moment in her quarters.

"I assume you'll be put out if I arrive at the Brightling home in torn linen and patched trousers."

He was trying to amuse her, she realized with a jolt. Trying to ease her mind. And she appreciated it. "I suppose you'll wear whatever you will, being a viscount and all, and I'll have little choice in the matter."

"We always have choices, Captain. Lambeth Gardens wasn't how I intended to spend my evening."

"Nor I," Kit said. "But it appears that's the evening we'll have." She looked at him, expected to see grim resignation in his expression. That was there, of course. But there was something else beneath it. Fear. And she recalled why he'd wanted to return to New London.

"You're going to look for your brother before the event," she said.

"I am."

"Would you like help?"

"Help?"

"In finding him. I'm a skilled fighter and a ranked officer in the Crown Command. I imagine I've spent more time in New London than you have. And, given my profession, I've seen a gambling hell or two. And I let you go on my adventures. It's only fair that you return the favor."

"Those were the queen's adventures. And no, I don't need assistance in locating my own brother." He pulled a pocket watch from his coat, checked it. "I'll ring for you at six."

"Try not to wear torn linens and patched trousers."

Grant leaned down, lips nearly at her ear and sending a thrill of something that felt like magic along her spine. "Do try to look a becoming escort for a viscount," he said, and walked away.

Kit blew out a breath. Perhaps he hadn't moved past that moment after all.

TWENTY-THREE

K it walked into the Brightling house with a frustrated disposition. Portnoy's was closed, having apparently devoted
itself to preparing for the Lambeth festivities, where Kit imagined it would sell cones of sweets to attendees.

She opened the front door, found herself looking down at a
girl in a simple pink dress, her blond hair a gleaming mass of
curls held back by a pink ribbon.

Mrs. Eaves had wasted no time, Kit thought.

"Hello," Kit said pleasantly. "Do I know you?"

Louisa's chin lifted. "It's me, Louisa. Mate of the *Diana*."

Kit frowned. "That doesn't sound familiar. You don't look
like a sailor."

"Well, I was," Louisa said, "before I became a prisoner and
was forced into a stupid dress." She pointed at her dress, stuck out
a boot. "It's a tragesty!"

"Travesty," Kit said, holding back a smile. "Or tragedy, depending."

"That's what I said. Did you bring a box from Portnoy's?"

Kit narrowed her eyes. "Who said I bring something from Portnoy's?"

"The twins. And they hide them so Mrs. Eaves doesn't find out, or it's right into the bin. And Mrs. Eaves doesn't cook very good things."

Louisa had been here for barely two hours, Kit thought, and already had the lay of the land. She could have been one of Sutherland's observing officers.

"Unfortunately, I didn't bring treats today. The treat shop was closed." She heard music from the parlor, and glanced over.

"That's Pari," Louisa said. "She's playing the pianoforte. She said she could try to teach me some but you have to sit still for so long."

"I had the same reaction," Kit said. "Other than the dress, how do you like it here?"

Louisa lifted a shoulder.

Time would tell, Kit thought, and walked to the parlor doorway, looked in. Pari sat in front of the pianoforte, hands moving across the keys. She was fourteen, with tan skin, long dark hair, and a slender build.

Kit closed her eyes to listen to the soft rise and fall of the melody, the little trills that sounded like birdsong. Kit couldn't play an instrument, couldn't hold a tune. Which made her appreciate it all the more.

When Kit opened her eyes again, Pari was smiling at her with a single lifted eyebrow.

"That was lovely." Kit went to her, took a seat beside her on the bench. "Who wrote it?"

"I did," Pari said. Hope shined in her eyes. "Did you really like it?"

"I really did. It was beautiful."

"Did you bring any pistachio nougats?" Pari asked hopefully.

Kit sighed. She was beloved for the narrowest of reasons. "Portnoy's was closed for the Lambeth celebration."

Pari clapped her hands together. "I think that will be magnificent, with fireworks and an orchestra, but Hetta says we're too young to go."

"You're too young," Kit agreed. Lambeth was for couples to steal time alone, whether or not beneath the watchful eyes of their chaperones.

Hetta appeared in the doorway, smiled at her daughters. "Good afternoon, Kit. Pari, that was lovely. Louisa, you look very presentable. Pari, might you take her upstairs for a bit so Kit and I can talk?"

"Of course, Mother." Pari held out her hand, which Louisa took without hesitation. "I've found a new book of pirate adventures."

"I've fought pirates before!" Kit heard Louisa say. "They were very fierce."

When Hetta's brows lifted, Kit shook her head. "She stayed in the hold, and didn't have so much as a glimpse of a pirate."

"That's a relief." Hetta walked to Kit, and they embraced.

"You look tired," Hetta said.

"It's been a very long few days."

"Then let's go into my study and have some tea, and we can discuss it."

⁓

Tea was served with milk and sugar, but Kit drew the line at sampling one of the dishwater-colored "nutritional biscuits" Mrs. Eaves had added to the tray.

"'Biscuits,'" Hetta said, eyeing them warily over the rim of her cup, "is a very generous term."

That confirmed Kit's suspicion of tastelessness. "Nutritional" was how Mrs. Eaves described food with no taste and little texture.

"The Guild has built a ship," Kit said, getting to the business of it. She told Hetta everything, from Queenscliffe to Forstadt and back, but for the kiss. Nothing good would come of sharing that, or dwelling on it. And by the time the update was complete, Kit was exhausted.

Roast beef, she decided. She wanted a slab of roast beef, delicate potatoes, crusty bread. None of which she'd be eating at home. And more, instead of considering how she might spend an evening at home after many days at sea, she had another mission—and a social event—to prepare for.

She'd take a lie-down, she thought, just a few minutes to rest before an evening of intrigue.

～～

Kit woke with arms and legs flung wide on the narrow bed, was momentarily confused about her location and the time of day. But the clock said it was time to make her preparations, so she rose, cursing under her breath.

She found Jane in her rooms, frowning over a metal stand that held small glass tubes, each half-filled with pale yellow liquid. "More sparkers?"

Jane glanced up. Her hair was pinned up into curls, and she wore a lavender gown barely visible beneath the enormous white apron. "You're awake. Hetta said you'd come back, but needed rest." She turned her cheek so Kit could press a kiss there.

"A bit," Kit said.

"And no, I'm not making sparkers at the moment. Were they useful?"

"Incredibly. They caused some damage to the pirate fortress at Finistère."

Jane's smile faded. "Blast. I was hoping to see that one day."

"It's still standing, if a bit worn. And 'blast' is the appropriate word for it," Kit said with a grin. "Much noise, much light. They helped us free the man we'd gone to save." Even if they hadn't been able to save him afterward. And that was still a pinch beneath her heart.

"I'm glad to hear it. It's been quite the week here." She poured liquid from one vial into another, so they shimmered and changed into the rich blue of deep waters.

"Oh?" Kit asked, watching as Jane added yellow powder to that mix, which turned it into a rather unattractive green.

"The twins are rowing over a book, Mrs. Eaves is furious at the green merchant because the quality of rutabagas is, and I quote, 'pitiable.' Astrid has attracted the attention of a member of the Beau Monde—a Lord Langley, who's five thousand a year and a fine estate in the Western Isle."

That was quite a lot. "And you?" Kit asked.

Jane smiled. "I've received a new apron"—she gestured toward it—"and mudwort I've been waiting on for months. I am a woman of simple pleasures."

"Are you wearing my pearl earrings?"

"Borrowed," Jane said. "Much like your gloves."

"You'll be a bad influence on Louisa. How has she been?"

"In the few hours she's been here?" Jane asked with a grin. "Absolutely fine. She'll be rooming with Marielle, who's with the governess."

278 | CHLOE NEILL

Jane stirred the green mixture so what appeared to be solid droplets formed and swirled in the liquid, and then looked at Kit. "You've done your duty. Now, get on with it."

Kit's brows lifted. "What?"

"You're pacing, which means you're feeling impatient, which means you aren't done with your current mission, or you've been assigned a new one."

"On occasion, your observational skills make me very cross with you."

"And which occasion is this?" Jane asked with a grin.

"I need to ask another favor."

"More sparkers?"

"Actually, yes. But not tonight. I need a dress. And an escort."

Jane put the tube she'd been holding into its slot in the stand, turned toward her, gaze narrowed. "For what?"

"I have to go with Grant to Lambeth to identify a traitor. I need a gown and a chaperone, lest our reputations become sullied." She said the last with audible sarcasm.

"Well, well," Jane said, staring at her sister. "Those are not words I'd have thought to hear from you. Accompanying a viscount to Lambeth."

"It's a mission from the queen direct, so I've little choice in it. Although I like fireworks, and there will probably be sweets. And spies. Could you be our"—she struggled to voice the word—"chaperone?"

Kit didn't like the knowing smile on Jane's face.

"May I amuse myself at your expense?"

"Do I have another option?"

Grinning, Jane slipped her arm into Kit's. "This is going to be great fun."

⤙⤚

They adjourned to Jane's bedroom.

"We have some choices." Jane kneeled in front of the trunk, began to sort through the dresses folded carefully within it. "White muslin?"

"Too . . . sweet. Can't I just wear my uniform?"

"No. Wearing uniforms for moonlight strolling is unimaginative, which we decidedly are not." She frowned down at a dress, then up at Kit, gaze narrowed as if she were evaluating a portrait.

"No baubles." She found another, pulled it out, shook free the folds. It was the color of the cold ocean, captured in undulating silk. Gold braid at the edges of the sleeves and golden embroidery rising from the hem in loops and swirls.

"That's beautiful," Kit said, taking it from Jane.

"It's blue," Jane said, rising to watch Kit move to the tall mirror, sweep the dress in front of her.

"I love it," Kit said.

"I hate it," Jane said.

And they looked at each other.

"It's the color of the sea," Kit insisted.

"But it's a poor color for you."

"I wear a blue uniform every day."

Jane's expression was unapologetic. "I know."

Kit rolled her eyes but returned the dress to Jane, who put it aside.

"Now," Jane said, pulling out a third dress. "This might be something."

It was silk taffeta in deep red that shimmered faintly in the sunlight. There was no lace, no rope, no "baubles."

"Too bold," Kit said.

"I don't think so," Jane said, and this time she rose, swept the dress to the mirror. "Not for you. Come here."

Kit walked forward, prepared to dismiss the dress out of hand. Until Jane held it up to her, moved aside so she could see. The color put a glow against her cheeks, made her gray eyes more noticeable.

"We're supposed to be inconspicuous," Kit said, but swung the hem around so she could watch its crisp movement. "This is quite conspicuous."

"Which is exactly why it's perfect," Jane insisted. "No one would suspect a woman on a mission for the queen wearing a gown as noticeable as this."

She had a point. "I don't think I've ever seen you wear this."

"It's Astrid's," Jane said. "She wore it last year, discarded it. I was going to reshape it for the twins, but haven't had the time." Jane looked at Kit, grinned. "She'll be furious if you wear it."

"All the more reason."

Mrs. Eaves stepped into the doorway, surveyed the pile of discarded dresses. "It appears the children have swept through here."

"We're finding Kit a gown for Lambeth Gardens. She'll be accompanied by a viscount."

The shock that paled Mrs. Eaves's face would forever be etched into Kit's memory.

Kit was bathed, rouged, and perfumed, her pearl earrings re-claimed, satin slippers located. She found a reticule buried in her trunk, and tossed in several coins and the smallest knife she could find. Principle of Self-Sufficiency No. 2, and one of her personal favorites: Preparation is worth its weight in gold.

She'd just come downstairs, precisely on time, when the footman opened the door, and Grant walked in.

There was no threadbare linen, no patches. His ensemble was uniformly dark—trousers, waistcoat, tailcoat, boots—and tailored to show every honed muscle. He had no coat, no walking stick, no frilled cravat, no gloves. None of the ornaments that members of his class often used to emphasize their style or wealth. He didn't need them. His hair was brushed back, his eyes bright. He looked regal . . . and dangerous. Particularly when his gaze followed the line of her dress, his smile warming until she thought the heat of it might scorch the fabric.

She met his gaze with an arched eyebrow. His smile was utterly unapologetic. And they stood in silence for a moment, the unspoken things humming between them.

"Lord Grant," she said.

"Captain Brightling. That's not your usual ensemble."

"No, it is not," Kit said. "Did you find your brother?"

"Not entirely," Grant said, voice tight. "He's been staying at our town house, but hadn't returned overnight, at least not before I left."

"Perhaps he'll return by the time we're done this evening," Kit said, then glanced over at the polite throat clearing. Jane stood in the doorway in pale blue silk, her hair curled and piled up and bound by a ribbon in the same color. Jane didn't care for social gatherings, Kit thought, but she could certainly fit the part when the need arose.

Kit gestured to her. "Lord Grant, may I present my sister, Jane Brightling? Jane, this is Colonel Rian Grant, Viscount Queenscliffe. Jane will be chaperoning us this evening."

They exchanged polite nods.

"So you're Kit's Jane," Grant said. "The genius behind the explosives."

"'Genius' is a very overused word," Jane said. "But not here."

Grant smiled. "I see Kit comes by her confidence naturally."

"We are well trained in the art," Jane agreed, and looked him over. "You're tall for a viscount. And appear strong."

"It's unfortunate I've a borrowed carriage, or you could give my horses the same review."

"I do enjoy horses," Jane said. "Which is not a familial trait."

Kit made a vague sound.

"I'll have to take you and your sister riding sometime."

"Not in this lifetime," Kit said.

"Hello," said a voice above them. "I didn't realize we had company."

She descended the stairs with the bearing of a queen, pale skin against deep blue velvet. Her dark hair was piled in a complicated knot dotted with paste diamonds. And there was cunning in her green eyes.

"Astrid Brightling," Kit said as Astrid joined them, proud that her voice didn't simmer with irritation. "Colonel Rian Grant."

"Ah," Astrid said. "Viscount Queenscliffe, of course."

She would note the title.

"Pleased to make your acquaintance, Ms. Brightling," Grant said, then offered a small bow as she made an irritatingly elegant curtsy.

"Kit mentioned you'd served aboard her ship. That must have been quite a change for a man used to very . . . different circumstances."

He slid a glance toward Kit. "It was an . . . enlightening experience."

Astrid's smile was quick. "Aren't you very gracious, my lord?"

"Ever so gracious," Kit said tightly.

"Are you going to Lambeth, Ms. Brightling?"

"Unfortunately, no. Lord Dartmouth's ball is this evening, and everyone will be there. Oh," she said, mouth forming an apologetic curve. "That was so thoughtless of me. I didn't mean to suggest . . ."

You meant exactly what you said, Kit thought but didn't bother to say aloud.

But she did find the information interesting—that the meeting at Lambeth had been scheduled at the same time as a ball, when so many of the Beau Monde—and New London's leaders—would be at Lord Dartmouth's. The crowds at Lambeth would be thinner, giving the traitors more privacy.

Had that been a lucky coincidence, or was the person who'd proposed the meeting place familiar with the Beau Monde social calendar?

Behind them, a door opened, and there were footsteps down the hallway. Kit wondered if every other sister in the house intended to greet Grant, when Hetta appeared.

"Are we so rude that we must greet our guests in the foyer?" she asked. But she smiled up at Grant. "My lord."

"Mrs. Brightling, I presume. And please, call me Rian."

"And you'll call me Hetta," she insisted.

"Is that my dress?" Astrid asked, her voice a fierce whisper as Grant and Hetta made their nods.

"Not anymore," Jane said with a smile.

"Your daughters," Grant said, "or at least the ones I've met, are very formidable."

"Then I've done my job," Hetta said. "And how are things in Queenscliffe?"

"For the moment, settled. But there's work to do yet."

Hetta nodded. "Isn't that true for all of us? That we try to move forward, but always find a bit more that needs repair?"

"Wise words," Grant said with a nod.

"And we've taken up enough of your time," Hetta said. "You've activities to attend, fireworks to see."

"So we do," Grant said, and offered his arm to Kit. "Captain?"

She nodded, and prepared for a very different kind of battle.

TWENTY-FOUR

The carriage was white and gleaming, the horses nearly the same, and far enough away from the velvet seat that Kit decided it was safe to ignore them. For now.

They bobbed across New London and the Saint James to the towering stone gates that led into the garden, where dozens of carriages were depositing those who planned to meet lovers, or enjoy supper, or take in the night air with a few thousand friends.

Grant offered the gold coins for their entrance fee, offered Kit his arm.

"Purely professional," he said, but she didn't care for the glint in his eyes.

"Professional," she agreed, and placed her hand atop his arm, could feel the heat radiating from strong muscle.

This is going to be a long night, she thought.

"This is going to be a very interesting evening," Jane said behind them.

Lambeth was large, nearly ten acres of tree-lined walks, colonnaded salons, theaters, and boxes.

They strolled the main walk, bounded by standing lamps that spilled light through the darkness, and watched couples do the same. Their chaperones—looking mostly bored or envious—walked behind.

"What time is our rendezvous?" Jane asked, and Kit felt Grant's flinch.

"I wouldn't allow her to help us without understanding the risks," Kit said.

"Ten o'clock," Grant said after a moment. "The pavilion is on the other end of the park."

"And a known location for illicit liaisons."

"Then it's a perfect location," Grant said. "We've some time before the rendezvous. I suggest we work our way across the gardens just as any other visitors, and watch for anyone unusual."

A harlequin ran past them, tossing an enormous hoop into the air and catching it on the run, to the applause of the viewers.

"More unusual than that?" Jane asked.

"Differently unusual," Grant said, then glanced at Kit. "Is that plan agreeable to you, Captain?"

"I have no objections," she said. At present.

They strolled leisurely down one tree-lined path and up another, pausing now and again to watch some spectacle presented for the visitors' amusement. Tumblers, dancers, actors, a man who shaved ice from a block in a sling around his waist into small paper cones. The weather was perfect, the elderwood trees bright with green. And Kit saw no one who appeared to be a spy.

Kit had grown used to trousers and boots—the comfort and the practicality—and had forgotten the discomfort of thin slippers on stone paths, the necessity of constantly lifting one's hem outside to avoid dragging it through dirt and puddles and mud. And being New London, there were puddles aplenty at an outdoor garden. The slippers would be a noble sacrifice to this evening of patriotism. It was unfortunate, Kit thought, that she hadn't borrowed the slippers from Astrid, too.

They made pleasantly vague conversation while they watched the surroundings, shared a cone of pistachio nougats—most of which went to Jane in payment for her toils—before they made their way to the towering pavilion of brilliant crimson and gold tile roofs.

"Perhaps a bench," Grant said, pointing to a small covered seating box a few yards away.

"That would provide a good view," Kit agreed.

"And ample privacy," Jane murmured as they passed another box, where a couple were very indiscreetly entwined. "Have they no homes?"

"They do," Grant said, following her gaze. "But they're both married, and their spouses would probably frown on it."

They took seats on the bench, Kit between Grant and Jane, and Kit nearly sighed in relief.

"Problem?"

"Shoes," she said, lifting a torn and soiled slipper. "Boots are better. But would have looked horrid with this dress."

"It is a very becoming dress," Grant said quietly. "And a very proper ensemble."

Kit was glad they sat in half shadow and he couldn't see the heat that she felt rise up her cheeks. It was enough that they were pressed leg to leg on the bench. She didn't need the reminder of their . . . compatibility. Compatibility could not overcome their positions, their divergent fates.

"And you look nearly proper enough to escort a captain of the Queen's Own," Kit said, tossing back the volley.

"Well met, Captain," he muttered, and stretched out his legs to wait.

At a quarter till ten, a man approached. The path had been quiet for some time, so while they kept their positions, Grant in his half-reclined pose, she could feel the tension enter his body again.

The man marched down the path, and as he passed beneath a light, she recognized his face.

John Stanton, the boorish man from the Foreign Office she'd met in the palace. The man Kingsley had protected her against. He nearly strode past them, and Kit was thrilled by the possibility they'd found one of their traitors—and he was a man she already loathed. Until he stopped, looked over, and peered at Grant.

"Well, well," he said, and strolled closer. "If it isn't the viscount, returned to New London." His voice was slurred, his steps unsteady, and he smelled of the arrack sold in the salon. Her excitement dissipated. Unless he was a rather remarkable actor, this wasn't their man.

Grant cursed, rose. Kit and Jane followed suit.

"Stanton," Grant said, and the men bowed. "May I introduce Captain Kit Brightling and her sister Jane Brightling? Ladies, this is John Stanton of the Foreign Office."

Jane curtsied. Kit didn't move.

"We're acquainted," Kit said. "Mr. Stanton has thoughts about Alignment, and felt free to share them in the palace one day."

"Oh?" Grant asked, and his tone had gone hard. "Does he?"

"Surprised to see you here," Stanton said. "Didn't know you were back in town."

"I've some business," Grant said. "Why are you strolling alone through the gardens?"

"Why are you escorting foundlings in the gardens?" Stanton shot back.

"Stanton," Grant said sharply.

"I'm not wrong," Stanton said. "Plenty of women of good breeding and character. And coin. I understand you need a bit of the coin."

Grant glanced at Kit. "I see you were correct."

"About?" Kit asked.

"The boorish behavior of the Beau Monde. I find myself rather embarrassed to be part of the same class."

Stanton snorted. "You're barely clinging to membership, given the estate and your brother." He looked derisively at Kit, gaze settling on her décolletage. "And she's certainly got no money to enrich your coffers."

Completely unperturbed, Grant cocked his head at Stanton. "You're a very small man, aren't you?"

"I beg your pardon?" Stanton's tone was all outrage.

"Oh, I don't mean in stature. I find that anyone with such remarkable rudeness has made a very small impact on the world. Has contributed nothing of use to it."

Stanton took a hesitant step forward, had to look up at Grant. "I ought to call you out."

"You wouldn't dare," Grant said, boredom in his voice. "And I've more important considerations. Be off, Stanton, before you say something you'll regret."

She could see Stanton considering it, debating whether instigating a fight with Grant would be worth the cost he'd likely pay. And apparently decided against it.

"Trash," Stanton said. "The entire lot of you." And he stalked down the lane.

"'*O goddess sighted*,'" someone called out, and a man, tall with a mop of blond curls, emerged from the darkness. "'*In thine bower innocent, in thine profile divine.*'"

Kit smiled at the man who made his way toward them.

"Kit Brightling," he said, giving her a gallant bow. "You look absolutely ravishing."

Dorian Marten loved women, horses, and money, if not necessarily in that order. And Kit considered him a good friend. In addition to reciting poetry, he'd built Marten's, the coffeehouse where investors bought and sold the risk of sailing ships and the merchandise they carried, and he'd done it despite his Beau Monde father's objections. His father, the earl, was opposed to Dorian having a trade, and disowned him for the effort.

"I know nothing about this week's Crown transports," Kit said. "So flattery will do you no good here."

"Flattery eases the way socially," he said, and glanced at Grant. "And I believe this man with the rather angry expression is Viscount Queenscliffe."

"Rian Grant, Dorian Marten."

"Marten," Grant said.

"I believe I've seen you at the Seven Keys," Dorian said, "although I've not had a chance to play you at indigo. I hear you've a very talented hand."

Kit looked at Grant. "You play?" Indigo was the favorite card game of soldier and sailor alike. Thousands of hands had been played in the *Diana*'s forecastle.

Grant nodded. "I enjoy a hand now and again. Marten's is an impressive establishment."

"I prefer to think so," Dorian said, gaze sliding behind Kit.

"My sister, Jane Brightling," Kit said.

"Enchanted," Dorian said, and bowed over her hand.

Apparently realizing, belatedly, that Kit and Grant stood together, Dorian cocked his head. "Have I interrupted a rendezvous?"

"A pleasant evening in the gardens," Grant said smoothly, smiling mildly, but his gaze on the rendezvous point. "With an escort. Are you strolling alone?"

"I had plans to escort a young lady," Dorian said, "but circumstances conspired against us. I decided to come alone, as one never knows what one might find in the dark. And in this case, it was a captain and a viscount." He studied Kit and Grant, and peered very carefully over his shoulder before turning back again.

"I have the sense I should continue discussing inane things while something important occurs."

"That is exactly what you should do," Kit said, keeping her own eye on the pavilion. "How is business?"

"Very well, thank you. I've a pistol if necessary."

Grant's brows lifted. "Why are you carrying a pistol?"

"One never knows what one will find in the wilds of Lambeth Gardens. Other than snogging marquesses," he said, and gestured in the direction of the amorous couple.

There were footsteps behind them. Grant put a hand at Kit's back, fingers warm even through the fabric, and leaned toward her. If she hadn't seen the approaching men—and they were men, or so it appeared—both in greatcoats over full dress—she'd have thought he was teasing her again.

"Do you prefer left or right?" Grant whispered.

She giggled—her first experience at the sport, and she found it unsettling—and watched as the two men neared the pavilion, eyed each other for a moment, then nodded.

"Right," Kit decided, as she could more easily pivot in that direction.

"You're *so* funny," Jane said, apropos of nothing, but linking her arm through Dorian's as if he'd just shared the most enjoyable anecdote. It hit just the right note, added just the right amount of show, and Kit decided her sister could join her for an operation anytime.

Kit nearly jumped when the first firework burst, light and sound filling the air. And she wasn't the only one. Despite having planned to meet during the fireworks, the men jumped apart, looked around.

"Go," Grant said, jumping toward the man on the left.

Eyes on the other one, Kit pushed off into a run.

This wasn't his first time at Lambeth, Kit thought. She chased her quarry down the lane, where he dodged left and into the forest that covered the northern end of the gardens. Three acres of trees, streams, meandering dirt paths. If she lost him in the woods, he was as good as gone. Which was undoubtedly his plan.

Kit followed him through a copse of hackcherry trees, their

white petals a carpet across the ground that sent their fragrance—vanilla and musk—rising into the air. Another firework whistled, casting green light upon the landscape and the man fifteen feet in front of her.

The man glanced back, and she saw the flash. Kit darted left, but heard stitches tear along her sleeve, then the *thwack* of the blade hitting behind her. She turned, found a blade still wobbling in a tree trunk. "You bastard," she muttered, but pulled out the knife, spun it in her palm, and took off again.

His legs were longer, but Kit was faster, notwithstanding the dress and slippers, both of which would undoubtedly be ruined by the experience.

She decreased the distance between them to twenty feet, then fifteen. He darted to his right, running around a small pool and fountain. Kit followed him down the stone path that surrounded the pool, leaned forward, pushed harder, narrowing the gap to ten feet, and threw the blade already in her hand. She gauged her distance and flicked her wrist, sending the knife spinning through the air.

It struck him in the calf. He screamed, limped twice, pulled out the blade, and tossed it aside. Then he darted into a tallgrass meadow that lined the south side of the path.

"Oh, bloody hell," she said, hearing Grant's voice in her head.

The grass was easily five feet tall, and impossible to see through. She stood at the border, worked to slow her breath and catch the sound of footfalls, of movement, of shifting pebbles or scratching leaves.

She heard nothing.

The man was gone. Swearing, Kit walked back to the spot

where she'd hit him, picked up the man's knife, and slipped it into her reticule.

⁓

Kit followed the same path back to the pavilion, found Dorian waiting with Jane, and Grant emerging from another path.

"Nothing?" Grant asked.

Kit kept her gaze steady. "Dorian, could you escort my sister home?"

Jane lifted her brows. "Am I being excused?"

"I believe we both are," Dorian said. "My carriage is waiting, and I'm happy to escort Ms. Brightling, although I'm very disappointed I won't have the details on"—he gestured at Kit and Grant—"whatever this is."

"The nation's business," Grant said.

Jane looked at Kit, who nodded. "It would be best," Kit said, "while we finish things here."

"All right," Jane said with a sigh. "But I'm owed a good adventure." She looked at Dorian, who held out his arm, and then placed her arm in his.

Dorian smiled at Kit. "I'll call soon, if you're to be in town for a bit?"

"For now," Kit said.

"What do you know about the dionic acids?" Jane asked as they strolled back toward the entrance.

"Nothing at all," he said. "Enlighten me."

"You and Marten are friends?" Grant asked when they were alone again, a rather steely tone in his voice.

"We are," Kit said lightly. "And will continue to be." Since she was entirely uninterested in pursuing that line of discussion with Grant, she gestured toward the pavilion. "I didn't see his face. Did you?"

"No," Grant said after a moment. "Mine was in shadow."

Kit nodded. "Mine wasn't quite as tall as you. Pale skin—I saw his wrist between coat and gloves, but nothing identifiable. Except that he was wearing a Guild token."

Grant's brows lifted. "That was bold."

"Or stupid, given it implicates the Frisian consulate." She pulled out the knife, offered it to Grant. "He'll also be hobbling, favoring his left leg."

Grant's eyes widened. "You stabbed him?"

"He threw that at me. I threw it back."

Grant's smile was wide and pleased. "Well done, Captain. I'll have it delivered, along with a report, to Chandler. And I expect the queen will want to speak with us tomorrow."

"May I confess something?" Kit asked.

Grant placed the knife inside his coat. "You're disappointed Stanton wasn't our man."

Kit looked up at Grant. "Terribly disappointed. It would have been so satisfying to see him dragged before the queen. Next money's on Thornberry."

"It's not Thornberry."

"He's an ass," Kit said.

"Inarguably," Grant said. "But they rarely make good spies. They aren't nearly charming enough, and can't keep their mouths shut long enough to obtain information."

That made a certain disappointing sense.

A *plink* echoed in the silence, the sound of a droplet hitting the earth. Kit looked down, and saw crimson against the stone, and the trail of blood along her fingers from the gash in her arm.

"You've been injured," Grant said, and pulled Kit bodily into the light, turned her so the wound was visible. Red striped her biceps in nearly the same position he'd been injured at Finistère.

"He got my sleeve," Kit said, turning to look, "but I only heard the seam rip. I didn't feel anything. It's not so deep." But she began to feel it now, as if awareness had deepened the injury.

"It's deep enough," Grant said. He pulled a handkerchief from his pocket, rolled it, tied it around her arm. Tightly.

"*Ow*," Kit said.

"Now you know how it feels," Grant murmured, then added a second knot. "You need a physick, but our town house is faster. It's just over Lambeth Bridge."

"I have a handkerchief," Kit said. "Hetta can take care of the rest."

"Oh, definitely not," Grant said. "I'm not turning you over to Hetta so she can run me through for getting her daughter sliced up."

"Afraid of my mother?" Kit asked.

"Yes," he said. "Let's go."

TWENTY-FIVE

The Grant town house was directly across the road from Victory Park, and was very posh indeed. Four stories of pale stone and a colonnaded portico, precise shrubberies outside.

The front door was thrown open by a man in black, with tan skin and dark hair. "Colonel, thank god. Lucien's here. I sent a runner, as he's—" The man stopped, cast a wary glance at Kit. "Perhaps we should speak privately?"

"Inside," Grant said, and the man stepped back to allow them in. "What's happened?" Grant asked, when he'd quickly closed the door behind them. "You can speak frankly in front of Captain Brightling."

"Your brother is upstairs, in bed. He'd been stabbed. It's not life-threatening," the man added, before Grant could bolt for the staircase. "A skim across the ribs. I treated him. He'll be sore, but should heal well as long as he rests and the wound stays clean. He's sleeping now. He was rather . . . inebriated."

"Of course he was," Grant muttered. "Who attacked him?"

"I'm not certain, Colonel. He didn't say."

Grant closed his eyes, seemed to reach for composure. "That's a rather miserable coincidence, as Captain Brightling also incurred a knife wound. Brightling, Will. Will, Brightling. Will, can you please fetch the kit? I presume it's already at hand."

Will's lips twitched, but he managed not to smile at Grant's dry tone. "Of course, Colonel. One moment."

While he moved through a hallway, Kit looked around. The foyer was large and lovely, with gleaming floors and pale gold walls. A wooden staircase, also gleaming, curved to the second floor, and rooms stretched along both sides of the foyer. But they were virtually empty of furniture.

"Lack of funds," Grant said, before she could ask. "It was either keep the furnishings, or keep Will. I made the better decision."

"A former comrade at arms?"

"We served together on the peninsula," Grant said. "He's saved my life more than once. He's now the family's majordomo, and runs our New London affairs. And refuses to call me anything but colonel."

"For sailors and soldiers both, the title matters."

"So it does."

Will returned with a basket of items, looked between Kit and Grant.

"Thank you, Will. I'll handle this, then see to Lucien."

Given the snarl in Grant's tone, Kit nearly felt sorry for his brother.

⌐⌐

Grant tended to Kit's wound with a bit more finesse in the town house than the park, carefully removing the handkerchief, cleaning the wound, wrapping it with clean linen.

"It's not terribly fashionable," he said, when the linens were tied off. "But it will keep the wound clean. Although you'll likely still scar."

Kit smiled. "It would hardly be my first. I consider them badges of honor."

"You would," Grant said, and Kit thought she heard a compliment in the words.

"Although I do usually prefer my scars be accompanied by some sort of success."

"You saw the Guild token," Grant said. "Got the knife, and wounded the man. That's significantly more than I accomplished."

"I'd have rather caught him."

"One step at a time," Grant said, and put the remaining items in the basket. Then he cast a wary glance upstairs. "I'll check on Lucien, then arrange your transportation home."

Kit nodded. He wasn't any more likely to find a hackney at this hour than she was, but she could admit to curiosity about the wastrel brother.

"That's fine," she said. "I'll wait."

And when he took the stairs to the second floor, she waited an honorable amount of time before creeping up behind him.

❧

She heard them in a bedroom, and watched through the crack in the door.

A man sat up in a small iron bed. Sun-kissed skin, dark blond hair that brushed his shoulders, blue eyes not unlike Grant's. Grant stood nearby, body rigid.

"Why are you in New London?" Grant's voice was low,

threatening. The thunder that preceded a storm about to break. "And what the hell happened to you?"

Lucien glanced toward the window. "I owe money to someone who has very little patience for delay. I thought it best that I handle it myself."

"Gambling?"

"Does it matter?" Lucien said, his voice carrying as much fatigue as Grant's carried anger. "He wants the money now, and I don't have it. I came to town to work out terms." He lifted his nightshirt, showed the bandage across his ribs. "That was not successful."

"'To work out terms,'" Grant repeated. "You hoped to gamble your way into good fortune?"

"Of course," Lucien said, smiling mirthlessly as he lowered the shirt again, grimacing with the movement. Grant walked to the other end of the room, Kit guessed to keep from laying hands on his brother.

"I hadn't planned on being stabbed, brother mine. But, as you can plainly see, I have once again failed to live up to the Grant name."

"What's his name?" Grant asked. "The man to whom you owe money."

"It hardly matters. I'll deal with my own problems in my own time."

"Given you're laid up in the family town house, your problems have plainly *become* our problems. You can't possibly think silence and denial are helping you, or us, or the family."

"We all have our secrets. I understand you've been working for the Crown."

If Grant was surprised by his brother's knowledge, he didn't mention it. "There's work to be done, so I agreed to do it. If you hope to obtain information you can sell, you'll find that well quite dry."

Lucien lifted a hand, let it drop again. "Just attempting pleasant conversation. I understand that's what families are intended to do—speak with each other about things other than debts and violence and memories of things past."

Grant sighed, the sound so heavy—so tired—Kit wanted to walk in, to offer comfort. But she knew comfort wasn't hers to give.

"Give me his name," Grant said again.

Lucien lifted his gaze to the ceiling. "Xavier Forsythe."

The man who ruled New London's criminal underground, Kit thought, and believed no crime was off-limits. Theft. Blackmail. Murder. He ruled his world from the Abbey, a tough neighborhood in the center of New London. A dangerous man, Kit thought. And not one to whom she'd want to owe a debt.

"And before you begin your lecture, I wasn't aware I was playing cards with his money. Not at the time."

"And yet," Grant said.

"And yet.

"If you want something to bargain with," Lucien said, then winced as he leaned over to sift through items on a small table near the bed, "you can use this." He held out his palm. Kit couldn't tell what he offered, other than it appeared to be metal. At the widening of Grant's eyes, he hadn't expected to see it.

"Dare I ask why you brought that here?"

"Because it's time you take it. It's time you wear it." Lucien held it up, looked it over. A ring, Kit thought, of gleaming gold.

"You were going to give Father's ring to Forsythe to clear your debts. Why didn't you?"

"Because apparently there are depths to which even I won't sink," he said. "And it's not Father's ring. It's the viscount's signet. You, being the viscount, should wear it." He took Grant's hand, pressed the ring into it.

Grant's fingers curled, went white around the ring. "I've no interest in wearing his gold. I put it away for a reason after he died."

Lucien looked up at him, and for the first time, Kit saw sympathy there. "Father was a hard man. A difficult man. And while he may have been a sublime failure at running his estate, he cared for the tenants. For those who made the land what it was. If the queen absolves the debt, so be it. If she doesn't, so be it. But either way, you've more than made up for what he did. You've worked to put the estate to rights."

Grant gestured toward the plainly furnished room, Lucien in bed. "And to what rights, what illustrious heights, have I brought it? I have a broken title. A broken land. A broken family."

"So maybe what we've done isn't working," Lucien said quietly. "Maybe there's another way." And then he laughed hoarsely. "And maybe I'll suddenly be a happy and industrious brother, and cause no further worry." His voice was bitter now, tinged with regret and what Kit thought sounded like resignation.

Silence fell heavy between them.

"There will be changes," Grant said.

And hearing the authority in his voice, Kit knew that was the last word.

⁓

Kit scurried back to the first floor, positioned herself in front of a very ugly painting, and was there when Grant returned after, she guessed, collecting himself.

Kit turned back, found his features expressionless, his hand still fisted.

"Lucien?"

"He's fine," Grant said. "I'll hail a hackney."

Kit glanced toward the stairway, hoped she looked sufficiently confused by his dismissal. But he walked to the door, opened it, looked back at her expectantly.

"I'm sorry to send you home alone. But I've matters to see to yet."

Kit nodded, walked outside, waited in silence—watching him—while he hailed a hackney. When a carriage pulled to a stop, the clacking of hooves echoing in the darkness, he gestured toward it.

She looked at him for a long moment, neither of them blinking. Neither showing weakness. And then she climbed inside. "I'll see you in the morning if the queen summons us."

She fully expected the queen would summon them. But she felt a keen ache at the possibility that the queen wouldn't, and this would be their last meeting.

He looked at her then, one hand fisted around the ring, the other fisted around the open door, and seemed as if he bore the weight of the world on his shoulders.

As the hackney moved forward, she watched through the window as Grant walked back to the town house, then stopped, hands on his hips.

She stuck her head out, thumped the carriage to get the driver's attention. "Pull up to the crossroads, and stop. Wait until I say."

He did as she instructed. Leaning out through the small window, she watched Grant pace back and forth, back and forth. Then he stopped, waved another hackney, and climbed inside.

Kit knew exactly where he was headed.

"I've changed my mind," she called out to the driver. "Follow that driver."

❧

The driver was discreet enough to work for Chandler, Kit thought, rather impressed. He followed at a reasonable distance as Grant's carriage bounced through Victory Park to the Abbey, where the buildings huddled closer along the narrowing road, all of it soot-stained and gray.

Forsythe hadn't spent his fortune improving the neighborhood.

They made a final turn into a narrow lane when Grant's carriage slowed, came to a stop in the middle of the block. Kit slipped her driver coins before jumping to the ground, wishing she were back in trousers and had more than the small knife in her reticule. But needs must.

Grant looked up at the building, a dozen columns rising to the second floor, two guards in front of it. It would have been garish in Victory Park, was especially so amid the surrounding poverty.

Kit watched from a sheltered portico as Grant faced the guards. Apparently unperturbed, they looked at him with no interest.

"I need to speak with him," Grant said, and when the guards made no move, took a menacing step forward.

Perhaps, Kit thought, Grant had simply been too angry to recall that he was alone, or that there was an easier way to get into a New London establishment.

Kit walked up, pulled gold coins from her reticule, held them up. "Perhaps this will ease the way."

Grant went rigid, looked at her with unmitigated fury. But before he could argue, the coins were taken, secreted away.

"Upstairs," one guard said as the other opened the door. They walked inside. Tobacco smoke, thick and pungent and sweet, slithered through the door like fog, added its miasma to the neighborhood. Music slid through behind it, a song played on a violin.

"I have notes of my own," Grant said in a furious whisper, "and could have handled that."

"I suspect you'll need the notes when we get inside. And you can pay back the coin."

"You shouldn't be here."

"You shouldn't be here alone."

Grant growled. "We will discuss this."

"Undoubtedly," she said. "But not now. At present, we're a united front."

They walked through the fog into Forsythe's world, which appeared to be home of the Isles' entire supply of gilt and velvet. Every stationary surface had been covered with one or both of them, from walls to ceiling to the gold-painted floors. Mirrors in gaudy gilt frames were the only other decoration on the walls; useless, given the haze that obscured the reflections.

Their progress through the foyer was halted by a stone fountain: a gold cherub urinating into a pool.

"I suppose you can't purchase good taste," Kit murmured.

They glanced at the staircase, which rose up and curved to the left. They made their way up, hearing whispered conversation and that same syrupy song, but saw no one else along the way until they reached the landing.

A woman—a very large woman—stood outside a set of closed wooden doors with velvet panels and gilt scrolling around the edges. She cut an imposing figure. At least six feet tall, her body was strong and curvy beneath trousers and tailcoat.

"What do you want?" she asked, her tone as indifferent as her gaze.

"To speak with him," Grant said.

Unlike the men downstairs, the goddess was smart enough to get to the point. She simply held out her hand. This time, without hesitation, he pulled a note from his coat, offered it.

She took it, gestured toward the door behind her. "Careful with your step, and your words."

They walked inside, found red carpet and swagged velvet. And behind an obscenely ornate desk—literally obscene; fornicating couples had been carved into the front panel—sat the apparent criminal mastermind.

Forsythe was, at first glance, a very common-looking man. Pale skin, dark hair. Average height, average weight. Small dark eyes over a nose flattened at the bridge.

"Rian Grant, the viscount without funds." He looked at Kit, brow furrowed and fingers linked. "I don't believe we're acquainted."

He spoke quickly, words clipped as if they'd been scurrying around in his head, eager for escape. He'd come from the west, his voice still lightly accented, before he'd made camp in the Abbey, and there'd been no stopping him.

"You don't need to be acquainted with her," Grant said.

Forsythe's brows lifted comically. "Ah, that's the way of it, aye? I see." Eyes bright with excitement, he leaned forward. "And to what do I owe the pleasure of this visit? Or shall I guess?"

"My brother was stabbed earlier this evening."

Forsythe pressed a hand to his chest, moved his mouth into a circle of shock as he shifted his gaze to Grant. "No. An assault in our beautiful city? Your poor, sweet, debt-riddled brother. How is he?"

"He survived." Grant's voice was cold, his expression equally so.

"I'm so relieved," Forsythe said, features twisting into faux concern.

"I'm sure," Grant said. "What do you know about the assault?"

"Well, nothing, of course. I've been here in my humble home." He spread his hands. "My customers and staff would be happy to confirm that, of course."

"He owes you money."

"Many people do," Forsythe said. "The Grant family has fallen so far since your father's death, don't you think? The older son come back from war a changed man. The younger son throwing away his potential. It's all so tragic," he said, with a dramatic slump of his shoulders. "Oh, but it was you that left him and went off to play soldier, wasn't it?"

Grant lunged forward. Or would have, if Kit hadn't grabbed his arm.

Gone was the playfulness in Forsythe's eyes now. Gone was the toying smile. And in their place was coldness and fury. Forsythe slapped a fist on the table. He leaned back and ran a hand through his hair. "This is no longer entertaining. State your business or get out."

"How much does he owe?"

Forsythe named a figure that had Grant's jaw clenching, and would have kept every resident of the Brightling house in Portnoy's for a year. But Grant stayed calm, pulled a stack of papers from his pocket, held it out toward Forsythe. And the man's eyes went wild, like a dragon scenting gold.

"The complete sum," Grant said. "Plus one percent interest."

"The rate is higher."

"One percent," Grant said. "Or I will make it my personal mission to make your life hell."

Suddenly interested, Forsythe sat back in this chair, steepled his fingers. "Your titled friends also owe me money, and even if they don't, I know their secrets. They won't raise a finger against me."

Grant's smile was thin. "Not the titled, Forsythe. The soldiers. Those I fought with at Contra Costa. Those who know how many didn't fight because they made payments to the right parties. Payments that were funded by this establishment."

Forsythe watched him for a moment, head bobbing as he considered. "That's an interesting threat. But do you really think anyone in the ministry would punish me?"

"Oh, probably not directly," Grant said pleasantly. "But how long do you think it will take for your revenues to go down when former regimentals are camped on your doorstep, watching everyone who enters, and your name has been so thoroughly dragged through the gutters that no one—no one—from the ministry would risk doing business with you any longer?"

Forsythe went rigid, hands shaking with anger. "You don't have the connections."

"Try me," Grant said. And given his perfectly mild expression, Kit surmised how Grant was good at playing indigo.

"Get out," Forsythe said.

"Say it," Grant said. "Say it, in front of my witness, that Lucien's books are clear."

Forsythe had gone so taut with quivering rage that Kit thought he might simply snap.

"Lucien's books are clear," he said, each word an obvious battle. "Now get the hell out."

✌

They didn't argue, and had only just emerged from the room when the sound of breaking glass echoed behind them. Having a tantrum, Kit guessed. A good thing there was decor to spare.

Kit and Grant moved swiftly back through the building, Grant fuming silently until they emerged outside. Kit breathed deeply of the fresh air, and followed him up the road, which was silent in the darkness but for the barking of a lone dog, the whispers of men huddled near a fire.

"You had no right," Grant said, his strides so long Kit had to nearly run in her dress and slippers to keep up. But she wouldn't ask for quarter from him. Not now.

"You could have trusted me," she said.

"It's not a matter of trust. It's not your burden to carry any more of my problems," Grant said, stopping short, turning to her. "For gods' sake. How much of the Grant family's misery do I need to spread at your feet? My family is a mess. My estate is a mess. For three years, I've worked to bring the estate back from the ruin made of it while I was gone. And yet, it remains—"

"A mess?" Kit offered, and enjoyed the heat that fired in his eyes. Better anger than this frustrated hopelessness. A good rage might burn some of it away.

"You don't understand."

"Being titled?" Kit asked. "Having the ability to settle your brother's debts by tossing down notes? Having the privilege of time to resolve those debts without his being thrown into debtors' prison?"

He stopped, looked down at her. "That's not making me feel better."

"It wasn't intended to," she said. "It was intended to make you think." She resumed walking.

He growled behind her, but followed. "I won't foist my problems onto someone else. There's nothing principled, nothing titled, in that."

"Have you demanded I pay his debts?"

"Of course not. I—"

"Then you've hardly foisted anything on me." This time, she stopped. "I've witnessed the facts of your existence, just as you've witnessed some of mine. And that they aren't my burdens doesn't mean I can't help."

"I don't need help."

She snorted. "You do if you think marching into Forsythe's lair alone was a good idea."

And then his hand was on her arm, long fingers sending heat across her skin. Kit swallowed hard, thought again of the kiss, scorching after her trip into frigid seas.

"No rules of engagement apply in Forsythe's world. You could have been hurt."

She lifted her gaze to his. "As could you. And you were angry, which is hardly an ideal way to strategize."

"I was bloody furious," Grant said, dropping his hand. "I'm sending him home as soon as he's well enough to travel."

"Will he stay if you send him back?"

Grant opened his mouth, closed it again. "I don't know. And that is a slice through the gut."

"He's not your responsibility."

"He's my brother."

"And an adult. I'm not suggesting you shouldn't care, or offer him help. But he's going to make his own choices, good or bad. That's not a failure on your part."

Hands on his hips, Grant closed his eyes, sighed heavily. "It's bloody irritating, Brightling, when you say insightful things like that."

Kit understood the storm had passed. "Let's walk to the circus. We can find a hackney home."

"Home being the key consideration," Grant said. "I think we've had enough excitement for one evening."

TWENTY-SIX

The summons came the next morning as she was pulling on her boots. She was mildly irritated at herself for being excited to see Grant again.

"*Viscount*," she reminded herself, and thought of the viscountess's rooms at Grant Hall, the fine fabrics and soft furnishings, and the misery of being captive inside that prison instead of on the sea, where she belonged.

She met him in the palace, just outside the throne room. They exchanged nods. His tailcoat was dark blue, a shade that nearly matched what she'd seen inside the Northern Sea.

"You're back in uniform," he said.

"It is a relief."

"It is a pity," Grant countered. "You were very fetching in red."

"I find the uniform suits me best," she said. And from the tension in his jaw, he didn't seem to care for the reminder of the obstacle between them.

"Lucien?" Kit asked.

"Was asleep when I left," Grant said. "I asked Will to keep an eye. Your sister?"

"Home safely, without even an improper word from Dorian, which is a rather remarkable surprise."

Grant bit back a smile. "I presume you managed not to follow another hackney on the return home?"

"I considered following the Earl of Glenndon," she said with a glint in her eyes, "but given he has nearly ninety years, I thought it would be a very dull trip. A woman must have standards, after all."

They were admitted with haste, found Chandler with the queen. Chandler in navy today, the queen in gleaming gold.

"The traitor was wearing a Guild token," the queen said with disgust when they reached the throne. Grant had apparently managed to send an update, Lucien and Forsythe notwithstanding.

"He was, Your Highness."

"Any possibility that you mistook a button or medal, or the token of some other merchant or organization?"

"No, Your Highness," Kit said. "I saw the eagle quite clearly."

The queen sighed heavily. "I'd hoped against hope the report was wrong. In matters as sensitive as this, one must confirm." She glanced at Chandler. "You've made discreet inquiries about the wounded man?"

"I have, Your Highness, and will advise."

The queen nodded, looked back at Kit. "I understand you were injured during the operation."

"A minor laceration."

"From the knife you collected and then threw back at the traitor."

Kit nodded.

"In that case, well done." The queen sat back, looked over Kit and Grant. "You've become a surprisingly reliable team. Your reliability, of course, is not surprising." The queen smiled. "But your ability to work together was."

It still surprised Kit.

"We know the Guild is involved in the creation of the ship, the passage of information to Gerard or his allies. That, in turn, implicates Frisia," the queen said, gesturing for Chandler to continue.

"They have a ship," Chandler said. "And apparently a ship that utilizes magic in some form. We need to know the Guild's plan. Where they intend to sail it, what they intend to attack. Those plans are likely inside the consulate, probably in the office of the Frisian ambassador."

"Once again," the queen said, "and until we identify the traitor within the Crown Command, we must impose upon you. Infiltrate the consulate," she said. "And find what plans you can."

The situation was too dire for excitement, Kit knew. The threat of war too serious. But Kit couldn't help but be . . . intrigued . . . by the possibility of sneaking through a foreign consulate.

"If you are caught," the queen said, expression grim, "your mission will not be acknowledged by me or the Crown Command. We will disclaim any knowledge of your activities. That is a risk you must consider. And because of that, if you wish to decline, that declination will not be held against you."

Grant and Kit looked at each other. Kit expected he saw anticipation in her eyes, and she saw determination in his. They nodded, looked back to the queen.

"Understood," Kit said.

"We can provide a plan for the building," Chandler said. "But it's not been updated since the war, so it may not prove especially helpful."

This time, Kit felt utter confidence. "I believe I know someone who can assist us."

⟿

It was the last town house in a row, situated on a narrow lane only a half mile from her own. White brick, with a door on the right-hand side and a small plot of flowers on the left.

Kit used the iron knocker—shaped like an anchor, of course—and waited for a response.

The woman who answered a moment later was tall and striking, with light brown skin and dark, gleaming hair in a sleek knot at the base of her neck. Her nose was straight, her eyes wide, her mouth a small bow.

"Kit! How lovely to see you." Her brows lifted at the sight of Grant behind her. "Is everything all right?"

"It is, Nanae. And I apologize for interrupting your time with him, but we need to speak with Jin."

"Of course. Come in, come in.

"Oh, hello," she said, with a grin that was as much interest and intrigue as surprise. "I don't believe we're acquainted."

"Rian Grant," he said, and made a perfect bow.

"Ah, the soldiering viscount," she said with a sly smile. "I'm Nanae Takamura. Please come in."

She stepped aside while they entered, and closed the door behind them. The foyer was small, a parlor to their right, a narrow staircase leading up to the second floor. A hallway led back to the kitchen.

"Our housekeeper, Mary, has the catarrh, so we're a bit out of sorts," Nanae said, then led them into the parlor.

Jin sat on a sofa of green velvet. With one hand, he cradled their youngest, Emi, who chewed contemplatively on a small toy. In the other, he held a small book. His older daughter, Saori, was curled on his other side, gaze on the book.

It was, Kit thought, a pretty perfect visage.

"I'd rise to greet you," Jin said quietly, eyes dancing with humor, "but there are two very heavy weights upon me."

He wore no uniform today, but buff trousers and a matching vest, his long legs booted and stretched out in the sunlit room. His long, dark hair was loose, framing his oval face. It was a side of Jin she rarely had the opportunity to see.

"We're sorry to bother you," Kit whispered. "It's just that we need your . . . unique advice."

His brows lifted with interest, his eyes alight with it. "I enjoy providing unique advice."

Nanae smiled knowingly. "Let me take the girls," she said, then lifted Emi from Jin's lap. "Come, Saori. Let's go have a bit of lunch."

She hopped off the couch and took her mother's outstretched hand, but looked back with wide eyes at Kit and Grant.

Kit watched them leave. And wondered, not for the first time, how difficult it was for Nanae to raise two children while her husband, her partner, was gone for months at a time, and she'd receive only sporadic updates about his safety. Kit wasn't sure how they managed it. The separation, the fear, the danger.

"All right," Jin said with a smile. "What are you planning to steal?"

"We aren't sure yet," Kit said. "But we'll find it in the Frisian consulate."

Jin's eyes went wide. "There are very few times that I regret the loss of my rather adventurous bachelorhood. This may be one of them."

"It would be a joy to have you along on our felonious adventure," Kit said. "But your place, for now, is here. However, if you've ideas, we could use them."

Jin's smile was bright and broad. "Oh, I have ideas. Take a seat," he invited, and waited until they had. "Now," he began, when his pupils were ready. "There are four means of ingress on the first floor of the building."

∽

It was specific. That was Kit's first and last impression of Jin's plan. It was very, very specific.

"He's put great thought into this," Grant said outside.

"He puts great thought into everything he does," Kit said. "He enjoys evaluation and consideration. But this particularly? Yes. Jin is as skilled a thief as you will ever meet."

"A good thing he's on our side."

"Yes," Kit agreed. "It is."

They returned to their respective homes, waited until darkness fell, and met outside the consulate, both in black. Kit had borrowed a jacket from a footman, paired it with dark trousers and boots. Grant wore a dark greatcoat over a dark ensemble.

"Are you ready?" he asked.

"I've been waiting all day. Finding evidence of treachery is more enjoyable than I'd have imagined."

"Yes," Grant said dryly. "It's only the being caught and imprisoned that ruins the mood."

The Frisian consulate was three symmetrical stories of columns and windows in white stone. As Jin had warned them, the main entrance was in the middle of the front facade, and was guarded by soldiers. So they weren't going in that way.

The consulate was the middle of three buildings that stood in a row. On the right, the offices of the Isles' revenue department, where taxes were levied, stamps were issued, paperwork was reviewed. It had its own entrance and, by some determination of the architects, a door in its basement that led into the consulate.

No one bothered to guard the paperwork, Jin said, and Kit and Grant walked easily inside the front doors of the revenue building, offered severe nods to the only human they passed as they moved through the quiet hallway and then down a flight of stairs to the basement.

They passed shelf after shelf of leather-bound ledgers in green and red, and more than a few spiderwebs, to the very back of the storage space. And the narrow wooden door that led into the consulate.

Carefully, Kit turned the knob, bracing her body as if to ward off the sound.

It turned silently, and she pulled it open, glanced inside.

From revenue basement to consulate basement, and revenue storage to consulate storage. More ledgers, more files, and more doors. They crept through tall shelves of ledgers and boxes to another opening, then into a long corridor with more locked doors.

It was quiet enough here that Kit could hear her own heartbeat, currently pummeling her ribs as adrenaline pumped.

The corridor ended in a simple wooden staircase. They stayed against the wall, moved upward to the main level, and waited just outside the doorway.

The building was silent. But as Jin had promised, it took only moments for slow steps and a bobbing light to come nearer, pause, pass. A guard on duty, making a search of the floor.

When silence fell again, they crept down the corridor, then to the grander wood and iron staircase. They took the steps two at a time, then peered around into the second floor, found it empty.

The ambassador's office was at the end of the hallway in a suite of rooms that overlooked the road, the palace beyond. They saw no one, and the door was closed, no light beneath. And as Jin had promised, unlocked. So confident were the Frisians that no one would make it past the guards.

Ironic that they could also use the advice of a thief, Kit thought.

Grant opened the door, and they slipped inside. He found a beeswax candle on a side table and lit it, and they looked around. Sitting room, necessary room, and office proper. The office was smaller than Kit had expected, but neatly appointed, with fine furniture and a desk of pale and gleaming wood.

Kit moved to the desk, and in the dim candlelight, began inspecting each pile. Found personnel records, budgets, summaries of foreign trade. Nothing even remotely resembling a state secret. Frustrated, she moved into the center of the space, turned a circle to take another look, and felt something shift beneath her feet.

There you are, she thought.

"Grant. Bring the light."

He moved over, the candle casting a circle of light over the floor.

Kit pressed a toe against the other end of the board, and it popped up, revealing a small, dark hold. "One of my favorites," she said, and reached inside, pulled out a small diary bound in black leather. And beneath it, two leather portfolios of papers.

She took those, too, closed the board again. From inside the first portfolio, she found a folded drawing. Casting a cautious glance toward the hallway, and finding it dark and quiet, she spread the document on the table.

It took a moment for Kit to parse what she was looking at; the shapes and lines were so foreign to anything she'd seen before. And then she understood.

It was a ship. An enormous one, nearly two hundred feet from bow to stern. Two decks of guns, and two spindly masts that weren't nearly large enough to move the bulk of it, and were disproportionately short. And between them, an apparatus. Some kind of machine, she thought, with gears visible, attached to a long cabinet.

A ship whose sails, perhaps, were only necessary in limited circumstances, so they needn't be as many or as large. A ship that relied on whatever was inside that box to operate.

She flipped through the other pages in the portfolio, but found no other schematics. Grant had done the same, shook his head.

"There will be another drawing," Kit said, pointing at the box. "Of what, exactly, this is, and how it operates. We have to find it."

Kit went back to the desk, looked through the piles again, hoping she'd missed something in her first perusal, because this was the information they needed.

Something clattered in the hallway. Kit blew out the candle, slapped a hand over Grant's mouth as they watched light glow beneath the door. The doorknob rattled once, then twice. Then the light faded again.

Then she pulled her hand away.

"I wasn't going to speak," he whispered.

"Abundance of caution," Kit said. "They might be back. We need to go."

"I'll take the portfolios," Grant said, and began to slip them inside his coat. "It will be easier for me if we're caught."

"Because you're a man or a viscount?" Her voice was dry.

"Both," he said evenly, gaze level.

Kit supposed she could appreciate the chivalry. But she didn't need to be coddled.

"We each take one," she said, and held out her hand.

He handed her a portfolio, and she stuffed it inside her coat, ensured the buttons were tied. Time to make their escape.

⌇

Another hackney home again, this time with Grant in accompaniment. He ignored her declarations that she could make the trip on her own.

"I'll be watching to see if we're followed," he said, and pulled out a small pocket mirror, which he used to survey the street behind him.

"Clever," she said, and was glad he'd thought of it, as she certainly didn't want to lead anyone back here.

She opened the door quietly, found Jane inside in her wrapper, toe tapping.

"You're late," Jane said as Grant followed Kit inside.

"I told you not to stay up," Kit said.

"It's so late," Grant agreed. "Surely you need sleep."

"Having your sister involved in sorting out treachery is not good for slumber." Jane's mouth thinned. "I like you, Colonel Grant, so I'll excuse your telling me what I do and do not need, given I've lived in this body for twenty-two years, so I'm fairly well aware of it."

Grant worked to bite back a smile. "I stand corrected."

Jane inclined her head. "Now that you're home, I'll just go to bed." She leaned forward, kissed Kit's cheek, then narrowed her gaze at Grant. "Go away," she said firmly, before turning on her heel and making for the stairs.

"The Brightling girls are very independent sorts," Grant said.

"We are," Kit agreed, then yawned hugely. "I'll admit to needing sleep, so we can spare that particular argument. Breaking into government offices is rather exhausting."

"There's little about espionage that isn't. One grows used to it." He turned for the door, then looked back. "You said I didn't trust you—about Lucien. I do trust you," Grant said. "But your bravery is rather terrifying."

That might have been the nicest compliment he'd given her.

She nodded. "Good night, Grant."

"Good night, Brightling."

TWENTY-SEVEN

She'd planned to review her portion of the consulate documents by candlelight in her own bed. But she fell asleep the moment she hit mattress and linens. When she woke, dawn light barely breaking through the window, her hand was still atop the portfolio.

Assuming the queen would summon her again soon enough, Kit pulled out the documents, began to review each one. Most were in Frisian. She recognized a few words, but only a few, and not enough to give context to what she was seeing. There were dated reports, ledger pages with entries, including one describing a ship called the *Julianna* that had made its way from New London to Pencester.

Wait, she thought. She knew that ship. Not a Crown ship, but a merchant. It was the ship Kingsley boarded the day Grant had joined the crew of the *Diana*.

"Coincidence," she murmured, as was the fact that it had sailed for Pencester, the city where the Cork and Barrel was located. She felt the tightness in her chest, but ignored it, focused on the words, on the documents.

And toward the back of the pile, found a letter on pale ivory paper, written in Islish. Very short, very brief.

C&B confirmed drop. Msg from Home rec'd.
Fleet locations to follow.

Cork and Barrel confirmed as a drop location, Kit translated from the shorthand. Message from home received. Fleet locations to follow.

It was signed, in a long and confident scrawl, *Chas. A. Kingsley.*

All the breath left her.

It had been Kingsley.

He'd passed information from the Crown Command—from Chandler's office—to the Frisians, the Guild, the consulate. And he was going to tell them where the Isles' ships were located. He was going to hand over to Gerard the location of the Crown Command's ships—the entire fleet. Given what they'd found at Forstadt, it wasn't difficult to guess why: so Gerard could plan for the launch of his warships—and their attacks.

And not just that: Kingsley had given up Dunwood's alias. Kingsley was the man intended to meet the dispatch at the Cork and Barrel. And it was Kingsley whom Grant had chased through the gardens, and who was arrogant enough that he'd signed a damned letter to a damned enemy.

Kit's rage was so hot, so bright, she thought the paper might ignite in her hands. She tossed the letter down with the others, shoved them into the portfolio, then paced to the other end of the room, back again, wondering, hoping, that she'd misread something, misunderstood something, and hadn't really seen proof that her friend was a traitor to his country. Fury tangled with guilt that she'd failed to see his perfidy.

But she realized there was nothing to do now but report, and stop him before he could hurt anyone else.

She dressed, put the message inside her coat, and left for the palace. She'd only made it to the street to find a hackney, when someone called her name.

"Kit, thank gods."

She looked up, found Kingsley striding toward her. And mustering every ounce of reserve, she schooled her face to blankness.

Furious though she was, the country's business didn't need to be conducted in the street. She linked her hands behind her back, squeezed her fingers together until they ached—until she'd regained some control.

"Kingsley," she said brightly. "What brings you here?"

"You do," he said, took a step closer, fear etched into his features. "Can we speak privately?"

Oh, we'll be speaking, you perfidious bastard, she thought. But managed a quizzical expression. "Of course. We can go inside."

She wasn't thrilled at the idea of inviting a traitor into her home, but she wasn't naive enough to get into a hackney with him. And most everyone was still asleep.

"I—" He looked up at the house, watched it for a moment. "Yes, that would be fine. That would be best. This isn't proper talk for the street."

Kit led him inside, and she was relieved to find the house still quiet. She gestured him into the parlor, closed the door.

"I'm sorry," he said, when they were alone. "I shouldn't have come so hastily."

"Of course," she said. "What's happened?"

He moved a step closer. "I've heard you were injured at some kind of stampede at Lambeth Gardens." He made a show of looking her over, but her bandages were hidden beneath her uniform coat.

Here to fish for information, Kit thought with disgust. He must have known the noose was tightening. She wasn't going to make it easy for him.

"Lambeth Gardens?" she asked with a laugh. "What would I be doing at Lambeth Gardens? I'm not exactly the strolling-couple type. Were you there?"

"No," he said, brow furrowed. "But I'd heard from . . . Chandler . . . that you were injured."

Flustered, she thought. And hadn't expected her to deny it. So she let it play out, wondering how long it would take before he pulled away the disguise. She let her eyes widen. "Chandler? Your Chandler? Why would he care if I went to Lambeth Gardens?"

He watched her for a moment. "I suppose I was confused."

"It's fine," she said, and watched his eyes. "But surely you didn't come all the way here to ask me about a rumor?"

"It's just . . . I was very surprised. And worried."

"I'm fine," she said. And thought there was no point in wasting more time. "But while you're here, what do you know about the *Julianna*?"

She gave him credit; if she hadn't been watching, she wouldn't have seen the hitch. But a man engaged in treason was probably well practiced in denial.

"The *Julianna*," he repeated, brow knit in confusion. "The ship?"

"The ship," Kit confirmed. "She was used to pass confidential information to Frisia."

"Confidential—for treason?"

His look of shock was perfect. So flawlessly executed she wondered for an instant if she'd been wrong, drawn the wrong conclusion. And then she thought of that tall and confident signature—*Chas. A. Kingsley*—and doubt slid away again.

She took a step toward him. "You were on that ship, Kingsley. You were on the *Julianna* to visit Pencester, to visit the Cork and Barrel, to obtain what messages might be waiting for you and, I presume, leave a few for the *Amelie*."

His eyes flashed. "You're making very serious accusations, Kit. Serious and offensive. If you were a man, I'd call you out."

"Call me out," she said. "I dare you. I've seen your note, Kingsley, your scrawl about providing fleet information to Gerard. Have you any idea how many sailors that places at risk? How could you?"

"Now wait," he said, and held up his hands. But she ignored him.

"Do you have any regret? Any remorse? Or are you so taken with Gerard that you don't care who you hurt?"

"You'd best watch your tone." Kingsley's voice was icy now. And, she thought, more honest. He made her stomach turn.

"Or what?" she said, taking a step forward. "I've never known you to take a shot, Kingsley. You prefer words and paper and intrigue, yes? So perhaps you'd like to try now?"

He looked at her for a moment, hatred flaring. And then it disappeared.

"Fine," he said with a haggard sigh. "As it appears you aren't going to back down, we'll go to Chandler, and we'll sort this nonsense together." He glanced at a sideboard where Hetta kept a bottle of scotch for guests. "Do you mind if I have a drink first? Soothe the nerves?"

Kit inclined her head, shifted to watch him as he moved across the room.

"There's a glass there," he said, gesturing to the side table, "if you'd like a drink, as well. I think we could both use one."

Instinctively, she turned toward the table. And felt blinding pain across the back of her skull.

Damn it, she thought, as she slipped to the floor. She should have seen that coming.

⤳

She smelled something sharp, bitter, and opened her eyes, found Grant on his knees in front of her.

"Hello," he said, voice bland. "Sit up slowly," he said, hand at her back.

Kit sat up, wincing at the pain in her skull. Her thoughts felt a bit slow, too. She reached back a hand, felt the hard knot. "It's Kingsley, Grant. The bastard hit me."

"So he did," Grant said.

Mrs. Eaves worried behind them, brow furrowed, fingers knit in concern. "Should I send for the physick?"

"No, thank you," Grant said. "I believe we'll be all right here."

Because Kit's mind wasn't as quick as usual, she looked at Grant for a moment. "Why are you here?"

"I found Kingsley's name in the portfolio, and came to tell you. Jane let me in, and we found you like this."

She looked up, found Jane behind him, still in her wrapper. It was still early yet, then. She hadn't been unconscious for long.

"The door was closed," Mrs. Eaves said, apology heavy in her voice, "or I'd have seen you sooner."

"Did you see him leave?" Grant asked them.

Both shook their heads.

Grant nodded. "Could you please both give us a moment alone?"

Mrs. Eaves lifted her chin. "That's hardly appropriate for two unmarried people."

"It's to do with the queen," Kit said patiently.

Mrs. Eaves arched an eyebrow, but nodded, then scooted Jane out the parlor door and closed it again.

"Did he tell you anything?" Grant asked when they were alone.

She shook her head. "He said he came here to ask me about Lambeth Gardens. He said he'd heard I was hurt. I asked him about the *Julianna*."

"The *Julianna*?" Grant asked, and Kit explained its involvement, then pulled out the message she'd found, let him read it, understood his muttered curses.

"His response?" Grant asked, handing it back to her.

"He denied any involvement. Suggested we go speak with Chandler to clear up the confusion. I turned my back on him for a moment, and then I was on the floor."

"Cowardly," Grant said. "To strike from behind."

Kit couldn't disagree, but that didn't diminish the embarrassment. "Did you know he was the traitor?"

That Grant looked surprised by the question calmed her some. "No. Why do you ask?"

"Before we first sailed on the *Diana*, it was obvious you didn't care for him." Or for my talking to him, she thought silently.

Just as it had on the dock that day, Grant's expression darkened. "I didn't care for him because he is a coward. He was stationed in the Crown Command personnel bureau before moving to Chandler's office. He was known to use his position, his influence, to affect the assignments of those he didn't like. There was no hard evidence, of course, that decisions were made based on his animosity, but soldiers who didn't give him the respect he believed he deserved found themselves in the most dangerous regiments, the longest assignments."

"Dishonorable and treacherous," Kit said. She took a breath, and when she thought her head was steady enough, offered Grant her hand. "Help me up?"

"Of course," he said mildly, lips just curved, and took her hand in his. His hand was warm, his grip solid.

"Let's go talk to the queen," Kit said as he pulled her to her feet.

~~~

Grant had already delivered his bundle of papers, including the ship drawing, to the palace. They were immediately escorted into the throne room, and walked inside to find the queen with Kess and Chandler. All three looked grim, and there were shadows beneath Chandler's eyes.

"It was Charles Kingsley," Kit said, offering the message she'd found. "He's the one who's been passing information to the Guild, to Frisia." And she and Grant provided the information they'd found.

Queen Charlotte read the note, slammed a hand on her throne. "That perfidious bastard." At least, Kit thought, they were of a like mind.

She offered Chandler the message, pierced him with a stare. Chandler sighed as he read it, tucked it into his coat.

"One of yours, Mr. Chandler," the queen said. "I find that very disappointing."

Chandler inclined his head. "As do I, Your Highness. He's served the office without rebuke or complaint in the years he's been there. That's not offered as an excuse. Merely an explanation. I can only offer my apologies to the Crown—and my promise that he will pay for his treachery."

"Where is he?" the queen demanded, looking back at Kit.

"I don't know, Your Highness. He confronted me at home, and knocked me out. He was gone when I came to." Kit rubbed the back of her head. The dizziness had mostly gone, but she could still feel the ache.

The queen's brows lifted. "And Hetta allowed him to walk away?"

"She wasn't yet awake, Your Highness."

"Find him," the queen said, and nodded at Kess, who hurried to the throne room's side door.

"Janssen is the name of the man you injured at Lambeth," Chandler said. "He's an attaché at the Frisian consulate, concerned mostly with information gathering and analysis. He appeared at the office yesterday, where his injury was noted. Apparently having feared he would be identified and have no bargaining power, he's made a full confession and thrown himself on the leniency of the throne."

"The throne," the queen said with narrowed eyes, "is not presently inclined toward lenience."

The side door burst open. Surprised by the noise, and careful of his queen, Chandler moved to block the throne from whatever threat might be coming. But it was Kess, hurrying forward with a note.

The queen leaned forward. "Kess?"

"He has absconded with a Crown ship," Kess said, nearly breathless, and handed a piece of paper to the queen.

Lip curled with disgust, she read it, then passed it to Chandler. Kit knew better than to interrupt their review.

"He stole a ship," Chandler repeated as he scanned the document. "Along with documents identifying the locations of all major squadrons in the fleet, which were apparently taken from the admiral's office."

"He's had a very busy week," the queen said dryly.

"The bastard," Chandler said.

"We do not disagree," the queen said, and looked at him, this time with sympathy. "The problem with espionage is that it's rarely what's obvious. It's what we cannot see."

"Which ship did Kingsley take?" Kit asked.

"The *Forebearer*," Chandler said.

"A schooner," Kit recalled. "Smaller than the *Diana*. Two-masted, gaff-rigged. No guns. She often carries medical supplies, has red jibs to signify." And she was too big for one person to sail, Kit thought, even assuming Kingsley had any skills. Which meant he had accomplices. "How many more are with him?"

"Based on the report," Kess said, "there were six. Including two current Crown Command sailors. They'd been on the *Julianna*."

"They'd been planning this," Kit said. "The *Forebearer* requires a crew. They'd need supplies, and the sailors would have to be ready, loyal." She looked up at the queen. "You saw the drawing?"

"We did," she said. "And it appears to match Dunwood's intelligence. Your thoughts?"

"A new type of warship," Kit said, "that's intended to be maneuvered by whatever magic-manipulating implement is within that cabinet."

"Then why the sails?" the queen asked.

"Likely to compensate in waters where there's less magic. It wouldn't be fast under sail, not a ship that large with only two masts, but it didn't appear to lack for guns. It would make up for speed with firepower."

"We searched for additional schematics," Grant said, "but found none."

"So Frisia has some sort of new warship, and Kingsley has a schooner, and they can sail the oceans together." There was disgust in the queen's voice.

"Where would Kingsley go?" Grant asked.

"*Forebearer* isn't an ocean-going vessel," Kit said, "so he'd be bound for somewhere relatively close. Narrow Sea, Northern Sea, a coastal port in the Western Isle or the Continent. Not farther than that."

"Montgraf," Chandler said. "Frisia. Perhaps some other island which Frisia is using to build or fuel their ships."

"He must be found immediately," the queen said, leveling her gaze at Kit. "Your mission, Captain Brightling, is to find Charles Kingsley and bring him home."

"We'll need more ships, Your Highness."

The queen nodded. "Leave those details to us. In the meantime," she began, then looked at Grant. "I presume you will not object to Colonel Grant's joining you again?"

"He has acquitted himself reasonably well," Kit said. "For a viscount."

Kess snorted. Grant rolled his eyes. The queen smiled with obvious pleasure.

"I'm not at all surprised to hear it. Grant, may we impose upon your kindness once more?"

"Your Highness," he said with a bow.

"Then I'll wish you fair winds," the queen said.

"Your Highness, I do have one small request regarding our personnel."

The queen's brows lifted. "Oh?"

"As you may know, one of our sailors, Mr. Cordova, will need a bit more time to recover from his injuries from the gun brig's attack. There was a midshipman on the *Divine*—Cooper. I believe she has significant promise. Presuming the *Divine* is amply staffed, I'd respectfully request her transfer to the *Diana* for this mission."

The queen's brows lifted. "You believe her promise will not be realized on the *Divine*? That's not very flattering to its very experienced captain."

That the queen chose *experienced* instead of *trustworthy* said much.

Kit chose her words very, very carefully. "I believe, Your Highness, given what I know of Cooper's personality, what I've seen of her file, that her particular skills and her professional development would be better served on a courier's ship, rather than a man-of-war."

The queen watched her for a moment.

"It so happens," she said, "that Captain Thornberry requested she be transferred off his vessel. There were concerns about her loyalties." She studied Kit's face. "You have no concerns?"

Very, very, *very* carefully.

"I have no concerns about her loyalty to the Crown or the Isles, Your Highness."

The queen's smile was sly. "Very well. Kess, if you'd contact the admiral regarding the paperwork?"

Kess nodded.

"Are there other favors you need granted, Captain?" The queen looked at least mildly amused. Better than entirely put out, Kit thought.

"Unless Crown provisions now include a substantial shipment from Portnoy's, Your Highness, I've no further requests."

"Watch your step, Captain."

"Your Highness," she said, and made her bow exceedingly reverential.

And was fairly certain she'd heard the queen laugh.

⌡⌠

The mission was revenge.

She knew it wasn't that simple, and that her own motivations didn't matter. The Isles mattered, and their security, and the safety of her crew.

"I need more explosives," she told Jane as soon as she returned home. Jane ignored the request, pulled Kit into her arms, squeezed her tightly.

"You gave me quite a scare, Kit Brightling."

"I know, and I'm sorry. I didn't think him dumb or rash enough to strike me in my own home."

Kit pulled back, wiped a tear from Jane's cheek. "But I'm fine now. And we're on the hunt."

"Thus the sparkers."

"Thus. Can I get more of them?"

"How soon?"

"Two hours?"

Kit's tone was hopeful; Jane's expression was flat. "Fine, but I expect compensation. I want a dozen pistachio nougats."

"I don't have any."

"I imagine Portnoy's does."

"Half dozen," Kit said. "When I return from this mission."

"Ten."

"Eight, and I get to read this week's penny romance first."

"Done," Jane said. "It's nearly always a wife at the attic anyway."

TWENTY-EIGHT

What with her appreciation of a member of the Beau Monde, the magical storm, and the betrayal by Kingsley, Kit was running out of things to be surprised about. She'd received the queen's more detailed orders, which advised the *Diana* had been fully provisioned and her hull patches already reinforced. Five additional ships would participate in the search. One would sail toward Forstadt, two toward Frisia, one toward Montgraf, and one toward Fort de la Mer. Captain Perez, Kit's former commander, would lead the fleet. And the queen gave Kit the option of coordinating with Perez and the other ships as Kit preferred, and of using her Alignment as she wished.

Kit knew it was likely the most freedom she'd ever be afforded in a naval mission, and she intended to take full advantage. She also intended to take advantage of Perez's experience, and sent the captain a message offering her thoughts.

And more surprising yet: When Kit walked down the dock at the Crown Quay toward the *Diana*, she found Captain Smith staring up at the ship. Smith's ship, the *Delphine*, was anchored on the other side of the quay.

"Go aboard," she told Grant. "I'll talk to her."

"I demand a full report," Grant said, but moved to the *Diana*.

Kit strode to the woman. "Captain Smith."

"Captain Brightling." She swallowed, looked visibly uncomfortable. Which Kit found fascinating.

"The *Delphine* was initially assigned to travel to Frisia, one of two ships with that mission. I requested, and both Admiral Lawrence and Captain Perez have granted, permission for the *Delphine* to escort the *Diana* and support her search for Kingsley."

Perez, the squadron commander. Lawrence, Tasha Howard's father.

"And why did you do that?"

"Because you were right about Forstadt, and they—and I—were wrong." She straightened her shoulders. "I don't enjoy being wrong, but I prefer to learn from my failures. And I imagine the odds of your finding Kingsley first are fairly high. You may need guns. I can provide them."

Kit watched her for a moment, taking the woman's measure. "You'll follow my lead? Sail where I direct?"

"Right behind you," Smith agreed. "In whatever measure you need."

Kit considered. "Do you have a spot on board where we could secure some prisoners?"

Smith's smile was wide. "I believe, Captain, that the *Delphine* can accommodate you there."

⁓

She checked the *Diana*'s hull, inside and out. The Queenscliffe repair had held, and the Crown's own shipwrights had reinforced it. The topmast they'd lost at Finistère remained secure, Tamlin already aloft. No Louisa this time, given the risk, and Kit expected the crew would miss the smallest sailor. But there was one new addition. She caught Cooper's eye in the crowd, and they exchanged a nod.

When Kit was content the ship was ready, she had Jin call the crew.

"Our mission is singular," Kit told them from the helm. "We will find Charles Kingsley's ship, and we will bring them home so Kingsley can be held accountable for his crimes against the Isles.

"We will be escorted by the *Delphine*." She lifted a hand before they could growl their displeasure, as lips were already curling. "*Escorted*," Kit said again. "We will determine our course. The *Delphine* will accompany us only to assist in the capture of Kingsley. The *Diana* leads this mission. And we will succeed in it."

She let them have their hurrahs before turning to Jin, Grant, Tamlin, Simon.

"Well, Captain," Simon said, his charts already spread on the steering cabinet. "Where are we going?"

"The queen has sent ships toward Forstadt, Frisia, Montgraf, Gallia," Kit said. "We go where we choose, where we think Kingsley is most likely to run."

"And where do you think that is?" Simon asked.

"Let's start with where I don't think he is. I don't think he's brave enough to run to Gerard. Kingsley is a coward, and while he may fashion himself to be a supporter and an ally, there's no protection Gerard can offer him on Montgraf. And if Gerard is smart, he'd disclaim any involvement in treason within the Isles. Not until his position is stronger.

"Not Gallia for the same reason. He may have contacts there, but there's no obvious Gallic connection to his treachery. Forstadt has been exhausted of its resources—magic, lumber, solitude."

"That leaves Frisia," Jin said, and Kit nodded.

"He's been working with members of the Frisian consulate. The Guild has funded the construction of the new warship," she added, thinking of what the queen called it, "and they'd likely have promised him protection in the event he was caught."

Jin snorted. "The Guild won't protect him from anything, especially if the queen offers a bounty for his delivery. The highest bidder always wins."

"Agreed, but they wouldn't have told him that. Quite the contrary—they probably told him he'd be celebrated as a hero." Kit paused, considered. "The *Forebearer* is ahead of us, but they lack an experienced captain, and the ship is slower than ours. We make sail, as quickly as possible, toward Hofstad, as that's where the Guild is headquartered. And we fly with all canvas. If we're lucky, we catch Kingsley before he reaches port, disappears into the countryside."

"Or gets a knife in the gullet," Jin said.

"As likely," Kit confirmed. And because he'd earned the right, she looked at Grant. "Thoughts, Colonel?"

His lips curved. "To Frisia," he said, "with the caveat that Kingsley is likely sailing on fear, and may not be thinking as rationally as we are."

Kit nodded. "Understood." And because she was captain, she resigned herself to the next bit. "I'm going to do the receipts. I'll come up when we've reached open water, if not before."

She gave the Saint James one final glance, then nodded at her crew, stepped toward the companionway, and heard Simon whisper behind her, "I don't know if I care for their agreeing so much. It's . . . off-putting."

She grinned all the way to her cabin.

⁓

Receipts. Tea. Receipts. Tea. A glance through the windows to check the ship's progress. Receipts.

This time, they reached open water before Kit's work was complete, so she stuffed it into the writing desk and returned to the deck as they passed Surrey-on-Sea, the Narrow Sea ahead of them.

It was time to check the current. She'd been anticipating this moment, and not entirely for the better, as she wasn't sure what she'd find. She waited until water surrounded them and they'd made the gentle turn to port across the Northern Sea toward the Frisian coast.

In short, she waited until she couldn't wait any longer, because if there was magic to be had, the Isles and the *Diana* had need of it.

She looked up, found Grant watching her. He nodded encouragement, and she nodded back, then closed her eyes.

She reached down, through water cool and clear, through darkness and light. And when she felt the current below her, nearly wept with relief. It was still weak, even this far from Forstadt. But it was whole. Thinner, she thought, as if the current from the surrounding ocean had spread to cover the deficit. She didn't know if such a thing was possible, had never heard of it. And while she was pleased at the regeneration—perhaps humans wouldn't destroy the world completely—the damage in this part of the ocean had been relatively minimal. She didn't know if larger wounds, if the removal of the current nearer Forstadt, could be resolved. A chilling thought, given they were more likely to need the magic the closer they sailed to Frisia.

So they'd use the advantage while they could, she decided, and opened her eyes to find Jin, Simon, and Grant staring at her.

"What?" she asked, a bit unnerved.

"You were muttering, Captain," Jin said. "Something about removal and regeneration?"

"The current is stronger here than it was," she said, straightening her jacket and hoping she'd not sounded like an idiot. "But I fear it will not last." She looked up at the billowing canvas, nodded. "Hold on," she said, and touched the current.

❧

As they sailed northeast, she touched the current sparingly, not wanting to hinder its healing. And although the first contact sent them running across the sea, the second attempt a few hours later offered little.

The *Diana* spent the rest of the day and night in hard winds, with much tacking and, at least from its captain, growing doubt that she'd guessed incorrectly and had chosen the wrong course.

"It's taking too long," she murmured more than once, squinting at the horizon as she searched for her quarry.

And then, at noon on the second day, Tamlin spotted the *Forebearer*'s red jibs.

"Treasonous bastard's sail ho!" was her alert. Which Kit found entirely appropriate under the circumstances.

Unfortunately for the *Forebearer*, either treasonous bastard and his accomplices were miserable sailors, or they'd faced down weather the *Diana* had missed entirely. There was a hole in the mainsail big enough to jump through, and the sails flapped rather pitifully.

Not even Kingsley had bravado enough to run from the Crown Command's fastest ship and one of its largest frigates. One shot from the *Delphine* over the port bow and the *Forebearer* turned into the wind, which rendered its sails useless. It was a sign of surrender.

"Damn," Kit muttered as they moved to intercept. "I was hoping for a bit of a challenge."

"Maybe he'll try fisticuffs," Jin offered hopefully, "and you can fight it out."

They came alongside, the *Delphine* to starboard and the *Diana* to port, and all the *Forebearer*'s sailors—including Kingsley—on deck with blades already down. Being the biggest ship, the *Delphine* would transmit the prisoners. The away team, some of whom Kit recognized from the island, prepared to muscle the sailors aboard.

"Take all but Kingsley," Kit told them, when she'd jumped the void onto the smaller ship, Grant and Sampson behind her. "We'll speak with him here first."

They followed her directions without complaint, pushed the prisoners onto the *Delphine* over the gangplank they'd erected between the ships, leaving Kit, Grant, and Sampson with Kingsley.

They searched him, tied his hands. Then searched the captain's quarters, put him there. Sampson shoved Kingsley into a chair. "Wait," Kingsley said.

They ignored him.

When she was confident he'd been secured, Kit met Grant in the corridor. "Search the ship. Find what you can. Perhaps he hasn't turned over any documents yet."

Grant nodded, glanced back at Kingsley. "I certainly hope, when I return, that he looks worse for wear."

She was so angry with Kingsley that the fury had gone hard and cold as ice. "You're a traitor," she said, when she'd calmed enough to speak coherently.

"You're naive," Kingsley said. "It is only a matter of time before Gerard takes the throne again."

"Because the Guild demands it?"

"They understand practicality."

"You have no loyalty to the queen," Kit said. "To the Isles. To its independence?"

He looked at her. "I have loyalty to myself, and I'm wise enough to see what's coming. Many on the Continent supported Gerard's rule, and they have the funds to see it happen. There's time yet for you to make the same decision. To accept his return, and put yourself in the best position when he does. I'm sure Gerard would find a use for the *Diana*, and for you."

"Ah, but that's the difference between us. I'm not a traitor, I don't trade lives for my own comfort."

"I've killed no one."

"Kingsley, you're well past *one*. You gave up Dunwood. You told the Frisians on Forstadt that we were coming. You intend to hand over to our enemies the locations of every ship in the fleet."

"There was a treaty. We're all allies now."

God, she wanted to wipe that smug smile off his weasely little face. But they didn't have time for this. For any of it.

"Where is the ship, Kingsley?"

He just shook his head, looked away.

"Where are the documents you stole from the Crown Command?"

Still nothing.

"All right," Kit said. "If you're so confident they're your allies, we'll leave you here, in the ocean, alone on this ship and tied to this chair, and see how long it takes for them to look for you." She looked at Sampson. "How long, do you think?"

Sampson just snorted. "Why would they turn around for him?"

Kit nodded sadly. "We agree there." She looked back at Kingsley. "Last chance."

"You won't leave me here."

Kit just sighed, gestured Sampson toward the door. "Let's go." And they walked out, closed the door behind them. Moved back to the deck, where the search of the ship continued.

"Anything?" she asked as Grant emerged from another companionway.

"Nothing. The ship was mostly empty—no cargo—and we've found no safes, drawers, loose boards, canvas bags, or anything else that might hold them. He must have met another ship."

Kit nodded. "Maybe the gun brig, or some other Frisian vessel, met him off the coast."

"Because they expected we'd look for him first."

"And they didn't much care whether he was protected or not," Kit said. "The intelligence is what matters."

"I presume he's given nothing up?"

"Nothing useful," Kit said, and the smile that crossed Grant's face was terrifying.

"My turn to try."

He was a coward. Despite the treason, the bravado, Kingsley was a coward.

One quick punch in the abdomen from Grant, and Kingsley doubled over, retched onto the floor. Grant looked at him with disgust. "Men have gone to their graves because of you, and you can't even take a punch. Just wait until you're in prison."

"To hell with you," Kingsley muttered.

Grant crouched in front of him, hands linked. "I'll ask you one more time. Where are the documents?"

"They're on the new ship—the warship. We met the convoy yesterday off Fort de la Mer and delivered them."

That explained why it took so long to find the damned *Forebearer*, Kit thought. "How many in the convoy?"

"Eight. Seven frigates and the warship."

Grant rose. "And where are they going, Kingsley?"

"I don't know."

Grant turned on him, had him hauled up and out of his chair before Kingsley could squeak a response. "Where are they going?" Grant said again, each word a low threat.

"Hofstad," Kingsley said. "They're going to Hofstad."

Still holding him up, Grant watched him, expression mild. "Keep going."

"The Guild headquarters—inside the castle. That's where the decisions are made. We were to rendezvous just off the coast. We deliver the documents first, then we travel separately to the rendezvous point to confuse anyone looking for us. Then the Guild gets us into the city."

Not just arrogant, Kit thought, but rather stupid if he thought the Guild had any intention of meeting him anywhere. They'd already gotten what they wanted from him.

Apparently reaching the same conclusion, Grant dropped him down again.

"What's the signal?" Kit asked. "The one you'd use to approach the envoy and not get blown out of the water."

"It doesn't matter. You'll never catch them. The ship is too fast."

"Let me worry about the speed," Kit said with a thin smile. "What's the signal?"

To punctuate the demand, Grant took a threatening step toward him.

Kingsley wiped his mouth. "Two pennants. Red above blue. If the plan is on, the response is yellow above blue."

"Any particular movements?" Kit asked. "Positioning of the ship?"

"No. Just alongside."

"You do understand the cost if you're lying?"

"It hardly matters to me," Kingsley said. "You're going to leave me here."

"Of course we aren't," Kit said, "we're going to take you with us on the *Diana*. So if you've told us the wrong signal, they'll be blowing you out of the water as well."

His face paled. "Two pennants," he said, and swallowed hard. "Blue above red."

"Much better," Kit said, and turned on her heel for the door.

"Can I have some water, please?"

Kit just snorted. He might as well have asked for tea with the queen. He was just as likely to get it.

"We'll see who wins!" Kingsley called out. "We'll see who ends up a prisoner when all is said and done."

"Yes," Kit murmured. "We will."

They'd found Kingsley and the *Forebearer*, but not the documents he'd stolen. And no sailor in the Isles fleet would be secure until they did. Jin took command of the *Forebearer*, along with a crew of sailors from the *Diana* and the *Delphine*. They secured Kingsley on the *Delphine*, and they prepared to sail.

Kit searched for the current, but knew what she'd find. A shadow of what had been before, the signature of what had been stripped away. It wouldn't help the *Diana*, but nor would it help the warship.

Four hours later, still no current beneath them, Tamlin called out, "Sails ho!"

Eight ships along the eastern horizon, running toward Frisia.

"Glass," Kit said, and without looking away, felt it placed into her palm.

She raised it, and stared. Seven of them were frigates. But the one in the middle was different.

Here was Gerard's warship. It looked in reality just as it had in the plans: cabinet across its middle, two stunted masts. Those masts were full of canvas now, the ship streaming toward Frisia under wind power. That, she suspected, because of the damage done by the explosion at Forstadt. The cabinet was scarred, a corner buckled where magic warped it.

Good, Kit thought. Maybe they'll have learned some lesson from it. She was relieved at the state of it, hadn't admitted until now that she'd been concerned—seriously concerned—about whether the *Diana* could survive an attack by the warship.

If they'd seen the *Diana*, they hadn't yet moved to attack. It was not logical, however, that two ships—three if the *Forebearer* was included—should attack a line of eight. Those odds were so unfavorable even Marten's wouldn't insure them. But they couldn't simply sail home, leaving Gerard's new navy to set its own course, wreak its own havoc.

They had to engage—not in a line, not with broadsides and cannons—but with ingenuity. With brains and speed.

And homemade explosives.

TWENTY-NINE

They settled on the *Diana*. The *Delphine* was too large, and they doubted they'd be able to convince anyone that Kingsley had managed to nab a frigate and enough sailors to crew it. And the *Forebearer* was unfamiliar and not as fast as Kit's own ship. If Kit wasn't going to have guns, she wanted speed.

Members of the envoy might have seen the *Forebearer* near Fort de la Mer. But the ship hadn't been there long, and while smaller than the *Diana*, it was similar enough in style that Kit thought they could make it work. Especially if the *Diana*'s jibs were switched out for the *Forebearer*'s red ones.

The *Diana* would sail forward, signal raised, no other identifying pennants, and no Crown Command uniforms visible. And then they'd unleash their secret weapon.

They switched the sails and raised the pennants, and Kit reclaimed her commander, leaving the *Forebearer* floating behind them as the *Diana* moved forward toward the southernmost ship.

The wind blew toward starboard, so they tacked against it until they were within one hundred yards and could see the hard-bitten crew looking back through their own glass.

And still no signal.

Grant stood at the helm, Kit behind him; the crew of the *Forebearer* had been almost uniformly male, so the envoy would have expected to find, at least, a man at the helm. Half the *Diana*'s crew was below, with only a skeleton assemblage on the deck to tend the sails, and those in their dirtiest slops.

The sea thundered beneath them as they moved, but the magic was still gone.

"Pennant's going up," Grant said, relief clear in his voice.

"Then let's get ready," Kit said.

"Reduce sail," Grant called out. "Come alongside."

"Beau Monde or not," Jin said as the orders were relayed, "the man can act at captain."

"Don't encourage him," Kit said, while Grant snorted in amusement. It was hard enough for her not to jump up and take charge.

The *Diana* slowed, and Kit ran a hand across the polished wood with affection. "I will make this up to you," she promised quietly. And this time, slipped the coin from her pocket and placed it for luck between the planks of the deck. Planks that plainly needed better caulking, but that was for another time.

They drew closer to the outlier ship, could see the guns clearly now. A dozen, mostly smaller, but large enough to do plenty of damage.

"Ahoy!" called out a bruiser of a sailor at the gunwale on the frigate. He looked more pirate than sailor, and Kit suspected he'd called Finistère home.

"Ahoy," Grant said.

"You're late," the bruiser said.

Grant gave the man an impressively imperious look. "I managed to steal a damn Crown ship and make my way here, didn't I? Do you think that's an easy task?"

"I think you'd best watch your tone, aye? There's nothing about you that's better than the rest of us."

"You can walk right into the sea," Grant said. "Are you ready or no?"

The bruiser looked at Grant, and the moment stretched taut as wind-filled canvas.

"Aye, I'm ready." Then he shifted his gaze to the *Diana*'s hull and then her rigging. "Seems I've seen this ship before."

Grant's look was flat. "Did you miss the bit where I said I'd stolen it? I didn't build it myself. Maybe you have seen it before."

The bruiser didn't look convinced. And when sailors began moving away from him across the deck, she knew they'd lost him. She didn't know why—although she wouldn't put a bit of lying past Kingsley—but they'd lost him. They'd be loading the cannons now, preparing to fire on the *Diana*, thinking it a usurper.

"Ready," Kit whispered, pulling down the cap she'd borrowed a little more.

"Captain!" August called out, and right on time. "Do we need to link up with this boat here?"

Every sailor on the other boat turned to where August stood in the bow, grappling hook in his wizened hand, swinging it around like a flail.

"Now!" Kit said, and sailors sprang into action to set the sails again.

Kit tossed away her hat, moved to the starboard rail, and pulled the sparker from her pocket. She had to wait until they were moving and the *Diana* wouldn't be damaged, but not so long that they allowed the frigate time to fire a broadside.

"Ready the damned cannons!" the bruiser yelled, and Kit imagined the activity below: Gunpowder cartridges pricked, and sparks prepared, waiting for the command to fire.

The wind caught the *Diana* and the sails filled, and she began to move, wind and canvas fighting friction, the pull of the sea.

The moment the frigate ran out her cannons, Kit tossed the sparker.

"Down!" she cried out as explosions rocked the sea.

The explosive hit the frigate's deck and shot out fire in all directions, sending wood and men and rigging through the air at the same time two of the frigate's cannons fired, sending balls straight at the *Diana*.

The noise was remarkable, and the *Diana* shook, shuddered, as a ball hit somewhere below, the sound of cracking wood loud as the felling of a tree. The second flew inches from the mainmast, ripping through the shroud and rigging. But the mast stayed standing.

"Get below and check for damage and injuries!" Kit shouted to Watson, then gripped Jin's arm. "Keep us moving!" she ordered, then ran back to the stern, aimed, and threw another sparker at the now-receding enemy. It landed near the wheel and roared, and shrapnel flew. There was another explosion below, three sequential pops, and flames emerged from the gun deck.

"The powder," Grant said quietly.

"Yes," Kit said, and made a silent *Dastes* for the lost, or those who'd be lost soon enough as the fire grew, consumed the ship.

Watson emerged from the companionway, a smudge of soot on her face. "Your windows are gone, Captain, and a good plug of the stern near the port side. But no fire, and the damage is well above the waterline."

"Two more ships giving chase!" someone called out, before Kit could respond. They looked back, found two of the line now raising sails and turning toward the *Diana*, two hundred yards back.

And on the other end of the line, the *Delphine*, now rushing toward the melee, Isles flag flying.

"Welcome to the ball," Kit said, and turned back to the helm. "Turn around."

Jin's head snapped toward her. "Turn around?"

"Turn around," she said again, more slowly. "They'll be faster than we are. We cannot outrun them, and we've no islands to run through, nor any magic to guide us."

Jin's gaze narrowed as he studied her. "You want to face them head-on?"

"No, but I want them to think we're going to," she said, and plucked the wax pencil Simon offered. He knew his captain well.

Kit sketched two slender boats in a blank spot on the cabinet map, the *Diana* some hundred yards away, her position roughly between theirs. "We make them believe we plan to sail through them, which would be ridiculous."

"Double broadsides," Grant said.

"I'm really very pleased with his nautical education," Simon said.

It was Kit's turn to snort. "When we get close, we veer starboard. They'll be planning to shoot us in the middle. They won't have cannons ready on the outside."

"And we use the explosives again," Jin finished.

"And we do." She put a hand on his shoulder, squeezed. "This is going to be close. But we can do it. *We will do it*."

Gods, let them do it, she prayed. Let her crew survive it.

Instructions proceeded down the length of the *Diana* as she streamed toward the ships, the crews near their bows screaming with raised sabres.

"Are they trying to intimidate us?" Grant asked.

"I'm not entirely sure," Kit said, and put a hand on the steering cabinet, and waited until she could feel the quiet of the slickest, fastest water.

"Starboard on my mark," she said quietly. "Three. Two. One. Mark."

The crew was ready, and the booms were shifted, the wheel turned hard, the shouts from the starboard ship turning to shouts of alarm and warning as they decided the *Diana* wasn't going to sail between them—she was going to sail into them.

Kit watched the starboard ship grow closer until it seemed the *Diana* would simply sail on top of it. And then their bowsprits passed like jousters' lances, and the *Diana* streamed by the ship.

But they'd been more clever than she'd thought. A cannon on the starboard ship's port side boomed only ten feet away from the *Diana*'s hull, and her responding heave sent a line of cold sweat down Kit's back.

She couldn't think about that. She could only think about her role. Her part.

Time seemed to slow around her, and she pulled out the last sparker, threw it over the gunwale of the enemy ship, and shouted out her warning.

"Down!"

She didn't know if anyone heard, but she instinctively covered her head, felt the concussion and the sprinkle of debris over her arms. She made herself breathe, then rose again and looked back.

She'd hit the ship in the middle of the deck; the mast was cracking, toppling, and pulling the rigging down with it.

Two ships down, she thought, and looked around. The *Diana* was still upright, the masts still standing. And no horrific injuries that she could see, although there were bruises and gashes and sooty faces aplenty.

"Kit."

The roaring in her ears slowed, quieted, and she looked down, found a hand on her arm. She looked up, found Grant staring at her.

"Are you all right?"

"I'm . . ." She shook her head to clear it. "I'm fine. It was the explosion. I think it rattled my brain a bit. The shot?"

Watson emerged through the smoke. "Into the hold," she said. "Foot of water already in the boat, but Oglejack's got sailors working the hand pumps, and he's sealing it over. No one was injured."

She looked toward port, found the *Delphine* engaged with another ship, and one of the others already on fire.

"Sails ho!"

Kit's heart sank. They'd been clever, but the *Diana* was taking damage, and they couldn't play this game forever. "More frigates?"

But it wasn't.

Kit turned around, and grinned at the answer. Captain Perez had gotten her note, and decided their following the *Diana* was the right course.

"About damned time," she murmured, grinning as four enormous frigates bore down on the enemy like sea dragons, whitewater streaming in their wake.

She could hear the shouts from Gerard's ships as they saw their new opponents, and then the melancholy quiet fell as they realized this would not be a simple return trip to Frisia. They'd have to face down the Isles' navy, or die trying.

Kit felt the tingle in the air even as Tamlin called out from the top. "Warship maneuvering!"

They all looked back toward Gerard's ship, the sailors that turned cranks to open the massive cabinet. The sides drew open like unfolding wings, revealing a dark labyrinth of metal gears and arms. Other members of the crew doused the sails.

"Bloody hell," Jin said. "What is that?"

"A kind of gristmill," Kit murmured, and glanced at Grant.

"What do you feel?" he asked, moving to her side.

Kit didn't need to reach out to the sea to feel it. "Irritation. And if you're about to ask me to explain, I couldn't possibly."

In seconds, the mechanics inside the cabinet rose into the air, the platform holding them lifted by metal chains and pulleys.

"How can they try it again?" Jin asked, staring at the chimera of ship and machine. "At least four dead on the island, and probably more we didn't find."

Her head began to ache again, but she pushed through the pain. "Because sailors, to them, are fungible."

Hers, however, were not. She looked around, surveyed her

battlefield. There simply wasn't time to change position and run from whatever force that infernal machine was about to unleash. So she had to protect her people.

"All hands brace for impact!" Kit called out, and the warning echoed down the line.

The platform stuttered to a stop. The gears began to spin, what little current remained in the sea seemed all devoted to that buzzing irritation. Or maybe that was simply her perception of the electrical nips that seemed to bite at her skin.

And then the nips stopped, and the gears stopped. And the warship was dead in the water.

Kit grinned. And then she began to laugh.

"What?" Simon asked. "What's funny?"

"There's not enough magic," Kit said. "They burned through the current at Forstadt, probably in the explosion. But you can't run a magic warship without magic, and that magic warship apparently requires a lot of it to operate."

"They have a very serious design flaw," Jin said, not bothering to hide his amusement.

"They absolutely do," Kit said.

"That's why they have envoys," Grant said. "If they'd sailed south, they'd have come upon stronger current, could have used that."

Kit shook her head. "They'd be too far from Frisia. That's where the money is, and that's where the decisions are made. The Guild doesn't want anyone else playing with their toys, at least until the issues are resolved."

She was disappointed she'd not see the warship in action. But she'd be very happy to keep the Guild from having its new toy.

Things moved quickly after that, as the conspirators' loyalty to Gerard didn't extend to death in deep and cold water. They surrendered almost as neatly as Kingsley had, but for the single ship that decided it could outrun Perez's present ship, the *Imperial*.

It was mistaken. Rather egregiously.

The remaining frigates were emptied of enemy combatants who'd been divided among the squadron for the return trip to New London.

Kit and Smith met Captain Perez and the others on the deck of the *Imperial*.

"Kit," Perez said with a smile, her tricorn hat cocked over short brown hair, her brown eyes canny beneath. "A pleasure to see you again." She extended a tan hand, and they shook.

"Captain," Kit said. "Thank you for the squadron. Your ships were very welcome."

"We do what we can." She cast her gaze to the warship, her smile falling away. "Do we take the monstrosity home, or scuttle it here?"

The queen would want the ship, the technology, both to keep the exemplar from Gerard and to study it. To learn from it. And, very possibly, to use it.

Kit was obliged, was she not, to send the ship to the Isles? To give the queen that opportunity? Perhaps. But that didn't eliminate the small knot of tension in her belly, her concern the world's relationship to magic would change.

She thought of the gristmill in Queenscliffe, of the magic she touched every time she tried to speed the *Diana*. She walked that line very carefully. Maybe the Isles could, too.

"We tow it home," Kit decided.

Decision made, Perez's smile went thin. "And as to the others? Do we prefer fire or powder?"

The question was probably rhetorical, but Kit made her answer.

"Burn them. Burn them, and let the ashes fall where they will. Don't give him a chance to raise them from the deep."

THIRTY

There was no parade when they slipped into New London again, when they rode the Saint James. It would only be later that the public learned of the battle that had taken place, of the treasure they'd brought home.

But the victory was enough for now.

They reached the Crown Quay, anchored, furled sail. Not for the first time, Kit expected she and Grant would part ways, if permanently this time. She'd have duties and obligations here—or wherever the Crown Command thought to send her. He'd return to Queenscliffe and the care of his estate, to keeping an eye on his brother. Their paths were different; there was only fate to blame for that.

But still, she felt that ache again, that little hollow in the center of her chest. And what good did it do, the ache? What purpose did it serve, when the only lives they could live were their own?

"You're welcome aboard the *Diana* anytime," she told him on the dock, working to keep up her smile.

He offered his hand, and it discomfited her that she hesitated before taking it.

Why? Because she didn't want to shake his hand? Or because she was afraid she wouldn't let go? She hated fear, so she took it.

"Good luck to you," he told her. "And fair seas."

But they stood there for a moment, hands still clasped, delaying the conclusion they assumed was inevitable, and considered what dangers the future might hold.

"And to you, Colonel Grant." With regret in her eyes, but feeling as if she had no other choice, she let go.

﹏

There was a knock at the door. The sisters rose as Mrs. Eaves opened it.

"This just arrived for you," she said, crossing the room in her efficient stride and offering Kit a letter.

It was from the queen—the seal, the ribbon, the thick, luxurious stock. And her heart tripped in fear that Gerard had already made his move, had already stuck fangs into some village along the Isles' coast. Had already committed violence.

She moved to the window, putting space between her family and the violence the missive might contain, and pulled away the seal and began to read.

Captain Brightling,

On behalf of Her Royal Highness Queen Charlotte, please accept this formal commendation of your recent service respecting the rescue of Marcus Dunwood,

securing the Diana *through attack and storm, and in
the recent halting of Gerard's new armada. In
anticipation of your continued service to the Crown,
you are hereby granted a commission in the Order of
Saint James, induction to be conducted at the palace
at eight o'clock this evening.*

Kit stared at the document, only realized then that her hand
was shaking around the paper. And it was a testament to her control that she didn't scream.

The Order of Saint James. It was both an honor bestowed by
the Crown for service to the Isles, and a group that closely advised the queen. Hetta was a member, and now Kit would follow
in her footsteps.

"Kit." Jane's voice was quiet. "What's wrong?"

Kit offered her the paper. That's when the screaming began.

"For gods' sake." Mrs. Eaves stepped back into the doorway,
displeasure pulling down her brows. "What is all this noise?"

Jane ran to her, put an arm through hers. "Kit's being in-
vested in the Order of Saint James. Can you believe it?"

"Hardly," Mrs. Eaves said, looking down her nose at Kit. But
there was pride in her eyes, and warmth that confirmed she was
proud, even if she wasn't willing to say it aloud.

"Well, well," Hetta said, coming into the room beside her. "I
believe a celebration is in order."

⁓

It was raining, of course. Pouring in sheets that beat horizontally
against the windows and turned the streets into a soup of mud

and rock and horse detritus. And cold on top of it, so Kit's breath fogged the air of the carriage.

But Kit didn't care.

The queen had sent the transport, and Kit was bundled into it with Jane and Hetta, who'd be her supporters and witnesses at the palace ceremony inducting her into the order.

Even Mrs. Eaves had taken special care with Kit's uniform. "You will not represent this family with scuffed boots," she'd said, and then gave them a zealous buffing.

"How are you feeling?" Hetta asked.

"Fortunate and excited and nervous."

Hetta, who sat across from her, reached out and patted her knee. "Very reasonable responses to a very exciting honor." As they rode toward the palace, Hetta's tone and expression were all joy, all pride. But the thoughts she'd passed along in private had been cautious.

"I am so proud," she'd said in her study. "Not surprised, but very proud. It is an honor to serve in the Crown Command, much less the order. It is an honor to represent the queen, to advise her." Her smile faded.

"But there is also a cost to bear. You will become . . . a symbol of the Crown, in some respects. And those who dislike the queen, who dislike the Isles, will consider you part of the Crown. Part of the queen's government. I wouldn't say that's dangerous, Kingsley's idiocy aside, but the scrutiny can be uncomfortable."

"You think I should decline?" Kit had asked.

"Not in this damned lifetime," Hetta said fiercely. "I'm merely telling you the things I wish someone had told me. I wouldn't have done any different, either," she had said. "But I'd have been . . . less startled . . . when confronted with my opponents."

Kit understood the honor, so she'd refused to give voice to her concern. But this close to the palace, to the ceremony, it bubbled out.

"The next war will use magic. Nations will fight for it, use it against one another. The land and people will suffer." She looked out the window. "We will use it, and I wonder if that's a cause I ought to support."

Hetta watched her for a moment. "Perhaps we might consider adding a new Principle of Self-Sufficiency. Principle number ten," she said crisply. "If you're the one who best understands the line between good and evil, it's your responsibility to keep watch."

Kit looked at Hetta now, was comforted by her confident and knowing smile, by the fact that she could look to Hetta for advice and counsel. It made an interesting circle—Hetta advising the king. Hetta raising Kit, teaching her to be the person she'd become. Kit advising the king's daughter, a queen in her own right.

"Okay," Kit said. "Okay."

~⁓

The rain had eased by the time they reached the palace. Kit climbed out first, helped Hetta, then Jane. The guards at the gate were too well trained to smile, but their eyes gleamed as Kit moved through the gate, followed by her family.

The palace doors were opened for them, and Kit wondered if that was because of her, or because she'd arrived with Hetta. Probably the latter, which would help keep her humble.

They walked into the rotunda, and Kit pushed her hair behind her ears, straightened her jacket.

And then stopped.

There were many others in the rotunda waiting to be escorted into the stateroom for the ceremony. But even with his back turned, she recognized him. There was no mistaking the set of his broad shoulders, the sun-streaked hair.

He glanced back, his gaze meeting hers.

And across that expanse of gilt and marble, they watched each other.

"Oh?" Hetta said, slipping beside her. "Did I not mention Colonel Grant has also been given the honor of induction in the order?"

The crowd shifted, moved, breaking the visual connection.

Kit glanced down at Hetta, noted the wicked smile in her eyes. "I believe you failed to mention that."

"Hmm," Hetta said. "It's very unlike me to forget a detail."

"Strategic to the last," Kit muttered, but let herself feel the jittery flutter in her abdomen. And let herself feel the uncertainty. The excitement. The fear.

The crowd shifted again, and he stood in front of her, eyes as bright as the sea, the heat in his gaze warm enough to spark flame.

"Captain Brightling." The words were low, infused with promise.

She smiled at him. "Colonel Grant."

The silver horns were raised, their song ringing across stone as the queen made her way into the room.

And they all turned to face their queen . . . and their futures.

⁓

When the toasts were made and the speeches done, and the glittering badges of the order—diamond circles crossed by a curve of the Saint James—were pinned to their jackets, Grant found Kit in the crowd.

"Colonel," she said.

"Captain. I thought I saw your mother and sister?"

"They've gone for more punch. Tepid though it is."

"Punch is always tepid," Grant said. "I came to congratulate you on your induction. Congratulations."

Kit nodded. "And to you. I imagine it will be difficult for you to serve in the order from Queenscliffe, will it not?"

"That's more obtuse a question than you usually prefer. But I'll answer it. For the time being, I'll be staying in New London."

Uncertainty and excitement flitted again. And while people moved around them in gowns and tails, and candles winked in chandeliers, Grant looked at her. She saw the promise—and the challenge—in his eyes.

"And the estate?" she asked, thrilled her voice didn't waver.

"My agreement to, shall we say, reenlist came with a side benefit—the absolution of the estate's debts."

That echoed the reward the queen had given to Kit, which she'd promptly donated to the Brightling house.

"I've hired Matthew to act as the estate's manager in my absence. He'll be teaching Lucien how to run it. And Will has a friend who'll be assisting with . . . security."

Kit grinned. "You hired a soldier to watch Lucien."

"In the guise of a bodyguard, should Forsythe or anyone else decide to intrude on his pastoral interlude. But essentially, yes."

"It sounds like you've managed those problems very neatly," Kit said. "I'm glad of it. And I hope it brings your family some peace."

He looked at her again. "Grant Hall will always be home, if a rather complicated one. It is, in a way, my touchstone. Much, I suspect, as the Brightling house is for you."

Kit nodded.

"Having a place to return after the war, after the pain and misery, had been a relief, even in its condition. But the thought of going back now . . . simply doesn't have the same appeal."

Kit stared at him, tried to sift through her tangled emotions, wondered how to align them.

Grant had opened his mouth to speak, when Chandler found them, his expression grim.

He offered no greeting. "With me, please."

They followed him into a small anteroom Kit hadn't yet seen. A room of soft carpets and fabrics, and a basket of needlepoint near a chair. A place, she thought, where the queen could find a few moments' peace outside the throne room.

"What is it?" Kit asked, when the other door opened, and the queen stepped inside, Kess behind her.

"We've just learned Gerard is gone," she said, eyes blazing. "While you brought home his warship, he and a loyal few managed to kill eight guards at Montgraf and escaped in a fishing schooner."

They all stood quietly for a moment, each considering what

the future might hold. The dangers they might be required to face.

"Our world has just become more dangerous," the queen said. "But never forget this—you've taken the first battle for the Isles. Now we'll see what comes next."

PHOTO BY DANA DAMEWOOD PHOTOGRAPHY

Chloe Neill—*New York Times* bestselling author of the Chicago-land Vampires novels, the Heirs of Chicagoland novels, the Dark Elite novels, and the Devil's Isle novels—was born and raised in the South but now makes her home in the Midwest, just close enough to Cadogan House, St. Sophia's, and Devil's Isle to keep an eye on things. When not transcribing her heroines' adventures, she bakes, works, and scours the Internet for good recipes and great graphic design. Chloe also maintains her sanity by spending time with her boys—her favorite landscape photographer (her husband), and their dogs, Baxter and Scout. (Both she and the photographer understand the dogs are in charge.)

Ready to find
your next great read?

Let us help.

Visit prh.com/nextread